PRAISE FOR TIM GREEN AND
THE RED ZONE

"Fast-paced action and a look at the darkest side of humankind . . . lots of surprises . . . a wild ride to the end."
—*Los Angeles Times*

"With this thriller it's clear that Green is now a player in the field."

—*New York Post*

"If you like thrillers, you'll like Tim Green's new book."
—*Larry King, USA Today*

"One is considered blessed with either brains or brawn. Tim Green has been blessed with both."
—*Bob Costas, NBC Sports*

"Plenty of raw action . . . Green's story tumbles in unpredictable directions, and—just as in chasing down a loose ball—it's worth following the bounces."
—*Cleveland Plain Dealer*

"Intriguing . . . good plot, well-paced, interesting characters. And you don't have to be a football fan to enjoy it."
—*San Francisco Examiner*

"THE RED ZONE should add to his accolades. It's an excellent story, well written . . . [with] a conclusion that is exciting and unusual."
—*Chattanooga Times*

more . . .

THE RED ZONE

ALSO BY TIM GREEN

Fiction

Ruffians ★
Titans ★
Outlaws ★

Nonfiction

The Dark Side of the Game ★
A Man and His Mother: An Adopted Son's Search

★Published by Warner Books

TIM GREEN

THE

RED

ZONE

WARNER BOOKS

A Time Warner Company

This book is a work of fiction. Names, characters, places and inci-
dents are either the product of the author's imagination or are used
fictitiously, and any resemblance to actual persons, living or dead,
events, or locales is entirely coincidental.

WARNER BOOKS EDITION

Copyright © 1998 by Tim Green
All rights reserved.

Cover design by Diane Luger
Cover illustration by Richard Newton

Warner Books, Inc.
1271 Avenue of the Americas
New York, NY 10020

Visit our Web site at
www.warnerbooks.com

 A Time Warner Company

Printed in the United States of America

Originally published in hardcover by Warner Books.
First Paperback Printing: September 1999

10 9 8 7 6 5 4 3 2 1

With love for my beautiful wife, Illyssa, the only person I know who could admire the artwork after the kids painted the kitchen table.

THE
RED
ZONE

Prologue

Dawn was nothing more than a pink glow behind the dark bank of clouds stacking up out over the ocean. A stiff offshore breeze had whipped the surf into a foam, and despite the time of day it was already quite warm. The storm was imminent. Sandy Kiffleman strode purposefully up the beach, her thin frame, freckles, and the red-orange hair tucked up under her hat giving her the look of a teenager. She was, in fact, a National Park Ranger. Hers was serious work, as serious as any other federal agent's. Although there were jobs within the National Park Service where the most challenging assignment might be dealing with a drunken camper or a hive of bees, for the rangers who patrolled MacCarther National Park, this was not the case. For a park ranger, South Florida was a war zone.

Her instincts were telling her something now, as she surveyed the beach. When she'd arrived at the north parking lot at five A.M., it was empty as it should have been. Overnight parking was not allowed. On a whim Sandy had pulled her truck off the blacktop where an overgrown track led to a clearing in the trees by the beach. Occasionally she would find a couple too cheap to spend fifty dollars for a motel room down the road. Instead of teenage lovers, however, she spotted a nondescript Ford Taurus backed into the bushes. If her dad hadn't raised her to hunt white-tailed deer in the hills of Pennsylvania each fall, she probably would have missed it altogether. But to her, freshly broken twigs were as obvious a marker as orange construction cones.

The hood of the car was cool. It had been there for a while. From the tags it appeared to be a rental. She thought it strange that someone with the means of renting a car would look to spend an illicit night on the beach with the sand fleas. Something didn't feel quite right. Although an out-of-towner might have reason to pull off the blacktop, attempting to hide the car in the bushes was above and beyond the call of breaking park rules. Besides, Sandy was paid to be suspicious. She pocketed her hand radio and instinctively felt for her Browning 9mm, before hiking down a short path toward the beach on foot.

She walked north for a mile, all the way to Lost Tree Village, an exclusive Palm Beach development, and back, but saw no sign of anyone. She decided to search the vehicle and to have someone call in to the rental company to find out who had leased the car. She was walking close to the surf where the sand was firm and was just about to turn back toward the parking lot and her truck when she froze. Like a ghost, a frogman had suddenly appeared knee-deep in the surf about a hundred yards up the beach. She could see he was carrying a speargun and there was a fish-laden net tossed over one of his shoulders. She cursed under her breath.

She'd seen many fools in her day, but this was a first: a guy spearfishing in a national park! Whoever he was, and whatever fish and game rules he was breaking, he was clearly not a smuggler. That is, unless the cartels had found a way to turn grouper into coke mules. As a precaution, Sandy unfastened the snap on her holster. She had no trouble imagining the gibes she would get back at the station if they learned she'd pulled her gun on a tourist for poaching. It was probably overkill, but Sandy always believed in having an edge. If she had to pull her gun, she would, and she wouldn't get caught fumbling with the snap either. Pulling the gun was something Sandy practiced in front of the full-length mirror on her bathroom door. Alone, of course.

When she'd covered half the distance between them, the diver looked at her and waved before plunking himself down in the sand to remove his gear.

"Damn fool," she muttered out loud.

"Sir," she said, stopping ten feet in front of the man, with her back to the ocean and the brewing clouds, "do you have some identification?"

The man looked up at her. His teeth shone like rich pearls in the early morning light. He had stripped down to his swim trunks. He was a big man, and muscles rippled in his arms, stomach, and chest. One of the fish lurched in the sack by his feet, and it made Sandy jump.

"You say that like I've done something wrong, officer," he said pleasantly.

"You have," she responded with a coldness that she didn't really feel, and pointed accusingly at the five large gasping fish at his feet, each one dying slowly from a bloody perforation in its midriff. "Those fish are going to cost you a hundred dollars each."

This obviously disturbed him.

"I . . ." he stuttered, "I really had no idea . . ."

"You had your car tucked away pretty nicely for having no idea," she responded without expression from behind her dark glasses. "Now, I'd like to see some ID."

"You know," he said apologetically, "I really don't even know how to use this thing. I kind of rented it as a lark . . ."

The diver touched the speargun casually as he referred to it. It almost seemed to Sandy that he was moving in slow motion as his hand tightened around the gun's rubber grip and as he swung its pointed broadhead toward her with his other hand. This was it. Sandy had secretly imagined something like this since first becoming a ranger. The motion of drawing her weapon was almost instinctive, she'd done it so many times. Her mind, though, moved faster than her body. Her limbs seemed weighted down. This was different from the mirror. Nonetheless, she got her Browning halfway out of its holster before the two-and-a-half-foot steel shaft shattered her sternum and ripped through her heart like a bolt of lightning lifting her off her feet and knocking her backward.

It didn't hurt. She was surprised more than anything, and angry with herself for not pulling the gun sooner, for becoming distracted by the smiling man and his easy way. It wasn't supposed to happen this way. She grasped feebly at the spear that protruded from her chest, but she lacked the energy to pull it free. He was standing there, above her now. And even before her vision faded to black, Sandy was aware that he was dragging her by the feet toward the surf and the incoming tempest.

Chapter 1

Madison McCall checked her watch as she hurried down the long corridor on the main floor of her firm's ornate offices. As usual, Madison wore clothes that were stylish, but that concealed her well-toned body. She didn't want to be regarded as just a body, or even a face, and she never had. Growing up, Madison was the girl who could have been the captain of the cheerleading team or Miss Texas. She never tried. When she was six years old she watched her father deliver a closing argument in a murder trial. Since that day, Madison knew she would be a lawyer. She was never smug about it, but as she grew up, other things just didn't matter as much as they seemed to matter to the rest of the girls her age.

Even now—especially now—it was hard to not notice the gleam in her pretty green eyes which were perfectly spaced above high, shapely cheeks. Her nose was just long enough to set her apart without detracting from her good looks. Her light brown hair was thick and soft, but she rarely let it down. Even with her hair up, Madison almost always drew a second look. At thirty-four, she was the youngest senior partner in her law firm. Her natural attractiveness, however, had nothing to do with her unusually rapid advancement. She had achieved that through her lawyering. Unfortunately, neither her looks nor her brains could help her now. She was late.

"Hi, Dotty, I'm running," she said with a quick wave over her shoulder as she passed in and out of a large wood-paneled chamber that faced a bank of elevators. Dotty, the scowling receptionist, sat like a foreboding gargoyle at her claw-footed desk in the middle of a thick blue oriental rug. She was an old crab, but even she seemed unable to help herself from smiling when Madison bubbled by.

Madison skidded to a stop on the marble floor in front of the wide double doors on her right. Absently, she brushed back a lock of her hair that had escaped its bun and fallen into her face. She took a deep breath, pulled open one of the doors, and stepped inside. She expected to be confronted with the disapproving scowl of Dorian Baxter, the oldest and most powerful man in the firm and one of the most respected attorneys in the state of Texas. She was also prepared for painful silence from the rest of the firm's partners as they looked on with pursed lips while Baxter berated her for being late. Instead, the six other partners on her firm's executive committee were clustered about Dorian's throne at the head of the conference table, standing anxiously like a handful of school-children waiting for the bell to ring.

Instead of frowns, she was met with seven benevolent smiles. Madison would almost have preferred frowns. There was only one other woman in the room, Isabelle Denofrio, and her smile was the weakest of the bunch. Madison quickly reviewed her life over the past month, searching for the one thing that had gone drastically wrong and resulted in the trap that was so obviously about to be sprung.

"Madison, good," Dorian Baxter said in his thick sonorous voice. "We were just talking about you."

"I noticed," Madison said. "That's what I get for being late."

Baxter was a large man with swarthy skin and flowing white hair. He wore a charcoal suit with a conservative tie and a bright white shirt, a modern-day monarch. It was rumored he was close to eighty years old, but he could easily pass for a healthy sixty. His pale green eyes were piercing, and left people with the impression that nothing could be hidden from him. The rest of the partners scattered to their respective chairs, still smiling and nodding affably at Madison. She found her own seat and pulled a pen and a yellow legal pad out of her briefcase, setting them on the table in front of her before she looked back up at Dorian with the same winning innocent smile she used when addressing a jury.

"As you know, Madison," Dorian began, before pausing to clear his throat, "this year the firm has had some of the worst financial difficulties in its one-hundred-and-thirty-seven-year history."

Madison wondered when he would get to the point.

"We're facing the unusual dilemma of having to look for places within the firm that we can cut," he continued.

This puzzled Madison more than worried her. Of course she didn't make as much money for the firm as some. Isabelle, who specialized in medical malpractice, could sometimes clear several million in a good year. As good as Madison was, the fact remained that criminals didn't typically have the resources to pay very big legal bills. Still, she had billed consistently for the past ten years and was careful to represent at least four paying customers for every indigent pro bono case she took on. She was easily worth her quarter-million-dollar salary. If anything, she had been expecting a raise.

"In that respect, one area in this firm stands out." Baxter held Madison's gaze with the cold certainty of an inflexible manager.

"I know it's difficult, still, for you to talk about Marty Cahn," Baxter said, clearing his throat politely, "and I respect that. However, this firm has to move forward, and it has been over a year since his unfortunate death."

Madison was sure the entire room could hear her heart beating. Marty Cahn had been her best friend, a tax lawyer with whom she'd gone through law school. His death had been sudden and violent, the result of his involvement in one of her murder trials. In fact, it was the trial of the man who was now Madison's husband. Any mention of Marty's name and death was loaded with emotion.

"However," Baxter's voice boomed after a substantial pause, breaking Madison's trance, "life goes on, and this firm goes on. It will after each of us has gone. And so, we would like you to seriously consider taking on one aspect of Marty's responsibilities that has suffered since his unfortunate demise.

"I'm referring to Marty's sports agency practice."

Madison's eyes focused sharply. She looked around the room to see that every other partner was staring at her.

"The fact is, Madison," Baxter said, "Marty was bringing in substantial revenue from the work he did for NFL players alone. He brought in almost twice as much money in that area as he did in his tax work, no small accomplishment, and all while expending a tenth of the hours. Unfortunately, without Marty, this source of revenue has dried up. Marty seemed to have a knack for winning over these players. The associate who worked for him obviously lacks those skills.

"We want you to take over the sports agency. And continue with your trial work, of course."

"No," Madison said without hesitation, looking bravely at Dorian Baxter. "I'm a trial lawyer. I'm one of the best in my field, and that is exactly what I want to do. It's all I want to do. I'm sorry."

Baxter pursed his lips and nodded grimly.

"I'm sorry, too," Baxter said coldly. He was not a man used to people saying no. "You see, we thought that with your marriage to Cody Grey and your affiliation with the NFL, and with the celebrity status that you've acquired in the last year since your husband's trial, well, we thought you could save some people's jobs."

"I really have no affiliation with the NFL, Dorian," Madison said as pleasantly as she could, "nor do I want to have. I don't think I'd be the person for that job. Is that all?"

"No," Baxter said, pushing a folder toward her across the smooth rich grain of the mahogany conference table. "Since you are refusing the direct request of this committee, you will be the one to tell Chris Pelo that he no longer works here."

Madison started to protest, but Baxter cut her off by raising his hand and his voice at the same time. "Let me tell you, young lady, that you're not the only talented trial lawyer I've seen. This isn't about what you want to do and don't want to do. This is about this firm and its well-being. You have the opportunity to help this firm in an hour of crisis!

"That you choose to take the path of self-service is a disappointment," Baxter said, his voice becoming appropriately sad, "but as the managing partner, I will not take it upon myself to terminate a member of this firm when his position could have been preserved with some good old-fashioned teamwork."

"Fine," Madison fumed, snatching the file from the table and rising to her feet. "But if you think that you can coerce me into taking on a specialty practice I have neither the background for nor interest in by making me do what is rightly your job, you're wrong. Oh, I'll tell Chris—and I'll tell him I'm sorry that he works for such a cold-blooded bunch as we obviously are, measuring our attorneys in terms of dollars and cents instead of their competence and integrity. One bad year, and we're already looking for who we can cut. Maybe he'll be better off elsewhere. Maybe we all would be."

Madison stormed out of the conference room and hurried back to her office, where she shut the door so she could stew in private. She didn't want to say anything else she would regret. It wasn't that Madison didn't think she was right. But, in a way, so was Baxter. Her firm did go beyond individual lawyers. The firm was an entity that had been there long before her, and would be there long after.

Madison remembered when she was first offered a job with Caldburn, Baxter and Thrush. It was the biggest moment of her life. It was her dream come true. Her father was a respected trial attorney in Dallas, and she could have easily joined his practice. But Madison had wanted to make her own way, and she knew that in Austin there were opportunities, if she was smart enough and good enough to secure them. When she'd first come to the firm out of law school, Timothy Pembrook, a lawyer whose skills even her father revered, had taken her under his wing, and by his death at the age of seventy-four, he had trained her to be one of the best.

Neither Pembrook, nor her father, had served two masters. They were trial lawyers and nothing else. Therein lay the conflict. The man who had given her career life by making her his protégé fresh out of law school was also the man whose focus was unwavering. Now she was faced with the choice of lending a hand to someone in need or maintaining the single-minded focus that had made her the best.

"Why am I even thinking about this?" she said out loud in a bewildered voice.

"Nancy," she said into her intercom. "Get me Chris Pelo, please. Tell him I need to see him right away."

"Yes, Ms. McCall," her secretary said.

Madison opened the file on the desk in front of her. On top was a termination letter. She glanced through the terms: three months' pay, one year of medical coverage for his entire family, prorated bonuses for this year. They were also letting him take the sports client list and the nontax files with him. It was all very fair, not something to be ashamed of. It was just business.

When Pelo walked through the door, it was clear to her why the sports agency was foundering. She wondered for the hundredth time why Marty had ever attempted to cultivate this man as an NFL agent. Pelo was forty-three. He wore an ill-fitting gray suit and a red tie that was too short, with a knot that was too big. Madison suspected that he grew his bushy mustache to draw attention away from his badly pocked skin. His hair seemed bereft of any style whatsoever, nothing more than a thatch. The only physical attribute he seemed to possess was a pair of deep-set eyes, bottomless black pools that focused with obvious intelligence. Madison knew that this guy was the last person ninety-nine point ninety-nine percent of all NFL players would even consider talking to about representing them. Agents in the NFL were a slick lot. Even Marty, with his angular frame and thick glasses, had cut an impressive figure because of his height alone. And Marty always knew how to put it on when he had to. He looked smart, and he was. Everyone around him sensed it. He knew how to dress and he knew how to order wine. Chris Pelo was the kind of guy who would have to prove he was smart, and NFL players didn't like to wait around for people to prove themselves.

"Sit down, Chris," Madison said after standing to shake his hand.

"I'm sorry I have to be the one to tell you this," she said, preferring to get straight to the point, "but the executive committee has decided to terminate the sports agency, and, along with that, your position . . . I'm sorry."

Only the turmoil in Pelo's eyes hinted at the agony he must be feeling. Outwardly, he was fine. Madison was impressed.

She handed him the file. It was business, she told herself that again.

"Is there anything I can do?" Pelo said. "I mean, would they reconsider, in any way, do you think? Could I work in another area? The tax department? Maybe even estate planning?"

Madison shook her head sadly. "I don't think so," she said. "They're planning on cutting back everywhere they can, Chris. I have to tell you that they wanted me to run this agency with you, but it wouldn't work. It was a desperation thing with the executive committee. It would only have prolonged the inevitable for a few more months. I'm not an agent. That's why they had me be the one to tell you, to punish me for not trying to become one. You know as well as anyone that it's not a thing you can do if your heart's not in it."

They both stared at the floor for a few moments before Pelo remembered himself and rose politely.

"Thank you, Madison," he said, extending his hand.

"Huh?" she said, caught off guard.

"No," he explained, holding up the letter, "not for this. I mean just thanks for treating me the way you did. I know the only reason I was in this firm was because of Marty. He was eccentric, let's face it. I'm a Mexican, middle-aged ex-cop trying to be a big-time sports agent."

Pelo let out a good-natured chuckle in honor of his old boss.

"But you were probably the only other person in this firm who treated me like I belonged here. You never acted uncomfortable when I passed you in the hall or met you in Marty's office. You acted as if I was just another lawyer. I appreciate that. Goodbye."

Madison almost stopped him as he passed quickly through her doorway. But then he was gone, and after a heavy sigh and a moment of thought, she lifted a thick trial file marked FEARS from her drawer and began to read through it.

Chapter 2

That same afternoon, in another office, in another state, a patient lay stretched out on a long leather lounge chair. Although the chair engulfed most of the people who lay on it, this particular man seemed to barely fit. His eyes were closed and his head was tilted back, exposing the long edge of a well-sculpted chin. Except for the gentle rubbing of one hand over the other in a repetitive motion, he appeared to be completely relaxed. A silver-gilded paddle fan turned lazily above him on the ceiling. Even the light in the room was soothing. The tall mullioned windows overlooking the Intracoastal Waterway were draped with two layers of heavy brown curtains that seemed like long eighteenth-century capes. Only the soft orange hues of the harsh sunlight outside were allowed to pass into the room.

The walls were lined with book-laden shelves, and an impressive collection of original pre-Columbian statues and masks was displayed throughout the room. The books were bound in faded red, brown, and green leather and emitted a musty smell reminiscent of an old library, a safe place. Jewel-toned Tiffany lamps adorned various carved wooden tables positioned among the richly upholstered furniture.

The doctor sat in a crimson wing-backed chair worn as comfortable as an old baseball mitt. Unlike everything else in the room, the doctor's face was severe. He had a bristling gray crew cut and wore a pair of chrome wire-framed glasses that seemed composed entirely of acute angles. His voice, however, was as gentle as the whispers of air stirred by the overhead fan.

The doctor surreptitiously looked at the clock he kept on a maple hutch just beyond his patient's line of sight. Time was almost up. And, as was always the case when time was short, his questions and comments became more pointed, more provocative.

"There are things you're not telling me," the doctor said.

The patient was silent.

"We've been over your feelings of guilt for what happened to your mother and brother many times, as well as the situation with your father, and even the woman and her boy," the doctor said. "But there seems to be something more, something you're not telling me."

"Yes," he finally said. "But it's not me. There are things that have happened, things that I think are going to happen, that I can't control."

"If you can't control them, then why do these things haunt you?" the doctor asked, knowing full well the answer.

"It's not me, but then, it is, isn't it? I mean, I know I'm responsible . . ."

"We've talked about your responsibility before," the doctor said. "There are some things we cannot control. Others we can."

"It's like the red zone. I think people are going to die."

"In your dreams?" the doctor said, puzzled.

"No, for real."

The doctor puckered his lips and said nothing. The things that were said to him by his patients were confidential. He had a duty to respect that confidentiality. He knew there was also a duty, if he could, to prevent harm to others. He was now hearing that people were going to die. Unlike many of his patients, the man before him was not prone to exaggeration. The doctor wanted to help people, but he shunned danger. He had a wife and a child. He had worked hard to develop the kind of practice that was safe from the dark things he'd learned about as a resident. A hysterical suicide was as close as he ever intended to get to violence.

"And you feel . . . responsible for this?" the doctor finally asked, tentatively.

"I will be responsible," he said with finality.

The doctor sat for almost a minute, watching the clock that would save him. He focused on the hands of his patient. The almost continuous motion of hand washing was a common neurotic manifestation of overwhelming guilt. This was easily understood. It was also a much healthier outlet than killing.

"We'll have to talk about this some more the next time," the doctor said gently. "I'm afraid our time is up. In the meantime, continue to focus your anger and your guilt and your negative feelings into your work. This is an advantage you have that many others do not."

The doctor liked to end on a positive note, so as he rose, marking the end of their session, he added, "It is a wonderful outlet."

The patient raised his bulk up off the chair with unusual grace for a man his size. The diminutive, sharp-looking doctor reached up and patted the big man halfway up his broad muscular back.

"Who do you play this weekend?" the doctor said, making light conversation as he ushered the man out the door, as if he hadn't heard what he clearly did.

"Atlanta," he answered.

"Ah," said the doctor, "the Hawks . . ."

"No," he said, "that's the basketball team. It's the Atlanta Falcons."

The doctor gave an apologetic shrug. Luther Zorn didn't care. He had yet to meet a shrink who was a true fan of the game. In a way, he thought that might be why he didn't mind talking with them.

Chapter 3

Madison rolled into the driveway of her new home in West Lake Hills, Texas. She lived with her husband, Cody Grey, and her son from her first marriage, Jo-Jo, in a gated community that had its own private golf course and country club. The house sat on a hillside and had a spectacular view of the Austin skyline. The hilly landscape was not at all dissimilar to that of Bel Air, the exclusive enclave adjacent to Los Angeles. The house, designed in the style of an elegant European château, was relatively modest for the neighborhood. Still, the lawn and shrubbery were impeccably sculpted.

As she pulled into the garage Madison saw that Cody's pickup truck was already there. She looked at her watch and realized that she was late. She hoisted her briefcase from the passenger seat of her Volvo sedan and hustled inside. Cody and Jo-Jo were halfway through dinner. Madison stopped to kiss them both before heaving a sigh and slumping down into her own chair. Their housekeeper, Bess, quickly brought Madison a plate of food.

"Mom, can I watch game film with Cody?" Jo-Jo asked before Madison had a chance to take a second breath.

Madison looked up from her plate at her husband. He gave her an innocent shrug.

"How about homework?" she said.

"Did it, Ma," Jo-Jo replied.

"All of it?"

"Yup."

"Okay," Madison said. "Who're you guys scouting this week?"

"We're playing Sam Houston this week and Cody's got a film of them slaughtering East Side," Jo-Jo said with an enthusiasm most nine-year-olds reserved for collecting snakes.

Cody was the West Lake Hills High School football coach. After playing for nine years in the NFL as a star defensive back for Austin's own Texas Outlaws, a ruined knee forced him to retire. While teammates dreamed of postfootball careers in TV or the movies, Cody's sole ambition had been to teach and coach high school kids. The West Lake Hills job opened after the former coach's failure to produce a winning team for six straight years.

Madison supported her husband completely. She admired his desire to work with kids and she knew he was more than just a coach to the players on his team and a teacher to the students in his classroom. She was even understanding when they had to cut their honeymoon short by a few days so he could return for summer workouts. Recently, though, their different career paths had been the source of some tension.

The biggest problem was the fact that she earned more than six times Cody's salary. Because his first wife had been so preoccupied with material wealth, Madison suspected that Cody had developed a subconscious aversion to prosperity. It also seemed to Madison that the physical infatuation they had enjoyed during the first months of their relationship was beginning to wane. Now, some of the realities of a marriage and its inherent compromises were beginning to set in.

Originally, she didn't have a hard time convincing Cody to live in their present house. But lately, he talked about wanting something a little more middle class. That, however, wasn't what Madison was used to, and it wasn't what she'd worked for. It took a lot of long hard hours to make her kind of salary, and she wanted to reward herself by living comfortably.

Cody, for his part, was suddenly concerned that they live more in line with how other high school football coaches lived. Football coaches, he had explained, didn't need much, just a couple of sweat suits, a windbreaker, and some sneakers in their closet, and a late-model pickup in the driveway. According to Cody, country club living and high school football were not compatible. It was one more reason for Madison to dislike the game. She considered it bizarre that both her husbands had been football players. She had no affinity for the game, or the stars it created. Still, she wasn't fooling anyone, even herself. There was also some indefinite quality about the kind of man who would play that game that undeniably attracted her.

Jo-Jo, on the other hand, had been an unabashed fan of the game since he knew what a football was. He was thrilled that Cody was the coach, and he talked incessantly about playing and coaching himself one day.

But Madison was happy that Cody and her son had a common interest, even if it was a game where young boys and grown men alike ran around on the grass trying to hurt each other. Football enabled Cody and Jo-Jo to form a bond much sooner than if Cody had simply been a high school history teacher and nothing more. That bond was critical to Madison because while she adored her husband, Jo-Jo was her only child and, despite her career, Madison had a distracting maternal instinct. That instinct told her it was critical for her son to grow up in a house where a man was present, and Cody was as good as any man she had ever known.

And of course she needed Cody for herself as well. As strong as she was, Madison wanted a man, one man, whom she could count on to be there with her through the good as well as the bad. It was hard sometimes, maintaining the precarious balance of hard-nosed lawyer and softhearted woman. Madison wondered if her two sides weren't mutually exclusive. She hoped not. She wanted Cody in her life.

Despite their problems, she loved him completely. She'd come a long way since her first husband. Jo-Jo's father was exciting and handsome, but he'd turned into a monster. Her first marriage seemed like another life altogether.

"Madison? Did you hear me?" Cody's voice broke through her reverie. She smiled at him, happy just to see his face looking at her. He wore his dark hair short and his deep hazel eyes seemed somehow to be lit from within. His tan face was marked with lines of care that sometimes made him look older than his thirty-two years. But still, he was handsome, strong, and above all, extremely kind.

"No, I'm sorry, honey," she said. "I was thinking."

"I said Chris Pelo called," Cody told her, roughly swiping something from the corner of his mouth with a napkin. "It seemed important. Is everything okay?"

Madison furrowed her brow. "Everything's fine," she said. "Except I'm not thrilled that Chris is calling me at home about something I wrapped up with him already at the office."

"Well," Cody shrugged, "maybe it's important. It sure sounded like it."

"I'm sure it's important to him," she said, taking another bite of her food.

"So, what's up?" Cody asked.

Madison sighed and set down her fork before recounting her meeting with the executive committee and how she subsequently broke the bad news to Pelo. When she was finished, she gave her husband a sad smile and continued her meal. She looked up after a moment of silence. He was staring at her.

"What?" she said.

"Nothing," Cody replied calmly, looking to her son. "You ready for some film, big guy?"

"Yeah!" Jo-Jo said, hopping up from the table.

"Okay, you go get the projector set up and I'll be in in a minute," Cody said.

"So, what?" Madison said when her son had left the kitchen.

"So, just that I'm kind of surprised, that's all," Cody told her gently.

"At?"

"At the fact that you could have helped Chris Pelo keep his job, but you didn't," Cody said frankly. "I mean, he's a hell of a guy. I just . . . I don't know, it's not like you, Madison."

Madison set her fork down on her plate a little harder than she meant to and it rang out loudly. "He's a hell of a guy? I don't know what that has to do with my career. You're supposed to be on my side, Cody. I can't go around saving everybody's job any more than you can."

Cody looked at her dispassionately and said quietly, "You're a little overexcited, aren't you? You sound like you're in court or something."

"Yes, I'm excited, Cody!" she said. "I'm excited because of what I said. I don't want to be Chris Pelo's savior. I'm a lawyer, not an agent. I have no intention of being an agent. If Chris Pelo decides to go into house painting, should I go out and buy a ladder and a can of paint in case he needs my help? Look at what you're asking—"

Cody held his hands up high in surrender as he got up from the table.

"I am on your side, Madison," he said. "I'm not trying to tell you to change all your plans, but I think you could do what you want and help him out without even breaking a sweat. He's a great guy. He just can't close a deal. He never could. That's why he and Marty were good together. If you just helped him a little, I think he could keep that thing going. I know when I was a player, I loved dealing with Chris. He was on top of everything. But it was Marty who got people to sign on. He did with me, anyway. You could do that, too. I think you know it already, though. That's why you're so upset."

Cody leaned over and put his hand on Madison's cheek before giving her a kiss on the forehead.

"Don't say I'm not on your side, Madison," he told her gently. "I'm always on your side."

Madison reached up and held his hand tightly against her face.

"Good," Cody said. "I'm going to go watch some film with Jo-Jo before he has to go to bed, okay? We'll talk later."

"Okay."

Madison sat alone in the kitchen for a minute pushing her food. Then she set her fork down again and got up for the phone.

"Hello?" came the thickly accented voice of Chris Pelo's wife.

"Is Chris there?"

"Yes . . . Please, *un momento*."

"Hello?"

"Chris, this is Madison."

"Madison, I know you don't like to be called at home, but I've got an idea," Pelo blurted out desperately. Before Madison could get a word in, he continued rapidly. "It wouldn't be much of a burden on you. I promise. Just please listen. Marty had a client. His name is Luther Zorn. He plays for the Marauders. He's a great player and his contract is up this year. I just found out that the team wants to redo his deal now, in the middle of the season. They want to renegotiate his deal before he becomes a free agent at the end of the season. If I can get him, just him, his contract alone would pay for the agency for the next three or four years. Just one contract! Now I know I can get a meeting with him, just based on my relationship with him in the past."

"Chris—" Madison tried to sneak a word in, but Chris was speaking too fast.

"Madison, I know you don't want to have anything to do with this. I know you're a trial lawyer and you're busy. I know all about the Fears trial. And the rape case. But I was thinking. I could help you make up for any time you spent on this by doubling up and helping you do legwork or research for your next trial. I'll do anything, and I know I can help some way. If you just help me close this deal with Zorn. It could legitimize me. But I'm not going to kid myself. I probably don't stand a chance to do it without some help."

"Chris, stop," Madison interrupted. "Let me talk. I hear you. I hear you."

"I know what it means, Madison, and I—"

"Chris! Listen to me," Madison pleaded. "I'll help."

There was silence on the other end of the line.

"Madison," Pelo said quietly, "I'm sorry I had to ask you like this and put you on the spot. I won't forget this. I won't."

Chapter 4

Across the Gulf of Mexico, on a sultry Florida night, two NFL teams battled each other as well as the humidity. The Florida Marauders were playing the New York Giants in a Thursday night game on cable TV. The home team was ahead, but only by six, and the Giants were threatening to score. The West Palm Beach Municipal Stadium was an open arena with a grass field, so grass stains marked the players' uniforms along with the brilliant spattering of blood from numerous open wounds. The only players whose bodies weren't slippery and slick from sweat were the kickers. They huddled on the bench like a pair of penguin chicks next to the cold-air machine that blew a cool misty fog out of a single eight-inch flexible pipe.

On the field, the Marauders' defense seemed to be losing its will. They had begun the current series of plays with the Giants backed right up to their own goal line and very little time in the game. But in every critical third-down situation, Dave Brown, the Giants' quarterback, came up with a big play. Everyone was tired at this point in the contest, and momentum was more important than even a roster of star players. The momentum belonged to the Giants. After a run that was stuffed for a loss, and a failed screen pass, again the Giants found themselves in third down with a long twelve to go. The goal line, however, was painfully close. They were on the seventeen-yard line: the red zone.

In football, once the offense crosses the other team's twenty, it is called the red zone because every move, every penalty, every inch, every detail, is critical. In a game of violence, nowhere is the primal urge to attack and defend more clear. Here is where the lust for blood boils most clearly to the surface. Here is where the winners are separated from the losers, the weak from the strong. Mistakes in the red zone are known to cost people their jobs, their careers, and therefore their lives.

Luther Zorn, the Marauders' inside linebacker and defensive captain, tapped into the violence within himself. He could do that, did do that, better than anyone in a critical situation. It made him a leader. It made him great. It made him dangerous. He popped himself in the forehead with the palm of his gloved hand, an old trick that flooded his system with adrenaline. He read the play hand-signaled in to him from the sideline and repeated it to his teammates before exhorting them.

"Come on! This is EVERYTHING, right here! This is the FUCKING game! Somebody's got to make it HAPPEN!" he howled, then broke the huddle.

The play called for Luther to take the tight end in man-to-man coverage. That was fine, but if he sensed his man was going to stay in and help protect the quarterback by blocking, Luther intended to take matters into his own hands. He would go for the quarterback himself. If the tight end set up like he was blocking, then released into the pass pattern late, it would be an easy touchdown and the loss would be on Luther's head. If Luther guessed right, however, he could make a play that might win the game.

He looked around him. The other linebackers on either side of him were lined up with their heads hanging low, sucking air into their lungs as if they'd just come up from a deep dive. The linemen in front of him were in three-point stances, their hamstrings hanging limp off their leg bones like water balloons. There was no electricity in anyone. Luther hit himself in the face one more time and glanced at the tight end. He was back on his heels. He'd stay in to block. Luther believed that sometimes in every game, as in life, someone had to step up and take a chance. Otherwise, you ended up just like everyone else, just like seaweed being washed along by the surf and the tides.

The ball was snapped, and despite what he was supposed to do, Luther blitzed up through the middle of the line, an apparition passing through the scrum of bigger linemen locked in a frenzy of violence. Like a guard dog at the back door, the fullback was instantly on his feet. Luther leapt with inexplicable grace, belying his size and strength. Then he was down, landing on his feet in the grass quite near the quarterback, whose eyes were now filled with panic at the sight of Luther so close. Luther took a swat at the other player with his heavy arm and the ball spilled from the quarterback's hands. A wave of players from both sides suddenly came crashing down around them both, swamping even Luther off his feet.

But even as he fell, Luther instinctively searched for and found the wayward ball. He pulled it into his body and held on as if his life was in the balance. The roar of the crowd echoed in his ears with a deafening intensity. When he rose from the pile of bodies with the ball in his hands, the noise became louder still. The enemy's last-minute drive for the goal line was foiled. The Marauders' offense would ramble out and run down the clock. They had won. Luther would get to keep the game ball. It wouldn't be his first, but he had no way of knowing it would be his last.

In the locker room, Luther knelt with the rest of his teammates to thank God for their victory. While one of his more religious counterparts droned on about the Glory of God and the forgiveness of sin, Luther thought about the serious transgressions he had committed in his own life. He had never given much thought to God. If in fact there was a God, Luther was certain that He hadn't given much thought to Luther. He learned that very early as a child growing up in the city. With a mother who was white and an abusive father who was black, Luther could not remember a day when he didn't feel completely alone, except for his mother and his younger brother.

Before he died, his father had been as great an enemy as Luther had ever known. Luther considered his early death a blessing. The only way he could ever figure that his mother had ended up with such a man was the mistake of his own conception. There were many things that haunted Luther, especially the way he had cowered while his father beat him and his younger brother. There was one particular incident that was so horrible, it repeated itself over and over in his dreams. Although there was nothing Luther could have done to protect his brother or his mother, it twisted his insides to think that he had never even tried. Then, mercifully, his father died of a gunshot wound, an unlucky bystander during a liquor store robbery.

But even then there had been no shortage of enemies for Luther. His mother didn't have to live in the world that he was forced to endure, a world somewhere between the blacks and the whites. Luther suspected that being spared that final humiliation was the thing that allowed his mother to keep her faith. Despite rarely having even enough food to eat, she always talked about God. For his part, Luther had listened, and nodded, and said the right words. But after years of going hungry, and years of being beaten either by his own father or the older boys in the neighborhood for the simple mistake of having been born, Luther knew that his mother's God could, or would, do nothing for him.

By the time Luther grew up and the neighborhood bullying ceased, it was too late. His mind was made up. Size and strength were his gods. He learned how to be tough and mean, and his own dominance allowed his younger brother to be spared much of the punishment from the neighborhood gangs. The only thing Luther regretted about his father's early death was that he never had the opportunity to protect the two people he loved by using against his father the brutal force he had come to wield so effectively.

But even though Luther became physically strong, he was never able to escape the scorn and derision from not only his peers, but neighbors, teachers, and even clergymen. Their abhorrence of him wasn't always obvious, but it was always there, and Luther knew it. He learned to act for himself and by himself and to advance toward the things he wanted in life with calculation and a disregard for others. In high school, he discovered football, a world where the color of his skin meant nothing at all. In that world, he could unleash his pent-up anger without being arrested.

Without football, Luther knew his path in life would have ended in prison. There was too much hatred inside him for it not to erupt. But with football acting as an emotional safety valve, Luther was able to function socially, to create and maintain the appearance of a pleasant and friendly young man. Even with football, though, he was sometimes pushed to a point where sanity was drowned out by his rage at having to pretend. The emotional turmoil created by carefully maintaining this outward appearance of calm and control was at times overwhelming. It had caused him to act erratically on occasion. Early on he was put into counseling, which had helped him. And, among other things, Luther was smart, so he did well in school. People who didn't know about his "problems" would marvel then, as they did now, at how such a model young man could play the game of football with such cold-blooded viciousness.

When the prayer was over, Luther stripped to his waist, then turned to face the onslaught of cameras and microphones that swarmed around his locker. The questions came at him from all sides. He knew that the group of reporters were nothing but hyenas that would snap him up the moment he stumbled and his career started its inevitable downslide. But Luther knew how to play the game. He put on one of his most patient smiles and began to slowly and carefully sort out the questions one at a time.

After the interviews, and a shower, Luther toweled off among the rapidly thinning crowd in the locker room. The equipment men were working like a busy colony of ants, tossing the last of the damp, stained jerseys into large canvas bins for cleaning. The jubilation of the win had already evaporated like a morning mist. The aches of torn and damaged body parts were settling in. Painkillers, splashed down with Gatorade, had yet to take effect. There was only one way to revive the excitement of the win and squeeze just a little more from it, like the pulp of an already juiced orange. Even though it was already late, Luther would join his teammates at a nightclub to rehash the game and further drown the nagging body aches with alcohol.

"Where's it at?" Luther said, directing his question at Antone Ellison, a defensive back whose locker was next to Luther's.

Antone was already dressed from head to toe in silk, alligator, and gold, and Luther could smell his distinctively thick cologne. Antone was one of the more anonymous members of the team, who rarely saw the playing field, a lifetime backup player who never fulfilled his college potential, but who nevertheless seemed to make the final cut year after year. Despite his skills on the field, he was the team's grand marshal off the field, the Marauders' unofficial social coordinator.

Antone's face broke into a wide smile. "Everyone's goin' to the Hot Tin Roof," he said with the smoothness of a cocktail lounge entertainer, "an' I *know* you goin' be with us, Luther. It ain't a real thang without the man, an' *you* the man."

Luther absorbed the information with a nod and slapped Ellison's suspended palm with an obligatory high-five before sitting down on his stool to dry off his feet. It was then that Luther noticed a small pink square of paper in the bottom of his locker. He scooped it into his palm and looked around furtively. Ellison had been hovering, but he looked away quickly and departed without another word. Luther opened his hand with the care of a small boy holding a butterfly and examined the note. It appeared to be a simple telephone message. Players had these pink slips deposited into their lockers routinely two or three times a week. Typically, the bigger the name of the player, the more phone messages he got. They were like fan mail.

People called the Marauders' offices all the time, looking for some way to get in touch with guys like Luther, or Gary Morris, the team's quarterback, for any of a number of reasons. Most of them wanted something. The unusual thing about the message Luther held in his hand was that the of-

fice had closed long ago. The secretaries upstairs didn't
work past five. There was no way a phone message should
have appeared in Luther's locker on Thursday night, after a
game. It hadn't been there before the game began. Luther
was sure of that.

Luther didn't know how the message had been delivered,
but he did know why it was there. His heart raced, and a
thrill not unlike the rush he had just experienced on the football field surged from the center of his body outward until he
was flushed with excitement. He examined the note. It was
written in her own hand. He knew she was somewhere in the
building, and he wondered if she could have come into the
locker room herself while he was in the shower to deliver it,
or entrusted someone else to do it. Either way, the obvious
risk she had taken to get the message to him made the
thought of a rendezvous all the more exciting.

Luther crumpled the note and held it tightly while he
dressed. When he was finished, he stood and with his free
hand began to carefully caress the hand holding the note. As
he walked out of the locker room, he tossed the crumpled
paper ball in the trash can, then made his way through the
heavy double doors that led to the stadium tunnel and outside into the muggy warmth of the Florida night. He had no
way of knowing that Antone Ellison would retrieve the
crumpled message from the trash only a minute after he'd
discarded it there.

Chapter 5

Luther pulled his black Dodge Viper into the north parking lot of MacCarther National Park and swung his car in a wide circle to illuminate the entire lot, making sure no one else was around. Satisfied, he pulled off of the blacktop onto an overgrown sandy track that led to the place where Sandy Kiffleman had parked her truck for the last time. Luther felt no need to pull the dark Viper into the undergrowth. Getting it out of plain view in the parking lot was enough to ensure that he would be safe from discovery.

Luther absently rubbed his hands as he made his way from his car down the narrow path that led to the ocean. The breeze rushed in through his nostrils and filled his lungs. The smell of the ocean to him now was as reminiscent of sex as the smell of cheap perfume on a whore. Above, the night sky was clear, the stars sparkled, and a sliver of moon hung in the east over the hypnotic surf. As sore and tired as he was from the game, Luther began to jog along the beach toward Lost Tree Village.

When he got to the private development, Luther slowed down so he could hear better. He removed a small canister from his pocket and gripped it tightly in his hand. The dogs, he knew, would come quietly. They would only begin to bark when they could see him. His scent, however, would bring them running. In fact, he hadn't gone more than a hundred feet before he was forced to drop to one knee and aim his Mace at a raving pair of rottweilers. The mist from his canister filled the air in front of him and the dogs sprang away from him as if they'd run into a rubber wall. Their shrieks of pain filled Luther with delight, and as they spun around madly tearing at their muzzles with their own paws, he approached them quickly and hit them point-blank with another shot of Mace. With the dogs trembling and whining in agony, Luther proceeded down the beach with a smirk.

He felt a sense of smug satisfaction at the sight of a white mansion whose shape loomed above the trees lining the beach. He'd seen teammates come and go through his years as an NFL player, many of them ruining their lives with drugs or alcohol. He understood the thirst for a high. But drugs were child's play compared to the violence of football, and certainly to the kind of excitement he was feeling right now, the arousal of danger and imminent sex.

Marble steps led up from the beach and through a bank of palm trees to a courtyard and swimming pool. The pool water was sapphire blue, illuminated by a set of lights below the surface. The white house with its ornate roofs and cornices rose up around this courtyard in a way that reminded Luther of a small but fine hotel.

"Luther?" her voice came down from the balcony above and resonated throughout the courtyard. Luther felt the same electrical surge pass through his body that he felt when he'd first read her note earlier that night.

He turned his gaze toward her. In the shimmering light from the pool he could make out her long tan figure, adorned in a white lace negligee. It was his favorite, and she knew it. He said nothing. He knew the way, and in a moment found himself standing there beside her in the warm damp night.

"Luther," she said once more, her voice spilling desire.

"You shouldn't have done this," he said to her, slipping his arms around the small of her back. "Someone could have seen you."

"I had to have you," she told him quietly. "I needed you."

"Where is he?" Luther asked.

"Gone for the night," she said. "It's safe . . . Kiss me, Luther."

She leaned up toward him as she spoke his name for the third time. It was the way she spoke that made it so perfect. Their lips locked instantly and voraciously and Luther felt her hands on him, tearing at his clothes, desperately searching for his flesh. Soon they were naked and entwined on the bed, like some eight-limbed being, moaning and heaving in the throes of certain death.

In a private Gulfstream jet over the Atlantic Ocean, Evan Chase leaned back into the deep leather chair and entwined his fingers underneath his chin. His elbows rested comfortably on the armrests of the chair. A full glass of single malt scotch poured over crushed ice sat in a crystal glass on the small table beside him. He was a man with everything but good looks. Despite a deep tan, clear blue eyes, and an athletic physique that belied his age of forty-seven, his bulbous nose and a close-set pair of eyes made him unattractive to women who didn't know about his bank account. Chase, if nothing else, was wealthy. And wealth, he knew, was power.

"We're talking about fifty million dollars, Evan," Martin Wilburn explained patiently. "Even you can't pretend that it's not a temptation."

"I didn't say it wasn't a temptation, Martin," he replied. "I've told you all along that it's a temptation. I've also told you all along that I wouldn't do it. Florida is my home. I'm not going to leave it for fifty million dollars or a hundred and fifty million dollars. I like it here."

Evan smiled. He was having fun. If he didn't enjoy this banter, he would have stopped all the discussion months ago, when his partner had first proposed that he move the Marauders from South Florida to Memphis.

Evan Chase had grown up in Florida, and it was where he'd made his name. After an All-America career as a swimmer at the University of Florida, Chase had gone on to win a silver medal in the 1972 Olympics. He parlayed that success and his education in finance into a successful real estate development company that specialized in residential subdivisions. Slowly and meticulously over the years he assembled a substantial real estate empire. In the mid-eighties, when his business was at its zenith, the Florida Marauders had come up for sale. It was the perfect continuation of a hometown success story. After buying the team, everyone who was anyone in South Florida, from Palm Beach to Miami, knew who Evan Chase was on sight. Evan enjoyed this notoriety as much, if not more, than his substantial wealth, so moving the team wasn't even a consideration.

He liked playing with Martin, though. He had to get some enjoyment out of the man since he so deeply resented having sold him a ten percent interest in his team. But, at the time, he'd needed cash desperately. Without Martin Wilburn's fifteen-million-dollar infusion, he stood then to lose his entire real estate empire as well as his team in the bargain. Now, though, with the recent upturn in the market, Chase was well beyond needing anyone's money, or anyone's help. Still, Martin was there, and he wasn't going away. Evan couldn't blame him for that. There were few investments surer or more lucrative than an NFL franchise. The Memphis offer illustrated that quite clearly.

"Let's stop talking about Memphis, Martin," Evan said over the whine of the jet engines. "Let's talk about our team. Let's talk about Luther Zorn. I told you I wanted him signed to a contract extension before the end of this season. How's *that* progressing?"

Chase let Martin handle the players' contracts in part because Martin could say things to players that Chase could only think. From the other side of a closed door, anyone hearing Martin's interactions with a player during a contract negotiation would know he was an egregious bigot. What they would never dream, though, was that Martin himself was black.

"He hasn't been able to give me the name of an agent, and he won't talk about it himself," Wilburn said smoothly, absently straightening the diamond ring on his left pinkie.

Chase narrowed one eye at his partner and took a sip of scotch before responding, "You're sure it's not because you're dragging your feet, Martin?"

"I simply don't think we should be staking our team's future on a philanderer," Wilburn said judiciously. Among other things, Wilburn tended to be a bit of a prig.

While Chase was examining his partner's expression, he failed to notice the almost imperceptible narrowing of his lawyer, Pat Rivet's, eyes behind his round gold-rimmed glasses. Otherwise, Rivet's face remained impassive as he looked on.

"What does Luther Zorn's private life have to do with leading this team to the Super Bowl?" Chase said contemptuously. "I'm talking about football here, Martin. Did you see that play tonight? Zorn is a demon. He's everywhere on that field. I want him locked in with this team for the next seven years and I don't care how much it costs. Just get it done or I'll do it myself."

Chapter 6

On their flight to West Palm, Chris Pelo presented Madison with a thorough report on exactly who Luther Zorn was. Madison read with some interest about Zorn's life.

"He's very handsome," Madison remarked freely to Pelo.

Pretending not to have noticed, Pelo leaned over to look at the full-color head shot that he'd included in the file.

"I guess so," he said, embarrassed that Madison would speak so directly. After all, she was a married woman. He himself was a devout Catholic and had some very old-fashioned ideas about sex.

"How did you get all this?" Madison asked, handing him the file.

Pelo shrugged. "On the Internet, I use it for everything. The way things are now, there's almost no information about anyone or anything you can't get through a computer if you just know how to access it."

"And you know how, obviously," Madison said.

"When I was an investigator, I found that knowing how to access information through different computer networks enabled me to process cases almost three times as fast as the people who were limited to file folders and phone calls."

"So how did you end up going from that, to this?" Madison said, looking curiously at her associate.

"Different, huh?" Pelo said with a boyish grin. "I started with the police force when I was nineteen. I liked my work there, but I knew I was going to need more than the pay and the pension of a cop if I was going to ever be able to pay off all the college loans I'd need for the kids. We've got five. I learned early on that, short of dumb luck, an education is the only thing that gets you ahead." He shrugged. "I guess I'm just like everyone else. I want my kids to have things a little better than me."

Madison nodded her head with understanding, even though she had grown up quite comfortably and never wondered for more than a minute about the ability to send any children she might have to college.

"So," Pelo continued, "I went to school during the days and worked the night beat as a cop. It took a while and it wasn't easy, but I got my undergraduate degree, and when I did, I was so used to the routine that I just kept going to get my law degree. By that time I was with CID, the Criminal Intelligence Division, and doing well. I was an investigator. I never thought I'd end up doing what I'm doing. But I met Marty during a big money-laundering investigation. We retained him for his expertise. He found out I was a lawyer and the two of us got along really well. I was up for retirement with a full pension at the time, and it was really Marty—well, you know how Marty was. When I first got to the firm, it was a real accomplishment. I was the first Latino to be hired, and anyway, I started out in the tax group and that was when Marty got me into this. Kind of crazy, really, I know. I know computers and the tax code—not exactly your typical sports agent.

"But like I said the other day, it's too late for me to start over now. I'm overqualified to start as a beginning associate . . . I suppose I could hang a shingle and do tax returns, but I've got two in college now and I'm still paying off on the first two, and I've got one more on deck. Not that he didn't mean anything but good, but you know Marty. He assured me we'd have this agency thing going forever. I'm sure we would have too . . ."

Chris Pelo's words hung in the stale dry air of the airplane cabin. Madison looked sadly at the back of the seat in front of her and Pelo excused himself to use the lavatory and give her time to reflect on the memory of their mutual friend, Marty Cahn.

When he returned, Chris sensed something different about Madison, as if her chin were more set and determined.

"I want you to tell me everything you know about Luther Zorn from your dealings with him, Chris. I want to know as much as I can. I don't think we have much time to convince him to let us represent him. If the Marauders want to redo his contract before the end of the season, he needs someone working on this yesterday."

Despite seeing his picture and despite everything Chris told her about Luther Zorn, she was still taken aback when he walked into the restaurant that night. They were early. Luther was late. Without trying, he drew considerable attention as he descended a small set of stairs and strode smoothly across the room to their table overlooking the ocean. As well as being six foot four with an athletic frame wrapped in thick cables of muscle, Luther was the only non-

Caucasian in the entire restaurant. But by the way he carried himself and by the jewelry he wore, he obviously belonged.

On his wrist was a gold presidential diamond-studded Rolex. In the open front of his olive silk shirt a single heavy gold Gucci chain rested against his unblemished skin. The color of the shirt brought out the green in his hazel eyes, and Madison couldn't help but stare at him as he unclasped his hands and extended one toward her. She took it. It was large and smooth and gentle, the hand of an artist rather than the paw of a bone-crunching linebacker.

"I'm Luther," he said confidently and quite unnecessarily. "It's nice to meet you, Madison. Hello, Chris."

When she released his grip, he reclasped his hands and rubbed them together gently before he sat down at the table.

Madison was taken aback by his confident manner and his refreshing politeness. There was no hint whatsoever that this same man had grown up in the garbage-strewn streets of a big city.

"Thank you," she said. It was her goal to impress Luther Zorn with her composure and her nerve. Chris, she knew, had already laid that foundation by briefing him on her accomplishments. Now it was up to her to convince Luther that her impressive résumé somehow made her the right person to negotiate a multimillion-dollar contract with people who did so on a daily basis.

They made small talk and ordered dinner. Luther chose a rich California merlot, and gallantly instructed the waiter to allow her to do the tasting. Madison did so with the aplomb of a countess, but underneath it all, she felt as though she was playing in a very intense, very complicated game with an opponent who had the advantage of having made up the rules. Luther watched her closely.

Madison drew together the folds of her blouse where it opened below the base of her neck before speaking.

"Congratulations on your win last week," she said, raising her glass. "Here's to continued success in your season."

"Thank you," Luther said quietly, then asked a series of pointed and intelligent questions about her background and her involvement with the NFL. He knew her husband was Cody Grey, and when she brought him up he admitted his fascination with her involvement in Cody's murder trial. Madison was hardly nonplussed by this line of questioning. That trial and its outcome had put her in the spotlight of the national media. The fact that Cody's ex-wife had a hand in framing him for the murder of an IRS agent made the trial a scandal of grand proportions. People were always curious about it.

Without waiting to be asked, Madison changed the subject, and began explaining why she should be his agent. She conceded that she hadn't been directly involved in such a contract negotiation, but went on to explain with confidence that negotiations were something she conducted on a daily basis where the stakes were always very high. To a man like Luther Zorn, loyalty would be more important than experience. With his background in mind, Madison felt that if she could convince Luther she would stick by him, that, more than anything, would win him as a client.

Madison recounted Cody's history, and how he had been abandoned in the final days of his career by everyone within the organization for which he played. The Outlaws didn't cut her husband because of the scandalous trial, but because of a ruined knee he had played on long after he should have stopped, a knee that now caused him to limp. She reminded Luther of several other well-known players in the league who had gone through difficult times in the latter part of their careers, being bought, sold, traded, and cut by teams who no longer felt their large salaries were commensurate with their skills on the field.

"I'm not as much an agent, Luther, as I am a lawyer," Madison told him. "Part of that, to me, means undying loyalty to my clients."

"I'm glad to hear you say all this, Madison," Luther said with a knowing smile, "because it confirms everything I've heard about you. When Chris called me a couple of days ago and mentioned you, I checked you out. I already knew about Cody and what you did for him. It was all over the news. But I checked deeper. I made some calls. You've got a big-time reputation. Some people say you're the F. Lee Bailey of the nineties . . . only with great legs," he added in a complimentary tone that in no way sounded lewd or inappropriate.

"The fact is," Zorn continued, "I want you to negotiate this contract for me. I want someone doing this who isn't motivated by greed or ambition. I'm also more than comfortable with Chris overseeing my financial affairs and my taxes. But as much as anything, I want to work with someone who knows what it feels like to be an outsider, and that's what you'll be when you deal with this team.

"Just like I'm an outsider here," Zorn said with a broad sweep of his hand around the dining room. "You'll be an outsider in my world, in football. Being an outsider makes you sharper than everyone else. It's always that way. You're more aware than other people, because you live in a constant state of awareness. That's how I live. The only difference for me is that it's an all-the-time thing. You'll only have to feel it while you're doing this deal. And you're right about loyalty. I expect it, and I know you'll give it to me. That's the deal. You stick by me no matter what. I don't want one of those deals where you represent me while it's good for you, then when I need you most, when I start to get old and worn out, you move on to someone else and stop returning my calls on the same day. I want your word on that."

"Of course," Madison responded without hesitation.

"Good," said Zorn, "then it's a deal. Chris, you send me the agreement."

"No problem," Chris said amicably.

Madison wasn't certain she was understanding him correctly. What he was saying was so sudden and so final that she had no idea how to react. She looked to Chris. Could it really be this easy?

"So," Madison said, trying not to balk, "you want us to represent you?"

Zorn gave her a puzzled and amused look.

"Yes," he nodded, and then added pleasantly, "that's what I said."

Madison couldn't help taking a deep breath and allowing a smile to creep into the corners of her mouth. She looked at Chris Pelo. He was beaming.

Chapter 7

To maximize their time in Florida, Madison and Chris arranged an impromptu meeting with Evan Chase the morning after their dinner with Luther Zorn. The Marauders' facility was part and parcel of West Palm Beach Municipal Stadium. Team offices were on the second floor, above the locker and meeting rooms where the players prepared for their upcoming games. The team facility was actually part of the stadium. The grass practice field adjacent to the offices was separated from the locker room by a wide parking lot. As they pulled into that lot, Madison and Chris could see the players out on the field going through some drills. Madison shaded her eyes and tried to pick Luther Zorn from the crowd in the field.

Upstairs, they were shown through Evan Chase's office and into a paneled boardroom. On their way through the owner's office, Madison couldn't help but notice all the

medals and trophies adorning the walls, reminders of Evan
Chase's athletic achievement. She thought about Cody, and
how he kept two boxes of this same kind of memorabilia
in a storage closet off the garage. The only way Madison
even knew he had it was because her son had recently discovered the stuff and gleefully confiscated four or five of
the gaudiest trophies to line his bedroom's dresser top.
That, Madison thought, was the appropriate place for such
things, on a young boy's dresser, not in a grown man's office. It said something about the man she was about to
meet.

A secretary politely brought some coffee and then disappeared, promising the owner's imminent arrival.

"So, what do you think?" Pelo said when they were all
alone. A long wisp of his dark black hair had fallen onto his
forehead.

Madison could see that he was nervous. This had been
Marty's territory.

"We're just breaking the ice," she told him.

Chris was nodding when the door opened and Evan Chase
entered. Beside him was Martin Wilburn, dressed sharply in
an Italian suit. Chase, on the other hand, wore a simple polo
shirt and khakis with black Gucci loafers and no socks.
What Chase lacked in attire, he more than made up for with
his presence. The owner's back was straight and despite his
homely countenance, he held his head high. His physique,
his tan, and his wavy blond hair made Chase look ten years
younger than Madison knew he was. He had an unnecessarily firm grip that Madison did her best to return. Then they
all sat down.

Chase disposed of Chris Pelo by staring silently at him
until he dropped his eyes and began to fidget with his tie.
Then he shifted his imperious gaze to Madison. She met his
eyes and held them in her own gaze as she spoke.

"Thank you for meeting with us on such short notice, Mr. Chase," she said. Madison's dark blue business suit and severe hair style couldn't hide her good looks.

"Not at all," he replied, flashing a perfect set of white teeth. "I've been after Martin to get this contract extension under way for a month. The only thing we've been waiting for was Luther to choose an agent. We'd like to see if we can't resolve this before his current contract expires at the end of this season."

"We'll try to work toward that goal," Madison said with a doubtful smile.

"I've got to say that I'm surprised at Luther's choice," Chase said, eyeing her hungrily. "You've never been involved with a contract like this before, have you?"

"No," Madison said calmly, still holding the owner's incessant stare, "but I've been in my share of boardrooms and I've negotiated for things of much greater magnitude than money."

"I wonder," Chase said with a sly smirk, "are you as proficient in the bedroom as you are in the boardroom?"

Despite herself, Madison blinked.

"I'm good at everything I do," she said evenly, recovering quickly and showing no emotion whatsoever, "and like anyone who's truly good at something, I don't have to talk about it."

Her lance hit its mark. Chase's grin momentarily drooped. From out of the corner of her vision, Madison could see the smug look her comment had elicited from Martin Wilburn.

"How much time will you need before we can begin to discuss the terms?" Wilburn asked, reining in his delight and tastefully shifting the conversation.

"I can meet with you by the middle of next week," Madison said. She'd move everything off for two weeks except for a suppression hearing in the Fears murder trial and the deposition of a key witness in her rape case.

"Thursday?" Wilburn said, looking up from his rich leather planner with one eyebrow raised above his gold-rimmed spectacles. He had the demeanor of a schoolteacher, but Madison thought she detected something vulpine and cunning beneath the surface.

"Anytime in the afternoon," Madison said.

"Fine," Wilburn replied, "I'll see you here at one."

Skupper had once been the captain of his own dive boat. The moniker came from his mate, a simpleton who died one morning when he fell off the bow of Skupper's boat as it left the Intracoastal. The boat's propeller clove the mate's head in two. That was years ago. Skupper, drunk at the time, lost his captain's license over the whole thing and had been land-locked ever since.

Now, Skupper was a gray-haired crust of a man. His Top-siders, once white, were yellowed with age, constant wear, and his refusal to wear a pair of socks. Everyone who ran a dive boat or a fishing charter out of West Palm Marina knew Skupper, and Skupper knew them. It was no secret that he could barely see through the set of glasses he wore, so thick they gave the impression that his eyes were the size of fifty-cent superballs. It was also no secret that Skupper sold tanks of oxygen to anyone who could pay his "no questions asked" prices.

Three days before Madison McCall was to begin negoti-ations on Luther Zorn's contract, a man entered Skupper's shop early in the morning to buy two tanks of oxygen at his price of two hundred dollars a tank. Normally a tank cost no more than seventy-five, but that was when the buyer could demonstrate that he was certified. "No questions asked" oxygen also had to be paid for with cash.

He had never been concerned about an uncertified diver being injured and coming back to sue him because he had nothing to sue for, nothing anyone could get at, anyway. Skupper's home was a small shack at the edge of the marina's scrap yard. His hoard of cash nearly filled the three plastic garbage cans buried beneath the floor of his shack. Nobody knew the money was there, and Skupper knew that the dirty lawyers could only sue you for what you had in the bank.

Skupper welcomed the tinkle of the bells at his shop door that morning with a disdainful grunt. He wasn't ready for any customers. It was five A.M., too early for even the most zealous charter captain to be up and about. Skupper looked up from a bait tank in the back. In walked a black man. It was still dark out, but he wore sunglasses, no less. Skupper's heart skipped a beat. He thought the man was there to rob him. But although he was scared, it also made him giddy to know that every dollar in his register had been carefully removed the night before and was now resting safely beneath his floorboards. That sense of security made Skupper bold, and he scowled at the man.

"What'ya want?"

The man's smile made Skupper want to spit. He couldn't express with words how much he despised blacks. This was the second one this fall. He couldn't tell for sure, because he was too far away to see, but Skupper wondered if it wasn't the same one. Black men weren't supposed to scuba-dive. They didn't like the water. Skupper knew that. He'd been around. He peered intensely through his thick lenses to take in the man's appearance. He wanted to see clearly. He leaned forward to study the face carefully and rudely.

"I want two tanks of oxygen," the black man said, and then added, "no questions asked."

"No questions asked?" Skupper raised an eyebrow and his voice cracked slightly.

"That's right," the black man said, holding forth four freshly printed hundred-dollar bills.

Skupper could actually smell the ink. It made his nose twitch and he breathed in deeply. The bigotry lacing Skupper's entrails like frosted outdoor piping melted at the sight of the money. He snatched at the four bills without noticing that the smile had left the black man's face.

"There's some tanks by the door there," Skupper said dismissively.

Skupper rubbed four flattened fingers over the bills to thoroughly soak up the ink scent before stuffing them into his pocket. He looked up when he heard the bells that hung from his door tinkle a second time. The man was already gone.

It was dark before the day was over and Skupper got back to the shack. He muttered to himself as he carefully removed his floorboards and unearthed the least full of his three cash-filled garbage cans. Skupper glared about his hovel suspiciously, imagining eyes where none could be. He laid his newest bills on top of the heap, then took the liberty to sink his hands deep into the dirty green bills. After replacing the top to the can Skupper fussed for some time, shifting his rickety old linoleum table and battered rusty chair until he thought the money was again well hidden.

Skupper then opened a can of peaches and gobbled them down with three stiff slices of Wonder bread. With his stomach full and his money safe, Skupper lay back on his ratty cot and fell asleep almost at once, a broad smile on his lips.

He awoke with a flash several hours later and felt the hot spray of blood covering his face. Skupper tried to scream, but the air only gurgled in his bloody throat. His eyes popped open and he could see a dark form above him in the light that fell through the window. A wet steel survival knife gleamed in the moonlight. In a panic, Skupper's body lurched from the bed toward his money. Someone held Skupper's head high in the air by his long greasy hair and hacked at his neck until his head pulled completely free. For an instant Skupper could actually see his body thrashing on the floor beside his bunk, its fingers groping instinctively for the familiar feel of the bills, before his brain ceased to function and his face froze in a horrible mask of death.

Chapter 8

Luther Zorn didn't plan on being with anyone forever. His mother had died in his junior year of college. She never knew that he had made it, that all the wildest dreams of his life had come true. At the time, he had nothing but a scholarship, a used Toyota that broke down about every fifty miles, and enough pocket money to buy pizza and beer. It made him ache when he thought about all the things he could do for her now. If only she were alive, she would have everything. Luther would have made her a queen. Worst of all, if she had fallen ill only a few years later than she did, he could have gotten her the medical treatment she needed and deserved. Medicaid didn't pay for certain tests, so the extent of her illness had gone undetected until it was too late. Her death had killed something inside Luther, and the damage left only a sliver of compassion in his soul.

That sliver, however, had a focus that was as clear as it was intense. Luther found a boy. His name was Jamal King. He was nine now, but when Luther first found him he was just seven, standing in a doorway. Behind Jamal dirty children ran through the cots that lined the walls of a decrepit schoolroom. The kids screamed and played their games with a viciousness beyond their years. It had been three days before Christmas. With about ten other Marauders players, Luther had visited a shelter in Broward County for homeless women and their children. It was pathetic. As impoverished and destitute as Luther and his mother and brother had been, they never approached the misery that flourished in that shelter.

The players did what they could. They donated money, they brought food and presents, they signed autographs for the kids. They even sang Christmas carols. But it was only for a few hours, one day a year. As suddenly as they came, the athletes and their wives would slide into the leather seats of their European cars and return to their comfortable homes armed with security systems. Those battered women and their children would remain in that run-down abandoned middle school, eating Cream of Wheat three times a day and sleeping in rooms that had once held classes.

While his teammates and their wives toiled decorating a ten-foot tree, and the bleary-eyed women wearing worn-out robes and men's slippers watched with skepticism, Luther locked eyes with Jamal. Even though he was only seven, Luther could see from his eyes that Jamal knew exactly where he was and exactly what had happened to him. Rage and shame burned bright. He also seemed precocious enough to know that his future wasn't going to be much better. Jamal was tall and skinny. His hair was long and unkempt. Luther couldn't help being reminded of himself. Then he saw the mother.

When he was all alone with himself late some nights, Luther would try to honestly answer the question of whether or not the mother had anything to do with what happened. He didn't know. He hoped he was a better person than that. Either way, Luther had returned to the shelter the next week after the season had ended. He talked with the director about getting the boy and the mother out of there. It hadn't been difficult. Money was all that was needed, and Luther had that. He intentionally feigned disinterest in the mother, instead focusing his questions and concerns on the boy. The director, a Catholic nun, seemed never to suspect he had any ulterior motives, and maybe he hadn't.

However, in a very short time, Luther ended up in the same place with the mother that he ended up with most of the attractive women who crossed his path. In bed. He couldn't help himself. Once he'd fixed her up with some nice clothes, a little makeup, and some self-respect, no one could fail to see Charlene's physical virtues. Her skin was a light creamy chocolate only slightly darker than his own, and her eyes, catlike, were emerald green. Luther bought a house for her and the boy to live in, a small two-bedroom ranch off Sunrise Highway in Fort Lauderdale. It was close enough for Luther to visit, but far enough away not to invite trouble.

He didn't always sleep with Charlene at the beginning, but after several months, he dropped all pretenses. She had come to expect to satisfy him with every visit, no matter what the time, day or night. And Luther believed, correctly, that she was more than pleased to do it. Luther treated the boy like a nephew, and the mother like an easygoing girlfriend. He could come and go as he pleased without a hitch. If he needed a sexual fix, he knew where to go. The arrangement seemed to work for everyone, in part because

Luther was careful to make sure the mother kept her expectations low.

Charlene had never been an addict or a drunk. She was simply a product of the projects, a girl with no particularly outstanding attributes. What she did have was more than her share of bad luck. Her husband, Jamal's father, had been involved in some shady business that she had never asked about or wanted to know about. They found his head one day in the Dumpster outside their apartment building, inconveniently burdened with three 9mm slugs. That was all there had been to bury. They never found his body. Except for her son, Charlene was left with nothing. She then went from man to man, never finding anyone who really cared about her enough to accept her son in the bargain, and ending finally with a handsome animal who beat her senseless while Jamal hid under the bed in tears.

To Charlene, Luther Zorn was a savior, and she worshipped him accordingly.

Tonight, however, Luther's thoughts weren't on Charlene. He was going to deliver a gift. It was something he wanted to do, and anyway it took his mind away from the upcoming morning.

When Luther came in from the practice field earlier that afternoon, he was greeted with another telephone message from her. Its meaning was clear, and left him with a high-octane mixture of anxiety and thrills.

As Luther rolled up into the small semicircular driveway in his Viper, he made a mental note to have someone paint the house. It was something Charlene, with her job as a sales-clerk in a department store, probably couldn't afford. It was also something she would never ask for. But it needed doing. Luther let himself in the front door and was not surprised to find Charlene and Jamal sitting at the kitchen table working through math problems. Both of them beamed when they saw him.

"Luther!" the boy yelped, jumping from his seat to slap Luther's hand and then hug him around the waist.

"Hello, Charlene," Luther said politely, then gripping the boy's thin shoulder tightly: "Hey, my man!"

Charlene rose and accepted Luther's kiss on her cheek before getting a can of beer for him from the refrigerator.

"Luther, you were great on Sunday! You were the greatest!" the boy crooned. "Wham! Right into the quarterback! Four times! You won the whole game! Everybody at school said so!"

Luther couldn't help his smile.

"And what about you?" he said. "I heard you got something to crow about yourself. I heard you got straight As. Is that right?"

Jamal was rifling through a drawer looking for the report card as he spoke. "It's right here, Luther! I did! See it! See it!"

Luther smiled at Charlene. He admired what she'd done with the boy. Luther had helped, of course. He bought Jamal books and gave Charlene strict instructions to read. A year ago he bought a computer and every kind of educational program available. Luther didn't see the boy without talking to him about the importance of education. But it was Charlene who was there day to day, helping Jamal to study, drilling it into him.

Luther sat down at the table and sipped his beer as he studied the report card. He fussed over the details of it for some time while Jamal looked on with a smile that left his cheeks aching. Finally, Luther set the report card down and began shaking his head.

"I'm proud of you, Jamal," he said seriously. Luther took a box out of his pocket. It was a small present, wrapped in colorful paper with a red ribbon around it. "This is for you."

Jamal looked at the gift with wonder. If Luther brought anything, it was usually something that Jamal needed. Except for his birthday and Christmas, Luther didn't bring trifles.

"Open it," Luther said, "it's for doing good."

Jamal tore into the package and pulled a gold chain from the box. He held it up to the light, marveling at the golden, diamond-studded "1" that hung from it. It was the most extravagant thing Jamal had ever held.

"Luther," the boy whispered, "it's the coolest!"

He'd seen the same type of chain around his mother's neck, and he knew that it also had come from Luther. Charlene's was more ornate, and the diamonds were bigger, but to Jamal, the pendant he held in his own hand might have been a crown jewel.

"That '1' stands for you. It stands for your mom. It stands for me," Luther said, looking intently at the boy. "When I was a boy your age, I didn't have a lot of friends, Jamal. I wasn't in a gang. I was a gang of one. That's what the one means. It means you're a gang of one. When someone tells you to do something wrong, you put your hand on this one and remember what I'm telling you. It's like a club. I'm in it. Your mom's in it. Now you're in it. It means you can be stronger than everyone else, Jamal. If you want to be like me, you have to be tougher than any gang member you'll ever meet. You have to be tough enough to be a gang of one. Anyone gives you any grief about that, you tell them Luther Zorn said that's the way it is. You tell them Luther said so . . ."

The words branded a mark in the boy's mind. That was what Luther wanted. He knew that the odds were against a boy like this, a boy with no father. Luther wanted to give him an edge. He looked up at Charlene. She wiped a tear from under her eye and said, "Come on now, Jamal. Say thank you to Luther and let's get to bed. You've got school . . ."

She looked to Luther to see if she was doing right. He nodded his head to her.

"Here," he said to Jamal, turning him around, "let me put that on your neck and then you do like your mom says."

While Luther fiddled with the clasp, Jamal held the jeweled "1" tightly. When Luther was finished, Jamal spun around and hugged him. Luther engulfed the boy in a mass of muscular limbs.

"Thank you, Luther," Jamal said, his thin boy's arms squeezing Luther's thick torso with all their might.

"Good night," Luther said, his voice uneven from the burden of emotion.

"Good night, Luther."

Charlene followed the boy with her arms folded carefully beneath her breasts, but stopped on her way out of the kitchen.

"Are you going to wait for me?" she asked with a sultry look that stirred Luther's blood. Then he remembered the message in his locker. He'd need his energy. He glanced furtively at the clock above the stove and thought about it.

"Yes," he said finally in a low guttural tone.

She smiled, then she was gone. Luther got another beer from the refrigerator before sitting down again to wait. As he sipped from the can, his mind churned. He thought about the things she would do to him, and he to her. It was the thrill he craved, the thrill he couldn't get enough of.

In twenty minutes, she appeared in the doorway to the kitchen wearing nothing but a black lace teddy. Luther stood, and they met in the middle of the kitchen floor. Slowly and gently, he ran his hands over her entire body, kneeling to touch her legs and buttocks. Then Luther kissed the soft flesh on the inside of her thighs and Charlene began to say his name the way he liked to hear it said. She implored him. She begged him. Suddenly, she felt herself being lifted off her feet as though she were nothing more than a flower. Luther carried her to the bedroom. After lovemaking that was as gentle as it was intense, Charlene fell asleep, wrapped in two strong arms with her face buried in the broad chest of the man who she thought of as a beautiful savior.

Sometime during the night Charlene awoke. She didn't know if it was Luther's leaving that woke her, but he was gone. She didn't know why he had left, but she wished that one day she would wake and find him still there beside her, like some implacable boulder unmoved by the outgoing tide. She sighed deeply and reminded herself not to expect too much. Already he'd given her more than she'd ever had before, from anyone. She lay there for a while, watching the paddle fan spin slowly above her bed. After some time she looked at the clock. It was 4:07 A.M. She rolled on her side and clutched two pillows to her breast. Thinking of him, she closed her eyes and fell back to sleep.

Chapter 9

The surf pounded gently against the sand and rocks as the sun rose in a shoal of its own red blood. Even though it promised to be a warm fall day, Evan Chase felt a shiver scamper up his spine. He twisted his head this way and that with two sharp cracks and tried to shake away the goose bumps that had crawled to the surface of his skin. Chase looked up and down the beach. There was no sign of anyone, not that there should be. That was the beauty of Lost Tree Village: even in the heart of overdeveloped South Florida, you could still feel like you were the last person on earth. He turned back toward the house. It sat above him in the glow of the dawn, a fortress of wealth and prestige nestled in a lush growth of tropical vegetation. He thought he saw the brief image of his wife in a bedroom window before the heavy gray drape fell back into place. He wondered if it had only been his imagination.

The water, although clean, gave no indication of what lay in its depths. The gleam of the rising sun kept its secrets hidden. Bottomless water was the one fear Chase had never been able to subdue completely. That was part of the reason he forced himself to endure it every morning. He relished the act of beginning each day with the conquest of the one thing that made his skin crawl. It was irrational, of course, like a child's fear of the dark. There was nothing there. There never was. This water was too clean and too clear to enable a shark, even if it did wander in past the reef, to mistakenly bump into him and attack. It was simply the fact that he couldn't see, that he didn't know—that's what got to him.

He forced himself into the deeper water and began to swim. The other reason for this morning routine was his physique—there was almost no fat on his body. His daily swim had ensured that for the past twenty-three years despite retiring from competition. He believed his physical fitness was in part responsible for his success. It made him virile. Women wanted him. Men feared him. As he pulled at the water with long, even strokes, Chase lost himself in his plans for the day. It was during this time of day that he also gained his edge.

His climb to the top had been a struggle. He'd always been smart, but he'd grown up in a trailer park in West Palm Beach. Overcoming the handicap of poverty had been a monumental chore. Athletics had enabled him to improve his life. Being an All-America, and then an Olympian had opened every door. Thereafter, he used his brains and his cunning to get literally everything he'd wanted. And he'd come far. He switched to a backstroke and smiled.

Suddenly, something ensnared his ankle, and his entire body lurched out of the water, instinctively, like some great tortured aquatic mammal. This only made him sink that much faster when he hit the water in a vertical position, the downward pulling at his ankle now dragging him toward the bottom, some twenty feet below. Chase fought against the pull out of sheer panic, swimming hard for the surface, desperate to pull some air into his lungs, as the grip around his ankle tightened.

His thrashing was a waste of precious energy. As he reached down to loosen whatever had caught his ankle, his panic was heightened when he saw the dark form of another human. He clawed at the two hands clamped tightly around his foot. One thought forced its way to the surface of his boiling terror: no one would dare kill him. This was to get him off balance. Someone wanted something from him, and they were trying to scare him. Enraged, he fought for the surface.

Then he became confused. He was running out of air. With renewed fear, he began tearing at the mask of the frogman. Before he could get a grip on anything, the diver kicked his powerful finned legs, propelling them both into deeper water. Bubbles spewed madly from the diver's mouth, like the exhaust from a burning engine.

With one last mind-rending struggle, Chase kicked madly. Then, against his will, his airway opened and seawater slammed violently into his lungs and stomach. The burning pain made him vomit and choke, and Evan Chase convulsed helplessly as he started to sink. In the shock of drowning, his once capable limbs could only twitch ineffectively. The frogman finally released his grip on Chase's ankle and hung suspended in the water above the convulsing man as he sank, an eerie apparition dispassionately observing a painful death.

After watching her husband leave for his swim, Vivian Chase lay back down to wait. An hour later she pulled on her robe and opened the French doors that led to the balcony. She stepped outside into the early morning sunshine. The sky's red glow had changed to a brilliant yellow, promising a hot day. Already the stone floor was warm to her feet. She could see only part of the beach through the palm trees, but she had a clear view of the steps that led from the ocean to the courtyard and the pool. Her eyes wandered briefly to the house that surrounded her like a fortress. She, like her husband, had come a long way. And, like him, she had a high opinion of herself and her cunning.

She was raised in a small town in upstate New York and the two things she remembered most were the cold and the squalor. The day after high school graduation, she bleached her brown hair blond, and left for Florida. She hadn't been back since. She started out as a waitress in Daytona, then gradually worked her way south, moving from waiting tables to dancing in a large strip club in Fort Lauderdale. She'd never gone in for the drugs or the sleaze of the stripping scene. Instead, she saved her money and worked conscientiously on improving her manners, her wardrobe, and her style. The other girls had poked fun at her ways. They called her "The Queen."

Onstage, her long silky blond hair and her tight tan body and slender limbs were guaranteed to fill her G-string with tens and twenties. Soon she had enough money to buy a classic white Mercedes convertible that she used to troll the exclusive nightclubs of Miami and Palm Beach on the nights she wasn't working. Vivian dated selectively. She wanted it all, but she didn't feel compelled to get it all at once. She believed that good things came with time.

After carefully considering her options, she focused her attentions on a young man who was neither overly attractive nor overly dynamic nor overly rich. Like a lioness, she had chosen one of the weakest of the herd as her prey. He was, however, very well connected, a vice president in his father's investment company, and a legacy member of the Palm Beach Meridian Club, the stuffiest and most discriminating social club in all of South Florida. It was there, as a wife, that Vivian set her real snares.

It was quite a plan, really, especially for a girl of modest beginnings. Her first husband's sole purpose was to legitimize her, and he did so completely. Once she was one of "them," she immediately went to work, poolside. Within a month she had three other men pursuing her aggressively, and scores of others flattering her constantly with compliments and stares, which she demurely acknowledged.

She was astounded at the shamelessness with which these men threw themselves at her. Two were married. But the richest, and most powerful of the three had been the one bachelor, Evan Chase. His desire, she knew, had been heightened by the knowledge that he was competing with others for the same prize. That was seven years ago. She had been twenty-three at the time. Surveying the expanse of the mansion, the towers, the balustrades, the balconies, and the columns, she supposed that crooked bunch of strippers had been right all along. She was a queen.

When Vivian's gaze drifted back toward the steps, she gasped. Luther had ascended the stairs and was starting down the walk toward the pool.

Vivian glanced around, then waved her arms wildly. She wanted to cry out, but the noise would draw the attention of anyone in the house or on the grounds.

"What are you doing?" she hissed under her breath. She ground her teeth, enraged at Luther's presence.

Luther looked up at her. She waved him off frantically. The fool!

"Go!" she mouthed silently, over and over, waving him back with her hands.

Luther appeared momentarily puzzled. Then he, too, looked quickly about before crouching down and jogging awkwardly away until he reached the stone steps that led to the beach. An instant later, he was gone.

Chapter 10

Madison never liked to begin negotiations without confirming the numbers and the opening position with her client, but it appeared that the present situation couldn't be helped. Chris Pelo had alerted Luther a week ago that they would be arriving Wednesday evening. The player agreed to meet them at the Royal Palm Beach Hotel, but never showed. Repeated calls to his home proved fruitless, and Madison went to bed angry with her client's behavior. Zorn's irresponsibility only further reminded her of why she didn't want to be an agent.

In the morning, Madison met Chris Pelo in the hotel restaurant for a late breakfast.

"Any word from Luther?" she asked as she sat down.

Pelo shook his head. "I tried first thing when I got up, and I tried his pager. I don't know what happened, but I'm sure that by now he's at the facility for practice.

"I wouldn't be upset about it," Chris added. "This is the way Luther is. He likes to have people just do their own job and he does his. That's what he was always saying to Marty anyway . . ."

"Well, you would think that he'd have more than a passing interest in the dynamics of a twenty-five-million-dollar deal, wouldn't you?" Madison replied, taking a sip of coffee. "But enough. I've had to baby-sit before. I guess I'll be doing it again. Really, if we get anything close to the deal I think we can get, you'll be able to run the agency without me, and they won't be able to say one thing about it at the firm. This contract alone could cover operating expenses for five years and still turn a profit."

Pelo brushed the hair off his forehead and offered a weak smile. "I was thinking we make a pretty good team the way things are . . . You hooked Luther just like that! I crunched the numbers, now you cut the deal."

Madison smiled graciously. "Thanks, but I've got two trials coming up that . . . well, whatever. Anyway, we were lucky with Luther. I don't imagine it usually happens this easily. Let's be thankful and move on. I know you don't mean to, but do me a favor, Chris: don't pressure me on this. You're starting to remind me of a trial lawyer," she said with a wink.

"Okay." Pelo shrugged, raising his hands in surrender.

When Cody walked through the door at nine o'clock that evening, Madison greeted him with a candlelit dinner in the dining room. The strain from a late afternoon coach's meeting, a long day of teaching, and football practice had left him feeling sapped. For her part, Madison had spent the day deposing a female stripper who provided testimony that her associate, a fellow stripper, regularly sold sexual services to patrons of the dance club where they worked. One of those patrons, a state senator, was Madison's client. He was being charged with first-degree rape. It was a tawdry case, but Madison believed her client was guilty of nothing more than illicit and illegal sex, not the violent crime of rape. Despite the emotionally grueling day, Madison made it home in time to do homework with Jo-Jo and put together a veal cacciatore dinner for Cody, his favorite.

Cody kissed her on the lips before slumping down in his chair. Madison poured him a glass of pinot noir and Bess served dinner. Cody could still eat like a professional athlete. The problem was that without the same regimen of running and lifting that had kept him fit during his years as a player, his intake of food was starting to show itself ever so slightly around the waist. Madison didn't mind, though.

She hadn't married Cody for his looks or his physique, although there were plenty of women who would have. She'd married Cody for his quiet inner strength, a strength unmarred by meanness or selfishness. It had been a tumultuous time when they first met. He had been devastated by his shattered marriage, his dying career, and the false accusation of a brutal murder. She had been in the middle of a vicious custody battle with her ex-husband. Their relationship had been a surreal calm in the eye of a dark tempest.

"What do you think?" Madison said to him after taking a taste of her own creation.

"I think we're going to get our butts kicked by Northside Friday night if my damn linebackers can't get their blitzes right," Cody said through a mouthful of food.

"No," Madison said gently. "I meant the dinner. What do you think?"

"It's good," he said, but left his words hanging.

"But what?" Madison inquired, curiously tilting her head.

"Well," Cody admitted, "you left something out. I didn't want to say anything, but something's wrong with it."

"I didn't leave anything out," Madison said, suddenly as angry as she was disappointed.

"Yeah," Cody said with a definite nod, "you did. It's different."

Madison thought, then said, "Well, I doubled the recipe for the sauce so you and Jo-Jo could have it while I'm gone later this week . . . maybe I didn't double the tomato paste."

"Yeah, that sounds like it," Cody said, shoveling in another mouthful of veal.

"But it's still good," Madison said.

Cody's face twisted painfully and he screwed up his mouth.

"Not really," he said. "But that's okay. I'm eating it."

"That's awfully big of you," she said sharply. "I mean, to suffer along through this crappy meal is really stoic. All that training and mental toughness from your playing days have really stayed with you."

"Hey," he said, sensing her anger, "I'm being honest with you. What do you want?"

"I want you to be a little sensitive. That's what I want."

"Look," Cody said, "you had a hard day. I had a hard day, too. Let's just forget it. I'm trying to be sensitive. I'm eating it, aren't I?"

"Cody, you'd eat ten pounds of dog food if I put it in front of you, so don't think you're doing me any big favors. There's nothing you won't eat."

"Hey, Madison, lighten up, okay?" Cody said with a scowl. "You cooked a bad meal. You asked me how it was and I told you the truth. You're the one who's always talking about the importance of being honest. Now I'm honest, and you're mad. I like to eat. I like to eat. Big deal. I work hard. You don't want to cook? Order in Chinese. How's that?"

"That's good. That's just what you'll get," she said.

"Fine," Cody said.

"Fine," she said back.

They sat in silence, Cody eating, Madison staring at her fork, which she turned slowly, end over end, with one hand.

Then he said, "What do you mean, 'while I'm gone later this week'? Where are you going later in the week?"

Madison laid the fork down. "I'm going to Palm Beach to negotiate Luther Zorn's contract. I told you."

Cody shrugged. "Oh yeah. I forgot. You know, the game with Northside and everything."

"Yeah," Madison said, biting her tongue to keep from throwing out some sarcastic comparison between his high school football game and her murder trial, rape case, and multimillion-dollar contract negotiation.

"I hope you're not going to make a habit of running off," he said. "You know, with this agency business."

"Well," she replied, "you're the one who wanted me to help Chris, so now I'm helping him. That's part of it."

"I thought you were just going to get these guys signed up," Cody said through another mouthful of food, "then Chris could take over."

"Well," she said, "Luther Zorn wanted me to handle things personally. That was part of the agreement."

Cody looked at her thoughtfully, but kept chewing. He didn't know himself well enough to know whether he was jealous by nature or still feeling the effects of an unfaithful wife in his first marriage. Either way, he knew better than to badger Madison about her fidelity.

"Okay," Cody said, getting up and walking around the table so he could kiss her cheek, "I'm sorry about dinner."

The gesture wasn't lost on Madison. The two of them could disagree, argue, or even fight, but in the end, Cody always seemed to be able to build a bridge between them and make it come out okay. Most men Madison had known or observed were just the opposite—once the battle lines were drawn, the only thing that they could send over to the other side was missiles. Cody was different, and at that moment, despite the rising tide of differences in their lives, Madison believed that they would be together, forever.

At the stadium, Madison and Chris stopped to briefly watch the team practice before going in to find Wilburn. Everything seemed to be in order. The players ran through their drills. Balls flew through the air with the frequency of a circus act. It wasn't too hard now for Madison to pick out Luther Zorn. After just one meeting, she had a sense for his frame and the way he moved. He was large, bigger than any of the other linebackers in the group that ran in and out of a maze of cones. But, while being the biggest, at the same time he was the most fluid. He moved with the ease and grace of a panther. She did notice that when he stopped anywhere for more than a minute he would begin to clasp and rub his hands gently.

"There he is," Chris said, as if they were on safari, sighting some elusive quarry.

"There he is," she replied, still unable to completely purge the annoyance from her voice. "Come on."

Inside the facility, there was an undercurrent of energy that Madison picked up on right away.

"We're here to see Martin Wilburn," she told the receptionist.

The wild-eyed look the girl gave her and the nervous way in which she announced their arrival confirmed that something was amiss. While they waited, Madison was acutely aware of the hurried steps, the urgent whispers, and the searching glances of everyone who passed by the lobby. It was as if the entire office was waiting for someone or something.

Finally, a pleasant-looking middle-aged woman appeared and identified herself as Martin Wilburn's secretary.

"I'm sorry," she told them with a pleasant smile, "but Mr. Wilburn will be unable to see you today."

This was the last thing Madison expected, but she didn't want to show it.

"Ellen, you'll need to tell Mr. Wilburn that I have re-arranged my schedule because of this meeting, and that this appointment was confirmed as recently as yesterday, and that I intend to see him if I have to wait until he gets in his car to go home. I would hate to have to involve Mr. Chase in this, but under the circumstances I'll have to, if he won't at least give me a personal explanation."

Confronted with those words, the secretary politely excused herself.

"What the hell?" Chris Pelo said quietly when they were alone again. He was more glad than ever that Madison was with him. Left to himself, Chris would have already been halfway to the highway. Madison, on the other hand, looked like she was about to cross-examine a witness.

"We'll see," she said quietly. "It may not have anything to do with us, but it better be something pretty damn big for him to send us back to Texas."

Through the large window in the lobby, Madison and Chris saw the sudden appearance of a dark blue, official-looking Crown Vic as it pulled into the lot below. In seconds, two men, clearly police officers, appeared on the carpeted stairs and walked purposefully into the reception area.

"Mr. Wilburn's office, please," the first one said. Both were well built, in their mid-thirties with dark suits and crew cuts. Both wore sunglasses.

The receptionist picked up her phone, but the officer cut her off by flipping his wallet open and showing his badge.

"Just show us the way, ma'am," he said. "We'll announce ourselves."

The receptionist pointed uncertainly in the direction of Wilburn's office and murmured some directions. Without missing a beat, Madison fell in behind the two policemen and, after a quick glance around, Chris followed as well.

Wilburn was standing outside his office with a cup of coffee in his hand, involved in an agitated discussion with his secretary. When Wilburn looked up and saw the officers, he glanced nervously about like a cornered rat.

"Mr. Wilburn," said the first officer, showing his badge, "I'm Detective Lawrence, with the Palm Beach County Sheriff's Department, and this is my partner, Detective Gill. We need to speak with you, sir."

"I need to speak with you also, Mr. Wilburn," Madison interjected, muscling her way into the group. "I did not come all the way from Texas to be put off without any explanation. If this is your idea of a negotiating ploy, I've got to tell you that my client will simply wait until the season is over and test the waters of free agency. We have no interest in playing games, Mr. Wilburn. Let me remind you, it was this team's idea to negotiate this contract, not my client's."

Wilburn seemed to have regained his composure, and he gave Madison a malevolent look.

"Detective, please wait for me in my office," he said, swinging open the door on his right. "I'll only be a moment with Ms. McCall. Ms. McCall, why don't we step into the conference room?"

Madison and Chris followed Wilburn across the hall into a long conference room furnished with a highly polished table surrounded by about twenty chairs.

"Would you like to sit down?" Wilburn said pleasantly.

Madison sat. Chris took the seat beside her, and Wilburn stood at the head of the table.

"Now, Ms. McCall," Wilburn said, "since form seems so much more important to you than substance, you can now say that we sat down face-to-face and had a meeting. As you should already know, I am not willing to negotiate with you at this time. Circumstances have, shall we say, suddenly changed? And your threat of taking your client elsewhere is music to my ears.

"However," he continued, "I think you will soon find that your client has concerns much bigger than his contract. Now you have seen me, and you know straight from me that the Marauders are no longer interested in pursuing a contract extension with Luther Zorn. Good day, Ms. McCall."

With that, Wilburn started for the door.

"I will be speaking with Mr. Chase about this meeting before the day is over, Mr. Wilburn. Obviously you and he are not on the same wavelength," Madison said forcefully, still in her seat.

Wilburn stopped with his hand on the doorknob and said with just the hint of a grin, "Obviously not."

Then he was gone.

Chapter 11

Martin Wilburn was able to convince the detectives to wait an hour before taking Luther Zorn in for questioning. Wilburn wanted his team to finish their practice without interruption. He had known the police would be coming. He'd spoken with Lawrence and Gill's superior that morning. The lieutenant had informed Wilburn of Evan Chase's death, as well as the fact that Luther Zorn was wanted for questioning.

"I'd prefer not to disrupt the entire team," Wilburn explained to Lawrence, "as long as it's not necessary for you to talk to him immediately."

"As I said," Detective Lawrence replied, "Lieutenant Kratch is running the investigation and he told us to check everything with you first, Mr. Wilburn. Right now, the coroner isn't even calling this a murder, although they say Chase was a pretty good swimmer."

"Yes," Wilburn assured them, "he was."

"Word is his wife was running around with Luther Zorn," Lawrence said, scratching his ear. "I guess that's why Lieutenant Kratch wants to talk to him."

"I suppose," Wilburn said. He knew about the affair between Luther and Vivian, and about their secret trysts. He was counting on that knowledge to give him leverage with Vivian, who would now be the majority owner of the team. In the last twelve hours, Martin Wilburn had moved from a position of weakness to one of strength.

The owner's death would be his windfall. Wilburn could now move the team. Of course, the better the team performed during the rest of the season, the easier personal seat licenses, season tickets, and luxury boxes would be to sell in Memphis. The better those sales went, the more money he would make on the back end. So, keeping the Marauders on an even keel was worth money to Martin Wilburn. As much as he despised Luther Zorn, he knew his importance to the team, and that it would pay to keep him playing through the season. Once the season ended, Wilburn would have no use for him. By then the deal would be in place, the team would be in Memphis, the money would be in the bank, and Martin Wilburn wouldn't care whether the Marauders won or lost.

Wilburn had been assured that very morning by Pat Rivet, the team's lawyer, that if Luther was charged and tried for the murder of Chase, the trial would be months in the coming. Luther should be able to finish out the season even if he ultimately ended up in jail. Next year, Martin could go get himself a different linebacker, a cheaper one.

Martin Wilburn's dislike for Luther Zorn actually had nothing to do with Luther's affair with Vivian Chase. Luther had insulted him. During a plane flight home from a game in Chicago, Wilburn had been playing cards with some cronies in the first-class cabin. Back then, when real estate was still bad, Chase accorded Wilburn more respect. Back then, Chase had needed him. As much as anything, Wilburn's friends were thrilled with the prospect of meeting the enigmatic Luther Zorn. Luther was a mystery to most people, an exceptional and violent player who avoided the attention of the media. Thus the mystery, and thus the fascination. Wilburn had assured his friends of a personal interview with Luther as part of the trip. During the card game he sent his assistant, Myron Spellman, back to the coach section of the plane to retrieve his player.

Myron returned looking very disconcerted.

"Where's Luther?" Wilburn snapped, momentarily looking up from his hand of cards.

Myron tried to bend down and whisper into Wilburn's ear, which was doubly embarrassing. Wilburn had pushed the younger man away violently and declared, "Say what you got to say! I don't want you whispering in my ear like a schoolgirl!"

Myron looked hopelessly at his boss and said in an apologetic tone, "Luther said he wouldn't come."

This news hit Wilburn like a slap in the face.

"You go tell that nigger, I own part of his black ass! If he doesn't want to wake up tomorrow missing a piece of it, he better get up here and say hello," Wilburn hissed. "See what he says to that!"

Wilburn saw that this tack met with nods of approval from his friends, two of whom were city councilmen, men accustomed to dealing harshly with sedition. Myron disappeared again, but returned more frazzled than before.

"He said he doesn't care, Mr. Wilburn," Myron dutifully reported. "He said you could go ahead and cut him . . ."

Wilburn didn't react. He simply told Myron to sit down. But he smoldered quietly for the next half hour, drinking

Wild Turkey straight up and losing three hundred dollars in pinochle.

"Excuse me," he said to his friends, getting up after throwing down his last bad hand. He then quietly made his way to the rear of the plane, leaving his cronies to whisper among themselves.

He found Luther sitting by himself, reading a book, not engaged at all in the celebration, gaming, and general tomfoolery that raged on around him.

Wilburn leaned over and whispered in Luther's ear. "You just fucked with the wrong man, you half-breed ape. I promise you, you'll live to wish you'd kissed my ass tonight instead of sitting back here like some Shaka Zulu royal nigger. Just remember this! There's still a slave system in this world, and my skin may be black, but I'm the master."

Luther had kept his eyes directed on the pages in front of him. His outward reaction was almost invisible, but Wilburn knew that the player had heard every word. Luther's eyes had frozen in hatred at the mention of the word *half-breed*. Wilburn muttered the word again, then turned and indignantly walked away. He had kept a close eye on Luther Zorn ever since. Now his observation was about to pay off.

Chapter 12

Luther was just pulling on a pair of faded jeans at his locker when Myron Spellman walked up to him and whispered that there were two detectives from the Sheriff's Department who wanted to speak with him upstairs. Luther coldly assessed Martin Wilburn's lackey to be sure that the message wasn't a simple ruse designed to fluster him. Myron looked fearful and out of place. He wore slacks and loafers and a sweater-vest over a button-down shirt. His glasses were almost identical to Wilburn's, thin and round and gold. He blinked nervously amid the throng of naked beefy bodies.

"Don't even think about lying to me, Myron," Luther rumbled, looking up from the seat in front of his locker. "I'll crush your skull."

Myron shook his head fervently, saying, "No, they're there."

"Who?" inquired Antone Ellison indignantly, walking up to his own locker from the shower as he vigorously swiped water from the backs of his arms. "Who's here to see the Main Man?"

He spoke as if no one had the right to see his friend and the star of their team.

Luther met Ellison's toothy grin with a dark stare. Even Antone could see that it was time to shut up.

"I'll be up when I'm dressed," Luther said calmly.

Luther tried to maintain his composure. He focused on his locker room routine: rubbing cream into his feet, powdering his skin, brushing his hair, pulling on his shirt, sticking his feet into his worn soft leather driving shoes. Then, after one final remonstrative glance at Antone, Luther was gone.

At the police station, while Martin Wilburn was breaking the solemn news of Chase's death to the team, Luther was being shown into a plain white room furnished simply with a table, three chairs, and a two-way mirror. Bright fluorescent lights hummed, and filled the room with an unnatural glare. Luther tried to remain calm, but was unable to keep from grinding his teeth and rubbing his hands under the table. His jaw was fixed, but his eyes darted nervously about the surface of the glass mirror. After what seemed like a long time, a tall lanky man in a dark olive suit entered the room and introduced himself politely as Lieutenant Kratch.

"As you know, Luther," Kratch said in a tired monotone, "you are not under arrest. You are not suspected of anything. As a matter of procedure, we have to ask you some questions to help us determine what may or may not have happened."

Kratch's face was gaunt. His short dark hair and five o'clock shadow seemed to highlight the bags under his bloodshot eyes. Otherwise, his skin was quite pale, especially considering the fact that this was Florida. In all, Kratch had the appearance of having just rolled off the couch after a fitful midday nap and he reminded Luther more of a ghoulish doctor than a police detective.

"What if I don't want to say anything without a lawyer?" Luther said with an edge to his voice that he wished wasn't there.

Kratch raised the dark bushy eyebrow above his one wandering eye as if this was something he had yet to consider.

"I would have to wonder then if I hadn't made some kind of mistake in not arresting you and charging you with some kind of crime," he said. "I think that would be a pretty good indication that something was amiss where before I didn't think anything was amiss. Is something amiss, Luther?"

"No," Luther said. "I just wanted to know. I don't know why I had to come down here to talk to you . . ."

The detective extracted a filterless Camel from a package he kept on the inside pocket of his coat and lit it.

As Kratch exhaled, he spoke.

"Well, it's so I can videotape this interview, Luther; it's simply a matter of policy for me. It's my normal procedure. I'm not really all that sharp, to be perfectly honest with you, I don't mind saying it. I think it's good for a man to know his weaknesses. Mine is my memory. I like to have things that I can go back to, to make sure who said what to me and when. You know, it beats the hell out of notes. Half the time I can't even read my own handwriting . . . Okay?"

Luther nodded. "Fine."

Kratch turned to the mirror and rolled off exactly who he was and who Luther was, the date, the time, and the fact that Luther acquiesced to the videotaping of the interview, that he was not under arrest, and that he was volunteering to talk. Kratch began by asking mundane questions about who Luther was, where he was from, his life history. Luther became frustrated and asked what the point was. Kratch raised his cigarette and apologized through the smoke, asking that Luther bear with him. Finally the questions came around to what Luther was afraid they would come around to.

"Now," Kratch said in the same tired monotone he'd used for the past twenty minutes, "do you have some kind of sexual relationship with Mrs. Chase?"

Luther stared at the detective. He wanted to smile. He wanted to be smug. It was, after all, a good one. Here he was, the prize stud, dipping into the boss's private stock. But Luther couldn't smile. He could feel that sickening sensation of fear crawling into his stomach. There was no thrill to go with it, though. It wasn't like sneaking around with the owner's wife, or running through a maze of three-hundred-pound linemen. Now, the fear stood alone. No one was supposed to know about Vivian.

"How did you know?" Luther asked. He wasn't going to be stupid and deny everything.

"It seems just about everyone knew except for Chase," Kratch replied pleasantly. "But that's the way it usually goes, doesn't it?

"So," Kratch continued, "how much do you know about Mrs. Chase—I mean outside the bedroom stuff?"

"Not all that much," Luther said, not certain how much he should or shouldn't divulge. "It wasn't a really big thing. We've been together a few times. It's not like it's some kind of full-blown affair. It's just a thing . . ."

"So you don't know about her past?" Kratch said.

"No," Luther said, wondering what that meant.

"How about her future?" Kratch asked.

"What do you mean?" Luther said.

"I mean that she stands to inherit her husband's entire empire, including the team, all told about five hundred million dollars."

"I hadn't thought about it," Luther said.

"Had she?"

"I don't know what you mean."

"Had she ever thought about it?" Kratch asked, exhaling a thick plume of smoke. "Or talked about it? I mean, about what would happen if her husband weren't around?"

"I don't know what you're getting at, Lieutenant," Luther said firmly.

"Oh, you know what I'm getting at," Kratch said in a friendly manner. "It's okay. We both know what each other is getting at, don't we? I'm not asking you to speculate on anything. I'm just doing my job. I'm just checking the facts."

"Well, there are no facts," Luther said, nearly wincing from the viselike wringing of his own hands.

"Fine, thank you, Luther. I appreciate your help," Kratch said, starting to rise, indicating the end of their interview. "Oh, Luther," he said, stopping as he reached down to butt out his smoke. "One last thing. Were you in the vicinity of MacCarther National Park this morning?"

Luther froze. His eyes narrowed.

"Of course not," he said.

"Yeah," Kratch smiled. "Just checking the details. Thanks, Luther. Hey, good luck in the game this weekend. Who are you guys playing?"

"Minnesota," Luther said suspiciously, shaking the detective's long-outstretched hand. "At Minnesota."

Luther drove less than a quarter mile from the police station before pulling into a vacant shopping strip. There was a pay phone hanging on the brick wall outside what used to be a drug emporium. Luther didn't want to use the cell phone from his car. He knew anyone could listen in.

"Hello?"

Vivian sounded tired.

"It's me," Luther said. There was silence for a moment.

"I need to see you," he said.

"I don't think that's a good idea," she said. "Why did you come to the house, Luther?"

"Why was I there?" Luther raged. "Why *was I* there? Why did you tell me to come, then wave me away?"

"I didn't tell you," she said.

Luther snorted at this. "Oh, this is great, Vivian! Why are you doing this? I got your note! I read what it said! Did you tell them I was there? They asked me, Vivian!"

"I didn't tell them anything!" she retorted.

"They know about us," Luther said flatly. "They know."

"Why did you come to the house!" Vivian demanded. "What were you doing here, Luther?"

"I was doing what *you* told me to do!" he bellowed.

"I didn't! I've told you to do a lot of things, Luther, but walking up off the beach this morning in broad daylight definitely wasn't one of them!" she said forcefully, then, "I have to go. Don't call again, Luther. Something bad is happening. Don't call me."

"Vivian, don't tell me—"

There was a click on the line. She had hung up.

Luther tried calling back. He got a busy signal. He tried again, cursing. It was still busy. "Damn!" Luther screamed, smashing the phone against the wall so hard that it exploded into half a dozen pieces.

Chapter 13

Kratch was a bass man. His fishing cabin on Lake Okee-chobee, which backed right up to a big hunk of state land, was remote enough so that only a handful of locals knew about it. There were plenty of fish, and it was quiet. When Kratch was out on his boat in the middle of that lake reeling in a lunker, he felt like he was part of the land. There was some Seminole blood on his mother's side of the family, and although Kratch looked as Anglo as Prince Charles, he fancied the Indian blood running through his veins.

Kratch was an experienced fisher. He knew well that you didn't just yank your line out of the water as soon as you got a bite. He knew that the real monsters would swim up to the minnow on your hook, take it in their mouth, then run with it for a while. A big fish would shake the minnow a couple of times to stun it, then, wump! swallow the thing whole. If you tried to set your line too fast with a big fish, it would spit that bait and run. Only if you were extremely lucky would you hook a big one without letting him run.

Kratch was going to let this one run. He'd felt the hit, but he wasn't letting on that there was a hook. Not yet. Not until it was buried in the gut. Then, he'd set the sucker, reel it in, and revel in the fight. Patience was essential. The thrill of the battle and the size of the trophy were the rewards. Kratch smiled to himself and tapped away at his keyboard, inputting the coroner's findings. Chase had in fact drowned; the marks on his ankle suggested he was struggling at the moment of his death. It was only one piece of the puzzle, but an important one. Reports were never fun, but they were essential. It was all part of the expedition. You didn't like to have to bail your bass boat either, but you did it. And while you were working, you thought about the big one.

Smoke crept toward the ceiling like a living thing. Kratch had his own office, and not just a cubicle like most other detectives. Kratch was the top man in homicide and he knew that to solve crimes you had to wade right into the muck. You had to wallow in it, rake your fingers through its murky sediments, dig in with your toes, and breathe deeply of the fetid odor. Crime was another world. Kratch was comfortable in that world. He could pass in and out of the real world and the criminal world like a warlock, and he liked the power it gave him. Those in the real world revered him. Those in the criminal world feared him. Those who knew him best did both.

He was an innocuous-looking character with a lanky frame and a vacant walleyed stare. In the early days, there were those who hadn't respected him because of his harmless, science-teacher appearance. His lazy eye created the immediate impression of intellectual deficiency. So, in the early days, he had to make examples of people, until gradually he became known as the kind of cop who would pistol-whip a brother and then plant a bag of smack on him, before charging him with possession, intent to distribute, and assaulting an officer.

Once, while investigating the death of a small-time crack dealer, some punk he was questioning told Kratch to kiss his black ass. Kratch beat the man so brutally he thought the little shit might die. Afterward, Kratch used his victim's gun to shoot himself in the head. He knew that his use of deadly force would have been condoned only if it were an act of self-defense. Of course, Kratch did nothing more than graze his own scalp. It healed in three weeks without a trace, but it looked real scary for the photos at trial. He'd bled like hell. The color prints showed a beleaguered Kratch with blood streaming down his face and into his eye and over his ear. The punk, who hadn't even been involved with the dealer, ended up doing ten to twenty in a maximum-security prison. That was Kratch. He always came out on top.

And, when dead bodies turned up, as they inevitably did in South Florida, Kratch was the man to find out how they got that way. He had a penchant for getting information no one else could get, and seemed to have a keen understanding of the criminal mind. As a lieutenant, Kratch had become more of an administrator now than he was an investigator. But, whenever a tough case popped up, Kratch always seemed to find his way into the middle of the investigation. Palm Beach County didn't have the same depraved reputation as Dade, but there were more than enough grisly murders to keep Kratch fishing year-round.

Chapter 14

Vivian was a prisoner in her own home. She'd made the necessary funeral arrangements, answered the necessary questions, and shed the necessary tears. Her tears, however, were more from anxiety and fear than grief.

Could it be? she asked herself. Was he really gone?

It was almost too good, and that's what scared her. That's what made her cry. It had taken her so long. She had endured so much humiliation and so much frustration along the way. Now, finally, she seemed to have it all. She wanted to flee. She wanted to get away from the police, the reporters, the funeral. Evan's parents would be there. They had never liked her. Who were they to judge? They were no better than her own stock, crude blue-collar people. Their only asset had been a son who was a self-serving egomaniac and who, with some luck and some ruthlessness, had become a multimillionaire.

Where Vivian really wanted to be was in Italy. There was a small town on the Amalfi coast, just south of Naples, Positano. That was where she belonged, on a terrace beside a pool, looking out over the emerald sea to the island of Capri, drinking the local wine, living. And wouldn't it be grand if Luther could be there with her? A scandal with his Moorish skin and his sculpted body. She, the American heiress. He, her kept man. But Luther was no one's kept man. And Luther was tainted. That was too bad. Vivian felt close to Luther. He was more like her than any other man she had ever met. Still, she would settle for just Positano. More than anything, Vivian wanted to be there. But there were motions that had to be gone through. She wasn't free, yet.

To help herself along, Vivian had begun drinking gin and tonics. No one could blame her for that, could they? She was trying to deal with the shock. The thought made her smile a wicked little smile. She pursed her lips, then fished the lime from her drink and bit into it. It wouldn't do for the help to see her socializing, or making plans, or smiling for that matter. That could be used against her. Instead, she sat alone on her bedroom terrace in an oversized rattan chair with her bare feet tucked snugly underneath her. Wearing a well-worn pair of jeans and an oversized cotton blouse, drinking gin and tonics, and staring at the endless surf. She looked quite forlorn. That was where one of the maids found her to announce that Mr. Wilburn and Mr. Rivet were downstairs to offer their condolences.

"Tell them I'm upset and don't want visitors, Amelia," Vivian said after a hard swig of her drink. "And please bring me another . . ."

Amelia returned after several minutes with her drink and the disturbing message that Mr. Wilburn and Mr. Rivet wanted her to know that it was quite important that they see her immediately, for business as well as personal reasons.

"I'm sorry, Mrs. Chase," Amelia fretted. "I told them they should leave, but they would not. No, they said I must give this message to you. What should I do, Mrs. Chase?" Amelia said, her blood rising. "You want me to get Hector and have Hector tell them to go? I think they might not be so stubborn with Hector . . ."

"No, Amelia. Thank you," Vivian said, exhaling a long low breath. "Go tell them I'll be down, and show them into the living room."

When Amelia had gone, Vivian stood up from the chair. She stumbled slightly, but steadied herself on the chair. She picked up her drink and started to bring it with her, but thought better of it and gulped it down instead before returning the empty glass to its place on a little wicker table.

"Gentlemen," Vivian said in a subdued voice as she stepped into the sunken living room with her head held high. They stood.

"Please," she said graciously, "sit down."

Both men sat without offering her any of the usual condolences. It made her uneasy to see them so callous. Vivian had never cared for Martin Wilburn, and she didn't trust him. Even Evan had been wary of him, and Evan hadn't been wary of many things at all. Swimming, for instance— he had gone swimming in the ocean in even the worst weather. People had warned him. He never listened. That was Evan.

"Vivian," Wilburn said, his voice echoing off the hand-carved vaulted ceiling, "come sit down with us. I want to make you an offer."

The room was large. Pastel paintings in bleached frames adorned the plaster walls. There was a large pink granite fireplace in the center of the exterior wall. Vivian could only recall building a fire there on one occasion. Wilburn sat opposite the lawyer on one of two facing white couches. Vivian sat in a high-backed chair and crossed her legs.

"What are you talking about?" she said, with as much disdain as she could muster. Talk of this nature with her husband not yet buried was gauche.

"I'm talking about a deal between you and me," Wilburn said. His face was expressionless. "I want the Marauders in Memphis. You want this team. I'll help you keep the team. You help me move it to Memphis."

"I can't think about this right now, Martin," she said somberly. "My husband—"

"Let me get straight to it, Vivian," Wilburn interrupted rudely. "We all know Evan's dead, and let's be frank, no one in this room is heartbroken. You don't have to play that game with me. Let's talk about the facts. You're having an affair with Luther Zorn."

He held up his hand to cut off her protest.

"Now, I don't know if it was you, or Luther, or both of you, but I do know something ugly is behind your husband's death. We're talking about murder."

Vivian blanched.

"How dare you!" she blurted, starting to rise.

"Sit down!" Wilburn commanded, rising to his feet and pointing toward her chair. "You'll listen to what I have to say! He was killed! It won't be long before Luther Zorn is arrested and convicted of murdering your husband, Vivian. I know you sent him a note, telling him to come here today! This morning! I can prove it! I have the note! I know all about how you have been contacting Luther Zorn, arranging to meet, using phone messages. I'm one step ahead of you, Vivian! So, sit down!"

Vivian plunked herself down on the chair so hard her teeth rattled. His words cut through her little alcoholic buzz like a cold bucket of seawater. She looked at Wilburn as a prisoner might look at her executioner. There were so many things she wanted to say, but none of them would come out.

"Good," Wilburn said calmly. "Now, no one else knows about these notes, and no one has to know. I don't want you to go to jail, Vivian. But even if you didn't go to jail . . . well, our good friend Mr. Rivet can tell you better than I that if you were found to have any involvement whatsoever in your husband's death, his will could be challenged. He has two parents who'd love nothing more than to get their hands on everything. You'd get nothing, and I want you to have it all, Vivian. I want you to have it all because you're going to do just what I tell you . . ."

Vivian looked at Rivet.

He nodded his head. "It's true, Vivian," he said finally. "Evan's alternative beneficiaries are his parents. They could have you disinherited, completely, even if you were never convicted of a crime. The burden of proof in a civil court is much less than that in a criminal court. And, if you were found to be an accomplice in a criminal court, quite honestly, you could receive the death penalty."

"Hah!" Vivian huffed in disbelief. "What the hell are you talking about? I may have been having an affair with Luther, but I didn't tell him to come here today, and I certainly didn't have him kill my husband! That's insane!"

"I have the note, and a pattern of notes that speak quite to the contrary," Wilburn said bitterly, still on his feet. "And when Luther realizes he's going to take a fall? Who knows? It wouldn't surprise me to see him bargain you away to save what he can of himself.

"But none of this has to be, Vivian," Wilburn said, his voice suddenly as pleasant as if the whole thing were nothing more than a bad dream. "I'm not asking you to do anything that isn't good for you anyway. You don't care about this team staying in Florida. It was Evan who cared about that. You'll make millions, as will I. That's all I want. That and control of this team, which would also be in your best interest. What, after all, do you know about running a football team?

"You see," Wilburn said gently, turning his gaze briefly to Rivet, then observing as Vivian digested what he said and made her calculations. "We're all on the same side here."

"What if, as you said . . . Luther tries to drag me down with him?" Vivian asked, mortified.

"I think when the police question you more thoroughly, which they'll get around to doing very shortly after the funeral," Wilburn answered, "you will break down and admit, despite yourself, that you saw the man who was your lover outside on the beach this morning. You'll sell him before he can sell you. That's what you'll do. That's the only way you aren't going to get dragged down with him. I have the note. Without that, it will be Luther's word against yours. That's no contest. No matter what you've come to think of him, he's still a black man, and he's still a football player, and this is still Palm Beach, not L.A. You, on the other hand, are a rich white woman whose husband has been murdered."

She felt as if she were entangled in barbed wire. She sat without speaking for a long while, pondering the possibilities, weighing the potential outcomes.

"All right," she said, finally. "I'll tell them."

"You can even suggest a polygraph," Wilburn said. "That's always a nice touch when you're telling the truth."

She nodded absently, thinking that she wanted a drink.

Rivet took a folder out of the briefcase that was sitting on the floor between his legs and handed it to Vivian along with a pen.

"This is a five-year contract that designates Martin as the president of the Marauders organization," the lawyer explained. "Nothing financially is being taken away from you,

Vivian. It simply lets Martin manage the team in the best interests of you both."

Vivian looked blankly from Rivet to Wilburn. Wilburn nodded and waited. She signed the papers. Martin Wilburn gripped his hands tightly behind his back but said nothing.

Chapter 15

Blood and cotton leaked out of Luther's nose, a steady stream of viscous blood running down his upper lip and draining into his mouth. He was gasping for air. The blood filled the cracks between his teeth and gave him the ghastly appearance of a well-fed vampire. His eyes had that wild animal look, wide open and extremely alert. He searched the sideline and found the defensive coordinator. The coach tugged on the bill of his hat, twirled both forefingers in the air, then made a sign as if to cut his own throat. Luther nodded and turned to his assembled teammates, ten of them, waiting for his words. It was a powerful feeling, but one that Luther took for granted. They were an impressive bunch, big, fast, strong, and mean. They looked to him for answers. They looked to him when things were going wrong and when things were going right. On the field of play, Luther dominated, physically and mentally.

"Switch coverage, tackles spin, cutthroat blitz," Luther commanded. "Ready, break!"

Eleven pairs of hands snapped sharply together in a unified clap. It was a comforting sound, like the beat of a war drum. To each man it meant that there were others beside him, others who would help. No one was alone.

To Luther it meant that his people were in sync. Each man had heard him. Each man knew the job he had to do. If someone lagged, Luther sensed it, and he did something about it.

There was not a thought, in any of their minds, of the brutal murder of the team's owner during the week. To most players, Evan Chase wasn't a person anyway. He was an overseer who made money on their efforts, their sweat, their blood. His death was nothing more than a subject for locker room conversation. For Luther, of course, Chase's death was much more significant. It was like a disease he had been exposed to, but didn't yet know if he had contracted. It was a bad thing that could ruin his life. Still, here, in the middle of a game, even for Luther Zorn, Evan Chase's murder was not a distraction. That was part of the beauty of playing the game. When you were in its midst, there was nothing else.

This game was in sudden-death overtime. Because Luther had broken the leg of the Vikings' star running back, their ground game was useless. They were trying to pass their way into scoring range. The impact of Luther's helmet, which had snapped the runner's tibia, had also jammed Luther's helmet down into his nose, rupturing it and causing it to bleed profusely. If not for the pungent taste of blood in his mouth, Luther wouldn't have given it a second thought.

Luther's men lined up. The Viking offense lined up. Luther barked out the formation, letting his men know exactly what they were up against, where the enemy was, how they would attack. Luther watched carefully. He'd seen this formation a hundred times during the week, sitting in dark meeting rooms, watching film of the Vikings' previous games. The formation shifted, and a receiver jogged from one side of the field to the other. Luther knew what it meant.

"Pass, pass, pass, PASS!" Luther yelled.

The ball was snapped and Luther turned his hips, as though he was going to drop back to help cover one of the wide receivers streaking by. He counted a beat, just enough to let the offensive linemen think he wasn't going to cross the line of scrimmage. Then he came, and he came fast. Two three-hundred-pound defensive tackles crossed paths in front of Luther and a hole opened up between the bodies. Luther never slowed.

Going through the line, he pumped his knees to avoid being tripped. A mammoth guard peeled off and slammed into Luther. Luther spun, using the guard's momentum to propel himself. He came clear again, and still the quarterback was holding the ball, unable to find a target. Luther leapt. The quarterback lurched and Luther was jerked backward in midair at the same time. His body crashed to the turf, the wind blasted from his lungs. He saw stars. He heard wild cheers. He rolled over and tried to raise himself off the field.

Whoever had grabbed him from behind was already gone. It didn't matter. There was no yellow flag. It should have been a ten-yard holding penalty. Offensive linemen weren't allowed to use their hands that way. This was not the time to be contemplating broken rules, Luther decided, assessing the situation.

The Vikings had completed a pass, but worse yet, Chris James, Luther's right cornerback and the team's best coverman, was also lying on the turf, writhing in pain. Luther jogged toward the other end of the field. He could see Antone Ellison running toward the huddle from the sideline.

Antone was the third-string cornerback, the team's last resort. James's normal backup had torn the cartilage in his knee only two weeks ago. Luther moaned. There were some Marauders who kidded that Antone had to have something on someone to have even made the roster. He was an average player during his prime, and that was several years ago. The Vikings would know Antone was an exceptionally weak link. Every team had extensive information on every other opposing player in the league. In that way, the game of football really was like a war. Everyone scouted his enemy. They would go after Antone.

Luther approached the huddle and looked Antone in the eye.

"Focus, Antone," he commanded. "We need you, man. You can do it."

Antone nodded, but looked nervous.

James was carted off the field on a gurney. Luther looked to the sideline for his instructions. The situation was desperate. Ten more yards, and the Vikings would be in field goal range. In sudden death, the first team to score won whether the points came from a touchdown or a field goal. The defensive coordinator waved his hand in a broad circle above his head. Luther closed his eyes briefly, as if meditating. A moment later they snapped open, sharp and clear.

"Storm the tower!" he barked. "Ready, BREAK!"

Eleven pairs of hands clapped as one. The defensive players made their way to their positions. The call was for an all-out blitz. Almost everyone would race for the quarterback. There wouldn't be enough offensive men to block everyone; so the quarterback would go down. The danger was that the quarterback would find an open receiver before he got hit, that he would pass for a touchdown. Because the defense was blitzing, the cornerbacks were isolated, one-on-one, man-to-man, with the receivers. They had to react to the hiccup-quick moves of the receivers and keep their bodies positioned between the receivers and the quarterback.

Luther took three quick steps toward Antone as he made his way toward the sideline, the perimeter of the formation. He reached around the smaller player and grabbed him by the face mask, pulling him face-to-face, the metal of their rubber-coated masks clanging mutely.

"Stick to him, Antone," Luther urged. "You cover this guy for two seconds! Just two seconds, and I'm buying you a big lobster dinner."

Antone smiled broadly and winked.

"You know I will," he said in the cocky manner of a Pro Bowl player.

"Yeah," Luther said, then jogged off to his own position directly opposite the center and the quarterback, who stood crouched behind him.

When the quarterback started his cadence, Luther edged up toward the line, coiling his muscles, ready to spring. Other defenders did the same, lining up all across the field in two- or three-point sprinter stances facing the quarterback. The ball was snapped quickly and the blitz began. Luther threw himself forward. There was nowhere to get through, so he launched himself up and over the struggling linemen. He could actually see the quarterback, and even though someone knocked his feet out from under him, Luther's leap was so powerful that he would come down directly on top of him. But that was only after the quarterback had launched the ball, downfield, into the waiting hands of the receiver who was racing past Antone Ellison toward the end zone.

The game was over. The Marauders had lost.

Chapter 16

On Monday morning, they came for Charlene at Lord & Taylor. She was behind the register, checking out a forty-something woman wearing a Rolex. The woman was purchasing two pairs of jeans and a belt. Charlene was happy for the commission. She wanted to be able to earn enough one day to support herself and Jamal on her own. It's not that she didn't appreciate Luther, or doubt that he would be there for them. It's just that one never knew. If nothing else, Charlene had at least learned that over the last nine years of her life.

Charlene's customer's eyes shifted past her and Charlene turned to see what had drawn her interest. Two men were approaching the register. They were dressed in dark suits and sunglasses and couldn't have stood out more if they were wearing clown costumes. The woman with the Rolex knew right away they were police, and when she realized they had come for Charlene, her mouth fell open. She hurriedly grabbed her bag and stepped away from the register. Detective Lawrence took out his badge and Charlene felt adrenaline race through her heart.

"Are you Charlene King?" Lawrence asked from behind his dark glasses.

"Yes," Charlene nodded. She was too afraid to speak. She could only think something had happened to Jamal. Tears welled up in her eyes. Still, she waited.

"Would you mind coming with us, Ms. King?" Lawrence asked. "We just want to ask you some questions."

Where Charlene came from, no cops ever wanted to just ask questions. The cops were there to harass people, to abuse people, to put people in jail whether they deserved to be there or not.

"Jamal?" she said weakly.

"Excuse me?" Lawrence said.

"Is it my son?" she said. "Is he all right?"

"Oh, yeah," Lawrence said in an offhand way. "No worry there. No, we just want to ask you a few questions about—"

Gill, Lawrence's partner, gave him a nudge.

"We just want to ask you a few questions," he repeated. "Would you mind coming with us? I don't think you want to make a bigger deal out of this than it is, Ms. King. The fact is, we have some questions that you probably know the answers to. It will look a lot better for you if you just come with us."

Charlene's eyes darted nervously around the store. Two other clerks were watching in shock, and her manager had a scowl on his face as he approached the register. Charlene was the only African-American in the women's clothing department. Her co-workers were assuming the worst. Her hands trembled as the manager completed the transaction for the woman with the jeans and closed the register.

"Charlene, what's going on?" he demanded. He was a short prim man. Like the two policemen, he wore a suit and had a grim expression on his face.

The detectives looked blandly at the manager, then at Charlene. She was wearing a miniskirt and a matching navy blue tailored jacket. Lawrence couldn't help admiring Charlene's long shapely legs and the way the material of the jacket was stretched taut around her breasts. When it came to a good-looking woman, Lawrence was color-blind. He wouldn't say anything to Gill, though. Gill was a spectacular bigot.

"I have no idea, Mr. Parks. These men are with the police and they've asked me to go with them," Charlene said, absently tugging her skirt down as she spoke. "They just want to ask me some questions."

"Is she in any trouble?" the manager asked with a scowl, pursing his thin lips.

Gill said nothing. He looked at the man with total disdain. He hated fairies, too.

Lawrence shrugged noncommittally. "We just need to ask her some questions."

"Is it all right if I go, Mr. Parks?" Charlene said pathetically. She didn't want to lose her job over this.

"If you must," the manager sniffed, turning to walk away, "then you must."

"Come on," Lawrence said, satisfied. He knew that Kratch wanted him to create a scene.

Charlene walked between them, keeping her gaze on the floor until they were out of the cool interior of the store and into the warm morning sun.

They got into the car, Charlene in the back, Lawrence and his partner in front. Lawrence sat in the passenger's seat and turned around to speak to Charlene. For the twenty-minute drive to the station, Lawrence questioned Charlene about her past and about her son and ultimately about her relationship with Luther Zorn.

"You've got kind of a checkered past, Ms. King," Lawrence said sadly.

Charlene gave him a panicked look. She knew her past was checkered. She knew her husband and the other men she'd been with had been in and out of trouble, even jail. And now she knew from the way things were going that something was wrong with Luther. She was so scared, she was afraid her hands were shaking. She tucked them underneath her legs and bit her lip in an attempt to control herself.

"Ms. King," Lawrence lied, delivering his final line, "I probably shouldn't be saying this, but from what you've told me about your son and how important he is to you, I think you'd better tell the lieutenant the truth about everything he asks you. If you lie, you may become an accessory . . . to murder."

Charlene winced as though Lawrence had struck her. Tears welled up in her eyes, but she choked them back.

"Did Luther kill someone?" she whispered in horror.

Lawrence looked to his grim-faced partner and then back at Charlene. "It's quite possible, Ms. King.

"Just tell the truth," he said, directing his attention back to the road, "and I'm certain everything will be fine. If you don't, I'd hate to think of your boy in some foster home somewhere . . ."

Charlene didn't conjure up any horrible images of brutal foster parents wielding leather belts and wooden paddles. Instead, her mind was filled with the image of Jamal, coming home from school, tossing his backpack on the kitchen table and smiling at her, happy and safe for the first time in either of their lives. For either of them to lose that, to lose each other, would be worse than death. To her it was unthinkable. She bit the inside of her lip until she tasted blood.

                         *   *   *

"Tell me about the red zone," the doctor said, his soothing voice washing over Luther like a quiet stream.

"The red zone," Luther said languidly. "How many times do I have to talk about the dream?"

He was lying on the big leather lounge chair with his eyes shut, his hands gently cleansing themselves of anxiety.

"You're still having it," the doctor reminded him. "As long as you're having it, you need to talk about it. It's part of who you are. We need to reinforce the bridges between the conscious and the subconscious until the free flow of information and emotion prevents things from rising up uncontrollably."

Luther was comfortable with the doctor's jargon. He had spent a lifetime listening to it.

Luther sighed. "My brother and I are playing with trucks. He has a beat-up old brown one; the paint is chipped and you can see the metal underneath. Mine is gold with red and green jewels on it, brilliant like a king's crown. We're on the floor of our bedroom, but it's dark, and the floor of the room is floating in space. My father is there. Just suddenly, he's there. And he has a hair dryer and he starts swinging it around and around his head by the cord, like a cowboy with a lasso. He comes at me, but I hold up my truck and the dryer explodes when it hits. My father is incensed and he keeps swinging the cord that has another dryer on it now, only it's shiny metal and its edges are sharp like razors. It spins faster and faster and he turns on my brother. My brother stands up and holds up his truck like mine, only his gets cut to pieces and the dryer keeps coming. My brother screams, but you can't hear it. You just see it. The metal dryer hits his head again and again and again and chunks of his head go flying everywhere like scraps of meat. My father keeps swinging and swinging until there's nothing left, just his body, only now I'm my father . . . everything is red. I see in red, like through glasses. It's the red zone."

The big room was quiet for some time, as if the doctor had been lulled to sleep by a bedtime story. The fan turned lazily above them. Luther opened his eyes to see the doctor looking at him in a strange way.

"What?" Luther said.

The doctor's hands were in front of his face, placed flat against each other with the tips of his fingers barely touching his nose. If the doctor wasn't a self-proclaimed atheist, Luther might have thought he was praying.

"So the dream is different, isn't it? Everything is still red, but you are your father now," the doctor said quietly.

"Yes," Luther said, shutting his eyes and lying back. "I am."

Kratch had wanted Charlene scared and desperate before he started talking to her. He wanted her to be thirsty. He wanted her electrolytes to be depleted. Little things like that always helped. Lawrence had done a good job. He could tell that she was scared already. She was too scared to have even asked if she could use the bathroom. She would sit until he came for her. Every so often, Kratch would send Lawrence in to tell her it would be just a little longer. He let Charlene sit for a good three hours in the glare of the bright white room before he entered and politely introduced himself.

"I'm going to videotape our interview, Ms. King," Kratch said mildly. "I hope you don't mind."

That seemed to alarm Charlene, but she nodded her head anyway.

"Good," Kratch said, turning to the mirror that covered the wall behind him. "I am Lieutenant Donald Kratch and I'm here with Ms. Charlene King. Ms. King has consented to this interview being videotaped. Is that correct, Ms. King?"

Kratch turned to Charlene and watched her patiently until she said, "Yes."

"And I have in no way coerced you to speak with me here today, have I, Ms. King?" Kratch said.

"No," she whispered, trying her best to resist another furtive glance at his wandering eye.

"You came of your own free will?"

"Yes."

"Ms. King," Kratch began, focusing his attention on her now and not the mirror, "how long have you known Luther Zorn?"

Charlene felt herself coming unraveled. Here it was. She knew what was coming. She had used the time they gave her to think. In some way, she was now going to have to betray the man she loved, her savior.

"About two years," she whispered, staring not at Kratch but at her folded hands, which twitched nervously on the table in front of her. Her nails were painted perfectly, half white, half pink, split diagonally along the length. Luther loved her nails like that. Since Kratch had walked into the room she had tried not to take her eyes off them.

"Please tell me how you came to know him and the nature of your relationship, Ms. King," Kratch said pleasantly.

Charlene felt ashamed as she told the story of how Luther had saved her. At the same time, she was happy to heap praise on Luther. They needed to know that. They needed to know how good he was.

"So you're not only very appreciative of all Luther Zorn has done for you," Kratch said, "it appears you're very much in love with him, is that correct?"

"Yes," Charlene nodded vigorously. "Luther is a great man."

"Now," Kratch said, the tone of his voice shifting ever so slightly, "Ms. King, in light of your feelings for Luther Zorn, I know you may not want to answer what I'm about to ask you honestly. I know how much Luther means to you, but it's very important that you tell the truth, Ms. King. It's very important."

Charlene looked up with her lower lip clamped firmly between her teeth. Her tears were evident now. Suddenly, Kratch's questioning took on a new tone. The inquiries came abruptly.

"Was Luther Zorn at your home last Wednesday night, November the seventh?"

"Yes."

"Did Luther Zorn spend the night?"

"Yes."

"Was he there in the morning when you woke up?"

Silence. Charlene may have worshipped Luther, but she would die before she put her son in jeopardy. She knew how important her next answer was. She knew about the owner's death. She knew when he'd been killed. It was on the news. She'd put it together in the three hours she'd been sitting there.

"I know Luther wouldn't do anything to hurt anyone!" she blurted out suddenly.

"Was he there in the morning, Ms. King?" Kratch demanded.

"No," she whispered.

"What time did you get up?"

"Seven o'clock."

"Do you know when he left?"

"No," she said, "not for sure."

"Do you have any idea, Ms. King? I want you to tell the truth, please. It's very important, Ms. King."

Charlene was sobbing now, but she choked out the words. She wanted to go home.

"I woke up," she moaned. "It was four-oh-seven. He was gone."

"So, Luther Zorn was at your home on Wednesday night when you went to sleep, but sometime before seven minutes after four in the morning, he left your house?"

"Yes."

"Do you know where he was going, Ms. King?"

"No."

"Do you know if he was driving his car, Ms. King?"

"Yes. He came in the Viper, and it was gone in the morning."

"Thank you, Ms. King," Kratch said, calmly, as if a storm had suddenly passed. "You've done the right thing."

Chapter 17

Charlene dreaded what might happen if Luther found out what she had done. For all the generosity he had shown her, she still knew that something deep and dark was lying dormant in Luther. Something that could hurt her. Something that, she suspected, if disturbed, would be more horrifying than any of the brutality she'd known in her past. That was saying a lot. She thought she saw this thing from time to time in Luther's eyes, lying there, coiled up, resting, but always there. She sensed its power, and she was afraid that now, after what she'd said to the police, she would feel its sting.

When Tuesday rolled to an end, Charlene began to relax. If Luther was coming, he would have been there by now. Luther was a creature of habit. Monday, the day after most games, was an easy day for Luther, where his work for the Marauders consisted of nothing more than watching film of the previous day's game and lifting weights. Tuesday was his day off. So, if she was going to see him at all, it was most likely to happen one of those two days. After Tuesday, his demanding practice schedule kept him away at least until the weekend. That was Luther's pattern. If she saw him again this week, it would be one of his rare Friday nights. It would be late. Luther, of course, had his own keys to the house, and on Friday nights, he might simply appear. He would usually be intoxicated. On those occasions, he would rise early the next morning and return to Palm Beach for a light practice on Saturday if the game was home, or head to the airport if the team was traveling. Charlene would wake and wonder if he had been there at all, or if it had just been a dream.

When Jamal was tucked away in bed, Charlene poured herself a glass of Chablis and sat down on the couch. She took a sip of her wine and exhaled deeply. Some of the tension left her. She checked the listings and turned on an old Bette Davis movie. It was Luther who taught Charlene to enjoy the old black-and-whites. At first, she had no interest in anything but color movies. But, because she would sometimes find herself sitting quietly beside Luther during an evening, she finally let herself enjoy the old ones. Now they were a habit. But the last day and a half of worry left Charlene tired, and soon she was asleep.

When she woke, it was almost three A.M. She yawned and rolled her neck, kneading it with her fingers to work out a kink. She shut off the TV and started for her bedroom. The wineglass, still half full, sat on the low glass coffee table in front of the couch.

Charlene went to the bedroom and removed her comfortable sweat suit before pulling on a big old jersey that belonged to Luther. It came all the way down to her knees, and the mesh material was worn smooth on the inside. It even smelled like Luther. She had actually pulled the covers up around her chin when the thought of the wineglass hit her. It would be fine to get it in the morning. The only problem was, what if Jamal got up before her? It wasn't a big deal. She'd had a glass of wine. Charlene rolled on her side with that comforting thought, proud that she'd rationalized herself out of having to move. One half a glass of wine. It was certainly not a major thing.

Ten minutes later, Charlene threw back the covers and cursed out loud. Every time she was just about to fall back into her sleep, the notion of Jamal finding the glass of wine would bump against her consciousness, ever so slightly, like a balloon gently bumping against a windowpane, and suggest that she was setting a bad example. Here it was, a weeknight, she had work in the morning, and she'd been drinking. She knew it was only half a glass of wine, but it would look bad sitting there in the morning light, the small semicircular smudge from her lips on its rim. She was sure of that now as she padded out to the living room in her bare feet. She picked up the wineglass and took it to the kitchen, where she dumped it out in the sink and placed the empty glass carefully in the dishwasher.

On her way out of the kitchen, Charlene heard a small noise in the garage. She stopped and listened. Yes. There it was again. She wasn't afraid. Her neighborhood, although modest, didn't have a crime problem. And, besides, she had nothing anyone would really want to steal. She opened the door slowly and reached around in the dark for the switch.

"Luther?" she said out loud.

Charlene sensed the large dark shape of a man. She turned to run, but a strong hand suddenly clapped across her mouth. Her neck was encircled with a muscular forearm that began choking her. She fell backward and tried to scream. She struggled wildly, but the grip on her mouth was so tight that the only sound she made was that of her bare heels thumping uselessly against the linoleum floor. A knee came up into the middle of her back, jolting her with pain and causing her legs to go limp. Her eyes were wide with shock as she felt herself being dragged slowly back into the garage. Upside down, in the dim light from above the stove, Charlene saw his face. The thing she had always feared more than anything was there, wild, foaming, let loose. The wide deadly eyes of a madman. Tears streamed down her face and her head moved almost imperceptibly from side to side before the lack of oxygen to her brain caused Charlene to lose consciousness.

When Lawrence pulled up to Charlene King's house, his heart skipped a beat. Two Sunrise police patrol cars filled the small semicircular driveway. The driver-side door of the first patrol car was wide open, as was the front door to the house.

"What the shit?" Lawrence uttered, looking sideways at his partner, who shrugged his shoulders.

Lawrence pulled over to the curb and he and Gill popped out of their car. The Broward County deputy sheriff they were with pulled in behind them. Lawrence looked back and waited for the Broward deputy, whose name was MacDougal. MacDougal adjusted his hat in the reflection of his car window before sauntering over.

"Looks like the locals got here before you," MacDougal commented smugly, eyeing the Sunrise cars.

"Really?" Gill said, deadpan.

"Let's see what's what," MacDougal said, puffing out his chest and heading for the door.

The three of them almost bumped into the Sunrise patrolmen coming out of the house with a little boy who was clearly distraught.

"Gentlemen, I'm Deputy Orin MacDougal, with the Sheriff's Department," the deputy said, extending his hand without a hint of the condescension he felt. It was ten times harder to be with the Sheriff's Department. Almost anyone without a criminal record could get a job as a local cop. But MacDougal wasn't the kind of guy to lord that over someone.

The Sunrise police seemed confused.

"I'm here to serve a search warrant with these detectives from Palm Beach County," MacDougal explained. "How about you guys?"

"We've got a possible missing person," the taller cop said. "Got a nine-one-one a couple of hours ago from this kid here. Says his mom was here last night, then, bingo, he wakes up this morning and nothing, no one. They live here together, alone. There's no sign of struggle or nothing. Bingo, she's just gone. Kid says the mom's boyfriend is Luther Zorn, the Marauders player. I don't know. I guess we'll try to get in touch with him, see if he knows anything about the mom."

Lawrence looked to Gill. Gill shrugged again.

Lawrence cleared his throat and said to MacDougal, "Well, Deputy, I don't know if it's got anything to do with what we're here for, but why don't we proceed with our search?"

Lawrence had been warned to conduct the search strictly by the book. This was MacDougal's jurisdiction. It made Lawrence sick, really, all the care and concern about doing everything just so. These days police work was more form than anything else. Killers roamed free because of undotted "i's" and uncrossed "t's."

MacDougal nodded. "We've got a warrant to search, so, we're gonna search the house. Um, I guess, well, what are you guys gonna do with the kid?"

"Taking him to Social Services, I guess," the tall cop said in an incongruously high-pitched voice.

MacDougal squatted down in front of Jamal and said, "Where's your mom at, pal?"

Jamal shook his head that he didn't know, but said nothing. He was fingering some kind of pendant that hung from a gold chain around his neck.

Gill gave a low whistle and quietly said, "Nice work, MacDougal."

"He don't say much," the tall Sunrise cop said.

MacDougal scowled and stood up before he addressed the tall cop. "Well, I better get your names in case I need to follow up."

"Go ahead on in," MacDougal said to Lawrence importantly, acting as if Gill was not worth noticing.

By the time MacDougal had all the information he thought he needed from the Sunrise police, Lawrence and Gill had already hit pay dirt. Gill was taking photos of some scuba equipment the two of them had found jammed into a trunk in a locked closet inside the garage. Lawrence leaned back against the maroon Toyota Camry that was parked in the musty-smelling garage.

"Got what you're looking for, huh?" MacDougal said, sidling up to Lawrence.

"Got just what we're looking for," Lawrence said grimly. Then he turned to MacDougal and said, "Nice work, Deputy."

MacDougal wasn't sure if Lawrence really meant it, or if he was somehow making fun. So, without a word, he opened the overhead garage door and went outside to sit in his car. When they were through marking the evidence and loading it into the back of their unmarked Crown Vic, Lawrence went over to thank MacDougal again through the open window of his Caprice Classic. MacDougal looked straight ahead, giving only a nod to let Lawrence know he'd been heard before throwing the Caprice into gear and driving off.

Lawrence slid into his own car beside his partner and said, "A different kind of guy."

"A dumbass," Gill said.

Even though it was November, the afternoon sun was bright and hot. Just the hint of a breeze wafted across the dusty dry grass of the Marauders' practice field. The horizon to the east was marred by an eight-lane interstate highway, raised above the swampy landscape. To the north was the West Palm Beach Municipal Stadium. Everything else surrounding the practice field, beyond the acres of parking lots, was overgrown wetland rich with green tropical vegetation. The cars cruising by on the raised highway glinted like broken shards of mirror on a slow-moving assembly belt. Not a single player noticed when several bulky white television vans and an unmarked sheriff's car exited the highway, spiraled down the ramp, and sped directly toward them.

Sweat ran down Luther's face and he drew deep breaths to recover his wind. They were nearing the end of practice and it had been a long day. The coaching staff seemed to be working them double time in preparation for the upcoming Dallas game. Opposite him, the team's third-string quarterback mimicked the cadence of Troy Aikman, the Cowboys' quarterback, whom Luther and his team would face for real this Sunday. The ball was snapped, and the Aikman stand-in pivoted, then handed the ball off to another third-string Marauders player, this one disguised in a number twenty-two jersey as Emmitt Smith. Luther knew from the formation and the complex pattern of movement in front of him that Emmitt's double, although moving to the right, would cut back to Luther's left. Luther changed his direction before anyone else and accelerated up to the line of scrimmage, meeting the runner in the hole and upending him with a tremendous crack. Luther's defensive teammates whooped out loud, even though it was just a practice play.

Luther allowed himself a smile and a few hand slaps. It was a good feeling to watch something time after time on the video screen, recognize what it was you had to do, and do it. It was a feeling of accomplishment that reinforced Luther's belief that with careful planning, you could negotiate your way through life as if it were a video game, scooping up treasures and deftly avoiding pitfalls.

He looked to the sideline for the coach to signal the next play. Luther's back was to the stadium and the parking lot where the TV vans were pushing their satellite output antennae slowly toward the sky. Reporters and cameramen unloaded like storm troopers and jogged toward the field, trying to catch up with the two detectives in dark suits and sunglasses.

Luther relayed the play to his huddled teammates. It wasn't that the players and coaches were unobservant. It just wasn't uncommon to see television cameras and reporters scurrying about like schoolkids vying for the first place in line. The offense ran another play. This time, Aikman's body-double threw a wobbling pass, a poor imitation of the real thing. Luther dropped into his zone to cover a tight end and watched the pass float overhead like a wounded bird and drop out of bounds near the detectives, who were advancing. Luther noticed them for the first time and froze. He knew instinctively what was happening, but he couldn't decide what he should do. This was one play he hadn't seen on film. It was something he hadn't even imagined.

Lawrence and Gill went for Luther. For all his prowess amid the cattle-sized men that huddled on that field, Luther seemed to be intimidated by the two men in suits. The cameramen tried to get close.

"Luther Zorn," Lawrence said, "you're under arrest for the murder of Evan Chase."

The words left everyone stunned and silent, and seemed to resonate across the field. Gill grabbed Luther's left wrist and twisted it behind his back. Luther spun toward the detective and swung a forearm into his shoulder, knocking Gill to the grass.

Lawrence grabbed Luther's jersey and tried to pull him down. Luther swung an elbow toward the detective's head, but missed. Then Luther broke into a run, churning his legs and digging up clods of dirt and grass against the weight of the detective, who held fast to his uniform. In an incredible display of balance and strength, Luther kept churning but twisted his body about in a full circle as he ran. Lawrence couldn't hold on. He fell to earth as Luther streaked for the opposite sideline. He passed his open-mouthed teammates and kept going, heading straight for the undergrowth. Cameramen jogged after him across the far parking lot as far as their untrained lungs would allow. Luther never slowed. He hit the treeline and disappeared. Gill and Lawrence were smart enough not to chase him. Instead, they scrambled for their car to call in a chopper and some dogs. Lawrence cursed himself and his partner. Kratch would kill them for this.

Chapter 18

Madison listened intently to the scrawny fifteen-year-old kid. They were separated by a small Formica table. The boy's wart-covered fingers fidgeted with the word *fuck,* which had been scratched into the pale yellow tabletop by some previous inmate. His dirty blond hair was greasy and too long. It hung down in front of his face like a tattered curtain. Madison had to control the urge to reach across the table and sweep it back. Behind the hair was a pair of electric-blue eyes, alert, but scared as hell.

The boy had killed his mother's boyfriend with a Colt .45 revolver. Shot him once, right through the heart, with a hollow-point slug. The incident took place when the mother sent the boy back to her boyfriend's apartment to retrieve her clothes. After the last of many bitter fights, she had finally decided to leave. The boy snuck in through a window and was stuffing his mother's clothes into a battered suitcase when the boyfriend caught him. The gun was in the drawer. The boyfriend, a big potbellied truck driver in his mid-thirties, advanced on the kid, scornfully taunting the boy, saying he didn't have the guts to use the weapon. The blond-haired boy had been beaten by the boyfriend before, and was deathly afraid of the older man. He shut his eyes and pulled the trigger. The circumstances seemed not to affect the sympathies of the Travis County DA's office. They weren't even conceding the bigger, older man's threat of violence. Nor were they conceding the boy's act of self-defense. They were going for murder, and under the new statutory guidelines they would press for the defendant to be tried as an adult. He faced life in prison.

This case was a free one, practically. Madison would be remunerated by the court, but only at the rate of twenty dollars an hour. Lately, she was able to bill her paying clients as much as four hundred an hour. Madison still took on pro bono cases, offering the best defense money could buy to those who often needed it most but who could afford it least. It helped her conscience, too, to know that people like Donald Fears paid the freight for kids like the one sitting before her.

Madison glanced surreptitiously at her watch. She had to get back to her office and wrap things up if she was going to make it home in time for dinner. It was already four-thirty.

"All right, Glen," she said. "I think I've got everything I need for now. Your mom told me she's trying to get together the money she needs for your bail, so hopefully we can get you out of here pretty soon. Are you okay?"

The boy nodded. He was naturally taciturn, and Madison doubted he would say anything but that he was okay, even if he was on a train bound straight for hell.

Back in her office, a memo from Chris Pelo stared at her from the middle of her desk. It was an outline for a plan to

recruit a defensive lineman named Clay Blackwell, who
played for the New York Giants. Madison glanced at it
briefly and sighed. She had to give Chris credit for his per-
sistence, and his planning. It was laid out for her exactly
when she should place calls to the player and what the theme
of each conversation should be, along with a list of points
that she should make sure to get across. When she learned
that Chris had done the same thing for Marty Cahn and that
the strategy had proved overwhelmingly successful, she
wondered at Chris's inability to make these contacts himself.

"Madison?"

She looked up to see Chris himself standing there in her
doorway.

"Chris, come in," she said, "I was just thinking that you
don't really need my—"

"Madison, you've got to see this," Chris said, cutting her
off and switching on a small TV that rested in the corner of
her bookshelf.

Madison looked to Chris for an explanation, but he had
his back to her and was watching solemnly as CNN came
out of a commercial. Madison's eyes widened and her
mouth slowly opened as she watched Luther Zorn being led
from a Florida swamp, handcuffed between two SWAT officers, still wearing his football pants and cleats underneath a
torn and filthy T-shirt. The anchorwoman's voice ran on
while pictures of helicopters flying overhead appeared on
the screen. The anchorwoman outlined the story of how the
star football player had broken free from local sheriffs who
had attempted to arrest him for the murder of Evan Chase.
The screen was suddenly filled with a flattering shot of
Chase, looking rakish and almost handsome. Then footage
of Luther's escape from the practice field was shown while
the anchorwoman explained that he had eluded capture for

over three hours by hiding in nearby swamps before being cornered by police helicopters and dogs.

Following a live report from a correspondent outside the Palm Beach Sheriff's Office, which detailed Luther's background, Chris turned down the volume and looked at Madison.

"Unbelievable," she whispered.

Chris nodded.

"I know what you're thinking," she said, looking at her phone as if she expected it to ring at any moment.

"I don't know Florida procedure," Madison said. It was the best she could come up with. "I've never tried a case outside Texas . . ."

Chris looked at her skeptically and said, "You can get local counsel to help you through the rough spots. Other famous lawyers have tried cases between states. It's not unheard of. If we try to back out of this, we'll never get another client in the league. Luther will make it known that we went back on our word, all our talk about loyalty—"

"We said nothing about representing him in a murder trial," Madison protested, but it sounded weak, even to her.

"We promised him our loyalty as agents, as attorneys," Chris said. "If a client got into a scrape with the IRS, I'd be expected to help them. That's the way it is."

Madison was quiet for a few moments. Then she said, "I don't really think I'm a 'famous' lawyer."

Chris said nothing. He just looked.

"Well?" he said, finally.

"I don't know," she said. "Do you think he planned it this way? All that talk about loyalty . . ."

Chris shrugged and gave her a pained look. "Loyalty is probably something a guy like Luther hasn't seen much of in his life," he said. "It's not that unusual for a player to demand it. Besides, it certainly wouldn't hurt your practice."

"I was surprised at how easily we signed him," Madison said, almost as if she was speaking to herself. "Chase was killed before the ink was dry on that contract, and I'm certainly better qualified to represent him in a murder trial than I am in a contract negotiation . . ."

"I don't know," Chris said, "maybe it's just a coincidence."

Madison stared at Chris and said, "You know as well as I do that what looks like a coincidence may really just be nothing more than careful planning."

Chapter 19

Aaron Crawford was a sad-looking man, with thick dark hair and fashionable silver-rimmed glasses. Despite his gloom, he looked quite a bit younger than his forty-eight years even though the meanness in his dark baleful eyes was immediately evident. He wore a pin-striped, double-breasted charcoal suit and a gold and black silk tie. He stood facing a window that stretched from the floor to the ceiling, his posture as stiff as the heavily starched collar of his bright white shirt. Although the evening sky was heavy with gray storm clouds, the window afforded a grand view of the city of Memphis. In fact, the view gave Crawford the distinct impression that he was standing on top of the city.

Crawford had his hands locked behind his back and his upper lip clamped between his teeth. As was most often the case, his plans were going well. However, as was always the case, he wanted everything, every single thing, to go his way. When that didn't happen, he was miserable. He prided himself on pushing people to their limits; and on having things exactly the way he wanted.

He had already raided and gutted Tyson Electronics, buying the company for less than its book value and then selling off all its assets. Never mind that he had cost more than two thousand people their jobs. Never mind that he had destroyed a successful company that had taken over forty years to build. Tyson had something he wanted. He made money on the raid, but the real prize was a piece of land that Tyson was planning on using to expand its operations. It was an enormous undeveloped plot adjacent to the highway north of the city. It was the perfect site for a sports stadium, a couple of hotels, a mall, a business park, and countless satellite commercial entities.

The entire project would be worth more than a billion dollars to Crawford, and the dismantling of Tyson made his entire investment, in effect, free. He had taken the company and the land right out from under its shareholders. This wasn't the first time that Crawford had raided a company for his own purposes. He allowed himself an evil smile. It was almost poetic that the linchpin to the entire project might be a football team named the Marauders. In a way, he fancied himself to be a marauder as well.

His intercom buzzed.

"Yes?"

"Mr. Wilburn is here, Mr. Crawford," his secretary said.

"Send him in," Crawford said, without moving anything beyond his mouth.

The great wooden doors swung open, revealing to Martin Wilburn an opulent office that was somehow different from the way he remembered. Maybe it was darker, maybe it was that the shiny assemblage of antique firearms that decorated the walls had been altered in some way.

"Sit down, Martin," Crawford said, his back to the man who controlled the Florida Marauders.

Martin sat down and stared at Crawford's small squared-off shoulders.

"How did your meeting with the sports committee go?" Crawford asked, without taking his eyes from the roiling storm clouds.

"I don't like the fact that suddenly they're talking about Arizona possibly coming in," Wilburn complained.

A small ray of sun broke through the dark clouds and lit a distant building like a shrine. Crawford smiled.

"You shouldn't like it," he said. "If Arizona is serious about moving, you may find yourself without a deal."

"You seem rather cavalier about it," Wilburn said stiffly.

Crawford turned around slowly. "My biggest concern is getting a team into Memphis. The Marauders would obviously suit my needs better than another, but my only imperative is getting a team. Your fortune, on the other hand, hangs in the balance," he added without emotion. "I personally think that's a good thing, Martin. Nothing motivates people like greed, and the harder you work at getting your team here, the better it is for me . . ."

Wilburn stared at the man without looking away. He'd known Crawford too long to be cowed by his wealth and his power.

"You said you had some advice for me," Martin said flatly.

"Yes," Crawford said, turning back to the window, "I do. These buffoons on this sports committee are more concerned with touchdowns than money. I suggest you focus your energies on getting your team into the playoffs. If you have a better showing than Arizona, it will give you the edge. No matter what they say about terms of the lease and the split on luxury boxes, the biggest concern with these people is that they have a winning team. They seem to think that matters."

"That has always been a concern with me. I've always worked to ensure the team was the best it could be," Wilburn said.

"But now you have a problem with your best player," Crawford said. "People tell me that without him, you may have problems winning these last few games and making the playoffs.

"As I said," Crawford continued with the wave of his hand, "all this bores me. But if the committee wants you to win, you should do what you can to win. It's better for me. And for you?"

Crawford let his own question hang like a spider twisting on a single thread before answering it himself. "Well . . . this may be your last chance, Martin. Who can say when a deal with this kind of upside will happen for you again? I'm aware of how you feel about this Luther Zorn, but don't let your emotions get in the way, Martin. That has always been your weakness."

Wilburn nodded to himself. "I appreciate your advice. I'll do what I have to."

Crawford nodded. He'd heard what he wanted to hear.

"And how is Vivian?" he asked as an afterthought.

"Vivian?" Wilburn said, unable to hide his surprise that Crawford would even ask.

"Yes, Vivian," Crawford said with a smile that Wilburn couldn't see. "I take it she's getting on through her . . . difficult time."

Wilburn didn't quite know how to answer.

"I guess she is," he said finally. "She seems to be doing fine."

"Good," Crawford said. "That's all."

Wilburn knew he had been dismissed, so he rose and left.

Chapter 20

Martin Wilburn wanted Kratch to conduct a low-key murder investigation, but that was just too damn bad. Kratch needed a conviction. That's what he was being paid for, not for the well-being of the Marauders football team. He wasn't waiting for the end of the football season, and he wasn't going to do things quietly. The more he could get out of Zorn, the better. It wasn't unusual for Kratch to get full-fledged confessions. That was good police work.

Part of getting a suspect to talk involved creating the right environment. Confusion, fatigue, guilt, and dehydration all helped. Kratch had timed Luther's arrest knowing he would be tired and dehydrated at the end of a long practice. It was an unusual opportunity for a cop. He also knew it would be especially disconcerting for Luther to be pulled off the practice field in the middle of broad daylight with the TV cameras rolling. So he did that as well.

Kratch tipped off all four local news channels and even put in an anonymous call to CNN's Miami bureau. He then sent Lawrence and Gill out to the Marauders' facility at around three in the afternoon. It was spectacular, really, and Kratch wasn't upset at all with the escape.

Luther's struggle, his break for freedom, the hunt, and the capture all made for good TV, and it all reinforced the idea that Luther Zorn was a killer. Kratch had chuckled through the smoky pall of his Camel cigarette as he watched the story unfold on CNN. He congratulated himself despite the irate call he got from the team's new president, Martin Wilburn.

Luther, unfortunately, had smartened up considerably since the last time he and Kratch had spoken. The first time they had talked, Luther hadn't been under arrest and the words spilled from him like an overturned bucket. The advantage of not arresting someone was that the police weren't required to give them a Miranda warning. If they talked voluntarily, as Luther had, and as Charlene had, there was no need to remind them about the right to a lawyer and the right to remain silent. The downside was that without arresting someone, they didn't have to come with you at all. Kratch was amazed at how many did come just because they were asked.

Now, though, Luther wasn't talking. In fact, he seemed to have taken his Miranda warning quite seriously. The only thing he would say was that he wanted a lawyer. Fortunately for Kratch, the only people who had contact with Luther at the station so far had been Gill and Lawrence, and they seemed to have developed temporary problems with their hearing. Kratch might have to have them tested. There was the risk that Luther might tell the judge he had asked for a lawyer long before he was given one, but the judge heard the same thing from almost every defendant. It was no big deal.

Most people under arrest couldn't resist the urge to talk. Even if they were innocent, and especially if they were guilty, it was a rare criminal who could resist the temptation to start explaining things. Once they started talking, you almost always got them. Sometimes it took people a little bit of time to want to talk. That's why Kratch was waiting. He figured he could let Luther sit for up to eight hours before getting himself into trouble over unreasonable police procedure.

Kratch's phone buzzed.

"Yeah," he said brusquely.

It was Gill. He said, "The lawyer's here, wants to talk with Luther Zorn."

"Stall," Kratch said and punched off.

He reached into his desk drawer and removed a cellophane packet. Inside, like a coiled snake, was a thick gold chain. Attached to the chain was a diamond-covered pendant in the shape of the number "1." To Kratch it was an insignificant trinket, but for Luther it was destiny. Kratch yearned to see Luther Zorn's face when he showed him the necklace. Sometimes a good shock to the system could jar loose all kinds of information. It was time to try.

Emmit Stone was the youngest sheriff Canal Point had ever known. It was his older presence, however, the permanent five o'clock shadow, his mild manner, and his receding sandy brown hair that made his youth tolerable. Every sheriff before Emmit had been a middle-aged, seasoned law enforcement veteran, most of them too tired for the constant strain of big-city police work. Emmit was just the opposite. Fresh out of the criminal justice program at the University of Florida, he had enthusiastically returned home to apply his newly acquired knowledge. It wasn't that Emmit didn't think big. He did. He no more intended to be the Canal Point sheriff for the rest of his life than he intended to turn to a life of crime. No, Emmit would do big things one day.

His goal was to become sheriff of nearby Belle Glade within five years. From there, after five more years, he would ascend into the upper ranks of the Florida State Police. Emmit planned to be the youngest colonel ever to head up the state police force in the state of Florida. They were ambitious plans, but he believed. That was Emmit, the kind of guy who expected to get someplace by toeing the line, doing as he was told, and showing up for work fifteen minutes early every day, the kind of guy who is almost always disappointed.

Emmit was not a man to learn in the ranks. He didn't think of himself as a patrolman. He thought of himself as a natural leader who should be in charge of something, no matter how small. Of course, in law enforcement the only place someone fresh out of school could be his own boss, no matter how good his grades had been, was in a place like Canal Point.

The downside of being your own boss was that you had to take calls late at night. When Emmit's phone rang, however, it wasn't a matter of annoyance to him. His wife might have sighed and rolled her eyes before answering the phone, but not Emmit. Emmit's blood tingled when the phone rang late. It might just be something good. And this time, as fate would have it, it was almost too good to be true.

"It's for you, Sheriff," his wife muttered sarcastically, handing him the phone from the couch where she sat spread-legged and pregnant, her hair held back in a faded blue bandanna like a kitchen slave.

"I'll take it in the kitchen," Emmit said, pulling his large thick frame from the couch and crossing the squeaky floor to the other room.

"Is this you, Sheriff?" came the voice from the phone on

the kitchen wall. It was a voice that Emmit recognized, but could not place.

"Yes," Emmit said, "this is Sheriff Stone. How can I help you?"

"I ain't saying who I am," the caller protested unnecessarily. His voice was an excited whisper.

"All right," Emmit said calmly. He knew how to deal with crazies. He'd taken all the latest psychology courses at the university. In fact, psychology had become Emmit's hobby of sorts. He had to keep it low-key, though, because Clara, his sharp-faced wife, was deeply born-again. She wouldn't hear of any influence on human behavior beyond God and Jesus Christ. Schizophrenia and manic depression were merely ills of the soul that could be eradicated through prayer. Emmit kept his mouth shut when it came to the power of prayer. Although twice her size, even now when she was a good seven months pregnant, Emmit was no match for his zealous wife when it came to authority. His came from textbooks. Hers came directly from God.

"Now I didn't kill *no* one," the voice hissed, "I want you to know that straight off!"

"All right," Emmit said, his heart pumping at the idea of a murder. "I believe you."

"Now, I don't want no questions about how I know, but I just know. I . . . I was out on route four-forty-one, a couple of miles north of town. Now, I just happened to turn down a dirt road right near highway marker thirty-seven. Now, I wanted to turn around see? I wasn't doing nothing wrong. I was just turning around. But . . . well, I went down in the driveway and kept going a little ways, just looking for a place to turn around, see?"

"All right," Emmit said patiently, still trying to put a face with the voice. He guessed the call was being made from some kind of restaurant pay phone. Emmit could hear the murmur of people and the faint clinking of silverware and plates in the background. There weren't more than about twenty-three hundred people who lived in Canal Point and, because of the heavy Southern country accent, Emmit was sure the caller was a local. He was probably calling from Lucy's. Emmit could call back and speak to Lucy herself to find out who had just used the pay phone.

"Well, so, Lord, I didn't do it, I swear, but you gotta go out there and see it, Sheriff," the man whispered. "You just better get out there . . . Lord . . ."

Emmit suddenly realized whom he was speaking with. It was like having the name of a song on the tip of your tongue and finally remembering it.

"Caleb," Emmit said firmly, "I told you about breaking into people's camps! Now, I'm warning you for the last time!"

"Damn it, Sheriff!" Caleb moaned. "I kept telling myself I shouldn't call . . . I didn't do it though. I just went down there—"

"All right, Caleb," Emmit interrupted. "I believe you, but I don't want you breaking in places anymore. Now, what did you see?"

"I can't tell you, Sheriff," Caleb moaned. "But I swear on my best coon hound, it weren't me."

Caleb Voles hung up before Emmit could say another word. Caleb was Canal Point's petty criminal. From time to time, when the welfare check didn't quite make ends meet, he was known to break into a fishing camp and steal tackle and whatever electronic equipment someone might have been foolish enough to leave behind over the winter months. Emmit was certain that whatever Caleb had found, he'd done so intending to commit a burglary.

Emmit walked back into the living room, tucking a loose shirttail into his pants.

"Gotta go check something out," he said with an importance he didn't quite feel.

Clara scowled at the TV and shook her head in disgust. She patted her hand gently against the cotton shift that in no way disguised her distended belly as if reminding him he was running out on two of them.

Emmit sighed and picked his hat off the rack by the door. "Don't wait up," he said quietly, closing the door on the sour pair of eyes that had followed him to the front porch.

There was only one lonely dirt road near highway mile marker thirty-seven. Emmit suspected Caleb chose this site for its remoteness. His headlights illuminated a thick steel post on either side of the drive. The chain that stretched between them apparently had been cut, probably by Caleb. The dirt drive was wildly overgrown. Saplings and crabgrass scratched and buffed the underside of Emmit's patrol car.

Emmit let the old brown Plymouth roll down the slight incline through the thick brush and trees until he rounded a bend and found himself in a tiny clearing, at the back of which rested a snug little log cabin. The cabin backed right up to the lake. As the dust overtook him, the beam from Emmit's headlights turned into a yellow haze that lit the front corner of the cabin and dispersed in the purple night that clung to the inky water. Only tiny white comet storms of bugs disturbed the stillness. Then Emmit noticed the posts off to the right, just out of the headlights' glow. They were tall, as tall as the cabin's dark shingle roof, long lean poles of knotty pine that were topped off with something that Emmit couldn't quite make out in the darkness. He got out of his car and removed the flashlight from under the front seat. He trained the white beam on the middle post and angled it up high. An involuntary cry escaped his lips when he saw the first head. Emmit staggered backward and pulled the Smith & Wesson .357 from his holster. He spun in a circle, peering at the darkness all around him with the gun trained on the beam of light. Small fearful whimperings involuntarily escaped his mouth. Emmit spun around several times with his gun and his flashlight before he calmed himself enough to look again.

There was a head on each of the three posts. They were in various stages of decay. Emmit was no pathologist, but one of them looked as though it had been there for some time. It was mostly a skull. The middle head was a gruesome grinning mash of rotting flesh and long gray hair. The third was fresh enough for Emmit to see that it belonged to the body of a young black woman. Its features were distinctly fine, even atop a pinewood pole.

Emmit vomited in the grass, and carefully wiped his lips with a thin white cotton handkerchief. This was the kind of thing he'd only read about. But he'd read extensively, so he knew that the person who'd done this was sick beyond reason. Most people would suspect that whoever had done this was some kind of raving lunatic. But that wasn't what Emmit thought. He was thinking some kind of psychotic disorder: a schizophrenic, a person who essentially had two selves, one that might function normally, if not successfully, in society, another that had the capacity to commit this kind of crime.

Emmit knew the drill. He would call the state police. They had the equipment and the labs to handle something like this. For all his thrill at the idea of investigating something of this magnitude and delving into the mystery of solving three heinous and horrible murders, Emmit was secretly relieved that he would have to pass this off to someone else. In fact, the three grisly heads made him wonder what had ever made him want to become involved in law enforcement in the first place.

Chapter 21

There were moments when Luther began to doubt himself, thinking that maybe he should talk, tell Kratch his story. Then maybe they would let him out. His sweat-soaked T-shirt had dried long ago. It was now stiff and scratchy and the smell was pungent enough for Luther to notice his own scent. He sat in the brightly lit room, still wearing his swamp-stained football pants and blackened rubber football cleats. He had removed his helmet and shoulder pads some-time during his attempted escape. Luther didn't know what the hell he was thinking about when he ran. It made him look guilty. It was a reaction more than anything. They caught him completely off guard. He was in the middle of a practice, in a zone. They came for him, and it just wasn't in his nature to capitulate without a struggle.

He probably could have eluded them for longer, but when he heard the dogs and saw the helicopters flying back and forth overhead, he realized he didn't stand a chance. Luther had turned himself in.

Luther's parched tongue shifted restlessly inside his mouth like a big cat in a small cage. He needed water. A small voice inside his head told him to give them what they wanted. Luther checked himself angrily, and bolstered his determination not to say anything without a lawyer. He now suspected that his first interview with Kratch had been a mistake. But, then, as the detective himself pointed out at the time, it would have looked very suspicious for Luther to clam up. Now, though, the situation had all changed. Luther was under arrest. The humiliation of being dragged from the swamp twisted his insides even now. Luther couldn't help fantasizing about the things he might have done if he'd kept running.

The door opened and Kratch stepped inside. Luther stared straight ahead. Kratch sat down in front of him and pulled something from his shirt pocket.

Luther's eyes came alive when he realized the chain dangling in front of his face belonged to Charlene. His heart raced.

"We found this in your car," Kratch said, and without expression he dropped it on the table in front of Luther.

Luther tried to swallow. His eyes began to mist over. He stared angrily at Kratch. Luther clenched his hands together and leaned forward, opening his mouth as if to speak. Kratch felt himself lean forward, too. Then Luther suddenly sat back and crossed his arms in front of his muscular chest.

"I want my lawyer," was all he said.

Many years ago, when he'd made the rank of investigator in the Criminal Intelligence Division of the police force, Chris Pelo moved his family from one of the Hispanic neighborhoods in the city out to the northern suburbs of Austin. Chris bought wholeheartedly into the American dream, and the suburbs were part of it. Chris liked to walk through the streets of his neighborhood late at night, when no one else was about. He took comfort in the way the dark maze of similarly constructed, similarly shaped homes rose around him like protective sentinels. Afterward, he'd stroll through the inside of his own house. Now, with four of their five kids gone, the four-bedroom house seemed spacious. Chris liked to assess what he had and remember at the same time where it was he'd come from: no money, a squalid shack in a bad part of town, the distinct smell of greasy tortillas and beans, a couple of scrawny laying hens pecking about in the small dirt plot out back, the broken seams of secondhand shoes, both his parents working as domestics in the homes of wealthy Texans in a manor on Town Lake.

Chris's family had been large, too, seven kids that survived their first year. Chris was thankful his parents lived to see what he had become, what he had. That was why they had worked so hard. They had worked themselves delirious so that the next generation of Pelos might have what they never could. This made Chris think about the generation to come. Each of his children would be college educated. One was already a lawyer. One was in medical school. In a way, it made Chris sad to think that his grandchildren would have little to strive for.

When he finished his rounds and turned off the computer his youngest son had left running in his bedroom, Chris undressed and slipped into a creaky old queen-sized bed next to his wife. She moaned softly and clung to him in her sleep. Her plump body warmed his back quickly.

Chris closed his eyes. It was midnight and he had to be up at five, but his mind couldn't seem to let go of the day's events. He thought about Luther Zorn and fretted over not having heard from him. Maybe he was wrong. Maybe

Luther didn't have plans to use Madison as his lawyer. If he did use her, it would present many more opportunities for Chris. He could capitalize on the publicity to expand the agency to new clients. It would be the second time in almost a year that Madison had come to the aid of an NFL player involved in a murder trial. She would become a legend, and there wouldn't be a single player he couldn't get to based on Madison's reputation alone. And murder trials were Madison's forte. She could do what it was she lived for and help his cause at the same time. Maybe the whole thing was too much to hope for. Chris opened his eyes and looked at the clock. It was just past one.

The phone rang. It was Luther.

Chapter 22

It was late when Vivian came to the jail to get him out. He was relieved to see her, but he was still angry over her betrayal. She told him not to worry. They were both silent as they sped through the night in her black Ferrari. They were soon in her bedroom. A warm ocean breeze gently wafted the heavy gray curtains on the balcony. One of the French doors banged quietly against the wall. Vivian stepped into her closet, and reappeared wearing only a white negligee. She couldn't have looked more perfect. Luther reached out to touch her breasts through the silky material. She gripped his wrists and pulled him toward her, pushing herself against the hard muscular bands of his body. Vivian pulled them both toward the bed, undoing his pants as they moved slowly and deliberately.

She hiked the negligee up over her breasts and around her shoulders and wrapped her long lean legs around the small of Luther's back as she fell softly onto the bed. Luther clasped his hands around her long slender neck and tightened them as the two of them became one. Vivian struggled, and a wicked smile crossed her face. Her smile caused the furnace in Luther's soul to rage uncontrollably. He seemed to leave his body and everything turned red. His hands wrung her neck tighter and tighter, as he worked them back and forth against each other like a player trying to get a better grip on a baseball bat. A blast of wind blew through the open glass doors. Luther watched from above as his fingers sank into Vivian's flesh, cutting off the blood to her brain. Her smile persisted; it was the smile of betrayal, of knowing that she had deceived him and mortally wounded him. Yet still she had the power to attract him. Luther bellowed with the effort of choking her, but his own sounds were drowned out by the deafening bang of the glass door against the bedroom wall.

It was a dream. Luther pulled himself free, springing from the narrow cot and finding himself mercifully awake in the confines of a dreary green cell. Someone was knocking on the door.

"Get dressed," came the rough voice of a guard through a vent in the Plexiglas window on the door. "Your lawyer is here."

Luther stood and quickly used the toilet. The speckled gray linoleum floor chilled his feet. He washed his hands. The tap water filled his nostrils with the smell of rotten eggs. Luther splashed some of it on his face before pulling on the top of the light blue prisoner's uniform he had been given. The officer waited and watched. Luther had been given his own cell to keep him away from the other prisoners, as much for the sanctity of the jail as for Luther's safety. There were always a few pieces of garbage who would mess with someone of Luther's stature just to have something to talk about.

Luther noticed that a plastic tray had been pushed under the door. He picked up two cold stiff pancakes and jammed them into his mouth on his way out the door. It was the first thing he'd eaten since lunch yesterday. He followed the guard down a long hallway that led to the conference rooms. These rooms weren't unlike the one Luther had seen the night before, except for the absence of the two-way mirrors. The room was empty when Luther sat down. A moment later the opposite door swung open and in walked Pat Rivet, the Marauders' general counsel.

Chapter 23

The long stakes were now down and the heads were gone. Emmit pulled up to the crime scene in his old brown Plymouth patrol car. The door lock was jammed and he had to reach inside the panel to jimmy it open. His fingers got greasy and he cursed silently to himself. His wife, Clara, had cured him of cursing out loud long ago. Emmit slapped the panel back in place and sheepishly looked around to make sure no one had seen him.

Emmit realized then for the first time how beautiful this spot really was. There were no other camps within sight. The cabin sat alone in a small cove; the only outlet to the big lake was between two fingers of land and rocks. Whatever happened here could certainly have happened without anyone ever seeing or hearing it. A thick patch of clouds stacked up over the horizon. Emmit lifted his chin and drew a breath from the westerly breeze that promised rain. Right now, though, the sky overhead was blue and the sun shone warmly in the grass clearing in front of the cabin.

The state police had a large trailer tucked right up under the edge of some scratchy pines. It was the command post for the investigation, and although the major in charge promised him he could come and go as he pleased, already Emmit felt completely out of place. He had not only lost control over the investigation, he was being effectively frozen out of the loop. Earlier in the day, when he'd gone inside the trailer, everyone stopped talking. For his queries Emmit got dismissive one-word answers.

Major Irwin Slaughter, whose barracks were a few miles south in Belle Glade, had almost as little experience with homicide investigations as Emmit. What he did have, though, was the equipment and the people to conduct a large-scale investigation, exactly what was needed to cope with three severed heads whose teeth had been carefully extracted, making identification difficult and highly unlikely. This was the most excitement Slaughter had seen in his two years as head of the Belle Glade post, and he wasn't about to share it with Emmit.

Emmit, on the other hand, had contributed everything he knew. And, with little more than that information, Slaughter decided he had solved the crime. Caleb Voles was already in the jail at the state police barracks in Belle Glade. Slaughter was ebullient. Solving grisly murders proved to be rather easy. He was convinced that either Caleb, or someone he knew, had committed the crimes and that he could sweat the answers out of his prisoner. Emmit tried to convince the major otherwise, but Caleb's rap sheet worked against him.

Emmit was given the menial task of checking the county tax rolls to find out who owned the cabin. When he delivered that information, no one even said thanks. The major simply grunted. In Emmit's absence, the team had already determined that the cabin was clean. Nothing in it suggested any connection with the crimes. Also, they had discovered a fresh campsite in the patch of woods surrounding the clearing. The campsite was located in the midst of a stand of thin dark pine trees just beyond the poles. There was an open fireplace and a well-used army-issue tent. Whoever had used the site seemed to have burned any useful evidence, but investigators were scouring the ashes and the surrounding area looking for footprints, scraps of paper, cigarettes, something, anything, that would tie Caleb to the crime.

Emmit had asked Slaughter if, for the sake of being thorough, he should follow up by locating and questioning the owners of the cabin.

"Sure," the major told him. "A good thing for you to look into, just to be thorough."

Emmit didn't like the way the message was delivered. It could be the major was simply preoccupied, but he suspected he was just being rude. He looked like the rude sort. He was about fifty with bags that hung from his eyes. He wore yellow-tinted glasses that were big, even for the major's large face, which reminded Emmit of a shovel, long and fleshy without any real definition between the chin and the neck. The major's hair was dyed black. It was wavy, cut short on top and the sides, but longer in the back. He was a disagreeable-looking man and always had a Pall Mall pinched between his middle and forefingers.

Despite Emmit's feelings toward the major, he knew he had probably been lucky to get any assignment at all. So, rather than moping around, he'd looked into the cabin ownership. And now he was back at the scene of the crime, without anything of substance to report. A Tennessee corporation called Ibex owned the cabin and used it as a getaway for company officers. Except for the late spring, when most fish were in season, it went unused.

Ibex was a small financial services company located in Memphis. It wasn't hard for Emmit to get ahold of the company's president, a man named Kevin Pallidan. Strangely, Pallidan seemed only slightly concerned that a crime had been committed on Ibex property. The police search of the cabin didn't faze him either. Pallidan asked only whether everything had been returned to its place. Emmit supposed it wasn't unusual for a man like that to be so cool. As the head of a corporation, he probably had many more important things to consider.

In an attempt to get some kind of reaction from Pallidan, Emmit had finally offered some specific details of the killings. That at least seemed to affect him. Emmit wondered to himself now why he'd done it. Probably just to let him know that Emmit was not some hick cop with nothing better to do. Slaughter had warned him against giving out any details, though, and that's why Emmit kept thinking about it. The major was of the mind that when something bizarre like this was leaked to the press, the crazies came out of the floorboards. Also, Slaughter seemed to distrust the media. Of course, Pallidan wasn't the press.

Also, Emmit figured it differently anyway. The press, he believed, could help them get a lead on the identification of the victims, especially the girl. He knew that the major had had a teletype sent out to all the other police agencies across the state, but that only meant that a connection could be made if someone was actively looking for a person whose description matched the limited information the forensic people had been able to glean from the heads. Emmit knew that even in a police department of five hundred officers, usually there was only one assigned to missing persons. The connection might never be made. The media, however, with three severed heads, would have a field day and publish composite pictures of the victims. That seemed to be the best way to proceed to Emmit. Find out where the bodies came from, and try to link them through the killer. The problem was, Slaughter thought he already had the killer.

Emmit wished there was a way to get Slaughter off Caleb Voles. He wished he could lie and say that something wasn't right with Ibex. He knew Caleb didn't do it. Emmit wandered down to the water's edge to think. There was a dock and a nice little swimming area. The shore was sandy, and the shallow water sprouted silky aquatic grasses and lilies. Little waves lapped gently on the shore, and the sand underneath the water's sparkling surface was ridged like an endless mountain chain.

Emmit squatted down to clean the grease from his fingers in the shallow water. He dug deep into the soft sand. When he clenched his fingers, the index finger on his left hand struck something metal. It was small and smooth. Emmit dug deeper, pulling it free with his fingertip. He used the water to wash away the glop of sand that came with it. It was a man's ring. Emmit took it from the water and it sparkled in the sunlight. It was a nice piece of hardware, gold with a single half-carat diamond in its center. Emmit read the inscription.

For a second time, he looked around to see if anyone had seen him. There were still lab people milling around the campsite, but no one was paying him any attention. Emmit's find was a Marauders championship ring from three years ago, when the team had won the AFC title. Even though they eventually lost the Super Bowl, Floridians had been bursting with pride because the Marauders were underdogs throughout the play-offs. Emmit wondered if the ring could have some significance in the case.

It was nowhere near the campsite, so he felt it would be best to keep it to himself. It would be a good lead to follow up on his own. He could check it out on the sly, and, if the ring did turn into something, he'd go to Slaughter and look like a hero.

Emmit drew a deep breath before heading toward the trailer to give his banal report to the major. He looked the ring over as he walked, but slipped it into his pants pocket before mounting the aluminum steps to the police trailer. He wore a dumb smile on his face because he was a huge Marauders fan and considered it a lucky omen to have found it.

Chris Pelo made the plane reservations and purchased their tickets over the phone with his credit card. He picked Madison up at her house first thing in the morning and drove straight to the airport.

"How'd you know I'd do it?" Madison asked as they rode against the flow of the morning traffic.

"I figured that if you'd defend Fears just because he was a client you helped with a DUI a few years ago, the loyalty issue would mean more to you than it would to most people, no matter how this thing looks for Luther," Chris said. "Then, well, this is what you do, and I know how you like to have a couple paying customers from time to time as well . . ."

"What made you ask for so much?" Madison said, still surprised. "What made you think he'd go for it?"

When he called at one A.M. Chris informed Luther that Madison's nonrefundable retainer would be one hundred thousand dollars.

"It's twice what you normally require," Pelo said simply, "so I knew it would make it easier for you to say yes and I figured he wouldn't mind too much either. He knows you're the best. When you've got the kind of money Luther Zorn has and you're in jail, there's not much difference between fifty thousand dollars and a hundred thousand dollars. All you want to do is make sure you get out."

Madison nodded. She didn't want to make too big a deal about the money, but a hundred-thousand-dollar retainer would go a long way toward making this job less painful. She appreciated the way Chris put it, too, in terms of the good work she could do for free when she did some dirty work for the big dollars. Madison checked herself. She hadn't meant to think of representing Luther Zorn as dirty work. She had no idea what had really happened. Just because Luther made a mad dash through a swamp to elude the police didn't make him guilty of murder.

The flights to West Palm Beach were quick, and Madison and Chris made it to the Sheriff's Department by just a little after one in the afternoon.

"Hello," Madison said boldly to a big, sloppy-looking desk sergeant with a thick walrus mustache. "I'm Madison McCall. I represent Luther Zorn. He's being held here, and I need to see him."

The cop looked at her in a funny way, then picked up a phone, taking only a split second to say, "Hang on."

"I've got a lady here who says she's Luther Zorn's lawyer," the sergeant said skeptically into the phone. "Yeah. You're sure? That's right. Okay. I will. Thanks."

Madison switched her briefcase from one hand to the other impatiently. She'd come a long way for a client interview and a bail hearing.

"He's gone," the desk sergeant said after he hung up the phone.

Madison simply stared. "We were told he was being held here until his bail hearing," Chris Pelo explained.

"Yeah," the cop told them, "I guess they had his hearing first thing this morning. He's out."

"By himself?" Madison said incredulously.

"Nope," the sergeant answered, "some hotshot lawyer got him in to see the judge just after breakfast and worked out the bail. Must have pulled some serious weight. You missed him by about an hour."

Madison turned to Chris in disbelief. He looked at her helplessly.

"I have no idea," he said apologetically. He felt like the boy who was caught crying wolf for the second time. He was crushed.

"Where is he now?" Madison demanded of the sergeant.

The cop shrugged and said dryly, "It's none of my business, and I guess it isn't any of yours either."

Chapter 24

Arnold Letterman was fifty pounds overweight and a drunk. He always had been. He always would be. He made it into the department because his mother's brother had been the mayor of Sunrise fifteen years ago when Arnold got fired from his job as a commercial light fixture salesman. Once on the inside, Arnold enjoyed the protection of a strong labor union whose power seemed to exceed not only that of his uncle but of common sense as well. Even before his uncle had been rendered powerless by a liberal Democrat, however, the department kept him pretty much out of the way. He handled missing persons.

Arnold knew the drill. It hadn't taken him long to figure out that when some people disappeared, it mattered; when others disappeared, it didn't. The ones who didn't matter far outweighed the ones who did, and the ones who did could usually be disposed of well before lunch, which often allowed him to get into a pint of Wild Turkey as early as eleven. No one was ever the wiser for it, because the world of missing persons was vague and totally disorganized. With no nationwide information bank, those in the know considered it a miracle whenever anyone truly lost was found.

It was quarter after eleven when a knock on Arnold's door forced him to stash his pint in the bottom drawer of his desk.

"One moment," he mumbled, then slipped out of his chair to unlock his door. "Come in," he said, returning to his desk.

Gerdy, the mail clerk, entered and handed him a two-page teletype.

"Confidential and priority. Straight from the troopers," Gerdy said in a gravelly smoker's voice that reminded Arnold of an old forty-five record played with a dusty needle.

"Thanks, Gerdy," he said, carefully directing the breath out the side of his mouth.

Gerdy, a fifty-nine-year-old widow with a ferocious case of varicose veins, looked up at him skeptically through her thick glasses and a mop of salt-and-pepper hair.

"All right, Arnold," she cackled, then shuffled out of his windowless office, closing the door behind her. She knew the drill, too.

Arnold locked his door and took a stiff drink before reading the teletype. Female, mid-twenties, African-American, brown eyes, black hair, time of death only three days prior, fax of photo upon request. It was pretty clear which file this baby belonged in. Arnold placed the two sheets together and carefully folded them, his tongue slipping out of the corner of his mouth. When he was finished, he took his best shot. His paper airplane landed right in the middle of the waste can by the door.

"Bingo!" Arnold barked, and took a double nip to celebrate.

* * *

Royal palms rose up on either side of the road as Madison and Chris pulled up to a guardhouse. The Palm Beach Polo Club was exclusive. The ten different television trucks waiting outside the guard's gate didn't fit the picture. They were parked haphazardly like emergency vehicles at the scene of an accident. Someone from CNN recognized Madison as they rolled past the trucks. The woman ran after Madison's car with a cameraman in tow. She stuck a microphone in Madison's face as she rolled the window down to speak to the guard. Like a flock of starving gulls, the other reporters swarmed the car.

"No comment," Madison said firmly, leaving no mistake about her position. She then identified herself to the guard.

They were allowed to proceed, and Chris scanned the decorative street signs, directing Madison. They passed riding stables and lush fairways sprinkled with middle-aged golfers. They entered a cul-de-sac, five enormous homes nestled into the sixth and seventh holes. It was the best real estate money could buy.

Madison drove into the brick-paved circular drive and under a spacious clay-roofed porte cochere supported by massive beige columns that rose twenty feet in the air. The house was magnificent. They got out and rang the bell. The enormous handcrafted bronze door swung open and Luther Zorn greeted them wearing a well-worn thick cotton Marauders sweat suit. Out of habit, not disrespect, he surreptitiously eyed Madison's attractive figure as she marched past him into the house. Chris took notice, but said nothing.

Chris had insisted on calling Luther the moment they left the Sheriff's Department. He reached Luther at home on his private number and Luther explained the situation. He told Chris that Pat Rivet had arranged a bail hearing that morning, and that although he didn't trust Rivet or anyone from the Marauders organization, he was more concerned with getting out of the jail. Evidently, Wilburn and Rivet had enough pull with the state attorney and the Sheriff's Department to keep them from putting up a fuss about bail despite Luther's attempt to avoid arrest. Even with the team's influence, bail was set at an astronomical two million dollars. The team, through Pat Rivet, also promised to pay the costs of having a federal marshal travel with Luther so he could leave the state with the team for their remaining away games.

"They're not on my side," Luther promised Pelo over the phone. "No matter what they say, I know Wilburn hates my guts, and Rivet is his lackey. They need me to win games. That's all. The coaches must have lobbied their asses off to get Wilburn and Rivet to lift one finger for me. So, I took their help and figured you'd call. I wasn't waiting around the damn jail any longer than I had to, Chris. You understand that. I need you guys, Chris. I didn't do this. I was in Fort Lauderdale with a woman. She'll vouch for me."

Pelo had understood, and even Madison seemed undisturbed by the confusion once she heard Luther's story.

Luther showed them to the kitchen where a Mexican woman served coffee on a thick oak table.

"This is Marla," Luther said, introducing them, apparently uncomfortable with having a domestic. "She kind of takes care of things for me around the house."

"Hola, Marla," Chris said with a smile, thinking of his own parents.

Marla smiled back, but left the room without a word.

Madison took out a yellow legal pad and her pen.

"No hard feelings about this morning, right?" Luther said.

"I would have done the same thing if I were you, Luther," Madison responded. "No one would expect you to stay in jail if you could get out. I just want you to be completely honest with me about everything, because no matter how important you are to the team, it still strikes me as odd that Pat Rivet showed up at the jail this morning with everything worked out, especially after your little adventure in the swamp. I need to know everything. I'm your lawyer. It's my job to defend you no matter what. So be honest. Tell me absolutely everything. It's critically important."

Luther looked out the window and seemed to be examining a foursome carefully putting on the seventh green. Madison noticed that his hands were dancing slowly together underneath the table.

"I had an affair with Vivian Chase," Luther said, then turned toward Madison. "I think she had her husband killed, and I think she wants it to look like I was the one who killed him. I think she set me up. I think she's telling them I wanted her husband dead, which is crazy. She's the one who wanted him dead. She used to talk about it. I might have said a couple of times that, yeah, it would be nice if he was gone, but that was it. I would never kill him. It's crazy."

"Did anyone else ever hear you saying something to the effect that it would be nice if he was gone?" Madison asked.

"No."

"Is there anything else that went on between you and Chase?" Madison prodded. "Did he confront you about the affair you were having with his wife?"

"He didn't know," Luther said. "I'm sure about that. He would have gone nuts if he did. Especially if he knew that sometimes I'd meet her in his house, in their bedroom."

"How did that happen?" Madison said, trying to keep the incredulity out of her voice. "Don't they have people working in their house?"

"I used to come in from the beach," Luther admitted. "No one ever saw me."

"The beach?" Madison said.

Luther nodded and said, "I think now that may have been part of the plan, to have me coming in that way. To show that I knew the layout, where Chase swam, all that. He drowned right offshore from where I would go to meet her."

Madison looked at him without saying anything for quite some time.

"What else?" he said. Her stare was making him uncomfortable.

"Tell me about where you were on the morning Chase was killed," Madison said.

"I was with Charlene," Luther said. "She's a girl I kind of helped out. She was in a jam a few years ago, kind of a battered woman thing. I got her and her son out of a shelter, got them a place, helped her get a job, you know. But somewhere along the line things with us got . . . physical. So, sometimes I would see her and spend the night. That's what I did that night. I went to see her and I stayed."

Madison nodded and asked for Charlene's last name and her address and phone number.

"What have you told the police?" Madison inquired.

Luther shrugged. "Nothing, this time. I kept telling them I wanted you."

"What do you mean, 'this time'?" Madison said.

"I mean," Luther said, "I spoke to this lieutenant, his name is Kratch, right after Chase died."

This disturbed Madison.

"He said he just wanted to talk to me," Luther explained. "I asked him what would happen if I didn't, and he told me he might think that I had something to hide, but that right then he was only checking some facts. It was really about my relationship with Vivian. He wanted to know whether or not she used to talk to me about her husband and about how she would get all his money if he was gone. He asked if I knew about her past."

"What did you say?" Madison asked.

"I didn't say anything," Luther told her. "I told him I didn't know what he was getting at, but he said I did. I did, too, but that was it. He didn't push it. He let me go."

"Was that all he asked you?" Madison wondered, jotting down some notes.

Luther nodded and then said, "He did ask me if I was there, on the beach, the morning Chase was killed."

"Why do you think he asked that?" Madison said.

Luther hesitated, as if calculating something very important. "I think Vivian may be trying to set me up. I think she may have said I was there."

"And that's how she's setting you up?" Madison said.

"I think," Luther told her. "I'm not sure, but that's what I think is going on. It's my word against hers if she's saying it."

"And you're sure about all this, Luther?" Madison said. "Everything you're telling me is the way things really happened? Everything?"

Luther's eyes suddenly seemed filled with dark twisting shapes, like the shadows of tortured men. "I told you," he growled. Then just as suddenly the fury was gone.

"Yes," she said quietly, standing her ground.

Madison wanted to look at Chris, to see if he'd seen the same thing she had, but she didn't want to drop Luther's gaze.

"All right," she said. She had more things she wanted to ask, but they could wait. Her first priority was finding out what the state attorney was going to be using against them. "Chris and I are going to the Royal Palm to check in. I'll be staying for the next couple of days. You can reach me there if you need me. I'm going to have to find some local counsel to get me through procedural technicalities. I'll have to file a motion with the court to let them allow me to represent you as an out-of-state attorney. It shouldn't be a problem. I'm also going to file a demand motion for discovery. I'm going to set up a meeting with the state attorney. When he sees I've filed for discovery, he'll know he's only got ten days to turn everything over, so most likely he'll be willing to sit down and talk. After that, I'll have a fix on what they've got."

"What do you mean 'discovery'?" Luther said.

Madison explained, "Discovery material is any evidence they have that implicates you. They have to turn it over to me by law."

"What do you mean," Luther said, "by 'anything'?"

"Anything they have that makes you look guilty," Madison told him. "Physical evidence from the crime scene, witness statements, investigative police reports, everything."

"You think they'll really do that?" Luther said. "Give you everything?"

"If they didn't," Madison explained, "and you were convicted, and we found out they had withheld anything . . . we'd get the conviction overturned and you'd walk. The prosecution knows this, and they'll rarely jeopardize their case by not disclosing information."

"You said something about some local lawyer, but you're the one who's representing me, right?" Luther said.

"Yes," Madison said. "You still have to sign a stipulation for substitution of counsel, which essentially fires Pat Rivet and hires me, but, yes, I'm your lawyer. I said I was, and I am. With luck, we can get this whole thing resolved without a trial. From what you've told me, it shouldn't be too hard to show the state attorney that prosecuting you will just be an embarrassment for everyone. Charlene King's story will help a lot.

"Just so you know," Madison said after a pause, "I'm going to have Chris handle the investigation, so you'll need to give him your full cooperation as well."

Pelo looked at Madison in surprise; this was the first he'd heard about handling the investigation. Normally, Madison would use one of the private investigators she kept on retainer back in Austin. Even for a case out of state, Chris figured she would use people she knew by reputation. But he was excited at the prospect, and it made sense. He had as much investigative experience as anyone from his years at CID.

"So, what should I do?" Luther asked.

Madison offered him a smile and said, "Just play football, I guess. You might as well carry on with your life as best you can while we're working for you behind the scenes. I don't want you to talk to the media. They'll be haunting you everywhere you go. This is big news, and you won't have much privacy for a while. But, if you don't say anything, they'll eventually go away . . . until the trial."

"I thought you said you could convince the DA not to take this thing to trial," Luther pointed out.

"I said, maybe," Madison replied. "I'm not making any guarantees either way. I've got to see what they have. The police must have something, or they wouldn't have arrested you."

"I guess if Vivian Chase is setting me up," Luther said, "then they might have almost anything."

"Well," Madison said, "there are some things that even a good frame-up can't do."

"Like what?" Luther said.

"Like put you someplace you weren't," Madison told him.

Chapter 25

The rain came down hard, splattering the dust in the parking lot, each droplet exploding outward, leaving thousands of miniature craters before turning the ground into a soupy mess. It was impossible to say where the mud ended and the puddles began. Inside the police barracks, the cinder block walls began to sweat. A small high window lined only with corroding iron bars allowed the free flow of air as well as some of the elements into the cell. The musty smell of the cell began to overpower even Caleb's own sour-smelling flesh. He'd been in jail for nearly two days. He couldn't remember going without a drink or cigarette for such a long time. He was beginning to hear voices. And, just moments ago, he was afraid that he'd heard his own voice answering them back.

Caleb was afraid to sleep. When it got dark, rats ran around the floor of the cell. He could hear them shifting in and out of the seams between the blocks, their sharp little nails scratching away at the mortar and stone. Occasionally, one of the bolder rats would nibble at the crumbs on his tray. When that happened Caleb would slam his tin cup against the wall. The clatter of tin against concrete would send them scurrying for cover like roaches surprised by a sudden burst of light. Because he was so tall, six foot eight, Caleb had to stick his knees straight up in the air to avoid hanging his feet over the edge of the cot. He did not want to give the rats an easy shot at his toes. The sounds of their nocturnal prowling kept Caleb awake the entire length of the night. During the day, he was so exhausted that he couldn't keep himself from dozing intermittently.

When the rain started, he was lying face up on the narrow iron cot, fighting sleep and trying to figure out if in fact he really did do what they were saying he did. It certainly seemed possible. There had been times in his life when he'd done things and then not remembered them. Caleb had fought in Vietnam years ago. Since then, he really couldn't vouch for much of anything. Once, after consuming a pint and a half of Yukon Jack, he went inside a Pizza Hut on the edge of Belle Glade. A young girl showed him and his ex-wife, Cherry, to a booth by the window. After Caleb ordered a cheese pizza and a pitcher of beer, he inexplicably lit the curtains on fire.

Caleb didn't remember the incident, and they'd called it an accident. The whole place burned down. Cherry told him about it later. She swore he did it, and Cherry never lied. Caleb thought about Cherry. He missed her. How long had it been since he'd come home to their run-down trailer and found her suicide note? Seven years? If there hadn't been a note, Caleb supposed they would have blamed that on him, too. The police chastised him for cutting her down, but what the hell was he supposed to do?

This, however, was a different story. They were accusing him and he didn't know if he did or didn't do it. He didn't think he did, but they were telling him that it happened that way sometimes. They were telling him they could get him some help, but he had to help them first. He wanted to help, and he wanted some help himself, mainly a quart of Yukon or a bag of reefer. What they said was starting to make sense.

Caleb heard the tinkling of keys and then the rattle of the lock. He looked up to see a tall, hard-looking trooper wearing a big pistol.

"Get up," the trooper said.

Caleb did, and followed him. He knew where he was headed and he knew who would be there. Caleb's limbs trembled and he swatted at his back where it seemed little crawlies were running up and down his spine. He ducked through a doorway and entered a small boxlike room.

Major Slaughter looked up at Caleb Voles through his big yellow-tinted glasses. Slaughter had three cups of coffee in his system and was determined to get a confession. It was now or never. He knew that the long arm of the Constitution could reach even as far as Belle Glade when it came to protecting criminals like the one before him now. Actually, Slaughter had no beef with the Constitution itself. He loved America. It was the countless Amendments and Supreme Court rulings that sickened him. The Constitution was fine in the beginning. The way Slaughter figured, if it needed anything different, God would have made it that way in the first place.

The major knew he had to indict the piece of white trash in front of him in a hurry. Or let him go. He'd delayed due process long enough in his attempt to get a confession. If he let it go any longer, Voles might walk on a technicality. Slaughter knew he was lucky to have gotten two days. Most criminals were smart enough to start crowing about a lawyer after about the first twelve hours. Voles was too dumb for that. He hadn't even blinked when they read him his Miranda. Once he went from being an arrested suspect to an indicted criminal, a lawyer would have to become involved whether Caleb asked for him or not, and Slaughter had never known a lawyer to advise his client to plead guilty. Lawyers were trash, too. In fact, the major knew for certain that it was lawyers who were responsible for fiddling with the Constitution in the first place, giving criminals far too much protection.

The major stared hard at Caleb, until he began to squirm. The rain still beat heavily on the roof above their heads. Slaughter pushed a typed-out confession across the table toward his prisoner. A clear plastic Bic pen was on top of the paper. Caleb could see that its back end had been gnawed, like a carrot in a gerbil cage, he thought.

"I want you to know something, boy," Slaughter began. "If you sign this, I'm not going to let them execute you. I'm going to make sure they put you in one of them loony jails with all the other crazies. It's not so bad there, Caleb. Kind of like a hotel, some people say . . . But if you don't sign this, Caleb, and admit what we already know you did . . . I promise you, boy, you're going to be sitting in the electric chair."

Slaughter let his words sink in. Caleb started to shake, just a little, but it gave the major confidence.

"I've got to tell you, son," he said in a low, almost compassionate voice, his head tilted down so Caleb could see the major's eyes clearly for the first time, peeping over the top of the glasses, "when they strap you in there, they have to shave your head because heat from the charge melts your flesh. If they left your hair on, they say you'd go up like a match.

"They stick a hunk of rubber in your mouth to keep your

teeth from shattering like old jelly jars," the major continued. "But the worst thing, I guess, is your eyes . . . They have to tape right over them, because when that electricity goes burning through your body, it blasts your eyeballs out of your head like a couple of champagne corks. Imagine that? They come busting right out of your head . . ."

Slaughter pursed his thick lips, wrinkling the expanse of skin under his chin, and shook his head in sad amazement.

"The tape keeps them from shooting across the room," he explained, "but I guess the blood comes shooting out of those eyeholes like geysers. Shit! I'd hate to have to watch you burn and bust apart at the seams like that, Caleb. I don't think you even remember what you did! I think one of them hotel jobbies for the crazies is where you should be. They drug you up like hell in there and I guess you just kind of float around, peaceful-like, I guess."

Caleb Voles tucked one foot up under his leg, biting his knee. He ran a yellow bone-thin hand over his face before forcing it through his thick tangled hair. He was shaking now. He was blubbering, too.

"Shit," Slaughter said, shaking his head sadly, "the state attorney can't wait to electrocute you. He wants your ass in that chair so bad . . .

"Well," he said, rising from his seat and reaching across the table to take the confession back, "I told him I wanted one last chance to save you before I turned you over to the court. I got no say in the matter once that happens. It's okay, Caleb. Maybe if I'd done those things I'd want to die, too. It's just such a damn ugly way to go! I can't imagine what it would feel like to have my head start burning up and my eyeballs exploding, choking on that big hunk of rubber . . ."

"No!" Caleb shrieked, jumping forward and grabbing for the sheet of paper and the pen that were now just out of his reach.

"No, please," he begged, looking up into the major's eyes. "Please, let me sign it."

The major watched without even a hint of a smile as Caleb Voles tried to scratch out a legible version of his name. Slaughter had no intention of intervening in the prosecution of Voles. That Caleb was freely confessing to the crime was proof positive of his guilt. Slaughter knew for a fact that he himself would never think of confessing to something he hadn't done, no matter what was promised to him. As far as the major was concerned, the confession added weight to the notion that the human garbage in front of him should be snuffed out as prescribed by law. He'd get the location of the bodies later. He already had the heads, and for now, those and a confession were all he needed.

When Caleb finished, the major yanked the confession from his hand and examined it. Satisfied he had what he needed, he turned without another word and left the room. Caleb looked after him in horror. This was not what he'd expected at all. The major should have said something reassuring. Caleb was filled with a terrible dread that what he'd just done was wrong. But, as had been the case throughout his miserable life, it was too late to change it. There was no sense in even hoping that things would come out all right. They never had. They never would. Caleb stared down at the mangled ballpoint pen that the major had left with him in his hasty departure and waited for the guard to take him back to his cell.

Chapter 26

The state attorney's offices for Palm Beach County were located in a relatively new building, a top-heavy, monolithic structure located near the courthouse. Chris Pelo thought that only a building bought and paid for by the government could turn out so drab and ungainly. Out front was an ascetic-looking pond with a single fountain that shot up from the middle of the murky water with all the fanfare of a forgotten garden hose. The parking lots were out back. On Friday morning there were a dozen empty visitor spots right up close, and Chris wheeled in between two yellow lines with precision.

Mark Berryhill's office was on the top floor of the building, affording him a less-than-magnificent view of the neighboring industrial district, the interstate, some power lines, and swampy vegetation. Berryhill was a young man, especially for such an important post. He had numerous diplomas and credentials, and his father had been the state attorney in Palm Beach for many years. Berryhill was a blond man of medium height with handsome chiseled features. The style and fit of his off-the-rack blue suit didn't quite match his athletic frame. Madison supposed he would have been more at ease in a sweat suit. Berryhill's large desk was covered with papers and files, all neatly arranged. Studio portraits of his wife and children lined his office bookshelves. Madison thought it was a good sign that the photos were placed in front of the political and legal memorabilia that inevitably clutters the office of any man involved in public life.

"Can I get you some coffee?" the state attorney asked.

"Yes, thank you," Madison said. Chris nodded as well.

"How do you take it?"

"Black," said Madison.

"Me, too," said Chris.

Berryhill nodded and left the office to get it himself. Another good sign. Still, Madison remained alert. She'd seen too many things to be lulled into complacency by good manners and an affable smile.

"Thank you for seeing me so soon," Madison said when they were all seated around a small conference table in one corner of the office.

"No problem," Berryhill said, taking a swallow from his own mug. "This is a very big case. I know your reputation, Ms. McCall, and I want to work with you as well as I can. As you probably know already, the state of Florida is one of the better places to have committed a crime."

"Or to be unjustly accused of having done so," Madison interjected pleasantly.

Berryhill stopped and seemed to smile despite himself. "Yes, that, too," he said. "Either way you look at it, I'm compelled to give you any and all discovery material I have: physical evidence, police reports, statements . . ."

The state attorney missed a beat.

"I see by your expression that you know all this. I didn't mean to lecture you."

"That's quite all right," Madison replied. "I appreciate your candor. I know from my local counsel that you have a reputation for being tough, but a straight-shooter, and a decent person as well.

"Even if you are on the wrong side of the aisle," Madison added. "I'd like to convince you not to go through with the indictment. It will mean a lot of very bad publicity for my client."

"Not go through?" Berryhill said, raising his blond eyebrows. "I've got the grand jury convening this afternoon. I've got your client in a vise, Ms. McCall. That's out of the question. With all due respect, this indictment is a slam dunk . . .

"Mel Rosen is your local guy?" Berryhill said, changing course.

"Yes."

"Good man, too," he said.

"Yes, he is," Madison agreed.

"Well," the prosecutor began, lifting the top page of a legal pad that rested on the table in front of him, "here's what I've got, Ms. McCall. Evan Chase was an Olympic swimmer. He swam every day along the beach where he lived. The medical examiner found extensive contusions on Chase's leg. Evidently he was pulled beneath the surface and held there until he drowned. Because Chase was such a strong swimmer, we believe that only a strong man using oxygen tanks could have accomplished this.

"I've also got Luther Zorn having an affair with the wife," he continued. "They both admitted it. I've got Luther at the scene of the murder. He denied it in his first interview with the police, but Vivian Chase saw him outside the house on the beach. After searching Charlene King's house, his girlfriend, we found the scuba gear we're pretty sure he used. Now, Charlene King herself seems to have disappeared and we don't know what's going on there, but before she did, she spoke to an investigator and confirmed that Luther was at her house the night before the murder. She also said he left her house no later than four A.M., which gave him more than enough time to get to the murder scene. When Luther was asked about this, he contradicted Charlene King and Vivian Chase. You'll get a copy of the videotape as well as a transcript of all the interviews. It's a lie, Ms. McCall. He was there, he had the gear, he had the motive, he lied to the police.

"Something else," Berryhill added. "The police found a necklace that belonged to Charlene King in Luther's car on the day he was arrested. She hasn't been seen since. I hope he didn't do anything to her when he found out she had talked to the police . . ."

Madison was jolted by the prosecutor's revelations, but she was conditioned to conceal her emotions. She quickly devised some rationalizations for the circumstances Berryhill described.

"You don't really have all that much, Mr. Berryhill," Madison said dismissively, scratching something into a pad of her own as she spoke. She wanted to float her ideas to see how Berryhill would respond. "Charlene King is a nonissue. She was Luther's girlfriend and a necklace in his car is easily explained. As far as anyone knows, she's hiding somewhere, unharmed. Everything else is circumstantial as well. The scuba gear means nothing. There are thousands of people with scuba gear. There's no way to prove it was even his. It wasn't in his house that you found it. By the way, please call me Madison."

"It was his house. He owns it. Charlene and her son just live there. Luther has a key. The suit is Luther's size, an unusually large size," Mark Berryhill said. "It had been used within the past two weeks. It was still wet."

"Has Vivian Chase indicted Luther in any other way?" Madison asked, outwardly unfazed by another blow to her defense.

"She told the police that Luther had spoken vaguely about how it would be good if her husband was out of the picture." Berryhill nodded. "She believed Luther had big plans."

"I think it was Vivian Chase who had the big plans, Mark," Madison interjected. "You better check her out before you go too much further with your grand jury. I think she may be lying about the whole thing. Luther could have left Charlene's house for any reason. Vivian is the only person putting Luther at the scene of the crime, and she has more of a motive for wanting her husband dead than Luther.

"Luther isn't in love with Vivian Chase," Madison speculated. "She's just another plaything for him. Otherwise, what was he doing at Charlene King's house in the first place?"

Berryhill seemed to consider this, but it was really something else he was thinking of.

"I'm sorry," he said, flipping his pages back toward the front of his pad. "I didn't mean to omit the parking ticket."

"Parking ticket?" Madison said with a scowl.

"Yes, a park ranger ticket," Berryhill said, finding it in his notes. "Luther Zorn's car was parked in the north lot at MacCarther National Park. The citation was for overnight parking. It was issued at six-fifty-three. The lot doesn't open until seven. You'll get a copy of the ticket along with the other material. Luther Zorn was there, Ms. McCall."

Madison blinked. She relied on every ounce of self-control to keep from showing the turmoil she felt. Luther Zorn had lied to her, extensively. It was the one thing she

could not accept. The only time Madison had withdrawn
from a case had been when her client lied to her. When she
discovered the truth, she was put in the untenable situation
of having to break her code of ethics and perpetuate the lie
herself, or destroy her client's case. She had chosen instead
to withdraw. It was never pretty when an attorney withdrew
from a client. In that case it was three days before the trial.
Dropping Luther at this point wouldn't be nearly as harmful.

"His car was there," Madison corrected him calmly. "That
doesn't mean Luther was there."

Berryhill shrugged. "Well, it certainly corroborates Vivian Chase's story in my mind, but that's arguable. That's
your job, after all, to argue."

Madison was steaming, but she comforted herself with
the notion that it might not be her job for long.

Major Slaughter made the evening news on ABC in Tampa
and Fox in West Palm Beach. It was a very big day, the
biggest of his life. He had cracked the brutal murders of
three as-yet-unidentified people. He solved the crime within
days of arriving on the scene. The people of Florida were
much safer knowing that law enforcement officers like the
major were out there, bringing criminals down with the
swiftness and certainty of a lion running down a gazelle.

It wasn't until the next morning that Caleb Voles was discovered in his cell. His pasty-looking corpse was drained of
almost all its blood. Fortunately, the big news was Caleb's
capture and confession, not his subsequent suicide. The network news trucks wouldn't be making the long trip to Belle
Glade twice in two days to fuss over a dead murderer. That
was good for the major, because it was certainly a mistake
to have allowed a man who was so obviously unbalanced to
keep a Bic pen. Its plastic casing, splintered the right way,
left Caleb with a cutting edge sharp enough and durable

enough to sever a vein in each of his wrists. He'd lain down in the dark to bleed to death. No one knew or suspected that the worst part of the whole thing for Caleb was that he was still conscious when the rats began to slink out of their holes to feast on the sticky crimson pool forming beneath him on the concrete floor.

The major's minor oversight regarding the pen in no way dampened his own spirits. He had to wonder at all the fuss people made over solving murders in the first place. It seemed pretty straightforward to him, and he hoped that in the future, when law enforcement people around the state had problems getting to the bottom of certain cases, they would think of him as a resource. He was a natural sleuth. Almost everyone who worked for him and with him seemed to agree.

The major was in full uniform, his polished black boots resting on the low windowsill, idly watching through the slits in his blinds as the coroner and his assistant loaded Caleb Voles's body into the back of their black station wagon. Voles's tall angular frame didn't want to fit into the back, even though the seat was down. Because the body was so stiff, the two men struggled for some time. The major whistled while he watched. That was how Emmit Stone found him, back turned, his feet on the window, whistling.

"Thank you for seeing me, Major," Emmit said hesitantly, removing his broad-brimmed hat.

"No problem, Sheriff," Slaughter said over his shoulder, watching as the coroner's car finally swung out of the parking lot and onto the boulevard. He could afford to be magnanimous. He felt a little sorry for the young sheriff, knowing how inadequate he must feel. He probably wouldn't have taken time out of his busy day to see Emmit, but he was curious about the purpose of the visit.

"I . . . I know this is going to sound a little strange to you, Major," Emmit began, creasing his eyes with worry, "but despite what's happened, I don't think Caleb Voles was the man who killed those people."

The major swung his head back over his shoulder to look at Emmit Stone, standing there in his office, with his drab chocolate uniform and his shiny brass star and one of the stupidest expressions of hope on his face that the major had ever seen.

"What?" Major Slaughter said, squinting his eyes and pulling his lips off his front teeth as though he had heard the sheriff incorrectly.

"I don't think he did it, Major," Emmit repeated apologetically.

Slaughter snorted and threw his feet down so he could spin around and face the sheriff.

"I hope you had to come into town to do some banking, son," he said, "because if you came here just to tell me that, you wasted your gas. Don't be a fool! The man confessed it to me personally! He signed a damn confession! Then he killed himself! What better proof could you ask for?"

"Major," Emmit stammered, "it's just that I've known Caleb for most of his life. He's had some run-ins, but nothing like this. Those heads . . . that was something an insane person would do. Caleb was a drunk, and a loser, but he never hurt anyone and . . ."

Emmit fumbled with something in his breast pocket, then held forth a large ring for Slaughter to see.

"I know I should have showed you this when I first found it, but"—Emmit's big round cheeks burst with color—"well, I didn't think it was anything then. I'm not sure if it is now, but maybe it is. I know Caleb didn't kill those people. He wouldn't, and if he did, he wouldn't have called me to tell me where to find them. It doesn't make sense . . ."

The major ignored the ring and glared at Emmit. "Let me tell you something, son. I've got a solved murder here. I've been getting calls all morning from people congratulating me. That man was as nutty as a pecan pie. Now, I don't know what the hell your problem is, son, but you best keep it to yourself, because if I catch word that you're trying to tamper with my work . . . the only law enforcement job you'll be able to hold down will be the night watch at a factory someplace north of the Mason-Dixon line. Now get the hell out of here before I decide to crush your balls just for being so stupid!"

Emmit's mouth fell halfway open, his face red enough now to have been blistered by the sun. He balled up the ring in his fist and turned to go, tripping on the carpet as he reached for the door.

Chapter 27

Martin Wilburn drove through the middle of West Palm Beach, past the Royal Palm hotel, and headed south on the intracoastal highway. After a while he made a sharp U-turn and pulled over to the ocean side of the road. A pay phone mounted on a concrete post faced the water. Wilburn got out of his new Jaguar and puffed warm air into his hands. The breeze coming in off the water made him chilly. He pulled his chocolate-colored suede coat close and scanned the area. He was just about right on time. He was three steps away from the phone when it started to ring.

"Hello," he said, picking it up.

"This is the wolf," said the voice on the other end.

"This is the panther," Wilburn said quietly. His mouth was twisted disdainfully at the ridiculous pseudonyms. Suddenly, though, he froze. There was a lumpy form on the bench that he hadn't noticed until now.

"Hang on," he said, setting the phone down on the dull chrome ledge of the box and walking around to the other side of the bench to get a better look. It was a bum wrapped in blankets. Only his tattered Converse sneakers, stuffed with newspapers, protruded from the nappy blankets that covered him. Wilburn brought his Bally loafer up off the sidewalk and nudged the bum with his toe until he stirred.

"Hey," he said, extracting a twenty from his wallet and waving it in the toothless grimy face that appeared between the folds of the blankets. "Let me have this bench to myself and go get yourself a good bottle."

The bum's weepy bloodshot eyes widened at the size of the bill. A dirt-stained hand shot out from the blankets, and he hustled to his feet and tottered off mumbling incoherently.

"I'm back," Wilburn said into the phone.

"What the hell was that about?"

"Nothing. A bum. He's gone."

There was silence, and then coldly, "We may have a problem."

Wilburn's blood raced. There had been so much careful planning. Things were going so well that bad news was almost inevitable.

"What?"

"I think your boy has lost control," the wolf said.

"He's not my boy," Wilburn protested. "Why?"

"We got a call from the sheriff in Canal Point near Lake Okeechobee. It seems they found three heads on three poles at a campsite near the fishing cabin."

"Holy shit," Wilburn muttered, his eyes squinting in disbelief. "Heads?"

"Yeah."

"That fucking psycho," Wilburn said, shuddering from a chill. "I said he was no good."

"I warned you," the wolf added.

"It wasn't my call, man! Shit!" Wilburn slipped ever so slightly into his street dialect. He did that whenever he was on edge.

"Chase is dead," Wilburn reminded them both. "That's the important thing."

"What's important now is that this whole thing doesn't blow up."

"It won't," Wilburn said with a confidence he didn't feel.

"Anything could happen with him."

"Hey, man," Wilburn protested, his voice approaching the pitch of a whine, "this ain't my fault!"

The wolf let that ride a moment before he said, "You got him out."

"I got him out," Wilburn said in disgust. "Everyone knew I was getting him out. I was told to get him out . . .

"What am I supposed to do about it?" Wilburn asked. "I can't control him."

"But you know who can."

"Hey, I can't control either of them at this point. I want that to be clear," Wilburn said.

"I just want you to know that you are the one being held responsible," the wolf said in a somber tone that was neither malevolent, nor a threat. That made his message all the more intimidating to Wilburn, because he knew the wolf meant every word.

"I'll see what I can do," he said with another slight shiver. "I have to go."

"Good luck."

"Good luck," Wilburn muttered after he'd hung up the phone. "Good fucking luck!"

Chapter 28

The Texas night was turning brisk and a wind whipped dust and straw wrappers through the air in a mad swirl. Foam cups spun and clattered along the ground, and crumpled hamburger papers blew like tumbleweeds. The sky above the huge banks of artificial light was as black as a crow's wing. Madison pulled her windbreaker tight around her and dipped her chin. Things looked hopeless. It was the game that would determine who got to play for the county championship. Cody's West Lake Hills Cougars were down by thirteen points, and there was a minute and a half left to play. Just to be in the hunt for the championship was incredible. Cody Grey had turned the team around in a single season. But, as Cody had reminded Madison, when it came to football in Texas, winning was the only thing.

Jo-Jo sat next to her in a gray hooded sweatshirt, his hands clenched, gnawing on the back of a knuckle. She could sense the same degree of tension in the ten thousand other people who had jammed themselves into the stadium to see the Friday night high school game. Madison couldn't believe the numbers, or the emotion. With so many things going on in the world all around them, how ten thousand people could turn out for a high school game in this cold was a marvel to Madison.

She searched for Cody on the sideline. His hands were on his knees and he was bent over, cap on his head, staring at his team with the intensity of a man about to sink a championship putt. He knew that despite the progress his team had made, most of the ten thousand fans would be disappointed all winter if he lost this game. He had almost done too well too soon, raising everyone's expectations.

The Cougar offense went to the line and set up. The opposing defense did the same. The Cougars suddenly shifted their formation, then shifted again. A wide receiver went in motion. The confusion of the defense trying to figure out how to play the changing formation was obvious. Even Madison knew enough to see that the opposition had left a split back out on the perimeter of the field completely uncovered. Without thinking, she held her breath.

The quarterback took the snap and dropped straight back five steps before launching the ball. He threw it high and long, well ahead of the wide-open receiver. The split back seemed to have a turbocharge. The boy accelerated toward the ball and just got there, catching it with his fingertips as he shot across the end zone. The stadium erupted.

Madison screamed wildly and hugged her son, who was jumping up and down with the rest of the crowd. After the cheering died down, Madison took her seat again and tried to compose herself. She blushed at her own outburst, then reminded herself that her husband was the coach. That was a better excuse for enthusiasm than most people had.

The Cougars lined up now for an onsides kick. The kicker was the key. He had to kick the ball ten yards for it to be a live kick. His own team could then recover it and put themselves right back on offense. Both teams knew that the kicker would boot the ball ten yards diagonally toward the sideline. This allowed his men to reach the ball at the same time as the opposition. For the kick to work, the kicker also had to put a top spin on the ball to make it bounce up into the air at the last second before it went out of bounds. If it did go out of bounds, it became the receiving team's ball. That critical bounce, if done right, turned the play into a jump ball between twenty-one heavily padded football players.

The Cougar kicker teed up the ball while his teammates clustered tightly on the opposite side of the field, facing an intimidating number of opposing players ten yards away.

"Mom," Jo-Jo said, grabbing her arm and shaking her so hard it hurt, "watch Kevin Delaney! Watch number eighty! See him, Mom! Cody hid him. He's right by the sideline near the kicker! Watch him!"

Madison knew that even though her son was only nine, he probably had a better understanding of what was going on than ninety percent of the people watching, maybe one hundred percent since he got the inside strategies straight from Cody. Madison did as her son said.

The kicker held up his hand and just as he did, the other Cougar players near where Delaney stood stepped back well clear of the sideline. The referee's whistle blew, but instead of kicking the ball toward the cluster of Cougars, the kicker ran laterally past the ball before turning to kick it back down the field toward the near sideline where Delaney had been hiding. The ball skittered twelve yards before Delaney caught up to it and threw himself down to recover the kick. Whistles blared in the air and the opposing coach stormed onto the field, shrieking at the officials. The crowd drowned out anything he might have been saying. Ten thousand West Lake Hills residents were bellowing and hooting as if they'd won a war.

Three plays later the Cougars were in the end zone and Cody Grey's name was on the lips of the entire town. Madison blushed and Jo-Jo beamed as they made their way with the rest of the throng toward the stadium exit. People were congratulating the two of them as if Cody had just been elected president.

As silly as it all was to Madison, she was very proud of her husband. She knew all the time and preparation he put into his team, and into their winning. And there was something she'd seen tonight that stuck with her, an idea that wouldn't go away. It was a simple thing, a cliché: Cody won because he refused to give up. He never gave up, even during the week, when there were no crowds looking on. It was the behind-the-scenes perseverance that counted. The trick play on the kick, and the crafty formation shifts, those were things that took determination as well as creativity. They were plays that had to be run over and over, beforehand, so the players could execute them the right way when the game was on the line.

Madison nodded and smiled at people as she walked. That's when things really counted, she thought, when no one was watching, just yourself.

Chapter 29

Luther boarded the charter plane and walked through first class. Everyone got quiet. Martin Wilburn was there with some of his friends. The coaches were there, and some of the media, too. No one met Luther's eyes as he towered past them behind a pair of funky dark gold-rimmed sunglasses, but when he passed, he felt their stares. He kept his chin held high and walked toward the back, thinking about how he'd like to just take them all out, every last one of them, staring at him like he was some kind of circus animal. In the front of the coach section, a federal marshal sat among the trainers and equipment managers. The marshal nodded curtly to Luther. He passed through the middle of the plane where most of the white players sat. They got quiet, too.

It wasn't that they hadn't seen him; they had. Luther had been at practice on Friday, and besides having to push his way into the locker room through a throng of media, the day hadn't been that much unlike any other Friday. But that was practice, where everything was routine and every minute was accounted for. The plane ride to San Francisco was a social gathering. Players talked and played cards and rolled dice. The whole trip took on a festive air. Luther felt like a rain cloud hovering over a reunion picnic.

When he got back to where most of his black teammates sat, he felt a little of the tension ease.

"Luther," one of the big defensive ends barked, "my man."

Luther nodded. Other black players acknowledged him, too. They knew it wasn't unusual when some shit went down to have everyone point a finger at the nearest black man. As far as they were concerned, the white man was prosecuting him for one thing only: screwing the owner's wife. And for that, with the exception of a few holy rollers, his brothers on the team lauded him.

"Luther."

"Hey, Luth."

"Blood, what's up?"

Luther felt the tension rush out of him like the air from a slashed tire.

"Hi, Luther," Bob Jenks said, looking up from a copy of *The New York Times*. Jenks was a big rangy tight end who wore round tortoiseshell glasses and who graduated magna cum laude from Stanford. He was one of the few whites who sat anywhere, sometimes with the brothers, sometimes with the whites. On the field, a player was just a player, but on the plane, in the hotels, or anywhere off the field, whites and blacks tended to segregate. Jenks was a rare bird.

Luther removed his glasses and winked at Jenks before sitting down across the aisle next to Antone, who was busy stabbing away at an electronic Gameboy. Luther wasn't crazy about sitting next to Antone, especially under the circumstances, but Luther, unlike Jenks, was a creature of habit. This had been his seat on the plane for the past eight years now, and he wasn't about to change it just to avoid Antone.

"Luther, my man!" Antone said, happy just to be there, as he should be.

"Hey, Antone," Luther said, taking a copy of *Sports Illustrated* out of the seat pocket in front of him and burying his nose in it to cut off any further conversation.

The brothers around Luther returned to normal and the volume of goofing began to pick up. Up front, the first-class passengers and the whites seemed to have trouble regaining their equilibrium. It didn't surprise Luther. They were always that way.

Chapter 30

After a weekend of celebrating her husband's big victory, and a rigorous Monday at the office, Madison returned to Florida on Tuesday morning with Chris. They weren't going to get the discovery material until Wednesday, but they needed to talk with Luther. On Friday, after they'd met with Mark Berryhill, they caught a plane back to Austin and hadn't had time to stop and see Luther. Madison could have called him, but on Saturday morning Luther flew with his team to San Francisco. She wanted to talk with him face-to-face anyway, not over the phone. She needed to get some things straight. She wasn't going to give up, but neither was she going to work with her client lying to her outright. Hidden truths were part of her business. She didn't like them, but she could accept them. Blatant, stupid lies were insulting. Luther must have seen the parking ticket on his car the morning of Chase's death and known that people would find out he'd actually been there.

Again, they met him at his home. This time, only three television trucks were waiting outside the security gates. Mercifully, the indictment had come down from the grand jury on Friday and the ensuing media storm had blown itself out over the weekend. Like all murder trials, Madison knew that unless someone was intimately connected to the case, they didn't give it a second thought unless it was force-fed to them on the nightly news or the front page. She also knew that, barring any abnormalities, people would stop talking about Luther and his indictment for murder within a couple of weeks. Even in the O. J. Simpson case, the scandalous speculation settled down considerably between the time of the indictment and the actual trial. It was a good thing for clients Madison had to defend. The best thing they could do while they waited for the trial was to stick as close to their normal routine as they could.

For Luther, that probably wouldn't happen until the end of the season, when he was no longer exposed to the media on a daily basis as a matter of course. She did believe the attention would subside, however, and sitting once again at his kitchen table, that's what she told him.

"Luther," Madison said after offering her opinion on the media, "before we talk about anything else, I've got to be completely honest with you." She stared flatly at him. "You lied to me, and I'm damn mad about it. I actually thought about withdrawing from this case—"

"Hey," Luther began, his face clouding instantly with anger.

She held her hand up, and with her sternest look got him to let her finish. "I said thought about it. And I'd have good cause, too. Don't make it worse by acting mad at me. I'm not the one who wasn't honest! Did you really think no one would find out that your car was at MacCarther National Park the morning Chase was killed? How could you even hope the police wouldn't know? And even if you could, why wouldn't you tell me?"

"I—" Luther started to say.

"Please!" Madison said. "Just listen for a minute, Luther. You need to listen to me. This is what I do. I know how all this works. You told me a few weeks ago that football was your world . . . Well, you're in my world now. This is the law, and I know it. You have to tell me the truth. I will defend you. That's my job, my sworn duty. No matter how bad things look, I will defend you with whatever means I can."

Luther's face softened, and he looked at her with a mixture of disbelief and uncertainty.

"What if I did it?" he said, stone-faced.

Madison looked to Chris and swallowed involuntarily. She hated this, but it was necessary. It was what she believed, anyway. It was what she had learned as a little girl growing up with a father who was a defense lawyer, and what was reinforced during law school. Strange things happened. Sometimes, even when everything pointed toward a person's guilt, there were nuances that equated to innocence, or at least a lesser degree of guilt. Every person deserved an advocate who would bring those points to the attention of a jury in opposition to the state prosecution. The state had so many resources and so much experience at its disposal that sometimes justice was subordinated by the zealous determination of the state to find someone it could point to and punish.

It wasn't the first time Madison had to explain her role to a client. It wouldn't be the last. She knew almost every guilty defendant lied about his guilt. She had never heard someone admit he was guilty. That was okay. It was for the jury to determine whether or not the defendant was guilty. Her job was to defend the accused individual against the state. What she did need to know, though, was all the facts.

"If you did it, and you told me," she said, "then I would withdraw. Some lawyers wouldn't. I would. But even then, I would not be able to tell anyone about your guilt. As your lawyer, I can never reveal any information you tell me that would be detrimental to your case. Even if I did, it could not be legally used against you. It's privileged information."

Madison let that sink in. "On the other hand, if you told me you were there, you pulled Evan Chase underwater, he swam away, and on his way toward the shore, he collapsed and drowned, I would have to defend you. I would. If you told me you were there, taking a serendipitous swim, and a paratrooper came out of the sky and pulled him underwater, I'd defend you. If you told me that you had said you'd do it, had planned it for six months, did everything necessary to kill him, but at the last second, you turned back and some- one else did it, I'd defend you. Do you understand what I'm saying, Luther?"

He looked at her hard. His handsome brow furrowed ever so slightly.

"Yes," he said. "I didn't do it. I really didn't do it. I was just asking."

"That's fine. I believe you. Now I need to know every- thing, Luther," Madison said. "I need all the facts."

Luther took a deep breath and spun his coffee cup around in its place on the broad round table. He was thinking, cal- culating. Madison didn't know whether or not he was the murderer, but as long as he leveled with her about the events of that night, it wasn't her business to wonder.

"I didn't know you couldn't tell anything I told you to anyone else. All this crap about things you say being used against you," Luther explained, "I just thought I was sup- posed to shut up about everything. I talked to that Kratch once, and I know it's going to come back to bite me in the ass. I told him I wasn't there, and now you're telling me that he knows, or they know, about the parking ticket. I didn't say anything because I didn't think anyone would ever know."

Luther looked intently at Madison. "Why would they know? It was a park ranger ticket. Why would the police ever know about that? Those two don't have anything to do with each other. I paid that ticket in the mail the minute I got home, and I figured it would go away. The cops never said anything to me about it. I figured no harm, no foul."

Madison looked at Chris. He was the ex-cop.

"He's right," Chris said after a moment. "Unless the ranger who issued the ticket contacted the sheriff's office, there would never be a reason for the Sheriff's Department to know about a ranger's parking ticket or really even think about asking. It's possible that a detective might have called the rangers and asked if anyone had seen anything out of the ordinary. But even that, I think, would be a detail pretty low on the list of priorities. The parking lot is almost a mile away from where Chase's body was found. We see the logical connection because we know that Luther would park there regularly to meet Vivian Chase, but no one else knows that. The logical presumption a cop would make would be that the killer was scuba-diving and lying in wait for Chase, and that he probably came by boat. If it was me, I'd be asking the Coast Guard and any local fishing charters if they'd seen anything unusual, not the park rangers. Unless . . ."

"Unless what?" Madison said.

"Unless the police knew Luther was going to be there in his car," Chris said.

"You mean someone tipped them off?"

"I don't know what I mean," Chris said.

"Well," Madison pointed out, "if Vivian told them Luther was there, and she knew that he normally left his car at the park, then one of the first things they might do is ask the rangers if anyone had seen anything."

"They might," Chris admitted. "But think about this: not only did a ranger see something, a ranger was there at the right place, at the right time, and he or she gave Luther a ticket seven minutes before the car could have been there legally."

"Documenting the fact that his car was there," Madison said, pondering the facts. "You think it was just a coincidence?"

"What was it you told me the other day about coincidence?" Chris said. "That sometimes it's just the result of careful planning?"

Madison nodded. "I think we'll be able to get a better handle on this when we see the discovery material. I'm sure a copy of the ticket will be in there. Then we can talk with the ranger who wrote it up and find out who made the connection between the ticket and the sheriff's office. In the meantime, we need to have a talk with Vivian Chase."

Madison took a mouthful of coffee and changed gears.

"Why were you there that morning, Luther?" she asked.

"What if it wasn't me?" Luther said.

"What do you mean?"

"I mean, what if my car was there, but I wasn't?"

Madison held up her hand to stop him. "You said that Charlene King was your alibi, but according to the state attorney, she has a different story."

"You don't have to worry about Charlene," Luther said confidently.

"What do you mean?" Madison asked.

"I mean you don't have to worry about her," he replied. "Charlene won't testify against me."

"The problem is," Madison said, "she already gave the police a statement."

"What statement?" Luther said, obviously shocked.

"Charlene King is missing," Madison said, closely watching the expression on his face, "but before she went wherever she went, she talked to the police. She told them you had left her house the morning of the murder by four A.M."

Luther seemed stunned and bewildered.

"The state attorney said the police also found a necklace of Charlene's in your car the day after she disappeared," Madison said, wanting to test his response.

Luther shrugged. "I don't know how it got there," he said, recovering.

"Could she have lost it at some earlier time?"

"Of course," Luther said.

"What about being on the beach the day Chase died?" Madison pressed.

"She sent me a note," Luther said, finally. "That's why I was there."

"Vivian?"

"Yes," Luther told her. "Vivian would let me know when and where she wanted me to meet her by leaving a phone message at the team offices."

"What?" Madison said.

"They were coded," Luther explained. "Anyone can call and leave a message at the office. I get ten or twenty of them every day from all kinds of people. The receptionist takes the message and writes it down on one of those pink slips. Vivian would leave messages in the name of Susan Smith. She sent me one the day before Chase was killed. It told me to meet her, in her bedroom, at seven A.M."

"Isn't that a little early for a tryst?" Madison said. "And a little risky?"

Luther hesitated, then said, "Yeah, but you've got to understand, Vivian's like that. She's crazy. She likes the excitement . . . I guess I did, too. Once, I met her in the ladies' room of a restaurant where she was having dinner with Chase and some friends.

"I'm sorry," he said politely. "I'm sure the last thing you want to hear about is Vivian Chase's sexual appetite. I didn't mean anything by it."

This was a very complex man sitting in front of her, Madison realized. And she had to admit that he made her more than a little nervous. She had never, however, shied away from anything because it disconcerted her. All Luther's enigmatic aura did was make her more determined to understand him. It was professional with Madison, not personal.

"Did you save the note?" Madison wondered.

"No."

She pursed her lips. "What about the scuba gear?"

"What scuba gear?" Luther said with a scowl.

"The police found some scuba gear in Charlene's house," she told him, "locked in the garage."

"What were the police doing in Charlene's garage?" Luther said.

"It's your garage. You own the house, don't you?"

"Yes," Luther said, "but they can't just go in there."

"I presume they had a warrant to search it, since it's your house, and you are a suspect," Madison explained. "It wouldn't be difficult to get one. So, is it yours?"

"What?"

"The scuba gear."

"No," Luther said. "I never owned any."

"Luther . . ."

"I'm telling you the truth, Madison," Luther said. "That's what it is."

"How do you think it got there?"

"I have no idea. I can't think of a reason, but I'm sure Charlene knows."

Madison pursed her lips and stuffed her doubts away.

"Can you dive?" she asked.

"Yes," Luther said, looking straight at her. "Last May, during an NFL owners' conference, Vivian and I went to West End in the Bahamas. It's a quiet out-of-the-way place. While we were there we learned to dive."

"And you think that's part of her setting you up?"

"Yes," Luther said, "I'm sure it is."

Chapter 31

Mel Rosen's offices were located in a shopping mall not far from Lost Tree Village. Madison got Rosen's name from her father. The two men had gone to law school together many years ago, and stayed in touch. Madison's father assured her that Mel was the kind of lawyer who would step back and let her do her own thing.

"He'll chart the waters for you," he said, "but he won't get involved unless he sees you headed for the rocks. He's a rare breed, a brilliant lawyer without a tremendous ego."

Her father hadn't exaggerated one bit. Rosen, a gnarled old stump of a man whose tongue was as sharp as his mind, gave Madison and Chris an office with two well-used desks facing each other. The room was drab and paper was peeling at the seams, but they had the use of a large conference room across the hall. The surroundings were austere, but in law, at least until you got to trial, substance always outweighed form. And, if Madison's father said Mel was the best, then Mel was the best.

On Wednesday morning, after repeated attempts to contact Vivian Chase, Madison held a brief press conference to try to put a positive spin on Luther's indictment. The conference room was packed with regional media from Orlando to Miami as well as a good number of national shows, including CNN and *Dateline*. Madison didn't want them hounding her and she knew the best way to diffuse the press was to give them a few calculated sound bites. It was important, however, to present her perspective on things. She still had to go through a jury and she didn't want the community opinion polluted by negative media coverage, a particular risk in a case like this involving a professional athlete accused of murder.

Madison kept her statement short and she didn't stray from her prepared comments when answering questions. She knew how a few misspoken words could cause more damage than saying nothing at all. When she was finished, Madison was confident that she had presented a credible alternative to the state's theory that Luther had killed Evan Chase. She made vague suggestions that there was a conspiracy to frame Luther Zorn for a murder orchestrated and committed by someone else.

By the time the press left, copies of the discovery materials had arrived at the office. Madison and Chris made another failed attempt to contact Vivian Chase, then set to work poring through the documents, making notes they would compare later. At one-thirty they finished and decided to review their notes over lunch. There was a family-style Italian place next door with cheaply upholstered red chairs and paper placemats decorated with colorful maps of Italy. Mel Rosen told them they couldn't miss with the vegetable pizza. Madison ordered a pitcher of Diet Coke to go with it. The lunch crowd was starting to thin out, and they had no trouble hearing each other across the table of their booth by the window.

"All right," Madison said, as both she and Chris spread notepads onto the table, "the big questions first. Number one, the ranger."

"What's his name? Putman?" Chris said. "I'll get in touch with him and find out if it was coincidence that he was there to give Luther a ticket or if someone tipped him off."

"Chris," Madison said, "if there was a conspiracy to frame Luther, couldn't this ranger be part of it?"

Chris nodded slowly, "I suppose anything's possible, but I doubt it. There would be no real need to get him involved. A tip-off would be enough. You know, a complaint called in to get the ranger on the scene. The difficult thing would be making sure the ranger was there when Luther's car was. That would be tough to arrange, but we'll know more after I talk with him."

The pitcher of soda arrived along with two tall red plastic cups filled with crushed ice and straws with just a small section of the wrapper still on them. Their waitress told them the pizza would be up in ten minutes. Chris took the cups and poured each of them a drink.

"Okay, second," Madison said, "Vivian Chase."

"We need to find out what she's got to say," Chris said. "I'll try to call her again tomorrow and if I can't get her, I'll try going out to her house. I have a feeling, though, that a deposition is the only way we're going to be able to get anything from her."

"What about Lieutenant Kratch's reference to Luther about Vivian's past?" Madison said. "Do you think there might be something there?"

"I'll find out," Chris said.

"I want you to find out what you can about Martin Wilburn, too," Madison said. "I know Luther is the fall guy, and Luther thinks it's Vivian, but what about Wilburn? From what I've read and heard, he's going to make a lot of money if this team moves to Memphis. I want you to see if Evan Chase was against that move for any reason. If he was, then Wilburn would have as good a reason as anyone for wanting him dead. Plus, I just don't like Wilburn. It was strange the way he handled our meeting. Find out what he's all about, Chris. Who knows? Maybe he's in on the whole thing with Vivian Chase."

"All right," Chris said after jotting down a note, "here's something. This Lieutenant Kratch. I think it's a little odd that he's handling this case. You don't normally see a lieutenant as the primary investigator in a murder. It happens, but it's strange. The other thing about the investigation is, why wasn't that scuba gear dusted?"

"Dusted?" Madison said.

"Yeah, if that scuba gear was found in Charlene King's house, or Luther's house, that's good for the police," Chris explained, "but it would be even better if Luther's prints were all over the stuff. I didn't see anything anywhere in those reports that suggests the stuff was even sent to the lab."

Madison frowned, "The police? You don't think . . ."

"I think everything," Chris told her, "and I think nothing."

Chris Pelo's blood was churning. He felt like a world-class skier back on the slopes for the first time in years. At his core he was an investigator, and it was all coming back to him without any effort. It was a state of mind that seemed completely natural.

"It could be that Kratch forgot to order the lab work because he's a little rusty," Chris explained, "being a lieutenant and out of the street game. It could be he has an unusual interest in this case. He took this case for himself. There are probably twenty guys he could have assigned it to.

Maybe he skipped over dusting the gear because he already knew nothing was there."

"Because?" Madison asked.

"Because he put it there," Chris suggested.

Madison was skeptical. "Do you really think?"

"It happens. Anything can. I've seen it," Chris said somberly.

"How do you think that gear could have gotten into Charlene King's locked garage?" Madison wondered.

"We need to ask Charlene King," Chris responded.

"Wherever she is," Madison said pensively. "That's a little strange, too, don't you think?"

"Again, maybe," Chris said.

"There's another big question," Madison said. "If Luther didn't kill Evan Chase, who did?"

"I thought that was for the police to worry about," Chris said. "We just need to show that it wasn't Luther."

"Sometimes the best way to show your client's innocence is by proving someone else's guilt," Madison explained. "Especially when everyone is so happy to pin it on the defendant."

"So who are you thinking?" Chris said. "I can't see Vivian Chase having the strength to pull off something like that, Wilburn either. Whoever did it had to know how to dive, and they had to be pretty damn strong, too. Chase was a strong swimmer, and he was fighting for his life. Not just anyone could have held him underwater like that."

"I don't know," Madison replied. "It's just something we need to think about as we're asking all our other questions. Maybe it was a professional. This was obviously premeditated."

The pizza came. Chris had a slice halfway to his mouth before he stopped and said, "Madison?"

"Yeah?"

"What if Wilburn, or Vivian Chase, or both of them, somehow convinced Luther to kill Evan Chase? What if he did, and now one or both of them is trying to hang him out to dry?"

Chris paused, then said, "What would you say if I said my instincts tell me that Luther would be the most logical third party for either of those two people to choose? He's certainly strong enough to have pulled Chase underwater . . ."

Madison stared at Chris for a minute, trying to gauge from his eyes just how much of what he was saying he really believed to be true.

"I'd tell you to stop thinking so much like a cop," she said finally.

"What do you think?" he said, then taking a bite and chewing while he waited for her response.

"As Luther's lawyer, I think Vivian Chase or Martin Wilburn likely set Luther up. They got him to the scene of the crime, tipped off the rangers that his car was there, and got someone else to kill Chase," Madison said. "If Luther didn't do it, and of course that's what we have to believe, I think there's a good chance either Vivian or Wilburn knows who did. Each of them has a motive, and each of them may have had the ability to get Luther to go to the beach that morning."

"How could Wilburn have gotten him there?" Chris said.

Madison hesitated, then admitted, "I don't know yet."

Madison picked up a slice of pizza and bit into it. Chris began chewing again as well, staring out into the parking lot where the heat shimmered like jet fumes on a runway. His faraway look gave Madison the impression that he was in some kind of a trance.

After a while she said, "What are you thinking?"

Chris's eyes came back inside the restaurant and focused on Madison. "You don't want to know," he told her. "I'm still thinking like a cop."

Chapter 32

Lieutenant Kratch agreed to meet with Madison in his office on Thursday afternoon. He had never refused an interview with a defense attorney. Kratch liked to know the enemy. When Madison walked through the door, Kratch was busy hammering away on his computer. A Camel cigarette hung from the corner of his mouth as he worked, and gray flecks of ash speckled his keyboard like dirty little snowflakes. Even Kratch couldn't keep himself from squinting through the smoke to get a better look at the attractive attorney. The springs in his chair screeched in complaint as he rose to shake her hand.

"Sit down," Kratch said pleasantly. His coat was off and the unbuttoned long sleeves of his rumpled beige dress shirt wheeled like signal flags as he turned with a gallant sweep of his arm, directing Madison to a beat-up chair alongside his desk.

Madison protested against the foul air with a gentle little cough, then sat. "Thank you for seeing me, Lieutenant."

"Please, call me Kratch," Kratch said as he politely smashed what was left of his cigarette butt into a glass ashtray overflowing with a mountain of ash. He looked up with a smile, showing Madison his big yellowing teeth, reminding her of a pumpkin-headed scarecrow. His left eye wandered her way and then back into space. She locked her own eyes on to the other side of his face.

"I have some information that I think you may find disturbing," she told him, getting straight to the point.

Kratch leaned forward, his tall pale brow furrowed with mock concern.

"As you know, on the day Evan Chase was murdered," Madison said, "Luther Zorn's car was nearby, in the north parking lot of MacCarther National Park near Lost Tree. Mark Berryhill, the state attorney, is convinced that Luther was also there. I'm not conceding that he was, but if he was, I think he was there because he was set up.

"What bothers me," Madison continued, "and I'm sure it will bother you, too, is that one of your detectives apparently called the ranger's station the day before to suggest that someone check the north parking lot in the early hours of the following morning. My investigator spoke with the ranger who responded to that call. He said the man who contacted him was a detective from this office, a Detective Gill, and that same detective called him the day after the murder to see if 'by coincidence' he'd seen anything unusual. Of course the ranger told him about the parking ticket. But it was Gill, twice."

Madison watched Kratch's face, carefully ignoring his bad eye. It was the rest of his expression that would tell her what she wanted to know. She was used to reading faces in depositions, during jury selections, and at trials. Kratch, however, puzzled her. She thought she saw uncertainty, but it might have been anger. Either way, the lieutenant was doing his best to keep his emotions in check.

"There's more," Madison continued. "Gill and his partner were the same people who found the scuba gear. I don't know if you're aware, but he never bothered to have that gear dusted for fingerprints. I checked with Mark Berryhill, and he said there was no lab report."

"Are you suggesting something untoward, Ms. McCall?" Kratch said slowly, raising an eyebrow as he spoke.

It was Madison's turn to lean forward. She set her jaw, narrowed her eyes, and spoke in a low firm voice. "I'm suggesting that you have a detective working for you who knew Evan Chase was going to be killed as well as the fact that Luther Zorn's car would be in that parking lot. I'm suggesting that he called the ranger's station to make sure that someone else would be there to confirm that Luther's car was on the scene, someone independent of the Sheriff's Department, who could issue a ticket or confirm the presence of a car like Luther's."

Madison had caught Kratch off guard, but he knew exactly how to deal with the kind of full-frontal assault she had just launched. His mouth turned into a sneer and his words oozed with contempt. "Let me tell you something, lady. No one, and I mean no one, comes into this office and accuses someone in my department of being involved in a conspiracy like this with the shitty little theory you're trotting out!"

Kratch pointed one of his long bony fingers at Madison's nose.

"You may be some kind of big-deal bitch lawyer in Texas, lady, but this ain't Texas. This is my territory you're in, and you better just take your theory and stick it where the sun don't shine. We don't have dirty cops in Palm Beach County."

Madison stood to go, but continued to hold the lieutenant's stare. When she felt certain that she'd communicated her determination she turned for the door. "I can see you've taken this personally, Lieutenant," she said. "I hope that doesn't mean that you're trying to do more than just protect one of your own. I dropped in on your captain just a few moments ago. He told me that you normally don't attend to individual cases, but that apparently when the call went out to dispatch a homicide detective in this case, you answered the call. Your captain said that it wasn't unheard of for you to do something like that. I understand it's not all that uncommon if you're close to a crime scene. But I wonder, why were you so close by when the call came in?

"Know this, Lieutenant," Madison concluded. "I'm not going away. And I *am* going to find out what the hell's going on."

If phone, fax, and modem lines could burn, Chris Pelo would have started a conflagration in Mel Rosen's offices. He spent all Thursday in high gear, making calls and darting through the Internet, accessing places that most people didn't even know existed. At seven-thirty that evening, he remembered that he was supposed to meet Madison at the hotel restaurant for dinner. He crammed a stack of printouts and fax sheets into his briefcase and headed for the door. Only Mel Rosen himself remained in the office. Chris could hear the low tones of a phone conversation through the closed door as he passed by the old lawyer's office on his way out.

Twenty minutes later Chris left his Taurus in the broad circular drive of the Royal Palm Beach Hotel. Liveried valets strode confidently in and out of the main entrance. Above was a brilliant gold dome bordered by an ornate pattern of red, blue, and green terra-cotta. One of the valets wished Chris a good evening and took his car. It was as fancy as anyplace Chris Pelo had ever seen, let alone stayed in. Madison, however, seemed quite at ease, even sitting alone in the elegant four-star restaurant waiting for him, sipping a glass of Chardonnay. Chris felt upstaged by the well-dressed diners, and by the regal bearing of the maître d' and the waiter. He loosened the tie around his neck and ordered a beer anyway.

"Sorry I'm late," he said to Madison as the waiter sauntered off for his drink.

"No problem," she said. "It gave me a chance to think. Let's order, I'm starved. Then we can talk about what we've got."

Chris nodded in agreement. There wasn't a single entrée on the menu that appealed to him, so he ordered chicken something.

Madison told him first about what she'd learned from Putman, the ranger, and then went on to describe her meetings with both Kratch and his captain.

"Sounds like Kratch has the latitude to do pretty much whatever he wants, a golden boy," Chris said. "When that happens with a cop, watch out. He can do no wrong. He's right, Madison, we're on shaky ground. We can't go accusing a police officer of being involved in a murder conspiracy for making a call like that to the ranger's station and then following up the next day with an inquiry. It's a reach, but it's plausible and the benefit of the doubt belongs to the police."

This disturbed Madison. "Chris, you were the one who said anything was possible . . ."

"I know, I know. But I said that between me and you—"

The waiter brought Chris his beer and poured an inch of it into a tall frosted glass before setting the bottle down on the thick white linen tablecloth. When he was gone, Chris took the bottle off the table and drew a long swig from it.

"I should have explained to you the way a police force works from within," he said, setting down his drink. "If Gill is a dirty cop who's involved in a murder, he's certainly not going to hesitate to fabricate some evidence to support his story. And, if Kratch is some way involved . . . he's a lieutenant. That's not a guy you want to mess around with, as he put it, when you're on his territory. A bad lieutenant is the kind of guy with the power to have you pulled over and arrested for the kilo of cocaine he had planted in your car. I'm sorry. I should have been the one to talk to Kratch."

Suddenly the subordinate was the master. Where Luther's world was football and hers was the courtroom, this world obviously belonged to Chris. As ugly and as frightening as it sounded, what he was saying made perfect sense. Crooked police were a hundred times more dangerous than the most ruthless criminals. They had the law on their side.

"So what now?" she said.

"There's nothing we can do about Gill and there's nothing we can do about Kratch," Chris told her. "Let's just move on. I've got some things you won't believe. By the way, Mark Berryhill called. He wants you to call him first thing in the morning."

Chris began recounting his day by informing Madison that Charlene King was still missing. He had no line on her whatsoever.

"The kid is in a foster home right now," he told her. "In fact, when I spoke to Luther this afternoon, he said he wanted us to start seeing if we can get temporary custody for him. I don't think the chances are very good, considering the fact that he's been indicted for murder. I told him that, but he insisted I try, so there's a woman in Mel's office who I've got working on it."

"I tell you what I can't come close to doing," Chris said in obvious frustration, "is get ahold of Vivian Chase.

"She's completely insulated," he explained. "She won't answer her phone, and when I went by to see her, they stopped me at the gate and said she wasn't accepting any visitors. I asked Berryhill about her, and he hasn't even spoken to her. He did say, though, that her attorney had informed him that she was going to be leaving the country but would make herself available upon subpoena. We may want to think about deposing her soon."

Chris then launched into the tawdry details of Vivian's past, the strip club, her first marriage, her divorce, and her marriage to Chase. "It doesn't make her a killer, but she's a climber, and a good one."

"It's certainly not inconceivable for someone like that to be involved in something like this," Madison commented.

"Yes, but wait until you hear about Wilburn," Chris said, stopping abruptly when the waiter suddenly appeared with their food. Neither Chris nor Madison paid any attention to what was being set in front of them. Their silence let the waiter know he was unwanted, and he quickly departed with a disapproving frown.

"Martin Wilburn," Chris began, "has a spotless past."

Madison's disappointment was evident. She was wrong again. She started in on her food while Chris spoke.

"In fact, he's too spotless," he continued. "I checked his real estate holdings and found that he owns an expensive condo on the Intracoastal in Palm Beach. The place has a mortgage with Gold Trust for about seven hundred thousand and change—"

"How did you get that?" Madison interrupted.

"Easy," Chris said. "Even a novice can get mortgage information on anyone in the country through Nexis online. The thing a lot of people can't get is someone's Social Security number, but I got into Gold Trust's records and got Wilburn's. Once you've got a Social Security number, and you know your way around the IRS information system and the FBI system, there isn't much you can't find out."

"That's kind of scary," Madison said in an offhand way as she politely dabbed her mouth with the napkin she took from her lap.

"It is," Chris told her. "Anyway, Wilburn was born and raised in Atlanta. He grew up in a rough section of town, but got a scholarship to a private school called Peers on the north side of the city. Wilburn went from Peers to Marist, and from Marist to Morehouse College. His freight was paid along the way because of his intelligence. After he graduated from Morehouse he went to Memphis State to get his MBA. For his first three years after graduating, he filed no income tax returns. I've got to believe he was involved in some kind of criminal activities. Drugs, prostitution, white-collar crime, who knows? Those are the only things I can think of that would explain no tax returns. That or being homeless."

"Why do you think he was a criminal?" Madison inquired. "You said he had a clean record."

"He does," Chris said, "but it wasn't always clean."

Madison was intrigued.

"You see," he explained, "there's a guy I knew from CID who has a brother that's a lieutenant with Memphis PD. The brother helped me get into their system. I figured, you know, I'd see what was up. It didn't make sense for a guy to go through all that schooling, stay in Memphis, but file no tax return like he wasn't making a red cent. Only someone with something to hide would do that.

"Well, when I punched up Wilburn's name in the Memphis PD system, I got an empty file."

"But why have a file at all?" Madison said, arching her eyebrow.

"Exactly, and my guy's brother confirmed that something was wrong. The thing is, sometimes when a bust is made, the DA will work a deal if the bad guy turns into a rat. The police will sometimes wipe his record clean. He gets off, but you get a bigger fish. It happens all the time."

"It never happened with one of my clients," Madison said. "I've never heard of that."

"It's not the kind of thing that happens once a lawyer is involved," Chris explained. "It's the kind of thing you do with a guy before the lawyers show up. If there's a deal to be cut, it's cut right away. This isn't the kind of thing anybody wants to go public with or have any kind of record of. It's generally a good policy because you can usually bring down a bigger criminal. If it's drugs, for example, you'll give away the street dealer if he can help you nail his distributor. But no one wants to make a big deal out of it because sometimes the small guy you let go ends up whacking some high school students as they get off the bus three weeks after you let him walk. It's bad politics, so if you do it, you do it quietly."

"So do you have any idea what Wilburn was up to?" Madison said.

"I have no idea," Chris told her, "but it gets better.

"After electronically dropping off the face of the earth for three years, Martin Wilburn reappeared as an employee of Ibex Corporation. Ibex started filing 1099s with the IRS for Wilburn where he worked steadily until about seven years ago, just a few months before he bought a ten percent interest in the Marauders, for fifteen million dollars in cash."

"So how could a guy who worked for three years, doing who knows what, then for several more for this Ibex Corporation, buy part of a football team?" Madison asked.

"Exactly," Chris replied. "I checked the newspaper archives and found that Wilburn was billed as a young black entrepreneur from Memphis who had recently moved his corporate business to West Palm Beach. He was a perfect candidate. He had the cash, he was black, which was good PR for the NFL, since players are always complaining that there's no black ownership in the league—and he was suddenly a West Palm resident. He had it all, and from what I could gather from the newspapers at the time, Chase needed the money because his real estate empire was floundering. Wilburn paid top dollar. Apparently no one ever thought to ask what his corporation did, or how he ended up owning it. The paper called Wilburn's company the Bonell Corporation, but as far as I can tell it was just a dummy company. Whatever assets it had were bought out by another corporation called Carnco. It's a privately held corporation whose only listed director is a lawyer from a big firm in Memphis. I have no idea who owns the stock. Bonell doesn't even exist anymore. There's got to be someone behind Martin Wilburn who's got all the money, but for some reason wants to keep a low profile."

"Can we find out who?"

Chris thought. "No. Whatever deal transpired between Chase and Wilburn and this Bonell Corporation is private business. It's not like the Marauders is a public company. And now, ten percent of the team is owned by whoever controls this Carnco. There are probably only a handful of people who know the truth."

"Chris," Madison interrupted, "keep going, but eat if you want to."

Chris looked around uncomfortably at their opulent surroundings.

Madison understood. She waved her hand and said casually, "Cody talks while he eats all the time. I could care less. Go ahead and eat while you tell me the rest."

Chris gave her a thankful smile and began scraping the gunk off his chicken. "This is the good part—of the story . . . and the chicken. The last line I really had on Wilburn was this Ibex Corporation. So, I called directory information in Tennessee and got the number for Ibex. I called and asked the receptionist who the president was, figuring he might tell me something about Wilburn. She told me the president was a guy named Kevin Pallidan. I called back a few minutes later using a different voice and asked for Pallidan like he's expecting my call. When I got his secretary I told her my name and that I was an attorney calling from Florida. Then she asks me if I'm with Sheriff Emmit Stone.

"I didn't know if it had anything to do with anything, but I figured what the hell," Chris said, pausing to wash down a mouthful of food with his beer. "You're going to like this. I told her, yes, I was with Sheriff Stone. I tell her I'm surprised he called himself. Then I ask her when he called. She tells me it was several days ago and I act puzzled before I ask her if he said where he called from. She says, 'Canal Point, I assume. Isn't that where you are?' I told her I was and she put me through to Pallidan. He wouldn't tell me anything. Said he was part of a new management team brought on board after Ibex was bought out three years ago. Said he never heard of Wilburn. I don't know if he was telling the truth or not. He seemed like a pretty cool customer.

"So, after that I called this Sheriff Emmit Stone in Canal Point. It's a little hiccup of a place and the guy acts real weird when I get him on the phone. He won't really tell me anything about why he's poking around Ibex. He acted spooked, I thought. Then, just before he hung up, almost as if it was an impulse, he told me that he might be able to help me more if I dropped by his office."

"Where's Canal Point?" Madison said.

"Not too far," Chris told her, "a couple of hours to the west on Lake Okeechobee."

"When do we go?"

"Tomorrow."

Chapter 33

Madison got back to her room a little past ten. She called home. Jo-Jo was in bed, but she spoke to Cody, who was in the middle of preparing his team for the county championship.

"I miss you, Madison," he told her in a tone that suggested a separation of months rather than days. "I know I helped get you into this whole thing, and I want you to do well, but I wish you were here."

"Cody," she said softly. "I miss you, too."

Madison went to bed feeling good about her marriage. She didn't feel good about much else. Chris's words about corrupt police made it hard for her to sleep. Every time she was about to drop off, the ghoulish image of Kratch invaded her consciousness and kept her mind turning. She finally comforted herself with the fact that she would speak with Berryhill tomorrow before she left for Canal Point. Unlike

Kratch and his captain, Berryhill was a lawyer, and even though he represented the state, he might be inclined to listen.

In the morning, Madison met Chris in the lobby. It was a busy place filled with people coming and going, beginning another sunny day in Palm Beach. Chris was easy to spot. His ill-fitting gray suit and stained red tie made him stand out from the well-dressed crowd. It didn't matter to Madison. She respected his intelligence and she greeted him warmly. Together they set out for the day.

The state attorney was sitting behind his desk, on the phone, his shirtsleeves already rolled halfway up to his elbows. It wasn't even nine o'clock. He hung up quickly and greeted them formally, asking if they wanted coffee as he inexplicably turned on the television set that rested on his bookshelf.

"I knew this report was coming on," he said somberly, "and since we were meeting today anyway, I thought it would be a good idea to get the whole thing out in the open."

The channel was set to the Palm Beach Fox affiliate where the leadoff story concerned an investigator who had uncovered some disturbing news about Luther Zorn's past.

"Luther Zorn's mental problems began in grade school," the blond correspondent stated as a school photo of Luther filled the screen. "Although he developed into a model student athlete, those who knew him best sensed a dangerous undercurrent of instability. In high school he began undergoing psychotherapy and continued to receive treatment through college. An official within the Northwestern University athletic department confirmed that although the secret of Luther's therapy was kept from the public, the entire staff and even many of the players knew about it. Marauders officials refused to comment on whether or not they had any knowledge of Zorn's condition. But, at least a few of Luther Zorn's teammates describe him as a loner, and insurance records indicate that Zorn has continued to seek mental health treatment under the supervision of Palm Beach psychiatrist Dr. David Weiss since joining the team nine years ago. I'm Arlene Taylor reporting. Kathy . . ."

"Thank you Arlene," the attractive but matronly anchorwoman said. "Joining us now in our studio is Calvin Ramsey, former Miami state prosecutor and now a criminal defense attorney. Mr. Ramsey, thank you for joining us."

"My pleasure." Ramsey was a balding, beefy man with a large nose and a neck that looked two sizes too big for his shirt.

"Mr. Ramsey, what does the latest information regarding Luther Zorn's ongoing psychotherapy mean to this case?"

"Well, depending on the extent of Luther Zorn's condition, it basically presents the defense with the option of a strong insanity defense against the charge of murder."

"Is this a course you yourself would pursue?"

"That's hard to say," Ramsey answered. "I don't know the specific details of the case. But if there were a substantial amount of evidence against the client, insanity is certainly an option that would preclude capital punishment. The defendant, however, in that kind of scenario, would not likely go free. He'd probably spend most of the rest of his life in a mental institution because of the gravity of the crime."

"So you're saying if Luther Zorn really did kill Evan Chase, this may be his best course of action?"

"Yes, it may be, again, depending on the weight of the evidence against him."

"Thank you, Mr. Ramsey." The anchorwoman turned from her guest back to the camera. "We'll keep you apprised of developments in this case as they arise. In Miami today, Cuban nationals vowed—"

Berryhill turned off the set and leaned back against the bookshelf, jamming his hands deep into his pants pockets.

"My investigator got to the school a little after this Arlene Taylor did," he said carefully. "Everything she reported is apparently true. I didn't know if you were aware of Luther's condition, whatever it may be. We haven't been able to determine what it is, but of course it's my ethical duty to make you aware of everything we find."

Berryhill stopped talking and watched. He was anxious to see how much of this Madison already knew and how much of it she was preparing to use. He was thinking of having to battle an insanity defense.

"This is the first I've heard of any of this," Madison admitted. "But I don't want us to get distracted. Chris and I still think there is some kind of conspiracy afoot here, Mark, and I hate to tell you that it may involve some people in your police department."

Madison outlined her findings regarding the parking ticket and their preliminary contact with the park rangers. She told Berryhill about the scuba gear not being dusted and concluded by recounting her meeting with Kratch.

The prosecutor's face seemed to grow heavier with each new bit of information. When Madison was finished, he seemed angry. "Ms. McCall, I don't know how this works where you're from, but I've got to agree with Lieutenant Kratch. This is the kind of thing that we get thrown at us all the time. A week doesn't go by when I don't get some kind of bad-cop accusation from a lawyer whose client was taken down in a drug bust. Unless you've got some real hard evidence, that's the wrong way to go about it in this part of the country."

"I can't give you the hard evidence that you're talking about right now," Madison said patiently, "but when I do, I hope you'll have the courage to do what's right."

"You worry about doing your job, Ms. McCall," Berryhill said curtly, "I'll worry about doing mine."

"I hope you will," Madison returned as both she and Chris got up to leave. "Thanks for your time."

On their drive to Canal Point, Madison and Chris went over the case again and again. They didn't notice the dark blue Crown Vic that had followed them out of the county offices.

"I just don't think you can rule out the fact that it may very well be Luther who killed Evan Chase," Chris finally said. He was obviously frustrated with Madison's adamant refusal to consider that as an option.

"Chris," she huffed, "that helps us in no way. Our job is not to figure out how Luther did it. Our job is to believe he's innocent and figure out how to prove that. I keep saying it—"

"I know what our job is," Chris protested, "but I'm talking about the truth. Job or no job, I want to know the truth."

Madison said nothing. She applied the brake as they entered the town. Chris was being pig-headed. There was nothing she could say if he was going to pursue that line of thinking. She squinted through her sunglasses as she looked up at the traffic light through the glare of the midday sun. When it changed she drove past a couple of two-story buildings on the main street before she found the sheriff's office and pulled into a metered parking space. Except for the make and model of the cars, Madison suspected the street hadn't changed in fifty years. The concrete sidewalks were brushed clean. The red and white pole in front of the barber shop turned without end. The diner had a pink neon sign in the window that said FOOD.

"He might be crazy," Chris said suddenly after Madison had turned off the engine. "I mean, he doesn't seem crazy. He seems perfectly normal. But . . ."

"Chris," Madison said, removing her sunglasses and turning toward him, "you can't just assume because someone has been seeing a psychotherapist that they're crazy. It's not fair . . . it's not ethical. We're still his defense attorneys."

"That's what I was getting to," Chris said. "I think we should think about putting together an insanity defense instead of just chasing theories. Why do you think Berryhill flipped on the TV? He wanted to see what your reaction was going to be so he could prepare for it. He expects you to go with an insanity plea. He's afraid of it. It makes the most sense for us."

"Unless we can find something more," Madison reminded him.

"Find something more," Chris said, repeating her words quietly, more to himself than to her.

"If Luther killed Chase, then you're right," Madison said, "insanity is the way to go. But we don't know the extent of his treatment. We don't even know what he's been treated for. It could be nothing more than depression. It could be some harmless phobia."

"He could also be schizophrenic," Chris pointed out. "He could have some sociopathic disorder, where he goes nuts, butchers everyone in sight, and then the next day he's normal again. That happens. I've seen it."

"And have a successful career as a professional football player?" Madison said.

"Or be a mathematics professor, or a doctor, or a lawyer, or a plumber," Chris told her. "It happens."

"Let's just follow through on what we've got," Madison said. "I still wouldn't put it past Wilburn or Vivian Chase to have some involvement, and if they do, and even if Luther is . . . unbalanced, then their involvement will only help to mitigate his guilt. Maybe they used his mental condition against him in some way. I don't know. Let's just see what business Wilburn's old corporation has with the sheriff. That's no coincidence."

They got out of the car and went into the sheriff's office. A woman in her forties with a beehive and cat glasses picked up an old brown phone that served as an intercom to Emmit's office. He had the door closed, but only a moment after she announced them, the sheriff appeared, filling the doorway like a child in a doll house, and ducking his head to come out and greet them. As they introduced themselves, Emmit Stone couldn't help himself from stealing quick glances at the street, as if he expected someone else to arrive at any minute.

"Come into my office," he told them. "Mira, hold all my calls."

Mira rolled her eyes. "All right, Sheriff."

Emmit's office was cramped, and after some hefty knocking of their knees and shins, Madison and Chris sat facing him across an old gray metal desk. The drab walls were bare except for Emmit's framed diploma and a picture of him struggling to hold up a monster gar fish on the end of a hooked gaff.

Before they could say anything, Emmit fished into the front pocket of his shirt and laid a big gaudy ring on the table in front of them.

"This is what I've got," he said. "It's a championship ring from three years ago when the Marauders went to the Super Bowl. I found it outside a fishing cabin a couple of miles from here. I also found three human heads stuck up on some pinewood poles."

Madison and Chris looked from the ring to each other. Without a word, each knew what the other was thinking. Madison picked the ring up from the table.

"Can I have this?"

Emmit shrugged. "Might as well, it won't do me any good."

Emmit then related for them the entire story, from Caleb's late-night phone call, to Slaughter's threat.

"I think whoever killed these people is still out there," Emmit concluded.

Madison turned to Chris. "Do you think one of those heads was Charlene King?"

"We've got a dangerous man on our hands," Chris said.

Madison shook her head in disbelief and then stared back at the ring. "Could anyone get one of these besides a player?"

"I checked into that," Emmit said, "kind of on the sly. The only people who have them are team members. Unless one of them sold it, which I doubt."

Madison sat staring.

"What are you thinking?" Chris asked.

"It's so damn complicated," she said. "I don't know what to think."

"Madison," Chris said, "it all comes back to Luther."

"I know," she said. "But there's more. Ibex owns that cabin. Martin Wilburn is connected to Ibex. Vivian Chase rolled over on Luther when she talked to the police. This Detective Gill arranged for Luther's car to be spotted, and then found the scuba gear in Charlene King's house. Would Luther kill Charlene King? It doesn't even make sense."

"Which Luther?" Chris pointed out. "The Luther we know wouldn't. Maybe there's another side to him."

"Maybe," Madison muttered. The three of them sat in silence. "But three heads?" Madison blurted incredulously.

Emmit shrugged. "No one has been able to find out. We put out missing persons descriptions over the telex, but like I think I told you, the teeth were removed. There's almost no way to know who they are."

"You said the woman's head wasn't yet decomposed," Chris said. "We can get someone to tell us from a photo if it was Charlene King. If it was, we'll know there's a link there. Can you get us a picture?"

"I can't get anything," Emmit said with a frown. "Slaughter has all the files. It's his investigation. There's no way he'll give it to me."

Madison shook her head and thought out loud. "We may be working against our own client, but we have to find out more. I still think it's Martin Wilburn. We need to solidify his connection with Ibex, this cabin, and those three dead . . . bodies or heads or whatever we're calling them."

"Maybe Wilburn controls Gill," Chris said to Madison as if Emmit wasn't even there. "And Luther."

"And Vivian?" Madison said.

"Maybe Kratch, too," Chris mulled.

"My God," Madison said. "What a mess."

"There's one guy who's not in on this," Chris said.

"Berryhill?" Madison said.

Chris nodded.

"You're right," Madison said. "And he can get those photos from Slaughter. The sheriff doesn't even have to be involved . . . Maybe I can cut a deal with Berryhill and get him to stipulate insanity."

"Whatever you do," Emmit interjected, "when you all see those photos, you won't wonder that whoever did it is flat crazy as hell."

Chapter 34

Even though Mark Berryhill had to stand up for the integrity of his policemen, it didn't mean he wasn't going to find out exactly what the hell was going on. Kratch was sitting in Berryhill's office with the door shut, explaining his side of it, when the prosecutor's intercom buzzed. He picked up the phone and asked his secretary what it was. He'd instructed her that he was not to be disturbed.

"It's Ms. McCall," she told him apologetically. "She says it's urgent."

"I'll take it," Berryhill told her.

"Excuse me," he said to Kratch.

"Yes?" he said into the phone.

"Mark, this is Madison McCall. I would have come to see you in person, but I'm in Canal Point and I'm on my way to the airport to catch a flight home for the weekend. I want you to know what I've found . . ."

"All right."

"Mark, first I want your word that if I tell you everything I'm about to tell you, you'll give me every benefit of the doubt in stipulating insanity . . ."

Berryhill raised his eyebrows at Kratch as if he was in on the deal, even though he wasn't. To no avail Kratch strained his ears to hear. The air vent above him was humming steadily, filtering out the conversation on Madison's end of the line. The exertion seemed to force his bad eye outward like that of a small-mouth bass.

"I've got to know more," Berryhill said. "I can't make any promises."

"Well, you think about it," she said, being deliberately vague. "But I may have a link to some other murders, and I'm pretty sure Martin Wilburn is involved."

"That's interesting," Berryhill said. "But I've got to know more. You've got to show me something before I start making promises and deals. I can't just say, yes, I'll stipulate insanity . . . The only thing I can tell you is that I'll be fair. I always am."

Madison was on a pay phone at the corner across from the Canal Point Diner. Chris stood outside the booth looking anxiously at her. She took a deep breath.

"I'll wait until I see you then," she said, deciding to feel him out face-to-face. "I'm on my way to catch the last flight to Austin, but I'll be back on Monday night. Can we meet on Tuesday?"

"How about ten o'clock?" he said.

"I'll see you then."

Berryhill hung up and considered Kratch. The detective stared back at him impassively.

"The plot thickens with Madison McCall," Berryhill said.

Kratch raised the eyebrow over his good eye.

"What do you know about Martin Wilburn?"

Kratch frowned noncommittally. "Not much. I've dealt with him some during the investigation."

"He was very interested in getting Luther Zorn out on bail," Berryhill mused.

"I presume that was because of the team," Kratch suggested.

"Madison McCall seems to think he's connected to Evan Chase's murder somehow."

"She thinks everyone is guilty except her client. The one who killed him," Kratch responded.

"There's more," Berryhill said. "She seems to think she's found some other murders that are connected . . . How, I don't know."

Kratch twisted his lips to the side in distaste. "I think she's full of shit. We both know that Luther Zorn is guilty. She's blowing smoke. They all do that, don't they?"

"Yes," he said distractedly, "they all do."

"I'll look into the situation with Gill a little more closely," Kratch told the prosecutor. "As I said, I'm sure it's a coincidence, and a fortunate one at that. It helps us nail Zorn."

When Kratch got out of the state attorney's office, he drove to the next intersection and stopped outside a Wendy's restaurant to use the pay phone. He dialed a pager number and then replaced the phone on its receiver. He leaned against the box, lit a Camel, and crossed his legs, waiting for a return call. A skinny black kid with a sky blue paper Wendy's hat came out of the employee's entrance on the side of the building. He had a quarter already pinched between his adolescent fingers. The kid had big droopy eyes and the hat sat at a funny little angle on his oblong skull.

" 'Scuse me, mister," the kid said.

Kratch smiled and exhaled his smoke in the kid's face. "Fuck off."

The kid licked his lips, then swallowed, glaring at Kratch, who never took his eyes off him. He just put the cigarette to his mouth and sucked in hard, making the ember on the end of his butt flare like a small orange spot of lava amid the dirty gray ash. Seeing that Kratch wasn't about to move, the kid turned and mumbled his way back inside.

As the heavy brown metal door banged shut, the phone rang.

"Gill?" Kratch said, snatching the phone to his ear.

"Yeah."

"Where the fuck did she go?"

Gill blew air out of his mouth into the receiver before he spoke to let Kratch know how bad it was. "She's in Canal Point."

"Canal Point?"

"Yeah, a couple weeks ago the sheriff there got a call from some nut job about three heads."

"What do you mean, three heads?" Kratch barked.

"Three fucking heads, cut off three fucking bodies, and stuck on top of three fucking posts."

"So?"

"So, the posts were stuck in the ground outside the fucking cabin."

"My cabin?" Kratch said incredulously.

"Yeah," Gill said.

"That motherfucking son of a bitch! I knew that psycho would fuck this thing up somehow! Three heads! Jesus! Who?"

"They don't seem to know," Gill said, "but I bet one of them is Charlene King."

"Damn."

"It might not be that bad," Gill said, relishing the good news. "This all happened a couple of weeks ago already. The state clowns had some major out there doing the investigation. They had all the troops, but apparently they were able to squeeze a confession out of the local dirtbag who found the heads. Then he offed himself in his cell."

"So, we're clear?" Kratch said. "They pinned it on the dirtbag?"

"We were clear," Gill said. "Until this little bitch from Texas started snooping around."

The brown metal door swung open in front of Kratch and out popped a short fat Wendy's manager wearing glasses and a bad toupee. He wiped the mayonnaise from his chubby pink hands onto his apron as he approached the pay phone. The kid peeped his head out from behind the door to watch. Kratch squinted his eyes through the smoke.

"You know what to do," he told Gill. "Call the wolf."

"You want me to have him send our friend after her?" Gill said, not wanting to make a mistake of that magnitude if he was misreading the situation.

"He seems to be offing everyone else," Kratch said, staring down hard at the indignant manager. "What's one more? I gotta go."

Kratch hung up the phone and stared.

"Are you finished now?" the manager said.

"Yeah, but it's broken," Kratch said from one side of his mouth. On the other side, the small remaining roach of his cigarette was clamped tightly between his teeth. Suddenly he gave the phone a violent yank, snapping it right out of the box. He handed the phone to the manager. "You better get it fixed."

The manager looked down at the frayed dangling wires that stuck out of the phone's metal casing like a colorful party favor.

"I'm calling the police," the manager said with conviction.

"I am the police," Kratch said, flipping his badge in the man's face. "Now who you gonna call? Ghostbusters?"

Kratch slid into his car and started the engine. The manager stood frozen in place with a dumb look on his face, the phone resting in his hand. Kratch rolled down the window with one hand while he placed a pair of mirrored shades on his face with the other. He threw the smoldering roach out onto the pavement.

"Scary, isn't it?" Kratch said, then drove off.

Margo had worked the ticket counter for almost two years, but her luck was terrible. Almost everyone else she knew in ticketing had met a celebrity of some kind or another during the past two years. Everyone but her. Several of her friends had seen Burt Reynolds. Almost everyone dealt with at least two or three of the recognizable names from the Marauders. One woman met Ted Kennedy. Not Margo. So, when a tall, good-looking black man with wraparound sunglasses suddenly appeared in front of her at a dead time of night, her heart jumped.

She pulled up an open first-class one-way ticket to Rio and asked his name, waiting and hoping. The man looked around.

"Bobby Allen," he said quietly, shoving twelve new one-hundred-dollar bills across the counter.

Margo's shoulders sagged. She printed the ticket and gave the man his change. He thanked her quietly and left. Margo shook her head. She had been certain he was somebody.

Around the same time that night, a man fitting the same description drove up to a 7-Eleven store not far from the airport to use the pay phone. The night was pleasantly cool, and the last of the dying insects from the late fall swam lazily in the white fog of the halogen lights that surrounded the parking lot. In front of the store a man in a cowboy hat with a gumball-sized wad of tobacco in his cheek sat idly watching the black man dial from the cab of a light blue pickup truck.

The man on the phone scanned the area from behind his dark glasses as he waited for someone to pick up on the other end of the line. He watched the cowboy lean forward and expectorate a long polluted stream of tobacco juice into a Styrofoam coffee cup.

"Yes?" came the voice on the other end of the phone, finally.

"It's me," he said.

There was a short pause. "Is everything all right?"

"Yes," the man said, watching a young woman emerge from the 7-Eleven lighting a cigarette from a fresh pack she had just purchased. "What do you want?"

"Madison McCall is getting too close," the voice said.

The man puckered his lips as if he'd bitten into a pickle after drinking a can of soda.

"She's the enemy, now?" he asked.

"She is."

"Then, that's that. What about the Mexican?"

"If he's there when you do it, take him out. Don't go to any trouble or added risk, though. He's not a threat."

"How many more will there be? It wasn't supposed to be this many," he said in a tone devoid of emotion.

"You agreed to stay in this until it was settled."

"I know that."

"One thing more." The voice was suddenly and uncharacteristically anxious. "I want you to leave her head alone. We don't need any more problems than we already have."

"I have to do this my way," the other man said, surveying the parking lot, his eyes briefly losing and then regaining their focus behind his dark glasses. "Don't tell me how to do it. You sit at a desk and you think you control things. You don't control things. I don't even control things. Things happen the way they do for a reason. No one can help it. No one can stop it."

"Just try to make them happen in a way that's not so messy."

"That's my business," the man with the sunglasses responded with unusual rancor.

"It's all our business now," the voice said, trying to sound authoritative, but unable to completely mask just a hint of timidity in his voice.

"You told me the cabin was secure," the black man pointed out. "You were wrong. You've been wrong about several things . . . and now Madison McCall."

"The cabin was secure," the voice reminded him. "You were camping out in the fucking woods, for God's sake, with three heads on posts!"

"I have to go," the man said. "I'll take care of everything."

He hung up the phone and looked at the cowboy, who quickly averted his eyes. The big black man got into his car and drove off.

A few seconds later another man in a cowboy hat and boots, wearing Levi's jeans, came out of the store with a twelve-pack of Pabst Blue Ribbon under his arm. He climbed into the passenger side of the pickup.

"What took you so long, Clint?" the first cowboy asked.

"No sticker on the fucking box," Clint explained. "The asshole behind the counter had to go out back and get the price. I don't know what the fuck he was doing back there."

His friend spit another gob of tobacco into the battered cup and wiped a string of juice from his mustache onto his sleeve. "You know who I just saw? Luther Zorn."

"The killer linebacker?" Clint said raising his brow. "No shit."

"I think it was him. He was on that pay phone. He was hiding behind some sunglasses, but I'm pretty sure it was him. Left just before you came out."

"Fucking asshole cashier," Clint said. He loved Luther Zorn, even if the guy had killed someone.

Chapter 35

Madison missed Cody's game. The last direct flight to Dallas pulled away just as she and Chris came racing to the gate from the main terminal. They were forced to catch a later flight to Atlanta and make a connection there for Dallas and then finally Austin. She didn't even get back in time to see the Cougars' opponent falling on the ball to kill the last few seconds of the game and secure their win, not that she would have wanted to. As happy as the community of West Lake Hills had been only a week ago, it was now despondent. It was just like in the NFL, the runner-up was regarded as no better than the lowest team in the league. Only the champions were lauded.

Chris drove her to her home. Jo-Jo had fallen asleep on the living room couch waiting for her, and Cody was sitting alone in his big leather chair in the semidarkness of his office. An open bottle of beer rested on his knee and two empty ones sat beside him on a lamp table.

"Hi," he said glumly.

"Hi, honey," Madison said, kissing him on the lips. "I'm sorry I missed it. I missed my connection. I'm sorry you lost."

She sat down on his lap, still wearing her suit from the day.

"That's okay," Cody said, shifting under her weight.

"Hey," she said, touching the end of his nose with her own and looking into his eyes, "you had a great year."

"I know," he said. "It's just how you feel when you lose, no matter what the reason, no matter how good things have gone up until that point, losing is losing, and it stinks.

"Besides," he continued, "I really thought we could win it. I was already psyched up about getting myself that new truck."

Madison closed her eyes, her forehead still resting against Cody's. Cody had been talking all season about how he would spend his ten-thousand-dollar championship bonus. It started as a joke. His team was so bad not even he thought he could get to the championship. Then, as the season went on, he really started to believe he had a chance of winning it all. Madison never said anything. He knew as well as she did that they could buy him five new trucks.

"Cody, I'll buy you a new truck," she said, regretting the words as soon as they passed her lips.

She felt his body stiffen beneath her.

She opened her eyes and said, "I didn't mean it like that."

Cody said nothing. He turned his head away and took a long pull on his beer.

"You just put your money away for you and Jo-Jo," he said, turning his attention back to her. "I'll take care of myself. I can get by with what I've got. I'll get it next year."

"Cody, please," she said tiredly. "I didn't mean to insult you. I just want you to have what you want . . ."

"What I want is to move out of this neighborhood," he snapped. "I don't want to have to go through a gate to get home. I don't want to have to live in a place where the only people not driving cars made in Germany besides me are the guys who cut the lawns and clean the pools. I don't want to have my neighbors ask me why I don't play golf or tennis. Shit! I don't want my kids growing up in this kind of world, Madison."

"Kids?" she heard herself say.

"Yeah, Madison," Cody said, his eyes digging deep into her own. "I want us to have kids. Jo-Jo's like my own. You know I feel that way. But I want kids."

Cody had mentioned wanting a bigger family from time to time, but never like this.

"We'll have to talk about it, Cody," she said.

"We are talking about it."

"I mean, I'll have to think about it."

"Think, Madison. Think about all those things," he told her, gently moving her off of him and rising to his feet.

"Can't we talk?" she asked, looking up at him.

Cody looked out the big glass doors that opened to the backyard where their pool was already covered for the winter and where the tall green shrubs were cut into symmetrical shapes. He could just make out the scene through his own reflection. Beyond the pool and shrubs lay the pond that you had to drive over to reach the seventeenth fairway. The moon shone like a new copper penny and left an electric trail of bronze light that spilled from the tee all the way across the water to the edge of their property.

"I don't see there being all that much more to say," he said, turning his attention back to his wife. Madison now sat with her stockinged feet curled up under her on the chair to draw the warmth from the spot where he'd been sitting.

"What do you want me to do?" she asked. "I make good money."

"Save your money," he told her. "I've said that to you before. I make enough for us to live. Let's get a little house somewhere in a nice neighborhood and let Jo-Jo and hopefully some brothers and sisters grow up like normal kids."

"There are normal kids here," she protested.

Cody looked at her quietly. "You know what I saw yesterday? Yesterday I pulled into the parking lot at school and Lizzy Shuler, the kid from down the street who's in my third-period class, she pulls up next to me in a new BMW 750. A 750, for God's sake!"

"Maybe it was her parents' car," Madison suggested.

"It said 'LIZZYS' on the license plate, Madison. Do you think that's reality? Turn sixteen and get an eighty-thousand-dollar car? The house I grew up in didn't cost half that."

Madison stood up and put her arms around Cody's waist. Looking up into his eyes she said, "I got a car when I was sixteen. I didn't turn out so bad . . ."

Cody couldn't help but smile.

"Let's ride this horse some other time," he said. "Tomorrow, maybe. We both had rough days. How was your day, anyway?"

Madison shut her eyes briefly. "I almost can't even explain it."

"Then don't," he whispered, pulling the comb out of her hair, letting it spill down around her shoulders like the crystal runoff from a sudden rain shower in a lush garden. He bent his neck and moved his lips closer to hers until they barely touched.

"What else have you got in mind?" she murmured.

"I missed you," Cody whispered. "I missed everything about you."

They kissed and Cody stood, scooping her up and carrying her upstairs. Madison relaxed in his arms and let him take her. It felt good to be in the arms of a strong man. Like a leaf clinging desperately to the branch of a tree, there was a certain tranquillity in finally letting go and being swept away by tempestuous forces that were simply stronger than she. Cody let her down gently and Madison sank back onto the bed, enjoying its familiarity. She opened her eyes wide, drawing in everything she could from the yellow swatch of light that lit their room from the hall. She removed her clothes unhurriedly, watching her husband as he did the same. When their bodies finally meshed, she felt the heat from his skin warming her like the summer sun emerging from behind a thundercloud.

Chapter 36

The sun was down in Florida. The Marauders had played to a tie with the St. Louis Rams, and the game was going into overtime. Luther Zorn sat heaving on the bench. He sucked pure oxygen from a translucent green mask. An extra quarter was hard on any player; for Luther Zorn, it felt like death. He played the first four with such intensity that he typically had only enough juice left to drag himself into the locker room and take a shower, no more. Adding to his fatigue, circumstances had made it hard for Luther to get the rest he required to be at his best. Now, a play-off position was at stake. If the Marauders' won, they would be guaranteed a wild card slot. Arizona, their closest opponent in the wild card hunt, had dropped their third straight, losing to New England earlier in the day.

Mercifully for Luther, the Marauders won the overtime coin toss. They would get the ball first. The defense would get to rest. Luther tried to draw deep from within himself. When things were at their most difficult, he had always been at his best. But not now. Too much had happened. There were too many distractions. Word of his ongoing psychotherapy had spread like a rampant virus. No one said anything to him, but even the brothers on the team were acting strange. There was a time when he had hoped that all the bad things would go away, but now they were only getting worse. He hadn't gotten much sleep.

He had a flash of panic. What if everything went wrong? There was no time for these thoughts now; yet, they bumped about in his mind like fat summer flies trapped in a jar. Luther needed some help. He needed to focus on the game.

"Scotty," he said, waving to the equipment man's son. "Come here, man."

Scotty pulled up short. Luther was one of a handful of guys on the team who always took care of him. Many of the players, despite their millions of dollars, were stingy bastards. Not Luther. Luther knew what it was like to bust your hump for crumbs. He slipped Scotty a twenty or a fifty at regular intervals just for packing the equipment in his travel bag after a game. So times like now, when he needed a runner or a favor, Luther knew Scotty would come through. Scotty didn't care about whether a guy was supposed to be crazy or a murderer or anything. If you took care of Scotty, he took care of you.

"What's up, big man?" Scotty drawled.

Luther pulled the sandy-haired young man close, until his chin bumped against the hard plastic shell of Luther's shoulder pads.

"Go into my locker," Luther whispered, "in my black leather shaving kit there's about four prescription bottles. One of them is real little, and the doctor's name on the label is Kauffman. Get one of those little green pills and bring it to me, but don't let anyone see you, Scotty."

Scotty nodded without another word, looking off into the mad sea of the crowded stadium.

"I'll be right back," Scotty said as if Luther had asked him for nothing more than a new chin strap. He turned and disappeared into the tunnel that led back to the locker room.

Luther waited for what seemed like a long time. He was glad to see his own offense moving the ball. He wasn't entirely sold on the act of popping a bean, but he would if he had to, if he couldn't find some deeply buried source of energy to get him through this game. In the fucked-up mess that was his life, here at least, Luther was in control. Here, he was the best, and here no one had to worry about him holding anything back or letting anyone down. Luther had no moral compunction about taking pills. Pills were good. He had played entire games on amphetamines, as had many of his teammates.

Only his own chemistry kept him from using them all the time. Luther could usually tap a source of violence that carried him through a game almost as well as any prescription drug. Also, the amphetamines let you down real hard. Luther would be sick for the next two days if he took one now.

Scotty returned as the Marauders' punt team was taking the field. Luther was still flat. Scotty laid the pill in his gloved paw and Luther put it into his mouth, crushing it into a wickedly bitter powder between his molars before washing it down with a mouthful of lime-flavored Gatorade. Crushed, the drug would absorb into his system faster. The punter got off a monster kick, and the concrete bowl of the stadium resonated with the crowd's deafening approval. The Marauders' punt coverage team had done all it could. The Rams were pinned down so deep into their own territory that the quarterback would actually have to stand in his own end zone. As Luther jogged out onto the field, he felt the drug begin to take effect. His heart jumped in his chest and his fatigue began to melt away. His face grew tight and his eyes more alert.

The first play came right up the middle of the formation. Luther let them know why that was a mistake by meeting the blocking fullback in the space between two linemen and hitting him with an impact that made the man's knees crumple like a paper doll's. With no place to go, the tailback was lucky to get the ball back to the line of scrimmage before Luther's teammates brought him down under a pile of sweat-stained bodies. Luther popped up off the pile and got the signal for the next play as his men huddled up.

The call was Mac Cross Cage, a run blitz. Luther smiled at his ten exhausted teammates as he called it out. It was the right call in this situation. If it worked the right way, it would put Luther in the backfield and, with his quickness, they would have a chance to win the whole thing right there. Even though tackling the opposing ball-carrier in his own backfield would result in nothing more than a two-point safety, it was enough. In sudden death overtime, it was the first team to score that won, no matter how they did it.

Luther broke the huddle and raised his fists to the crowd. He had the power of a conductor imploring his percussion section. The mob thundered on command. The noise made it all the more difficult for the Rams' quarterback to bark out his signals so that his offensive teammates could hear him adjust the play. This would give Luther and the Marauders a split second in their favor, and in the game of football that was enough.

When the ball was snapped, the offensive tackle was slow off the ball, the noise having forced him to rely on peripheral vision to see the snap of the ball instead of the quarterback's count. He lunged at the defensive end to keep him from racing into the backfield. The lunge left a gap too wide for the guard to close without blocking the blitzing outside linebacker, leaving a space Luther Zorn could drive a truck through. It was a chain reaction.

The play was going to Luther's right. He darted past the quarterback, who had handed off the ball. The runner was heading for the sideline. If he passed the outside "cage," the defensive end, he could severely damage the defense. The cage wouldn't hold him completely, but it caused him to hesitate. That was all Luther needed. He leapt through the air and smashed into the running back's head, bringing him down in a tangled pile of limbs in the end zone. The official behind Luther threw his hands up in the air to signal a safety just as the official in front of Luther threw a flag. The game was far from over.

Luther sprang from the grass. He got within inches of the official's face demanding to know what the penalty was for.

"Face mask," the ref barked at him. "Fifteen yards!"

Luther knew what that meant. The penalty would move the Rams fifteen yards ahead, safely out of danger's immediate grasp. Luther screamed at the referee until two of his teammates pulled him away.

Luther resisted wildly and one of the other refs threw his flag straight up in the air before taking another hold on Luther's arm. Fifteen more yards. Luther spun on the man, shaking his grip and picking up the official's flag. He grabbed the ref by his shirtfront and pulled him close, slamming the flag down the front of his striped shirt and screaming at him like a madman. It took three teammates and three officials to drag Luther toward the sideline. He was ejected from the game, and the officials refused even to start the action again until Luther was packed safely away in the locker room.

Luther's hands trembled uncontrollably. He felt as if he might vomit, but he kept his head high as he was led away from the bench and toward the locker room by a teammate, two state police, and one of the assistant coaches. The mob booed as he disappeared. Luther had no idea whether they were jeering him or the official who made the call. He didn't care. After everything that had happened to him already, it didn't even matter.

Above the fray, Martin Wilburn sat with a passive face in Evan Chase's luxury box. It was Vivian's now, but lately she seemed to have no taste for excitement. In fact, Wilburn and Rivet had recently given her permission to leave the country. So now the box was filled with Wilburn's cronies and connections. More important, the three most influential members of the Memphis Citizens Sports Committee were sitting beside him, shifting nervously at the sudden change in fortune of Wilburn's team. That was what it was now, his team. No matter who owned what stock and which corporation, the Marauders were his.

If his players won this game, Martin was almost certain the men from Memphis would lock in. If they locked in, he would be set for life. His contract with Aaron Crawford gave him forty-nine percent ownership of Carnco, the shell corporation that owned ten percent of the team, but only if he delivered the Marauders to Memphis. Wilburn knew that he was a puppet. And that Pallidan, the wolf, was working more strings than just his.

He also knew that Crawford was pulling Pallidan's strings and ultimately everyone else's. Crawford was too smart to involve himself directly in any kind of dirty work. He was twice removed from it. If anything ever went down, Crawford would be insulated not only by lawyers, but by layers and layers of corporate veils. That certainly allowed for the possibility that Wilburn could be hung out to dry. If anything went sour, Crawford would cut him loose without thinking twice. Wilburn had seen him do it before. But Martin was so close he could smell the money.

Ten million dollars for him personally. That was the kind of money Wilburn had dreamed of. He had lived well these past few years, but the money had never been his, and he knew if the show ever ended, so would his part in it. Before long, though, he could do whatever he wanted without having to pay homage to anyone. Ten million was "Fuck You" money. He wanted to continue to run the team, but it would be a simple diversion from his life of leisure. He'd even pay himself a handsome salary to do it.

It was ironic that within the last few seconds he had watched Luther Zorn almost cost him that opportunity. Luther Zorn with his temper, with his uncontrollable emotions, with his own special form of insanity. Luther was the one who had given him the opportunity to win or lose everything. Without thinking, Wilburn found his favorite matching grooves in the molars on the left side of his mouth and set his jaw.

Without Luther, the Marauders' defense deflated. The Rams drove down to the twenty-yard line and set up to kick a field goal. Wilburn couldn't bring himself to look at the men from Memphis. There would be no sympathy from them. They would simply wait another week, to see how the race between Wilburn's team and Arizona played itself out. Fortunes changed suddenly in the NFL.

The ball was snapped and an unexpected wave of Marauders defenders broke through the middle of the Rams' formation. They blocked the kick, and Wilburn took it as a sign when Antone Ellison scooped up the floundering ball from the turf and scrambled seventy yards for a touchdown.

Wilburn jumped up and began hugging the men from Memphis. They were almost as happy as he was. They would be bringing a play-off team home to their city. A team like that would make the medicine of increased taxes, and the cuts in local programs needed to pay for a new football facility, that much more palatable. Everyone loved a winner.

Chapter 37

Madison sent Chris to Memphis on Monday to try to find someone who worked at Ibex during the same years Martin Wilburn had been there. She had to appear in court that afternoon with her fifteen-year-old client for a preliminary hearing that would determine whether or not he would be tried as an adult for shooting his mother's boyfriend. Madison fought hard, but lost. The wheels of justice were turning against young defendants accused of violent crimes. She viewed her client as more a victim than a perpetrator, but the laws were written to punish, and it was a rare thing for the law to distinguish between different sets of circumstances.

When she checked in with her office, Madison learned that Luther Zorn had called three times, insisting that he needed to speak with her immediately. She tried first to reach Chris in Memphis, but got no answer. Madison then returned Luther's call. She sighed with relief when she got his answering machine. She hadn't yet figured out how she was going to handle Luther, but he was her client, and she owed him a meeting. She left a message that she would be staying at the Royal Palm that night and if he wanted he could have breakfast with her there at nine. She didn't feel uncomfortable with meeting him in the hotel's restaurant for breakfast. She would certainly be safe.

As an indulgence, Madison decided to take a late connecting flight to Palm Beach that went through Atlanta. It was a long trip, but it would enable her to steal a short evening with Jo-Jo and Cody.

Julie Tarracola believed there was nothing she couldn't sell and nobody she couldn't sell it to. She was only thirty-five, but was already the top salesperson in North America for Mayburn Chemicals. She was exhausted after traveling all the way from a conference in Tokyo, stopping only to change planes in Los Angeles. But when an opportunity arose, she was never one to balk, because of mere physical discomfort, no matter how tired she might be. Julie was about to close a ten-million-dollar deal with a soap manufacturer in West Palm Beach. You didn't tell someone like that to wait, and you didn't close a ten-million-dollar deal from a Holiday Inn, so she took herself directly to the Royal Palm Beach Hotel. She needed rest and needed to wake up in a place that bespoke luxury and power.

"Do you have any rooms available for this evening?" she pleasantly asked one of the men at the front desk.

"I'm sorry, madam," the man answered in a thick German accent, "we have no vacancies tonight."

Julie quickly summed up the situation. The young German had an air of punctiliousness that suggested a subtle approach.

"Oh," she said, bewildered, "I'm certain I have a reserva-
tion. I didn't even think to ask. It would probably be under
my company's name, Mayburn."

The man at the desk smiled appreciatively and checked a
box of file cards for reservations under the letter "M." Julie
leaned over the desk and stole a glance at the first name that
appeared.

"Hmmm," the man said searching through the *M*s again,
"we don't seem to have anything under Mayburn. Could it
have been made in your own name?"

"It could have," Julie said hopefully. "Madison McCall?
Is it there?"

"Let me look . . . I think, yes! Here it is, Ms. McCall," the
man said, smiling. "How would you like to pay for that?"

"Company credit card," she told him. The card was billed
directly to her company and did not have her name on it.

"That will be fine."

Julie passed him her corporate card and watched as he absently ran it through for approval. When she got her key, she
followed a bellman straight to her room. He hung her garment bag and placed her suitcase on a little stand inside the
closet. Julie tipped him well and hung a DO NOT DISTURB sign
on her door as she watched him leave. She was exhausted,
but her scam to get a room left her heart pumping fast. She
felt as if her blood were laced with amphetamines, and she
needed to slow herself down.

She grabbed her purse and headed downstairs. Just off the
lobby there was a softly lit bar with padded crimson-leather
stools and booths. The woodwork was a rich mahogany, and
the polished silver surfaces of the light fixtures reflected
muted waves of color. It was an elegant but comfortable
place. Julie sat at the end of the bar, hanging her purse from
the back of her high-backed bar stool. She ordered a double
scotch and soda. The long plane flights had left her dehy-

drated and tense. Three drinks later she was relaxed, perhaps too much so. She paid her tab and rose, stumbling against a portly man in a tan suit. His indignant face was so red he looked as if he were about to explode.

" 'Scuse me," she mumbled, aware from her slurred words that she was completely drunk. Embarrassed, she tucked her head and hurried as best she could for her room, forgetting her purse.

At her door, she took the room key from her pocket and fumbled with it a moment before letting herself in. She opened her suitcase and took out a sleeping mask, which she strapped around her forehead. Then Julie found a bottle of pills in her briefcase. She struggled to remove a Halcion from the childproof bottle, then changed her mind and took two, washing them down with half a bottle of Perrier from the minibar. She pulled on her pajamas, got into bed, pushed the mask down over her eyes, and lay back to wait for the pills to knock her out for the night.

Chris Pelo followed Kevin Pallidan home. Pallidan had refused to meet with Chris when he showed up at the Ibex offices just after lunch. Two hard-looking men had escorted him quickly and quietly out of the lobby and into the parking lot, where they waited for him to drive off. Ibex's operations were located in a suburban office building surrounded by dark green Scotch pines. The brick and smoked-glass building didn't hint at the nature of the business conducted there. The cars in the parking lot were unexceptional. When Chris had entered the reception lobby, he was greeted with the suspicious stare of a receptionist who was clearly unused to visitors. His next contact was with the two heavies who came spilling out of a black-lacquered door only a few short minutes after he asked to speak with Kevin Pallidan.

This reaction piqued Chris's interest like nothing else could have. From the appearance of things, it would have surprised Chris if Ibex was anything more than a two-million-dollar-a-year company. The offices weren't shabby, but in an area where space was cheap they were small. That Chris was seen to the door by two thugs was odd, too.

Chris had observed that the parking spot closest to the entrance was marked with a small sign bearing Pallidan's name. A new black full-sized Mercedes sedan filled the space. After his ejection Chris waited in the parking lot of a small strip center on a low rise of land that anyone leaving Ibex had to pass. It wasn't until after dusk at six-thirty when the black sedan pulled out onto the street. Pallidan sat in the passenger's seat next to one of the men Chris had seen earlier in the day.

Chris's surveillance experience from his days in CID made it easy, even in the dark, to follow Pallidan to an affluent neighborhood about twenty minutes away from Ibex. The Mercedes disappeared into a stark contemporary home set back from the wide street and lit by soft yellow lights hidden in the well-groomed shrubs. The home was nothing Chris Pelo would ever want to live in, but its striking angles reminded him of something from the pages of an architectural magazine. He pulled his own car around the corner and parked on the street. He took a small army-green backpack from the trunk and walked to the yard opposite Pallidan's house, where he tucked himself into a small cluster of evergreens.

Chris waited, hoping that the man who had driven Pallidan would leave. After about ten minutes, he did. The fourth of four garage doors yawned open and the security guard emerged behind the wheel of a dark blue Ford Explorer. After ten more minutes, Chris took a deep breath and started across the street. The phone box was easy enough to find: the two-and-a-half-foot metal stub protruded from the ground behind a bank of shrubs that concealed the electric transformer. The shrubs provided Chris with a nice cover.

He held a small red penlight in his teeth so he could see as he opened the transformer and began cutting and splicing the wires that led into the house. He hadn't run a phone tap in over six years, so he rechecked his connections three times. The unit he'd borrowed from his partner was state of the art; not only compact but with a voice-activated recorder with a tape that would allow him to hear an hour and a half of Pallidan's phone conversations. The only drawback to it was that he would have to retrieve the unit in order to hear what had been said. He tucked the wiring and the unit back into the box and closed it.

Chris looked around nervously and tried to think of a way out of what he now had to do, but there was none. If he wanted to guarantee some action, he'd have to stir things up with Pallidan. He would have much preferred to fade away into the shadows. That was something he was comfortable and familiar with. On the other hand, he knew exactly what Madison would do, so when he emerged from the bushes he marched right up the walk and rang the bell. It was some time before the intercom beside the door squawked and Pallidan asked who was there.

"My name is Chris Pelo," Chris said with as much force and confidence as he could muster.

The box simply went dead. Chris stood and waited. He shifted nervously from foot to foot. He thought about how wonderful it would be if Pallidan would just come out and answer his questions. He rang the bell again. There was no answer this time. When Chris heard the screeching of tires about three blocks away, his stomach sank. He started to retreat down the walk, but was only halfway across the street when a pair of headlights came racing toward him. The Explorer squealed, lurched sideways, and shuddered to a stop. Before the truck even stopped shaking, the security guard from earlier in the day was out on the pavement with his weapon drawn.

"Stop!" he commanded.

Chris halted in the middle of the street and raised his hands over his head. He'd seen enough to know that a situation like this was exactly the type where people got killed. The guard approached and spoke into a handheld radio. Before he reached Chris, another car pulled up quietly behind him.

"Who are you, mister?" the first guard asked.

"My name is Chris Pelo," Chris said.

"The guy from today, Marty," the second guard, who was out of his car now, said disgustedly.

"You were told that Mr. Pallidan wouldn't see you," the one named Marty said. "What are you doing here?"

"I thought he'd talk to me at home," Chris said simply, lowering his hands now that the situation was getting a little more under control. "I'm a former cop from Austin. I'm a lawyer, and I need to talk to Mr. Pallidan about one of my clients."

"Mr. Pallidan doesn't want to talk," the second guard said gruffly, stepping in front of Chris now with a malevolent stare. "So you just take yourself back to Austin. If we have any more problems with you, the next time we're not going to be so polite. Do you understand that?"

"Yes," Chris said, trying to keep his voice from shaking, "I do. But you tell Mr. Pallidan that if he doesn't speak to me, I'll just have to subpoena him. One way or another he and I are going to talk."

With that, Chris brushed past both the men and started up the street toward his car. The two guards followed him to his hotel. Chris worried the whole way back, wondering how long the two thugs planned on following him. If they didn't let up until he left town, it would be hard to get back to Pallidan's phone box and retrieve the tape. In the morning he'd have to take a drive and find out.

Chris never thought he'd wish for it again, but right then, he wished he had a badge. When you had a badge you had clout. Now he had to play by a different set of rules. He was in a city he didn't really know much about, trying to drum up information from a man who was obviously well insulated. Chris left the thugs in the parking lot and checked his messages at the desk. There were none, so he went into the restaurant and had half a roasted chicken and a milk shake for dinner. When he was finished, he returned to his room and called Madison at the Royal Palm. There was no answer, so he selected a pay movie that he watched until he fell asleep.

By the time Madison approached the front desk at the Royal Palm, the man who had been duped by Julie Tarracola was long gone. So was almost everyone else. When she was told she had no room, Madison was incensed. It was after midnight, and she had hoped to get at least some rest after her dogleg trip through Atlanta. It wasn't happening at the Royal Palm though. The short, sharply dressed man behind the desk wore a little mustache that quivered with anxiety at the predicament. Madison insisted he call the manager, but he was the manager. Unfortunately, he was also the type of man who reacted aggressively in an adverse situation, which explained why, after fifteen years with the hotel, he had risen no higher than night manager. Instead of apologizing profusely because there was nothing he could do, and explaining that there was no way he could wake a guest who had already been given a room, the man began to challenge Madison.

"I'm sorry," he said curtly, "I don't even know if you are really who you say you are."

"Not who I say I am?" Madison said incredulously. "Not . . . I have credit cards and a driver's license, and just about everything you can name that proves I am who I say I am. Are you kidding me? Do you know what your boss is going to say to you when I tell her or him how you've just treated a regular guest of this hotel?"

"Madam," the man hissed, "please, control yourself. I have to ask you to lower your voice."

"Lower my voice?" Madison said. "It's after midnight. You gave away my room. Now you're saying you don't believe I am who I say I am, and you want me to lower my voice?"

The manager pursed his lips and abruptly turned and walked away, disappearing through a door that was cut into the wooden wall behind him.

Madison huffed and waited for him to return. After five minutes she realized that he had abandoned her. She looked around helplessly. The only people about were a handful of hotel guests who made a quiet path from the grand entrance or the elegant bar to the bank of elevators. Madison had never experienced anything like it. She turned to go. If she wasn't getting a room here, she figured she had better find a place where she could, and soon, if she wanted to be rested at all for tomorrow.

There was a single valet, who didn't seem to understand why Madison was leaving after having just arrived. Finally she was able to get her car back, and he loaded her bag back into the trunk. She pulled out onto the empty road and comforted herself with ideas of the letters she would write and the phone calls she would make to see to it that the night manager who'd just insulted her was fired by the end of the week. She hadn't gone four blocks before she spotted a big black and yellow Walk Inn sign. She sighed heavily and pulled in. A sleepy middle-aged woman with long stringy gray hair heaved herself up from her chair behind the desk with a plaintive moan. She gave Madison the heavy brass key to a room out back by the Dumpsters where a derelict was noisily going through the day's refuse. A nearby transformer station droned on with a persistent hum, softening the derelict's stream of curses over not having found anything of particular use or value. Madison hauled her garment bag out of the trunk and up a flight of loud metal stairs to her corner room. She glanced nervously at the bum and opened the door as quietly as she could.

Tired as she was, Madison unpacked her suit for the next day and hung it in the hollow wood-board closet. Everything else she left scattered on the sagging double bed near the door. She didn't plan on being there more than one night, so there was no sense in unpacking everything. After getting ready for bed, she lay down on the bed nearest the bathroom and pulled the covers up tight. Then she dialed home to let Cody know she had arrived safely. He was asleep, of course, but the sound of his voice somehow made her feel safer in her less-than-illustrious surroundings.

"You're fine," Cody murmured sleepily. "Don't worry. Go to sleep."

Like every well-planned crime and every military operation, good intelligence made the difference between success and failure. The killer came in through the window, knowing it was the easiest way. He placed a handle with suction cups on each end in the middle of the windowpane and deftly cut a wide square of glass. He set it down with the nonchalance of a repairman who had been called in to fix a washing machine. He removed the handle and stowed it in a shoulder bag that was slung across his chest.

He moved like a cat, a big man with the stealth and grace of a much smaller one, and climbed through the opening into the hotel room. He knew she was here, and he knew she was unprotected. There were two beds, and at first he thought she was in the one closest to the window. But it was only her things, scattered about in a heap. She was buried to her chin in covers on the bed across the room from him.

He had no real inclination to do this job. But things seemed to have gotten out of control and he was backed into a corner. There were other people involved, other things at stake. It wasn't that he cared so much for other people, but there was one person he did care for, the one who had gotten him out, worked the system to set him free. That was worth something. It was worth a lot. He didn't have the kind of spirit that could be confined. For his continued freedom, he would continue to hold up his end of the bargain. He went into the bathroom, quietly cut down the shower curtain, and folded the plastic over his arm like a fancy waiter. By the time he went back into the room and stood over her, his eyes had adjusted well enough to the darkness to make out the general shape of her face.

In his mind he punctured the barrier between the conscious and the subconscious, opening a flow of translucent crimson fluid that was always there, waiting only to be let loose. It spilled over him, washing the vision behind his closed eyelids in blood red so that violent memories of the past swirled into the present like a film montage. In the context of everything that had already happened, this was just another frame in the red zone.

With the disinterest of a butcher, he opened his eyes and pulled the stainless-steel blade from its sheath. In one movement he covered her with the shower curtain, bent down, reached under the plastic, and cut through her windpipe and the major arteries and veins in her neck. With his free hand he pinned her head down into the bed. As her body began to thrash reflexively, he lowered his weight onto her frame, holding her as still as he could while the spray of blood splashed against the underside of the curtain.

Chapter 38

Cody already had Jo-Jo out the door and on his way to the bus. The sun was coming up hot orange and promised to burn off the December chill that had set in overnight, frosting the grass and shrubs. Cody was stuffing some midterm papers into his briefcase when the phone rang. He presumed it was Madison. He remembered her calling late last night, but not clearly. She probably realized he had been in a fog and was calling to let him know that everything was fine.

"Hi," he said cheerily.

"Cody?" the voice was not Madison's. That and the tone disturbed him.

"Yes?" Cody said. "Who's this?"

"Cody, it's Chris Pelo."

Pelo was choking on his own words, and Cody's stomach seemed to fall like a clod of dirt cast down a well.

"Cody, I, I . . . I don't know how . . ."

"Is it Madison?" Cody demanded, his voice breaking in the middle of her name. The thought of a car accident came immediately to mind. "What happened? Tell me!"

"She's dead."

Cody said nothing, unable to take a breath.

"No," Cody finally said, "she's not . . ."

It was something he couldn't believe. He suddenly seemed in the midst of a nightmare, suspended in a liquid, and the only thing more sluggish than his mind were his weighted limbs.

"I'm sorry," Chris said. "I'm so sorry . . ."

It was the pain in Pelo's voice that cut through Cody's haze.

"How?" Cody heard himself say.

"They think it was Luther Zorn," Chris said, not knowing what to say, but not wanting to be deceptive. He added, "With a knife. He's gone completely crazy. They can't find him. What should I do?"

"No," Cody said after a moment. "No."

Chris Pelo heard the line go dead. He rubbed his hands over his face and pressed his palms into his eyes. He was sitting on the bed in his Memphis hotel room, dressed for the day except for his jacket, which he had slung across the back of a chair. It was only just seven in Memphis. He had risen early and called to fill Madison in on what he had learned before she met with Berryhill.

When there was no answer in her room, Chris asked to be connected to the restaurant. Madison wasn't eating. He called her room again. The operator told him a wake-up call had been scheduled for six-thirty and that no one had answered that either. Chris asked to be connected to the front desk where he insisted that someone from security be sent to check on her. When the security guard went to the door, he heard the clock radio playing loudly and after repeated knocks, he became concerned and let himself in. He found her body, without its head, lying in a swamp of blood-soaked bedsheets.

It was all his fault. He was the one who had worked so hard to convince Madison to help him. If he'd left it alone, she would be back in Austin, working on some other case. He would have been back in Austin, too, looking for a job. He was overwhelmed with guilt.

Chris picked up the phone and called his wife to make sure she was okay. There was no reason to believe she wasn't, but after all that had happened, Chris couldn't shake the conviction that no one was safe.

Luther no longer knew who was his friend and who was his enemy. Everything had fallen apart. Nothing was as it had seemed. He had a 9mm Beretta stuck into the waist of his jeans, even though he was simply having a cup of coffee and making a show of reading the paper over a plate of eggs and bacon at his own kitchen table. He wore nothing else besides his pants and his gun. He could tell that the firearm and his half-naked body were making his housekeeper, Marla, nervous. He didn't have the energy to care.

Luther had arrived home very late. Exhausted, he fell right to sleep. But only three hours later sunlight splashed his face like a bucket of briny water. Exhausted, Luther's mind would not let him return to sleep. He could not stop thinking about Madison McCall.

The phone on the wall rang. Marla was cleaning the stove, and she looked questioningly at him. It was his private line. He let it ring three times before asking her to answer it.

"Hallo," she said quietly, then looked at him. "Is Ms. McCall . . ."

Luther rose from the table and grabbed for the phone.

"Hello," he demanded, "who's this?"

"Hi, Luther," came a woman's voice, "it's Madison. I know we were supposed to meet for breakfast at the Royal Palm at nine, but I got here late last night and they gave my room away for some reason. I'm at the Walk Inn down the road. We can meet here; there's a Denny's next door."

"I'm not sure . . . exactly . . . when I can get there," Luther stumbled. "What room are you in? I'll come get you."

Madison hesitated.

"Shit, Madison," Luther growled, "you're my lawyer. I'm not crazy. I'm not going to hurt you. Where the hell are you? I have to see you."

Madison finally spoke. "Room . . . two-seventeen."

"I'm on my way," Luther said, and hung up the phone.

The water dribbled out of the shower, and it took Madison a while to rinse the shampoo from her hair. When she finally stepped out onto the clammy tile floor, she felt rushed. She didn't know how long it would take Luther to get there, but she certainly didn't want him arriving before she was dressed. For all her anxiety though, Madison was dressed and packed well before there was any sign of Luther. She pulled the beige curtains aside and peered into the parking lot. The bum from the night before was gone, and the lot was deep in the heavy shadow of a neighboring building. No cars came in or out.

Madison sat down on the bed and took out her planner. As she did, the Marauders championship ring fell out onto the bed. Madison picked it up and tucked it into the inside pocket of her blazer. She wanted to remember to show it to Berryhill. Whether it was incriminating to Luther or not, Madison had a duty to disclose it. She would not risk her career by tampering with evidence. In the planner she'd written Chris Pelo's hotel number in Memphis. She tried to dial, but for some reason the call wouldn't go through. She hit the button for the Walk Inn's operator. After fifteen rings she was greeted with a disgruntled hello.

"I need a long-distance operator," Madison said pleasantly. The operator clicked her over without another word. Madison got through to the Memphis hotel and asked to be connected with Chris's room.

"Hello," he said, sounding incredibly despondent. Madison was disturbed by his tone.

"Chris, it's Madison," she said carefully, not welcoming the bad news that she sensed was coming.

"Chris?" she said. He hadn't responded. She heard him murmur something in Spanish. "Chris?"

"Madison?" he said, his voice ripe with disbelief. "Where are you?"

"I'm in Palm Beach," she said. "They gave away my room last night at the Royal Palm, so I'm at a Walk Inn down the road . . . why?"

"My God," Chris exhaled, "Cody . . ."

"What's wrong with Cody?" Madison panicked.

"Nothing," Chris assured her, "he's fine. It's . . . I thought. Whoever was in your room last night at the Royal Palm was killed. Everyone assumed it was you. There was no way to know, really. She was decapitated."

"My God."

"I'll call Cody right away. Madison, I can't even tell you how . . . Madison, I'm so glad you're all right."

"Oh, no," Madison fretted to herself, and then, "Chris, I called him."

"Who?"

"Luther."

"From where you are?"

"Yes. I told him to come meet me."

"Madison, he's gone completely insane. He killed whoever was in your room. Get out of there! Go! I'll call the police for you, just get out of there! Call me later! Go!"

Madison's hands shook as she replaced the phone and gathered her things off the other bed. She didn't think to look out her window. She simply flung open the door and ran right into Luther. Madison recoiled as if she'd bumped into a hot stove. Without thinking she was back inside her room. She slammed the door against the foot he'd gotten across the step. The door bounced back at her and Madison flung all her weight against it to keep him from coming in. Luther was caught off balance, but only momentarily. He forced the door open with one quick jolt from his hand and Madison was thrown across the bed. Luther slammed the door behind him. Madison screamed and scrambled for the phone. Luther reached it at the same time and yanked it out of the wall, tossing it aside where it smashed helplessly.

She saw the gun sticking out of his pants.

"Luther, no!" Madison shrieked.

Luther was on top of her. Her fingernails tore through his shirt, raking his thick muscles and leaving deep bleeding welts. Madison fought, but Luther was too big. He engulfed her thrashing body, pinning her arms against the bed, covering her mouth with his large hand. She bit into him, hard, but he only gripped her tighter. Madison could feel Luther's blood running freely into her throat and she gagged. The nausea sent Madison into shock. She looked up helplessly, an animal caught in the jagged jaws of a steel trap. His eyes were crazed with fear and determination.

Chapter 39

Kratch was sitting in the front seat of his car with the door open. He was parked haphazardly in the elegant circular drive of the Royal Palm with one foot resting outside on the rich clay paving stones. Lawrence and Gill were inside wrapping up the details and getting everything under way with the lab people and the coroners. It was all for show. He knew exactly what had happened, and now it was simply a matter of putting the pieces of the puzzle into place. Kratch had dispatched squad cars to Luther's home at the Polo Club. The officers reported that the guard had seen Luther leave only a short time before. Kratch was now filling out a report of his own. He was keeping close tabs on everything, since this would be considered part of his ongoing investigation of Luther Zorn.

Fifteen minutes ago, he had spoken to the hastily assembled press, indicating that he had put out an all-points bulletin for the immediate apprehension of the star football player. He was dangerous and deadly and to be considered heavily armed. Those were Kratch's words of warning to the press.

Kratch also strongly intimated to the law enforcement community that they shouldn't hesitate to use deadly force in apprehending Luther.

Suddenly, the radio in Kratch's car crackled with a general call for a code red response to the Walk Inn. The Walk Inn, Kratch knew, was a few blocks away. More details spilled from the radio, an urgent call regarding a wanted suspect.

Then Kratch heard Luther's name. He mobilized instantly, reacting as instinctively as a hunting dog picking up a fresh scent. As he pulled out onto the street, Kratch fumbled with his handheld radio and barked at Lawrence and Gill to get their asses down from the hotel room and follow him immediately to the Walk Inn. It was the kind of opportunity Kratch knew fate pitched at you every so often. It was the chance for him to nail Luther Zorn. There would be no fuss, no muss. With the three of them to back each other up, Luther could be eliminated and the case could be closed. It would be the best thing. Everyone would win.

Cody didn't sit around for long. Everything that had seemed important to him over the past year dissolved instantly. Madison was his world. Even when he'd struggled against her. Even when he'd envied her success as he foundered as a low-paid teacher and coach, she was his lifeline. Madison was better and stronger than anyone he'd ever known. He needed her.

In his mind, Madison had been indestructible. Her death left him floating in a universe devoid of meaning. He desperately grasped for some solid ground. Cody's mind was racing. He hit suddenly on the idea of revenge. *If Luther Zorn had killed his Madison, then Luther Zorn had to be exterminated.* Cody kept a .357 locked in his dresser drawer. He retrieved it and shoved the gun into a bag with some other things. Offering no explanation, he arranged for one of his assistant coaches to take care of Jo-Jo, then set out for the airport and Palm Beach with the dark shadow of death in his eyes.

Because Luther had a gun pointed at her, she listened.

"It's not me," he said.

Madison looked him bravely in the eye and said, "Luther, I know it's not you. I know you can't help what's happening. I can help you, but you've got to let me."

"You don't understand," he said. Luther grabbed his own face with his enormous hand and gripped it as if he was trying to wring out a washcloth.

"My God," he choked, "I don't know how to stop it . . ."

Luther's head jolted upright and his eyes were immediately alert. Outside, the screams of approaching police sirens could be heard.

"God damn you!" Luther said, believing she had led him into the trap.

"Luther!" Madison begged. "Stop it all! Give up! You can't keep going like this!"

"I can!" he said, pulling her off the bed by her arm and brandishing the Beretta in his free hand. "You're coming with me."

Suddenly Luther let her go, shoving her away from the door. She watched as he picked up a book of matches resting on top of the TV. He struck one of the matches, then lit the entire book before tearing the mattress off the bed and sticking the burning book into the loose sheets. The blanket melted away, but the flames licked hungrily at the sheets and the mattress. Black smoke curled up toward the ceiling and the smoke detector over Madison's head wailed loudly. She considered escape, but Luther turned his attention back to her before she could move.

Dragging Madison with him, Luther rushed outside and down the metal steps. He pulled her into the dark space underneath the stairs and clamped one hand over her mouth, resting the gun in the other hand, which was wrapped around her chest. A thick hedge hid them, but Madison could make out the shapes of the police cars as they careened into the parking lot and screeched to a halt.

Kratch saw smoke pouring out of the hotel room. He jumped from his car and dashed up the stairs with Gill close behind him. Lawrence remained in the car calling the fire department.

As the two detectives banged up the metal stairs above them, Luther lifted Madison from their hiding place and carried her toward his car, now loosely sandwiched between the two police cars.

Lawrence saw Luther appear suddenly from nowhere. The shock made him hesitate an instant, allowing Luther to shove Madison through the driver-side door and start in after her.

Lawrence began firing his weapon, and bullets zipped by Luther's head like deadly wasps. Madison shrieked, and Luther felt a primal scream erupt from the depths of his own chest as he dove for the ground. From that level Luther could see Lawrence's feet and ankles. He aimed the Beretta carefully and pulled off three quick rounds. The detective's feet disappeared, and suddenly, as if part of a staged magic trick, Lawrence's entire body lay still as a stone exposed on the pavement. Blood spread from his nose and forehead where he had hit the car door on his way down, knocking himself unconscious. Luther's amazed stare disappeared with the pain of a bullet tearing through his trapezius muscle and shattering his collarbone.

The shot came from above and behind him, and the impact rolled Luther partially under his car. With a rush of survival adrenaline, he burrowed into the impossibly low space, scratching and clawing his way underneath the car until he emerged from the other side at the same time Madison came spilling out of the passenger door on top of him. A fusillade of bullets rained down on the hood of the Viper. Gun smoke mixed with the smoke from the fire now billowing from the burning room on the second floor.

Luther waited. When the gunfire stopped, he continued to wait. Only when he could hear the clanging sound of the detectives' footsteps on the metal stairs did he scramble to the other police car where Lawrence lay unconscious and bleeding. From behind the detective's car door, Luther rose with his arm strapped around the front of Lawrence's chest, using the bloody detective as a shield. Luther aimed the Beretta at the two detectives and they stood frozen halfway between the stairs and the Viper.

"Don't move!" Luther commanded. "Drop the guns!"

Both Kratch and Gill had their pistols leveled at Luther, hoping he would give them a clean shot. Madison could see Luther, but not the police. She instinctively ducked her head between her hands on the pavement.

"I said drop them!" Luther screamed.

"Easy, Zorn," Kratch said, looking for even a small opening. It just wouldn't do if he shot his own detective, although Kratch was hard pressed not to open fire. He would gladly kill one of his own men in order to bring Luther down, if he thought he could get away with it.

"No!" Luther bellowed. "Drop the guns!"

Still Gill and Kratch held their weapons.

Luther fired a low shot, hitting Gill in the leg. Blood and bone dust sprayed out of the back of Gill's pant leg and he dropped to the ground like an impaled nightcrawler.

Kratch dropped his gun immediately and held up his hands. "Okay. Okay, Luther. Take it easy."

"Now pick his sorry ass up," Luther commanded, "and toss me the keys to your car."

Kratch tossed Luther the keys. Luther dropped Lawrence where he was and rounded the Viper and opened the trunk to Kratch's car.

"Put him in there! Now!" Luther commanded as Kratch approached, supporting the wounded Gill. "And you get in there, too! Now, Kratch! I'm just looking for an excuse to waste you right here!"

Kratch squeezed into the trunk and Luther slammed it shut.

Luther spun around now and bellowed at Madison. "Freeze!"

She was halfway across the lot.

"Get back here!" Luther ordered, letting a shot go in the air just to let her, too, know he meant business.

Madison returned, carefully crossing the parking lot with Luther's gun trained at her chest. She wished there was a way she could delay him until the fire trucks arrived. She could hear their wail in the distance. She looked down at Lawrence's body lying in a puddle of blood and thought better of it.

"Get in the cop car," Luther told her, "in the back."

Madison did as she was told. Luther got in the front and hit the locks. A cage separated him from Madison.

"You're bleeding," she said as quietly and gently as her nerves would allow. "You can't get away, Luther. Stop this now."

"Shut the fuck up!" Luther screamed, spinning around in his seat to glare at her as he started the car, then raced out of the lot and onto the street. Luther listened carefully to the radio for clues that would help him to avoid capture. Madison sat silently. She couldn't believe how calmly Luther drove, carefully putting as much distance between them and the Walk Inn as was possible without turning on the car's sirens and racing through red lights. After some time, Madison realized Luther was heading for the highway. They reached 95 and headed south. She choked down her hysteria like a wave of vomit.

"May I ask where we're going?" Madison said quietly after a while, the tears welling uncontrollably in her eyes.

Luther seemed to relax just a little. "We're going as far from here as we can get before I hear them start looking for the car on this radio."

As soon as he spoke, both of them could hear the excited chatter on the radio describing the car and putting out an all-points bulletin.

"Shit."

Luther got off at the next exit and headed west, checking his mirrors constantly. Soon they were beyond the heavy development and into an area that was dusty and overgrown with trees and scrub brush. Luther pulled off the road onto a dirt path. The path cut through the trees and eventually opened up into a cleared area of grassy fields. The path itself made a wide loop in the grass. Graying wooden stakes topped with crude fluorescent orange ribbons sprouted like brilliant tiger lilies. The stakes marked what had been planned as a residential development. On the high ground in the farthest corner of the loop, Luther pulled into the grass and backed the car carefully out of sight.

Luther turned off the car and dropped his head onto the wheel. Morning light filtered in through the gray-green camouflage of the foliage. The engine ticked quietly as it cooled. Madison eyed the oozing wound in Luther's shoulder. Blood trickled in a thin stream out of the meaty red and purple hole and spread in a great reddish stain across the back of his shirt.

Without a word, Luther ducked down in the front seat and rustled around in the glove box. He pulled out a white tin emergency first aid kit and spilled its contents onto the seat. He tore open his shirt, methodically washed his wound out, smeared it with an antibiotic cream, packed it with gauze, and taped the whole thing down. The entire time he worked, Luther made no noise. He only winced silently, gulping down the pain in great swallows that caused his Adam's apple to bob like a cork. His stoicism only served to further Madison's fright.

Suddenly Luther heaved an agonized sigh and lifted his head.

"I want you to listen to me," he commanded, peering intently at her through the cage.

Chapter 40

About six years ago a Navy SEAL lieutenant was stationed on an aircraft carrier in the middle of the Persian Gulf," Luther began. He looked at Madison to see if she was following him. She nodded for him to go on.

"The lieutenant and his men were flown into Iraq late one night and dropped about a mile from shore with their gear and a couple of inflatable rafts. The night was black, but these guys were able to navigate by the stars. They stashed the boats on the mainland and located a narrow river that flowed through a steep ravine into the Gulf, and followed the river upstream for several miles. The walls of the ravine got higher and higher. By the time they came to a steel suspension bridge it was about five hundred feet up on either side.

"The sun was coming up by the time they reached their target, so they stopped and dug into the thick vegetation surrounding the bridge, putting up trip wires around their perimeter for security. They slept through the day and when night fell, two men were sent to reconnoiter the area. After about two hours, one of them came back in a panic. They had been told that the bridge would be guarded by two infantry platoons, but the scout saw an entire battalion of tanks and light infantry, and two dozen support choppers on the north side of the ravine. Someone asked if they should abort the mission, given the inaccurate intelligence and the odds against them. At the same time, the second scout appeared and reported that a regiment of elite Republican Guards was camped out on the south side of the structure. The mission had suddenly turned suicidal, but the lieutenant knew he had to take out the bridge. There were fifty mobile SAMs positioned throughout the desert to the south of the bridge that needed to be isolated and taken out before any bombing raids could be launched on Baghdad. With the bridge out, the fifty mobile SAMs would effectively be neutralized. But someone had messed up in a big way, grossly underestimating the strength of the troops guarding the bridge. The lieutenant wanted the ship to send in some F-18s to knock out the copters and decrease the effectiveness of the pursuit that would be undertaken by the Iraqi forces once the bridge was blown.

"He had to get to the top of the ravine in order to radio the ship. It was a long climb but his anger carried him to the top quickly. He put on a pair of night-vision goggles as his sergeant set up the transmitting disc. The lieutenant could see tanks, tents full of men, and the nearby helicopters. When the sergeant had the communications unit up and running, the lieutenant called in to the ship. The ship's communications commander lit into him immediately. Their mission was supposed to be blacked out. The lieutenant barked at him, telling him, in code, that there was an emergency situation. The communications commander left his transmitter open while he raised the ship's admiral, complaining to the senior officer about the lieutenant's breaking the blackout. The stupid prick mentioned the name of the bridge," Luther said, shaking his head sadly.

"The lieutenant went ballistic. By the time the admiral was on the line, the Iraqi choppers were already in the air. The admiral screamed at the lieutenant that he didn't give a damn if the whole Iraqi army was there, he wanted that bridge down. The lieutenant cut him off in mid-sentence and tossed the radio on his back, as he saw big searchlights begin to sweep the banks of the ravine from the bridge. Two copters flew up over the lieutenant and his sergeant, and down into the ravine where they began to use their own searchlights to scour the foliage. Big guns traced every movement of the lights."

Madison stared, open-mouthed, as Luther raced through his story. She knew now that something terrible was about to happen, but still couldn't figure out what it had to do with Luther.

"Just as one of the copters located the lieutenant's men," Luther continued, "a missile went up and the copter burst into a ball of fire. A fist-sized chunk of shrapnel hit the sergeant in the face, killing him instantly. A moment later, other copters were swarming like hornets around a kicked-up nest. Another missile went up from the other side of the gorge and another helicopter went down. Troops began pouring over the side of the ridge in a full-scale assault. The lights now had completely illuminated the gorge, and the lieutenant could hear the screams of dying men as they were cut down by gunfire. The lieutenant headed toward the bridge, picking his way through Iraqi troops until he found a crevice between some rocks and a concrete abutment that helped support the bridge.

"He stayed there all through the next day. He had some rations in his pack, but his only source of water was a patch of green slime that oozed from the rock wall. When night fell he climbed out of his spot and out as far as he dared onto the underpinnings of the bridge, in the midst of the criss-crossing searchlights. All his men were dead. He was determined to blow the bridge with his own single block of C-4. He stuck the detonation device into the center of the plastique and made his way carefully through the lights and troops about a tenth of a mile down the ravine.

"In two hours, the sun came up again. As it did, the lieutenant made out a strange sight by the north entrance to the bridge. It looked as if the Iraqis had erected ten large match-sticks in a semicircle near the road. When there was enough light, the lieutenant put his binoculars to his face and discovered the twisted bloody heads of his men stuck on top of tall poles. Something inside him snapped. In the early after-noon, a convoy of fuel trucks crossed the bridge. The lieutenant detonated the C-4. The combined force of the C-4 and exploding fuel trucks destroyed the bridge, blanketing the horizon with fire and smoke. To escape, the lieutenant threw himself into the river.

"Six days later, he wandered into an American army out-post in Kuwait. Two weeks after that, he was back on board his ship, receiving a hero's welcome. The next morning they found the communications officer's head stuck on the short flag mast on the admiral's bridge. No one had any reason to suspect the lieutenant, but when guards caught him sneaking into the admiral's quarters two nights after that, dressed in black and armed with a razor-sharp survival knife, they put him in chains and had him flown to the psychiatric ward at the U.S. hospital base in Germany. He was twenty-three, and they said he'd completely lost his mind."

Chapter 41

The sun was high in the cobalt sky, and even though the temperature was in the seventies, it was hot inside the car.

"Can you open a window?" Madison said. A bead of sweat trickled from her hairline to her jaw before she reached up and dabbed it with the back of her sleeve.

Luther was shaken from his trance, as if he'd forgotten she was there.

"Sure," he said, turning the key in the ignition and cracking all four of the windows about two inches.

"Thank you," she said.

Luther seemed not to hear her. His eyes again looked past her, out of the back window of the police car and into the horrors he had just described.

"I couldn't see him for three years," Luther told her. "I don't know where my brother was or what they did to him. I was the only one who cared. Our mother was dead. They kept putting me off, saying Leeland was involved in some secret military operation. Finally, I got a lawyer and used some pull I had with a senator and they had to let me see him. It was bad.

"He was in a state institution outside Atlanta, a maximum-security facility for the criminally insane. It looked like an inner-city high school, all red bricks and a flagpole out in front. But it was in the middle of nowhere, and it was surrounded by a double chain-link fence with dogs and concertina wire and the latest in surveillance stuff. Even my brother couldn't get out of there, and God knows he tried.

"By the time I got to him, he was spending a good portion of his time in a straitjacket. About the only way they could get him to take his drugs was by injecting him, and even that was a battle. Anyway, when they let me see him he was chained to a chair in the middle of a padded room. He was in the jacket, and the leather muzzle they used to cover his mouth was hanging around his neck like a broken dog collar. They had taken it off so he could talk to me. Normally, they said, they had to keep his mouth covered because he once tore someone up with his teeth."

"My God," Madison said.

Luther's eyes seemed to zoom in and out of focus.

"When I talked to him, he started to cry. I know it was partly from the drugs, but I started to cry, and let me tell you, we weren't like that. We were raised to keep that stuff bottled up. We'd get whipped for crying. But neither of us could help it. I asked him what the hell had happened, and he told me it was all lies. He said he was sent on a bad mission and a lot of people had been killed. He told me the part about the heads. I knew that from the doctors and the story they'd given me. Everything pretty much matched up, but he swore the thing about the communications commander wasn't true. He said he had been infuriated at what happened to his men and that he promised the navy he was going public with the screw-up that cost eleven men their lives. It was just more bad decision-making up high in the military. You've heard of that kind of stuff before, everyone has. A lot of it happened over there. We lost more guys to friendly fire than we did to the Iraqis.

"He told me that it was the admiral of the ship who made the mistake. He based the whole decision on old intelligence reports and failed to double-check anything through navy intelligence. He had broken standard procedure and faced a discharge, the end of his career, maybe even a court-martial.

"My brother told me that they had been drugging him for three years and calling him crazy and it was all a sick cover-up. I told Leeland I would fight them. I told him I could get the best lawyers. But he said it would be too late. He begged me to do whatever I had to do to get him out. He begged me."

Luther sighed and pushed the base of his hand into his eyes one at a time, giving each a violent rub. Then he looked directly into Madison's eyes.

"He told me that they were going to lobotomize him. He said if I didn't do something, the next time I saw him—if ever—he would be a vegetable. I swore to him I'd do something. Before I left, I talked to the doctor who talked to me when I arrived. He danced around the lobotomy thing, saying that they would do everything they could before they resorted to something that radical, but that my brother was an incredible danger to himself and others. I told him I found that hard to believe. The doctor told me Leeland had a violently acute case of post-traumatic stress disorder, and that he had lucid moments when he appeared perfectly fine, but that for the most part he was incredibly dangerous and a sociopathic killer. I was told I could see him again in six months. Even my lawyer told me there was pretty much nothing I could do. Apparently they had done everything by the book. My brother was in there and he wasn't coming out. If they determined he needed to have part of his brain hacked out, they could do it . . .

"When I got back I tried to think of how I could get him out. No one could help me, though. I had used up my marker with the senator just getting in there to see Leeland. The lawyer told me it wasn't possible. The whole thing had been mandated by a navy tribunal, and it was all legal. Everyone seemed to think my brother was desperately manipulating me. I didn't think so, though."

Luther sighed and shook his head before continuing.

"At the time, I had been seeing Vivian on and off for about three months. We were getting pretty close. One weekend, we went away together to St. Bart's, just for a couple of days on the beach where we didn't have to worry about anyone seeing us or knowing us. Chase was in Hawaii on business. We both knew the kind of scum he was, and we never felt guilty about what we were doing. Anyway, she asked me why I wasn't myself and I told her. I asked her if she could help. She told me that if Pat Rivet couldn't help me that no one could.

"I was desperate, and she said Rivet was a guy who got things done one way or another, that's why he was Chase's attorney. She said she thought that as straight as Rivet pretended to be, before he came to work with Chase, he supposedly worked for the mob in Miami. He was no stranger to breaking rules. I asked her to find out if he would help. I knew Rivet, but I don't think the two of us ever said more than three words to each other the entire time I'd been with the team. She set up a meeting for me with him when we got back. I told him my problem, and he said he couldn't help me but he might know someone who could. That was it. He never said another thing about it to me.

"I began to think it was all bullshit. Then, about two weeks later I got a call from some guy who I never heard from before or since. He said he heard I had a problem with my brother and I needed it solved. I told him I did and I asked him who he was. He told me that wasn't important. I didn't know what to do. I had to get my brother out of there. They were going to kill him, or as good as kill him anyway.

"This guy asked me if I wanted to get him out. I told him yes. He told me that he could get him out, but that my brother would have to do a job. I didn't know what the hell that meant, and I asked him. He told me it would require the skills my brother had learned as a SEAL. I asked if it was some kind of underwater demolition or something like that. He told me 'something like that,' but that it was none of my goddamned business. If I wanted my brother out, I had to write a letter telling Leeland to do whatever job that was asked of him by the people who got him out. I did that. What else could I do?

"I asked when I could see him again, and he told me when my brother was done with his work, but that afterward it would be best if he left the country. He told me that if they got him out once, they wouldn't be able to do it again. That was early last summer. I asked Rivet about it, but he said he didn't know a thing, said he had no idea what I was talking about. He knows, though. A few weeks later I called the doctor who spoke with me at the hospital, but he told me my brother was no longer at that hospital. I didn't know what the hell was going on. I didn't know if my brother was in or out, or dead, or what.

"I got that lawyer who helped me get in to see Leeland to ask where my brother was. He finally found out that he had escaped. They said no one knew how. They said there was a warrant out for his arrest with the FBI and the Georgia Bureau of Investigation, but it didn't seem to be a big priority on anyone's list. That was the last I heard from, or of, my brother until a few weeks ago—not that I've heard from him now, but I'm pretty sure he's behind all that's happened."

"You're telling me that your brother is the one who's killing everyone?" Madison said.

Luther nodded.

"I think so. When Chase was killed, I had a bad feeling. I think probably Vivian and Rivet got together to use my brother to have him killed. She's rich now. She has everything. She used to talk about how great things would be without Chase. She knew I would never do anything about it. When she heard the story about my brother and the kind of things he was capable of . . . I don't mean as a crazy killer, I just mean as a navy SEAL, I think she figured it was her chance. It makes complete sense, the drowning, the scuba diver. My brother was trained to do that kind of stuff. Vivian hooked me up with Rivet. She sent the note. She got me there. She rolled right over for the police, telling them she saw me. She set me up. Now she won't even see me. I tried calling her, but I can't even get her on the phone. I went to her house, but there were armed guards all over the place, and no way to get to her without causing some serious trouble."

"And your . . . brother," Madison said, "why didn't you tell me this from the beginning? It doesn't make sense. I told you you could trust me."

Luther shrugged.

"I didn't tell you from the start because I figured you'd get me off and everything would work out. That's why I wanted you. You're supposed to be the best there is. I didn't want you or anyone looking for my brother. I figured if he bumped Chase, everyone would have what they wanted and they'd let Leeland just disappear. I didn't want him to get caught or captured or whatever. If they caught him, I knew what would happen. I couldn't live with that."

"And now?"

Luther sighed heavily. "I think he may have killed Charlene. He would never have done it if he had known who she was or what she meant to me. But how could he have known? I also think he may have killed whoever was in your hotel room last night."

"How did you know about that?" Madison asked suspiciously.

"I heard it on the radio on the way over to the hotel," Luther said.

"You just started shooting at the police, Luther," Madison said, still skeptical.

"That one cop shot at me, Madison," he said. "I didn't even raise a finger. He just saw me and pulled his gun and started trying to kill me!"

Madison fumbled with the inside pocket of her blazer. She took out the ring and passed it through the cage.

"What's this?"

"It's a championship ring. I want you to put it on."

"Why?"

"Just do it, Luther," she told him. Madison bit the inside of her cheek and watched as Luther slowly stuck the end of his ring finger into the smooth circumference of the brilliant yellow metal. Halfway down, it stuck.

"Doesn't fit," he said, looking curiously at her.

Madison could see that. She exhaled slowly, as if she'd just heard some good news she'd been waiting for.

"Who else would have a ring like this?" she asked.

"Anyone on the team," he said. "We all got them."

"What about Rivet?"

"Sure."

"How about Martin Wilburn?"

"Yeah, everyone gets one, the equipment manager, the trainers, the coaches, Wilburn and Rivet, too. Anyone who has something to do with football operations. Where'd you get it?"

"It was found outside a cabin," she said. "The same place where three severed heads were found on top of some wooden poles."

Luther's face crumpled.

"Jesus. That's what they said he did on that ship. That's what happened to his men. But why would he? Was . . . Charlene?" He choked.

"I don't know. I would think probably yes."

"But why?" Luther anguished.

"I think we should just turn you in, Luther," Madison continued, "and let them find your brother. If he really is out there, and sick, he needs help. You need help. You're bleeding."

"A lot of things aren't right," Luther said, shaking his head and waving off his injury in a way that suggested he was no stranger to pain. "Someone, somewhere, is pushing all the buttons. I have to find out who it is. If I don't, I'm going to end up in the same kind of place my brother did. I'm a black man with a gun and a history of psychological counseling. The police already think I'm a killer. I just shot a cop. You think anyone will believe he tried to kill me first? They may never find my brother and they may not want to. I make a nice story, and I don't want to spend the rest of my life in jail, or worse. I've got to find the people who are using my brother and get to Leeland myself. If I can do that . . ."

"Then what?"

"If I can do that, then maybe my brother can get away and I can expose whoever's behind this. All of them."

"I don't think your brother's getting away would be good for anyone, Luther," she said gently.

"He's my brother, Madison," Luther said flatly. "The other problem is you."

"What do you mean?" she asked.

"I mean, you're better off if everyone thinks you're dead."

"Why?"

"Look, for whatever reason, Leeland was ordered to kill you," Luther said. "Right now, he and everyone else think that's exactly what happened. If you turn up, it will be all over the news. Everyone will know. I'm just saying, my brother is not a guy I'd want coming after me, police protection or not. He's like a heat-seeking missile. He was a SEAL captain. You don't get to be that unless you're pretty damn dangerous."

Luther's stare gave Madison cause to think seriously about what he'd said. She could call Cody and Jo-Jo and let them know she was fine. Cody could call her parents and her sister. Otherwise, everyone else could think she was dead. Luther was right. The last thing she wanted was to have to look over her shoulder every minute wondering when Luther's brother was going to blast through a window or a door with the intention of killing her.

"I know where we have to look," she said finally.

"Where?"

"Memphis."

Chapter 42

Mark Berryhill was stunned to hear the news of Madison McCall's death. He turned off the television and sat at his desk for a moment thinking of his own wife and children. He made a resolve to spend more time at home. The intercom buzzed, and his secretary told him the coroner was on line one.

"Yeah, Art?"

"Mark, I know this isn't your territory, but I talked with the sheriff's office, and Lieutenant Kratch, who's running the investigation, suggested that you might be able to help us get in touch with Madison McCall's next of kin. There was no identification in any of her things. I don't know if the killer took her wallet or what, but all I've got to go on is her name from the hotel registration. I don't even know where she's from."

"She's from Texas—Austin," Berryhill told him. "She worked for the firm of Caldburn, Baxter and Thrush, and she's married to the former Texas Outlaws player Cody Grey. He's the one you'll want to get in touch with."

"No chance you'd have a home number or anything? I'm going to need an identification, Mark. I don't know if there are any prints on file in Austin, but if not, the husband will have to help me determine if it's really her, even though I can't imagine who else it could be."

The state attorney thought about that, a man having to identify his wife's headless corpse. He shifted in his chair as if someone had run a cold, smooth cube of ice down his spine.

"No," he said. "I don't have a home number. But I've got her office number. You can call there, and I'm sure they'll know how to get in touch with her husband."

Berryhill read off the number from the business card Madison had left with him. The coroner thanked him, and Berryhill replaced the phone. He wondered what horrible dementia could have caused Luther Zorn to do such a thing to Madison McCall.

Well, it was going to make his job easier. McCall was a fine lawyer. But Berryhill would gladly have faced the challenge of battling her in court if it would undo the horrible thing that had been done to her.

Leeland Zorn aimed carefully. The best shot was one that hit the brain stem. He pulled the trigger, and in a blur the spear shot through the head of the large grouper. Leeland allowed himself to exhale, and a storm of bubbles rushed from his regulator toward the surface seventy feet above. He reached between the arms of coral and tugged heavily at the spear that protruded from the fish, lifting both as he flogged toward the pale green glow of the surface.

With some effort he hoisted the fish over the side of the boat, then mounted a small platform at the stern where he began to remove his gear. He actually enjoyed the way he was living right now. He didn't have to think of money. They had given him more than enough to buy the old boat, a used car, and the supplies he required. As long as he had the speargun he would never go hungry, and his preferred dwelling was a tent. He felt trapped in any kind of building. When his work was complete, he would, in all likelihood, head to the islands. He could live even farther from civilization. But he wasn't finished doing what he had promised his brother.

By the time Leeland had his gear stowed and the motor running, the sun was high in the azure sky. He took a seat and chugged inland. The smell of spent gas filled his nostrils, and he bumped the throttle to outrun the fumes, heading toward land, where he would weave his way through the Intracoastal Waterway and west on the canal that would take him all the way to the big lake.

It would take less time if he drove, but he didn't like being in the car any more than he liked being inside a building, and the boat was a much less conspicuous way to travel. Six months ago it was the rental car that resulted in his need to kill the young ranger. In a boat he could avoid any police roadblocks, and in the open air there was always a way to escape. Leeland had no intention of ever being held captive again. Before that happened, he would impale himself on his survival knife. He had envisioned this act over and over so many times that he knew he could do it quickly, easily, and without hesitation, driving the point of the blade from just behind his collarbone down through the top of his rib cage and into his heart with one quick thrust the way the Gauls did so many centuries ago.

In a strange way he anticipated that moment. At times he was acutely aware that only the primal and inexplicable instinct to survive kept him from turning the almost constant rage he felt toward his own person. Killing was his only solace. When he extinguished the life from others, the animal within was soothed, and for a short time afterward he felt as if everything was quite good.

It was bright on the water now, but Leeland would have worn his dark wraparound glasses anyway. He didn't want people looking in at him, and it made him feel much better to have them on when he encountered other human beings. He passed the early afternoon motoring through the canal, ignoring the occasional fellow boaters he saw. Finally he was through the lock and able to open his throttle and race into the expanse of Lake Okeechobee. It wasn't long before there was no land and no other boats in sight. Leeland lost himself in a fantasy that the entire world was covered in water and everything besides him and the fish below the surface had been destroyed. A broad grin broke out across his face, but, still, something hidden behind his eyes flickered like the tail of a rattlesnake. Whatever it was, it wanted nothing more than to come out.

Kratch hung up the phone impatiently. He had work to do and didn't want to be bothered with things like body IDs and medical updates. It was, however, good news he had just received. Lawrence's doctor had assured him that, although his detective was still unconscious and had a bad concussion, he had stabilized. Lawrence had just come out of extensive surgery to remove one of Luther Zorn's 9mm slugs that had shattered his ankle. More orthopedic surgery would still be necessary.

Gill's wound wasn't life-threatening either, but it was certainly substantial. Some significant arteries and veins had to be cauterized to stem the bleeding, and his shattered femur also required some extensive orthopedic hardware. Both of

Kratch's men would be out of commission for quite some time.

Kratch had other help, but it wasn't quite the same. He didn't like this at all. He would prefer to have three guns blazing when they found Luther Zorn, not just his one.

While his two best men were undergoing their operations, Kratch had mobilized the entire Sheriff's Department and the state police as well. Kratch had issued urgent bulletins over the police wire requesting that every law enforcement office in the state be on the watch for Zorn and the missing police car. The local television news divisions and CNN were flashing shots of Luther's face on the screen hourly. It wouldn't be long before they found him.

Kratch lit a Camel and sucked angrily. It was a blunder to have let Zorn escape. Not only that, but he had two men down. Well, every cop in Florida knew that now, and the likelihood of Luther being taken alive was greatly reduced. Any good cop who had a shot at a criminal who had already gunned down one of their own would take that shot if the situation allowed it. The endless ringing of phones and the frantic bustle of cops outside his office door annoyed Kratch. He wanted a few moments to think, so he shut the door. If at all possible, he wanted to be on the scene when Zorn was pinned down.

Kratch looked at the phone, trying to figure out whom to call next. It rang suddenly. It was the desk sergeant.

"There's a man named Cody Grey here to see you," the sergeant said, and then in a lower tone continued. "Says you'll want to talk to him. I guess that woman killed at the hotel was his wife . . ."

"Send him up."

Kratch had no idea what to expect. Normally, the last thing he wanted to deal with was a raging husband bent on finding his wife's killer. But right now one more free-floating radical might just improve the chances of Zorn's being gunned down. That was his ultimate goal.

Cody rapped on Kratch's door.

"Come in," Kratch said, not bothering to get up.

Cody stepped into the office and shut the door behind him.

"I'm Cody Grey."

"Yes," Kratch said, chain-lighting another Camel before stubbing the butt of the first one out in his mountain of ash, "I know who you are. What do you want?"

Cody was taken aback by the rude cop. He wasn't expecting the sympathetic comfortings of a priest, but he wasn't expecting this either.

"I want to know where Luther Zorn is," Cody said, gritting his teeth the instant the words passed his lips.

Kratch looked at him and shrugged. "If I knew that, I sure as hell wouldn't be sitting here."

Kratch leaned over and slid open the lower drawer on the side of his desk. Without a word he took out a hand-held radio and put it down on the edge of his desk. Cody looked from it to the detective.

"What?" Cody said, baffled.

"That's a police radio," Kratch said as if he was instructing a teenager on how to tie a fly. "What you want to do is take that and keep it on channel two. Luther Zorn won't get far. I don't know what you've got in mind, and I don't want to know. If anyone asks me, you took that radio when my back was turned. You have no right and no authority to interfere with the lawful apprehension and arrest of Luther Zorn, but I can tell you this: when it all goes down, it's going down big. This fucker shot two cops, and when we find him, there'll be so many people around that no one will know who's who. I don't know, you might get a chance . . ."

Cody looked at him carefully. "Why are you doing this?"

Kratch's good eye stared right back at him. "Mister, I don't know you, and I don't care to. But that's got nothing to do with any of this. I know I'm a police officer, but this Luther Zorn is a sick son of a bitch. He's an animal. If someone raped my wife and did what that fucking animal did to her . . . I'd kill him without a doubt . . . I really couldn't blame you for doing the same."

Kratch could see the pain and the anger churning in the eyes of the man before him. It was a volatile mixture of toxic waste and poison. The rape was a lie, but Kratch knew it was an effective one. He doubted Cody Grey could pull off anything that would really help him, but it was certainly worth having another person out there with the same murderous intentions as Kratch. Kratch knew well enough that you didn't tear up a free lottery ticket. Sure, you probably wouldn't win with it, but you never knew until the game was up. It never hurt just to wait and see.

Kratch scribbled the name of the coroner and some simple directions to the morgue. He tore the instructions off the top of his pad and pushed them across the desk to Cody.

"I'm sorry to have to ask you to do this," Kratch said, not sorry at all, "but we need you to identify your wife, Mr. Grey. I'm not going to lie to you. Luther Zorn decapitated her, and he appears to have taken whatever purse or wallet she carries with her as well, so we'll need you to identify the body."

Cody pursed his lips and his face twisted involuntarily. He took the note and, without another word, he left Kratch to his investigation. Kratch watched him go with his good eye, and when the door shut he said to no one but himself, "This crazy bastard might be just what the doctor ordered."

Chapter 43

Chris had no luck trying to reach Cody, and the Palm Beach Sheriff's Department wasn't helping him with information of any kind whatsoever. No one seemed to know exactly what had happened at the Walk Inn, or if they did, they were so concerned with having two officers down that they weren't bothering to talk with an out-of-town lawyer pumping them for information. Instead of sitting alone in his hotel room, Chris decided to go retrieve the recording device tapped into Pallidan's home phone.

After making sure he wasn't being followed, Chris stopped off at a uniform supply store in a run-down Kmart shopping center. There he purchased a gray repairman's uniform with a matching gray cap. It was probably unnecessary, but since it only took him an extra fifteen minutes, he figured it was worth reducing the likelihood that any neighbors would call the police if they saw him emerging from the bushes in Pallidan's side lawn in broad daylight.

Chris rode into the exclusive neighborhood warily eyeing each house for signs of life. Except for an old woman walking her dog at the far end of the street, there was no one. Chris pulled up in front of the house just beyond Pallidan's and removed his briefcase from the front seat. He marched right up the lawn as if he had every right in the world to be there. He correctly suspected that any security people Pallidan had would be with him at the Ibex offices.

Seven minutes later, Chris got back into his car and drove off without a hitch. As he drove along he was able to use his free hand to fit the wire of a small earpiece into the recording device and switch it on. He rewound the tape to the beginning. It clicked off automatically after only a few brief spins. Chris cursed under his breath. If he had spooked Pallidan in any way, it certainly hadn't spawned an excessive amount of phone calls to the outside world. He pushed the play button.

The distinct sound of digital numbers being punched into the phone rang out in his ear. Later, he could feed those tones into his computer and have it interpret the actual numbers being dialed. The phone began to ring. What followed was only a series of more touch tones as Pallidan contacted someone using what Chris presumed was a paging service. There was a brief pause in the tape before Chris heard ringing. It was an incoming call, and Pallidan picked it up on the first ring.

"Hello."

"This is the panther."

"This is the wolf," said Pallidan. "I have a job for your boy."

"I think we're at the end of the line with him. I think you need to find another guy." The incoming voice was obviously perturbed.

Pallidan was silent for a moment, then he spoke. "I didn't ask you what you think. I want him up here. The Mexican is here, and he's not going away. I want him out of the game. I want your boy up here right away."

The voice sighed. "He did the same thing to the lawyer. He took her head."

"I don't care if he eats their eyeballs! I want him here and I want this Mexican taken out. You said he'd stay out of this once she was gone. He came to my house for God's sake!"

"Your house?"

"My house!"

"Shit."

"Take care of it," Pallidan said. "We're very close."

"I hear you."

The line went dead and the tape ended. Pallidan had made one call only, and it was to have Chris killed. Chris looked around nervously, wondering if Luther Zorn wasn't already on his way to Memphis. It was hard to believe that whoever these people were, they controlled Luther Zorn to such an extent that they could send him from state to state like a contracted hit man. In fact, it made no sense at all to Chris. That wasn't the profile. Luther was supposed to be a crazed killer, not the kind of hired gun these two men were talking about.

He wondered about the man who called himself the panther. It was a voice he'd heard before, but whose? Chris replayed the message. It was Martin Wilburn. He drove back to his hotel and flipped on CNN as he dialed the number of the Palm Beach County Sheriff's Department. He asked for someone who could tell him about the shooting incident at the Walk Inn. While he was on hold, the double line beeped in his ear. He switched over and was relieved to hear Madison's voice.

"What happened?" he exclaimed.

"I'm fine," she said. "Have you gotten in touch with Cody?"

"Not yet. I can't reach him."

"Jo-Jo?"

"No."

"Chris, please," she said. "You've got to find them and let them know I'm all right."

"I will. I will."

Madison then briefly described the story Luther had told her. Then she explained that Luther had dropped her off to get a rental car before returning to his nearby hiding place.

"We're coming to Memphis," she said. "I want you to use your police contacts to find me a doctor somewhere between here and there so we can stop and get Luther patched up. He's been shot, and I don't want to risk having Kratch get a line on us by stopping for a doctor anywhere in Florida."

"Madison, wait a minute," Chris said, "why are you coming to Memphis?"

"Luther wants to find his brother. The answer is—"

"I know how to find his brother," Chris interrupted excitedly. It made sense now. "It's Wilburn. He's the one. I tapped Pallidan's phone. He pages Wilburn and gives him instructions. Wilburn is the one who has been directing Luther's brother."

Madison paused to digest that information.

"It was Wilburn," she said to herself out loud. "How does Kratch fit into this?"

"If Kratch's man really did just start shooting at Luther at the Walk Inn," Chris said, "then it sounds like Kratch fits right into the middle of it. You need to stay away from him, Madison. If he's in deep, he'll shoot Luther and you if he gets the chance. There's nothing as desperate as a dirty cop. Nothing. Cops know what happens to them in jail. Kratch will kill everyone before he takes a chance of that happening, I promise you. We need to call the FBI. This thing is interstate, it's in their jurisdiction, they can neutralize Kratch."

"I don't want you to do that yet," Madison said.

"Madison—"

"What if Wilburn has already gotten to Luther's brother? What if Luther won't talk to the FBI? Then both you and I have death warrants out on our heads with a very dangerous, very capable killer. We need Luther to get to his brother before his brother gets to you, or me."

"He can't get to us if we're protected," Chris said, but his words faltered. Even from the short version of Leeland Zorn's story and the brief history that Chris was already aware of suggested that, in fact, he could get to them, any time, any place. A heat-seeking missile was the right analogy. Luther's brother was a heartless killer.

"How are you going to get Wilburn to tell you where the brother is?" Chris asked.

"I'll leave that to Luther," Madison said.

Chris started to remind her that she could be considered an accessory to whatever crimes Luther Zorn might be about to commit, but then he remembered whom it was he was talking to. Madison had probably forgotten more rules of that game than he had ever learned.

"If he won't talk," Chris said, "I want you to call the FBI right away."

"I promise. And you get out of wherever you are. Don't make it easy for him to find you if he's already on his way. Let me know where you are by leaving it on my machine at home, and, please, find Cody and Jo-Jo."

"I will."

"Thank you, Chris."

"Madison?"

"Yes?"

"Be careful."

"It's too late for that."

*   *   *

Leeland held Julie Tarracola's head between his knees and carefully extracted her teeth with a pair of battered gray pliers he'd taken from the tool chest in his boat. From the water, he appeared to be nothing more than a local fisherman gutting out his catch with practiced care. The boat itself was hidden in a nearby labyrinth of mangroves. For his own part, Leeland sat on a fallen tree at the water's edge where a swampy river opened with final relief into the gaping Okeechobee. After the cabin incident, Leeland had moved to the almost entirely uninhabited western shore where the demarcation between swamp and river and lake was sometimes uncertain.

He had found a high spot one hundred paces in from the shore among a cluster of banyan trees, and that was where he pitched his tent. After the tiny sucking pop each tooth made as it was removed, Leeland took care to pitch it into the mouth of the roiling muddy river before returning to his trophy. It was probably an unnecessary precaution, removing the teeth of his latest victim, but thoroughness was part of his training as an elite soldier and, since the Gulf, little details stuck to his conscious mind, building up like plaque on the inside of an artery, until their importance was undeniable.

When the teeth were removed, Leeland took the head and carried it into the undergrowth. Within twenty minutes it was securely mounted on a post that rose about fifteen feet above the small clearing that was his new home. He gazed appreciatively at his handiwork. His smile drooped when he heard the muted staccato cry of his electronic beeper. The proximity to the last call he'd gotten told him right away that something was wrong. After his first mission to reconnoiter Chase's swimming area, he hadn't received a page for months. And, although his most recent assignments had come in a matter of weeks, never had he been paged twice within a matter of hours.

He threw himself down inside his tent and rolled over on a small cot while he fished through a backpack for his beeper. He found it and held it out in front of his face to read the numbers that had been entered into it from some unknown place on the planet. He committed the numbers to memory and cleared the device. He'd have to turn right around now and go back to Canal Point on the other side of the lake.

Leeland closed his eyes. He hadn't slept in more than thirty-five hours. He decided to nap for twenty minutes before he made the call. As he drifted off into sleep, images of incredible violence filled his mind. He saw his men and others being hacked and twisted. He saw himself in a carnival of blood. The visions didn't disturb him in the least. He was quite used to them by now, and he knew that if he simply watched on, his mind's projector would stop and he would be left alone, and in relative peace, in the black void of sleep.

Chapter 44

Martin Wilburn stood alone in the middle of his living room. He watched the clouds beyond the skyline of the city. They were high horsetails, advancing at a visible rate. A storm had been forecast. He finished giving instructions to Leeland Zorn and then hung up the phone. He knew the whole thing was unraveling. Still, there was time to stop his deal from falling completely apart. If Leeland could eliminate the troublesome Mexican, then there should be no more obstacles.

Of course there was still Luther, but that was Kratch's job now. And as much as Wilburn disliked the unsavory cop, he was admittedly effective. Wilburn was confident that if Luther survived, he would be convicted of murder. All of them, Wilburn especially, had worked hard to see to that.

Crawford had warned him about framing Luther, about getting emotional. He told Wilburn months ago that it was unnecessary, but Wilburn hadn't been able to resist.

It was so simple for him to use the same code that Vivian had been using to lure Luther to their various rendezvous, thereby placing him right at the murder scene. Not only had it been easy to set Luther up, it made complete sense to Wilburn. It threw the police off the trail of everyone but Luther Zorn. And made sense emotionally as well. Luther Zorn deserved to be put in his place. He was much too full of self-importance for a poor ghetto kid who hadn't even finished college.

Wilburn strolled out onto the deck that overlooked the choppy aqua-green water of the Intracoastal Waterway. A long red cigarette boat crept by pounding the serenity with its Glass-pak mufflers. The noise and the distracting sight prevented Wilburn from hearing Luther Zorn kick open the inside door to his condo. Luther crossed the wide living room, dodging the squat handcrafted pieces of furniture as if they were fallen men on the football field. By the time Wilburn sensed his presence, Luther was on him and clubbing him in the back of the head until he fell to the floor.

Wilburn's cries were drowned out by the throbbing sound of the big engine beneath them. Luther dragged the team owner back inside the condo, sliding the glass door shut with his foot. He placed his knee squarely on Wilburn's spine. Wilburn twisted his face and winced in pain. Luther pinned his head sideways, with his palm pressed flat and hard against Wilburn's ear. He jammed the gun into the side of his nose and leveled the barrel off so that if he pulled the trigger, Wilburn's brains would be sprayed for twenty feet over the thick Berber carpet.

"You crazy bastard!" Wilburn protested. The eye that wasn't squeezed into the carpet rolled in total fear between the gun and the outer limits of his vision where he could just make out the edges of Luther's face.

Luther jammed the gun harder into his nose. "Tell me where my brother is," he commanded.

"You're crazy," Wilburn said, his voice rising and breaking, blood spilling in a small but steady stream now from his nose. "I don't know what you're talking about! You're crazy!"

"You're right," Luther said, pushing the end of the gun into Wilburn's nose until he whimpered in pain. "I am crazy! We're both crazy, aren't we? That's what this is about, you piece of shit . . . you . . . you . . ."

Luther started to shake with rage. His voice broke abruptly in a high-pitched animal noise. Tears were in his eyes as if he was about to cry. He cocked the hammer of his Beretta. The metallic clank of the weapon had the clarity of a heavy tool dropped on a steel surface.

"No!" Wilburn shrieked, desperately closing the eye Luther could see against the noise of the explosion and his own death. "I'll tell you! I'll tell!"

"Tell me then!" Luther raged.

"I don't know where he is," Wilburn whined, "but you can call him. You have to page him with a sky-page. He'll call back. That's how I get in touch with him. I don't know where he is!"

"Give me the number," Luther demanded, thrusting again with the Beretta.

Wilburn recited the number. Luther kept the gun on his face, using his free hand to undo his own belt. He removed a roll of duct tape he'd hastily secured there.

"Put your hands behind your back," Luther commanded, lifting his weight off Wilburn's quivering body. He set the Beretta down and sloppily wrapped the owner's wrists until his hands were bundled in a ball of silvery tape. He then began wrapping Wilburn's ankles, working his way up past the knees and securing the hands to the legs. Then he used a length of the wide, sticky tape to cover Martin's mouth.

Luther picked up the gun and moved toward the phone that rested on an end table. There was a pad of paper there, and he wrote down the number Wilburn had given him. He dialed the pager and then hung up to wait for the callback.

He wasn't at all surprised to find enough Percocet in Wilburn's bathroom to ease the pain of his throbbing gunshot wound. The team doctors, he knew, dispensed medicine liberally to everyone within the organization, not just the players. Percocet, an opium derivative, was as strong as anything you could get anywhere. Luther washed two of them down with some tap water, then made his way back to the living room. He untucked the bulky new shirt Madison had purchased for him at a nearby Marshalls before sitting down on the couch to wait. Wilburn watched him warily from the floor. Luther raised his pistol and sighted down the barrel of the gun. Wilburn's eyes snapped closed and he turned his head away as fast as he could.

It was easy for Leeland Zorn to remain inconspicuous in Canal Point. The black population, supported by the enormous sugar mill nearby, was big enough so that he could move through the town unnoticed. It was also not unusual for blacks from the Palm Beach area to bring their battered old boats up the canal to spend a day fishing out on the lake.

Leeland had plunked himself down at the counter of a side-street diner and ordered a cheeseburger with fries when the pager went off again. The waitress, a dark three-hundred-pound woman in a bright lime-green dress, looked accusingly at him over her shoulder and clucked her tongue. Leeland pulled the beeper from his backpack and quickly shut it off. He looked and saw that it was again the man who called himself the panther. Leeland snickered. He'd like to meet this panther some day. He'd show him a panther.

"Be right back," he said to the waitress as he rose from his seat.

"I don't want to eat no cheeseburger of yours!" the waitress barked with an angry scowl. "You better be back!"

Two wrinkled old men in a tattered booth looked up momentarily from behind their menus. Leeland turned and stared until the big woman averted her eyes and began flipping through her pad as if she were looking for something important. He made his way outside toward the pay phone on the edge of the dusty parking lot. He loaded a stack of quarters into the machine and made the call.

"Hello?"

Leeland looked off into space when he heard the voice. He felt suddenly small, acutely aware of the size of the sky around him and the universe beyond that. He felt swallowed by a time warp.

"Hello?"

"Luther?"

"Leeland . . . where are you, man?"

Chapter 45

Leeland would meet Luther at his camp. Even though he trusted Luther, he insisted that his older brother might be followed. The location of the campsite would assure that no intruders would arrive unnoticed. Luther began to argue, but then he stopped. He wrote the directions on the pad, tore off the top sheet, and jammed it into the front pocket of his pants. He checked around the room, looking for anything he might have missed, anything that could possibly help Wilburn to escape. There was nothing, so he turned and left, pulling the door shut behind him. Luther had broken both locks and splintered the interior molding on his way in, so the best he could do was to leave it only slightly ajar.

"Did he tell you?" Madison asked anxiously as he slid into the front seat of their rented light blue Town Car. She had waited for him there. She didn't want to know what it was he was doing inside.

Luther nodded. "Yeah. I got ahold of Leeland. He's meeting us out on the far side of Lake Okeechobee." Suddenly he hit the dashboard in front of him with his fist. "Damn, we need a boat. What the hell. He just rattled off the directions like it was no problem. I didn't even ask him how we were supposed to get across the water."

"I think I know someone who might be able to help us," Madison said as she started the car and pulled away from the curb.

"Who?"

"It's the sheriff there—"

"No way!" Luther protested. "We're not bringing in the law. That's not happening."

"I think we can trust this guy," Madison said. "He's a small-town guy. I'm just saying, if we need a boat . . ."

Luther looked at her and shook his head.

"We need it . . ."

They drove toward the lake through the residential developments of West Palm. As they left the last gas stations and fast-food stops behind, the sky opened up around them like the view from a wide-angle lens. Sugarcane fields and swamp stretched to the horizon. High-tension wires hung suspended from towers that straddled the landscape like columns of giant metal soldiers. Before long, the mill appeared on the horizon, a black hulk belching smoke and unseen poison into the water.

Luther leaned back and let the Percocet and the slap of the tires against the ridges in the pavement lull him to sleep. Madison looked over at the profile of his handsome face. He hadn't said two words about the pain of his wound. Knowing what she knew about the kind of men who made their living playing football, it didn't surprise her. In her mind she reviewed her own goals: to stop the killing, to exonerate Luther, and, if she could, to convince Luther to persuade his brother to give himself up peacefully. The man belonged in an institution. She was certain that with the right representation, Leeland could be cared for and possibly even rehabilitated. The first priority, though, was to defuse, as Luther had put it, the heat-seeking missile that was hunting for her and Chris Pelo.

Cody Grey clenched his teeth as the stainless-steel drawer rolled open.

"I'm very sorry, Mr. Grey," the coroner said in a quiet, gentle voice.

Her body lay there, covered with a sheet. The pungent smell of formaldehyde filled Cody's nasal cavity, sickening him further. He swallowed bile and fought to control his heaving insides. The blood left his face. The coroner lifted the bottom edge of the sheet and slowly pulled it upward.

It was a magic moment for Cody Grey. A strange form of life burst inside him, laced with hope, anger, and fear.

"That's not her," he heard himself say.

"What?" the coroner said, lifting the sheet all the way above the corpse's blue-pink breasts and blinking at Cody through thick bifocal lenses. "Mr. Grey?"

"That's not Madison. That's not my wife," Cody said. The bloom inside him was beginning to fade. If the woman in front of him wasn't Madison, where was she?

Antone wore a bright purple suit and lots of gold jewelry. He stepped out of his red Lexus and handed the keys to a sorry-looking white kid with pimples and long, crooked teeth.

"Make sure you leave plenty of space on either side," Antone commanded imperiously, spitting out the word *space* and slipping the kid five dollars.

Inside the restaurant, Antone approached a table where three men sat talking. There was one empty seat, and Antone took it. The men paid no attention to him. It was disconcerting, even to a character as apparently cool as Antone.

He ordered an iced tea with lemon and stirred in two packets of sugar. Finally, the smallest of the three looked up at him.

"You're late," he said flatly.

Antone flashed his biggest smile and shrugged.

"Traffic," he said.

"Where's the money, Antone?" another asked.

"Yeah," said the first.

"Well, now, that's what we got to talk about," Antone said, gesticulating dramatically with his hands and fingers as he spoke.

The small man followed the acrobatic movements of Antone's fingers, as if something interesting might come from them.

"Talk."

"What I need from you brothers is some more time," Antone said glibly. "It takes time to build a network, and that's what I'm building for you. A man can't build a network overnight, and I got to use product to lure people in. That's where it's at. I'm building a network. What I need is time and some more smack. That's what I need . . ."

The three of them stared at Antone in disbelief.

"You want more?"

Antone nodded. "I'm building a network."

"You said that. You've been saying that. I don't want no motherfucking network, punk," the little man said, narrowing his eyes and lowering his voice. "I want my money, and I want it now."

Antone feigned confusion, "Hey, blood. I thought we were partners. I thought we were in this for the long term."

"*We* are," the small man said, nodding at his two companions. "We're the ones taking the heat from the fucking

Colombians and the Jamaicans. We're the ones putting up the money and the blow. You were the guy who was going to open up the Marauders to us for some clientele and a spot to clean up some of our money. *We* haven't seen shit so far from *you*, and now *we* want our money. *Today.*"

Antone tried to smile, but he felt as though he'd taken an arrow in the throat. A nerve in his eyelid began to twitch. These were not good people. They would kill him. He knew that. He wanted to reason with them, keep things going a little longer.

The fact was that Antone had been so busy being a big shot with the drugs they'd given him that he hadn't really taken the time or the care to establish himself as a supplier. He thought it would be easy. He thought his buddies would come to him, but the fact was that most of the guys on his team, while they'd gladly accept some free blow on occasion, were not the kind of guys to develop habits. Now he needed money that he didn't have. He wasn't going to bullshit these guys. He knew how they'd react to that, and while Antone was cocky and obnoxious and ballsy, he wasn't stupid. He had reached the point with these people where they were apt to kill him if he looked at them wrong.

"I'll get the money," Antone said confidently. "Hey, Ramone, I'm sorry man. I am. I thought it could work out. I thought I could get something going, you know. I know I can help you clean some money. That's one thing I know I can help with."

Ramone stared at him coldly. "You get us our money back, and we'll talk about it. Meantime, we got business to attend to."

"Sure, blood," Antone said, raising the glass of tea halfway to his face before setting it back down amid the slight tinkle of rattling ice cubes. "Sure."

"Today, Antone. I'm not telling you again."

Antone got up to leave, and he left fast, afraid that a bullet might find the back of his head. He checked his rearview mirror for several blocks before he felt relatively certain that he wasn't being followed. There was only one place Antone could go for the money he needed. The good news was that, as dire as his circumstances were, he felt pretty good about his ability to get his hands on some quick cash.

He called the Marauders facility from his car phone and learned that Martin Wilburn was not in the office. He swung left at the next intersection and headed back toward the water. In ten minutes he was looking at the broken door of the owner's condo. He looked around, then let himself in quietly.

"Shit," he said.

Wilburn looked up in wide-eyed panic. Blood trickled from his nose across his cheek and into his ear. When he saw it was Antone, he went berserk. Antone struggled to get the tape off his head. Finally, he went to the kitchen and found a steak knife. As he cut the owner loose, he tried to think of what might have happened. He hoped it was something really bad. The bigger the favor he'd done by arriving to save the day, the more likely it would be for him to get his money. He cringed when he jabbed into Wilburn's wrist, spilling blood onto the carpet. Wilburn didn't even seem to notice.

"Hurry up!" he barked.

Antone freed Wilburn's hands.

"Get me the phone," Wilburn commanded.

Wilburn dialed the phone, sitting on his living room floor, while Antone cut furiously at the bands of tape around his feet and legs.

"Lieutenant Kratch," Wilburn said, then waited.

"Kratch," came the lieutenant's voice.

"It's me, Wilburn."

"You're not supposed to call me, dammit. We've got channels that—"

"Luther Zorn just left my house."

"Zorn?"

"He tied me up. He made me give him the pager number and he spoke to the brother."

"Jesus."

"He's going to meet him," Wilburn said. "You'd better get there. Quick."

"Where?"

Wilburn hesitated only briefly.

"Get me that pad, Antone," he said.

Antone looked up as if he hadn't been listening.

"Huh?"

"That pad over there on the table," Wilburn ordered, his wrapped legs preventing him from getting it himself, "get it!"

Antone brought him the pad, and Wilburn held it up in the afternoon light that shone through the big bay windows in a way that enabled him to see the imprint left from Luther's writing on the page above. He read the instructions that Luther had received from his brother.

"I'll need a fucking compass," Kratch said, more to himself than anyone. "Okay, good, anything else?"

"No. He's got a gun."

"I know that," Kratch said. "He shot both my men."

"Is this going to work?" Wilburn wanted to know.

Kratch had already hung up the phone. Wilburn didn't care. He wanted Kratch to get to Luther before Luther got to the brother. If he didn't, things were going to get ugly.

"I gotta ask you something incredibly important, Mr. Wilburn," Antone said suddenly, out of nowhere.

Wilburn looked up. He'd forgotten he wasn't alone.

Chapter 46

Cody called home from the coroner's office. There was no answer. He called his friend and assistant coach Jimmy Spence, who had Jo-Jo at his house.

"Madison's alive," Spence told him before he could say a word.

"How did you know?" Cody asked, dumbfounded.

"Chris Pelo called. He's been trying to reach you. He talked to Madison. She's—"

"She's all right?" Cody demanded.

"Yeah, Cody. She's okay. She's—I guess she's with the guy they thought killed her, Luther Zorn."

"Zorn?" Cody said, out loud. "Zorn?"

"Do you have a number for Chris?" Cody asked.

"No," Spence said. "He didn't say where he was and he asked me not to say anything to anyone but you about Madison."

"Jimmy, thanks. Let me talk to Jo-Jo," Cody said.

Jo-Jo got on the line. Cody told him his mom was alive and that he'd find her. The boy was in tears, more from confusion than anything. Cody talked to him for a few minutes until he calmed down.

"I'll find her, Jo-Jo. I'll find her."

Next, Cody called Madison's office. When he asked Madison's secretary if she'd heard from Madison, the secretary acted as if she was talking to a madman.

"She's alive," Cody told her. "Where's Chris Pelo?"

He got Pelo's number in Memphis and abruptly hung up on the secretary. He called the hotel, but Pelo had checked out. Cody set the phone down. He looked around the small windowless office. A skeleton hung in one corner, and an old pair of sneakers sat by the heat vent on the floor.

"Kratch," he said suddenly to himself.

"Thanks," Cody said as he bolted past the coroner who was standing outside the office.

Cody made his way to the parking lot and jumped into his rental car. He started toward the sheriff's office, then realized he was going the wrong way. He spun around at the next light. Tires and brakes howled as two cars turning into the intersection veered to avoid an accident. Cody punched his accelerator, leaving blaring horns in his wake.

As he wheeled into the sheriff's parking lot, he almost hit Kratch head-on.

"Kratch!" Cody heard himself yell, trying to will Kratch into making eye contact.

The detective's face was intense. Cody could see his scowl through the reflected light of the windshield. Kratch niftily avoided Cody without even slowing down and pulled out into the traffic with his tires squealing. Cody slammed his own car around, banging the undercarriage on the curb as he went up and over it. He barely noticed the impact. He did not want to lose sight of Kratch.

The detective's dark blue Crown Vic turned onto Southern Boulevard and headed west. Cody lost sight of Kratch at the turn. He ran a red light with his horn blaring and veered through traffic, cutting someone off to make the turn onto Southern. Kratch's car was already out of sight. Cody hit the accelerator. The road was straight and flat. Cody could see the next four lights in a row. They were all green. The fourth one turned red. Cody pressed on. Suddenly, a red flashing light jumped out at him from the traffic ahead.

It was Kratch, using his car light to get through the red. The third light changed. Cody jumped onto the median to get around the stopped traffic. Angry horns blared. He forced his way out into the intersection. His heart pumped in his chest like a sledgehammer. Cars shrieked and skidded; two collided, with the smash of large cymbals. Glass exploded. Steam hissed. Cody moved through the chaos untouched and punched the accelerator again once he got to the other side. The fourth light changed back to red again by the time Cody got there. He flashed his headlights and leaned on his horn, forcing people out of his way. By the time he hit open road, he could just make out the form of Kratch's dark blue sedan in the distance. The car's light was off now as it raced westward through the verdant cane fields and swampland. Cody bumped it up to ninety and still he couldn't close the gap.

He saw it coming. He leaned on his horn and flashed his high beams. It was no use. A slow-moving dump truck suddenly pulled out from a side road. Another car was coming in the opposite direction so he couldn't pass the truck. Cody locked up the brakes and closed his eyes. The car seemed to lift up off the pavement and float. The front of the rental car smashed into the back of the truck and crumpled like an accordion.

Madison pulled into a parking space directly in front of the sheriff's office.

"I don't like waiting in the car," Luther grumbled.

"It's best," she told him. "I'll be out in five minutes. If he can't keep the whole thing quiet, we'll find another way, but believe me, if we can get his help, we'll get to your brother a lot sooner and a lot easier. Where else are we going to get a boat?"

Madison didn't tell him that she was also counting on the sheriff for a certain amount of protection should Leeland lose control.

Inside, Mira, the secretary, looked up from a paperback novel and pushed the cat's-eye glasses up on her nose.

"I'm Madison McCall," Madison reminded the woman. She didn't look the sort to have remembered.

"Sheriff's out," Mira said, bored. It was evident that she hadn't heard the news that Madison had reportedly been killed, either that or she didn't much care.

"Is there any way we can get in touch with him?" Madison asked. "It's important."

Mira rolled her eyes before picking up the old rotary phone. "I'll call him.

"Yeah, it's Mira," she said into the phone, "is the sheriff there? Well, tell him he's got someone here to see him," she said impatiently, "it's official business, I guess. Okay, thanks."

Mira handed the phone to Madison.

"Hello?"

"Emmit, this is Madison McCall."

"Huh?"

"It's Madison McCall, I'm Luther Zorn's attorney—"

"Yeah, I know," Emmit said. "You're in my office?"

"Yes, I need to see you right away. I need some help."

"I thought, I mean, I heard on the news—"

"Yes," Madison said, "I know. I'm alive, though."

At this Mira rolled her eyes twice. Madison turned her back.

"Can I meet you somewhere?" she asked.

"Yeah, well, I'm right across the street," Emmit said. "Come on over."

Madison walked into the diner. Every person, except an old fisherman at the counter, turned to stare. Emmit rose like a telephone pole from his booth in the back and stepped out into the aisle with an embarrassed smile. His cheeks turned pink as all eyes went from Madison to him. It was a small town, and he knew his wife would hear about this before he got home.

"Hello," he whispered in a low conspiratorial tone that made Madison glance around. She wondered why, if he was so uncomfortable, he hadn't simply met her outside.

They slid into the booth, and she leaned across the table toward him, bumping her forearm into the pewter stand that held the large but nearly empty glass of a chocolate malt. A young bucktoothed waitress hovered.

"Nothing for me, thank you," Madison said, dismissing her.

When the girl was out of earshot, Madison leaned forward and explained the situation as simply as she could. She wanted Emmit's word that he wouldn't call in any other law enforcement people before she told him what she needed.

"So you're saying you're in a pinch?" Emmit said. He felt like a drunk on his tenth drink. It was too late to go back. Everyone around him would be talking, he knew, but he couldn't take his eyes off Madison McCall. People would talk regardless, so he simply enjoyed the thrill, a woman of her caliber asking him for help, the chivalrous knight.

"I am."

"All right," Emmit told her. "I think you should try to convince this guy to turn himself in and you definitely need me with you. I don't have to tell you how dangerous he is. But, yes, whatever it is you need from me, I'll do, so long as it isn't illegal."

"I need a boat," Madison said.

"A boat?" Emmit raised his eyebrows to the upper edges of his pie-shaped face.

"Yes, Luther's brother is camped out on the west shore of the lake. The only way there is by boat. Can you help?"

"I've got a boat," Emmit said.

"Can we go now?" Madison asked.

"Yes," Emmit said, getting up abruptly. He flipped a ten onto the table and fumbled for his hat. Instinctively, he also felt for his gun, patted it gently, then left it alone. He strode out of the diner, ducking his head and blushing as if to give silent apology to the patrons who knew him and suspected he was up to no good.

Madison and Luther followed Emmit in their car to his house. They waited for him parked in the stone and oil street. He had a sixteen-foot tri-hull with mottled olive-green seats in its open bow and a ninety-horse Mercury outboard strapped to its stern. Emmit hitched the trailer right up to his old Plymouth cruiser. The house was partially blocked by an old oak tree that wept Spanish moss, but Madison heard the screech of rusty springs as Emmit's wife barreled through the screen door and out onto the porch in a pink cotton maternity jumper.

"Emmit!" she shrieked. "What on God's green earth are you doing with that boat?"

Emmit stood in the driveway and pulled off his hat like a

kid caught in the act of shoplifting. He shifted nervously from foot to foot and puckered his lips before building up his resolve and answering her firmly with a single word: "Business." Then he plunked the hat back on his head and got into the Plymouth without another word. Madison started her car and fell in behind Emmit as he eased out of the driveway and down the street back toward the middle of town and the public boat launch. Emmit's wife, pregnant and irate, was too dumbfounded by the unusual happenings to speak. She simply stood there on the porch with her fists clenched, a disheveled strand of dark hair on her forehead, and her mouth hanging open.

Chapter 47

For some reason, the air bag hadn't deflated and Cody was pinned in his seat. The stink of the bag's explosive fumes made him gag. The shock of the impact made him wonder what the hell he thought he was doing, chasing a policeman across the state on the hunch that it had something to do with his wife. He felt blindly for his duffel bag on the passenger seat next to him. The impact had thrown it into the dash, but it rebounded right back into the seat, only upside down. Cody got it flipped over, and after struggling with the zipper, he pulled out the .357.

The driver of the truck, a haggard old black man, peered in through the cracked window. "You okay, son?" he asked.

"Get back!" Cody shouted as best he could into the bag.

The man stepped back and Cody aimed the gun, closed his eyes, and fired. The shot made the man outside jump. The bag deflated. Cody pulled it to one side and started the car. The engine caught. He threw it into reverse and backed away from the truck, which appeared to have sustained nothing more than a bent car-catcher, the metal bar that extended down from its rear bumper. Cody rolled down his window.

"You okay?" he asked the shocked truck driver.

The man nodded, too stunned to speak. Cody put his car into drive. It rattled and shook, but it went. He pulled around the truck and went as fast as the crumpled car would take him in the hopeless pursuit of Kratch.

The road turned bumpy and rough, making Cody's wobbling front end that much harder to control. Engine warning lights lit up the dashboard like a video game. Fortunately, it wasn't more than thirty minutes before the highway turned right into the main street of the small town called Canal Point. Cody's head swiveled from side to side, as he looked desperately for a sign of Kratch or his car. He came to a small intersection, Route 441 going north to the town of Okeechobee or south to Belle Glade. Cody stopped and looked both ways. He hated coin tosses.

It made more sense at least to take the main street to its end. It looked as if the water was right up ahead. Cody rolled through the intersection. The street rose up to the height of a big levee and ended finally at a public boat launch. There were a few vehicles there, mostly pickups and an old Plymouth police car, parked in the shade of some large oaks, each with an empty trailer behind it. Off to the right and halfway down the east edge of the bank, there was a little marina, built from faded barn board, that sat on a small cove where the canal and the lake met at the locks. There was a single gas pump on the side of the building that looked as if it could service both cars and boats. An old circular white Texaco sign, now faded yellow, swung in the wind from a bent and rusty pole. Outside the old gray building, amid more sun-faded pickups, sat Kratch's now dusty Crown Vic. Cody eased off the main road and down the bank into the dirt spot next to Kratch's car, then got out and made for the low shabby building.

Kratch almost ran him over on his way out of the marina.

"Hey," Kratch said in surprise. "What are you doing?"

In his hand he held a package that contained a compass he'd just purchased.

"I saw you come out of the station and I followed you," Cody said. "I tried to catch up."

Kratch's good eye assessed the battered front end of what he presumed was Cody's car. He shook his head in disbelief.

"What do you want?" Kratch said impatiently.

"I want to know what you're doing," Cody said. "I thought it had something to do with Madison, the way you came out of the station. We almost ran into each other. Madison's alive."

"What?" Kratch said, his genuine surprise as evident by his expression as by the tone of his voice. "What?" he said again.

"Madison," Cody told him excitedly, "that wasn't her in the morgue. I just came from there. She's alive. I think she's with Luther Zorn. That's who you're going after, isn't it?"

The wheels in Kratch's head spun so fast it made him nearly giddy.

"Yes," he said finally, "I know where he is."

"Then Madison must be there, too," Cody said. "I'm coming with you."

Kratch looked from Cody to the docks, where a teenage attendant was filling a rental boat with gas. Kratch took a pair of sunglasses from the inside pocket of his coat and put them on his face, hiding his wandering eye.

"Then come on," Kratch said before turning to make his way down a rickety set of stairs to the dock.

Cody raced back to his car and pulled the .357 from the front seat. He jammed the gun into his pants. Kratch was watching him from the dock below, but when Cody started to descend the stairs, Kratch turned his attention to the attendant, who was running through the operations of the battered old Boston Whaler. Kratch nodded to the kid and told him he'd rented before. He loosened his tie and took off his coat. The kid's eyes widened at the sight of Kratch's leather shoulder strap and the big Glock that rested under his arm.

"I don't know if you know it, mister," the kid said, tugging at a faded old John Deere hat that he wore backward, "but they're calling for a storm, so I wouldn't want to go too far if I was you. I don't know if Clive inside told you. Clive, he rented to a guy the day one of them hurricanes blew through, Andrew, I think. The guy was from Ohio, and, hell, they never found him. Clive didn't care . . . he's got insurance and all. It's supposed to be bad is what I'm saying . . ."

Kratch looked off to the west. The wind was stiff and something was brewing on the horizon, there was no doubt about that. The rest of the sky was clear though, except for the high ceiling of wispy clouds that did very little to fend off the glare of the sun.

"Thanks for the tip, kid," he said.

Kratch fired up the boat's engine without another word. When Cody stepped off the dock and onto the boat, Kratch barely gave him time to take a seat before he reversed out of the berth and slammed the boat forward toward the lock that would raise them up from the canal to the level of the lake.

Cody watched the murky water churning in the wake behind them. The kid stood next to the pump, watching them. Their boat idled into the cavernous lock, and Kratch tied up to one of the mooring lines that hung down from the concrete walls like stray threads.

The lock's twenty-foot steel doors swung slowly toward each other. Just before they closed completely, Cody glanced back again and saw that the kid was still standing there, only now he was pointing toward the western sky. Thunder rumbled in the distance.

Cody turned to see if the kid saw something new that he hadn't. Everything looked the same except for an angry crow that was perched on the highest peak of the dockmaster's shack cawing furiously at them all. Before Cody could turn back to see if that was where the kid had been pointing, he heard the dull gong of the heavy doors locking into place with the synchronization of the gears in an enormous clock chewing up time.

Chapter 48

The sun dipped suddenly behind the fast-moving front of dark clouds. The light became otherworldly. The air was heavy with the smell of the oncoming storm. The darkening sky rumbled discontentedly and lightning cast itself down from the gloom at irregular intervals. Madison set her jaw and pursed her lips. She whispered a silent prayer. The closer they got, the more she sensed the imminence of danger and the more she was convinced that something was about to go terribly wrong.

On the shore, Leeland stood erect in a pair of camouflage fatigues and an olive-green tank top. His size and musculature were not at all unlike Luther's. He had the three of them fixed in the sights of his binoculars. Emmit idled down, and Luther waved his hand in greeting. A broad smile lit Luther's face, but Madison could see the tense lines of worry at the corners of his mouth. The wind, strong all the way across the lake, began now to roar. Random flecks of rain spattered them along with small twigs and leaves. The boat rolled up onto the shore atop the crest of its own wake. Leeland caught the bow and lifted it, pulling the boat even farther ashore with almost inhuman strength. Luther hopped over the edge, splashing into the shallow water, and Madison started to climb out as well. Luther turned to help her.

Instead of coming to meet them, Leeland circled around the other side of the old boat until he was even with Emmit.

"Hi," Emmit said with an embarrassed smile.

"Hi," Leeland replied, as he pulled a Browning 9mm from the back of his pants and put a round through the sheriff's left eye. The back of Emmit's head exploded, and he fell to the floor of the boat in an unkempt heap of long limbs. It was as quick as it was unexpected, and the frozen expression on Emmit's dead and damaged face still registered the smile of his greeting.

Madison screamed, "Oh, my God!"

Luther clutched her to him instinctively.

"Jesus!" he moaned. "Leeland, what . . . what, man? Why? Put that gun down!"

Leeland rounded the front of the boat, leveling the gun at Madison as he did. His face registered nothing more than the pleasant smile of a man who was glad to see his long-lost brother.

"It's a trap, Luther," Leeland said matter-of-factly. "These people are working against you. She's in on it, man. Step back and let me do her."

Madison cringed and hid her head in between the bands of muscles in the middle of Luther's back.

"She's with me, Leeland!" Luther screamed. "Stop it, man! Stop it!"

"Luther, it's a trap, man. Move out of my way," Leeland

ordered. "They told me. They told me all about her, and that guy's a cop."

"I know he's a cop," Luther said in disbelief. "He was helping us, man. He gave us his boat. Oh, Jesus, Leeland, man, you killed him . . ."

"She's in on it," Leeland said, unfazed.

"She's not," Luther pleaded. "It's them. They're fucking us, man. They're trying to get me put in jail."

"It's her!" The brother pointed with the barrel of his gun, his face now locked in a scowl.

"It's not!"

Leeland fumbled with his free hand. From his front pants pocket he extracted a folded letter. He held it out as proof positive.

"It's right here, man," Leeland said. "You told me to follow these people. You told me I had to do what they said. You told me they were helping us both and I could *trust* them, man. *Trust* is a big word, big brother. *You* told me to trust them, and they told me to kill her!"

"Leeland," Luther said, dropping his voice, but filling it with passion. "It's me, man. It's Luther. Listen to me. I'm telling you, forget the letter. Listen to *me* now. *Listen!*"

Leeland looked at him.

"Well," he said, regaining his smile with a shrug and jamming the gun back into the waistband of his pants, "you can't be too sure about the cop anyway. You can never trust those people. I know, believe me. It's better this way. How the hell are you, brother?"

Leeland hugged Luther warmly. Madison stepped back a pace into the ankle-deep water and fought the urge to run.

Leeland looked at her over his brother's shoulder. Up close, Madison could easily tell from his eyes that Luther's younger brother was completely deranged.

"Sorry," he said, smiling at her. "It's Madison, right?"

Madison nodded. "Yes."

She was shaking and couldn't help herself from stealing an occasional glance at the figure of Emmit Stone lying in the bottom of the boat. She half expected him to get up and say it was all a joke.

"Okay," Leeland said, stepping back from his brother's embrace. "Who's who, and what's what? What do you need me to do now?"

"I think you should turn yourself in," Madison blurted out. "I can help you. You need help."

Leeland's eyes narrowed and he looked from Madison to his brother.

"This is what you call help?" he said.

Luther shot her a glance.

"She'll help," he said. "She's my lawyer. That's just what she thinks."

"It's what I know," Madison said firmly. "And now, I'm more than your lawyer, Luther, I'm an accessory to aiding and abetting a murder if I do anything but turn your brother in to the police. You'll be a defendant, too, Luther, and I can't defend you if you are.

"This," she said, pointing to Emmit's body, her voice quavering, "is something I've witnessed with my own eyes."

Luther looked at her as if she must be the one who was crazy. Leeland just smiled.

"A bold chick," Leeland said matter-of-factly. "So, what are we going to do? Should I kill her now?"

Luther came to life. "You've got to get out of here. I mean out of the country, Leeland. I've got you a ticket to Rio, and I've got a bag of cash back at my place."

"I've never been to your place," Leeland said. "Just tell me where it is, and where the cash and the ticket are, and leave the rest to me. If we're going to move, we've got to move out quick. When this weather hits we're not going to want to be out on the water."

"Can we beat it?" Luther asked, looking up into the dark sky, the wind whipping at his face.

Leeland looked up as well. A bolt of lightning lit a horizontal crack in the dark clouds to the west.

"We can if we move now and take my boat."

"What about the sheriff?" Luther asked.

Leeland shrugged. "Just leave him."

Luther turned to Madison. "If you can't help us, can you at least not hurt us?"

Madison looked at him for a moment, then said, "I'm not going to get myself killed, if that's what you mean."

"Good."

"Smart chick," Leeland said with a wink. "You two wait here. I'll break my camp and be back. My boat is around the bend up the mouth of this river."

"I'll come help you," Luther said.

"No," Leeland said, his eyes distant, "you wait here. There are things you don't want to see."

Luther frowned and tried not to imagine. He looked over to read the expression on Madison's face, and when he looked back his brother had disappeared into the jungle of overgrown trees.

"This is bad," Madison said flatly, staring again at Emmit's body, her brown hair twisting wildly in the wind. "This is very bad."

"There's nothing we can do," Luther said. "I can't let them take him, Madison."

"That's the right thing, Luther," Madison said, moving up past the bow of the boat onto the dry land.

"Do you think he'd let them take him alive?" Luther said angrily. "He won't. And he won't hesitate to kill either of us if we try to stop him, either. I hope you can see that!"

"Yes," Madison conceded, "I can."

For all her legal training, this was one situation for which she saw no solution whatsoever. Luther's eyes widened and Madison heard a rumbling that was not thunder.

"Oh shit," Luther said. Madison spun around. It was Kratch standing at the helm of a battered Boston Whaler humping up and down over the foamy chop. Beside him, with a gun in his hand and a look of hatred on his face, was Cody.

Chapter 49

At first, Kratch wasn't sure exactly how he was going to pull it off. He did know, however, the minute Cody Grey told him that his wife was still alive, that he was going to get a chance to win the whole pot. It wouldn't be easy, because if the brother was around, he'd probably kill Kratch before he could sneeze. That was okay. Kratch wasn't as uncomfortable with the notion of a quick death as he was with the notion of doing time in a state prison. They'd maul him in there, and then kill him anyway. If Kratch was going to go down, he'd go down shooting.

When he saw Luther and Madison on the beach, alone, it was almost more than he could have hoped for.

"Just keep calm," he told Cody over the drone of the engine and the howl of the wind. "Don't worry about anything I say or do. My whole purpose is to get him away from your wife, even if I have to take him out to do it."

Cody looked from the beach to the policeman. Kratch had taken off his sunglasses and replaced his suit coat. The gun was hidden, and his wandering eye made it impossible for Cody to judge the man's truthfulness.

"It's okay!" Kratch howled over the choppy waves at the two figures turned toward him on the beach. He held his hands open to show that he meant what he said. "I don't have a gun! Everything's okay. We just want to talk with Luther."

"Madison!" Cody called to her above the din of the oncoming storm.

"Cody!"

Her voice sounded small and pathetic. Cody grabbed the gunnel of the boat firmly to avoid being tossed into the water by the chop that had now become a rolling mess. Kratch drove the boat straight up onto the sandy shore about twenty paces from the sheriff's boat. The motor spit mud and water into the air behind them with a terrible scream until Kratch mercifully cut the power.

"Calm," Kratch said to Cody.

Cody jumped out of the boat, soaking his shoes and the bottoms of his pants. He held the .357 up in the air and churned toward his wife, never letting his eyes leave her fearful face. Luther Zorn filled his vision as well. Luther had instinctively raised his hands over his head. The Marauders player stood there, looking over his shoulder, frozen by an indecision that Cody prayed would last at least long enough for him to get to his wife. Cody's instincts still told him that Madison wouldn't be safe until he had placed himself physically between her and Zorn.

The sand beneath his feet kept giving way. Cody couldn't move fast enough. He saw Luther's Beretta stuck haphazardly into the waist of his pants. He reached Madison and grabbed her with his free arm, pulling her tight and burying his face in her hair and breathing deep.

"Madison," he choked, "my God."

"I'm all right," she said, touching the side of his face as if he was a small child. He drew back just far enough for her to look up into his eyes. Cody swore he heard the bullet zipping through flesh and bone before he heard the actual explosion from the gun. Madison's face suddenly ran red with blood and tissue. Without thinking, Cody yanked her to the ground, as if he could undo what had already been done.

Kratch let Cody get to his wife. Even Luther was distracted by their embrace, and Kratch pulled out his own weapon. He leveled the barrel at the center of Luther Zorn's back and pulled the trigger. The big gun kicked back. The bullet shattered Luther's spine and tore through his left lung, exiting with a splash of gore that covered Madison McCall's face. The big player was lifted to his toes by the impact of the bullet, but just as quickly dropped motionless to the ground.

Kratch advanced quickly. In the moments after a traumatic event, the man with the most wits about him held a tremendous advantage. Cody was on top of his wife, shielding her uselessly, his own gun forgotten in the sand. Kratch scanned the trees quickly as he moved, assuring himself that Luther's brother was not within range. Then his attention returned to Cody, whose head was still down, frozen in shock.

Kratch got to Luther's body and, after a brief struggle with the inert weight, was able to reach the Beretta and pull it free. He jumped up and stood with one foot on top of Cody's gun. Now the couple was completely defenseless. He had Luther's gun. With that gun, he could kill them both.

Kratch panted from his exertion and forced himself to rethink everything he was about to do. He had a moment, and he knew that a moment of forethought was always more valuable than years of hindsight. He wanted to make sure there was nothing he'd forgotten. He looked around and quickly composed the tale he would tell:

He'd say that the moment before they'd beached the boat, Cody jumped overboard and fled to the side of his wife, despite Kratch's warnings. Kratch stumbled and fell when the boat hit land. When he regained his feet, he jumped over the side and advanced toward the three of them on the beach. As Kratch approached, he realized that Zorn had his gun out. The player executed Madison McCall and her husband at close range with two quick shots before Kratch could draw his own gun from its holster and gun down the mad killer. Everyone was dead.

The problem Kratch saw immediately was the angle of the bullets. If he were to shoot Cody and Madison where they lay, the picture wouldn't fit. The forensic people would know that they had been shot as they lay helplessly on the ground. Kratch was too careful for that, and he smiled outwardly at his own cunning. A flash of lightning accentuated his demonic grin.

"Get up," he commanded.

Cody looked up, his eyes glazed. Madison was more alert, and she struggled beneath him.

"I said, get up!"

Madison got her arm free and wiped the bloody mess of tissue and gore from her face. She coughed and gagged at the taste of Luther Zorn's flesh in her mouth.

"Madison," Cody asked, "you're all right?"

"I'm all right."

"Now!" Kratch bellowed.

Both turned their eyes to him.

"What are you doing?" Cody said in disbelief. "Put your gun down."

"Get up before I put a bullet in your wife's head right

where she is," Kratch threatened, stepping back just beyond the fallen body of Luther Zorn.

They rose to their feet and Kratch let out an evil chuckle. The wind blew his hair off his face and his bad eye rolled maniacally in the flashing light.

"So smart, weren't you?" he said, raising his voice above the wind. "You and your enchilada partner, then your fuck-ing cowboy husband. You people deserve to die!"

"You're insane," Madison whispered. She felt the mus-cles in her husband's body tighten like the string of a bow being drawn taut. She knew he was going to do something, and it made her panic.

"They'll catch you," she said loudly. She wanted to keep Kratch talking. "You can't do this. Don't do this. They'll know it was you!"

Kratch raised the gun, pointing off into the sky for an in-stant to display it.

"I didn't kill you," he said with mock simplicity. "Luther Zorn did. This is his gun."

There was a sharp electric whine, and then the hollow splitting sound of an enormous coconut being cracked open with a single crushing blow from a heavy mallet. The spear from Leeland's gun pierced Kratch's skull; half of the gleaming metallic shaft protruded from the front of his head, half from the back side. It looked like a joke store prank, too comical to be real. Kratch looked dumbfounded. He tried to turn the gun back toward his victims, but only managed to shoot off one harmless round before staggering and falling dead at their feet.

Leeland's primal wail cut through the howling wind like an evil banshee.

"Noooooooo! Aaaawwwwwww!"

The sound sent a shiver down Madison's spine. Leeland burst from the trees and ran straight for the broken body of his brother. He bent over Luther and tore off his own shirt. Madison thought it was out of grief, but then she realized that Leeland was using the cloth to plug the bleeding holes in his brother's body, front and back. The rain suddenly came down in sheets.

"Luther, Luther, Luther, noooooo!" the insane man agonized as he held Luther's head in his hands and began kissing his face.

"My Luther, my Luther, my Luther . . ."

Then Leeland looked up, his eyes ablaze, rainwater dripping from his face. He looked straight at Cody and Madison.

"Kratch killed him," Cody yelled above the storm, as he instinctively pulled his wife closer.

"He's not dead!" Leeland insisted. "He's not dead yet. Help me!"

Cody picked up Luther's legs while Leeland effortlessly carried the bulk of his brother's body by hooking his hands underneath Luther's armpits.

"To the boat!" Leeland wailed.

Madison followed the two men across the muddy sand in the torrent of rain. They loaded Luther's body gently into the center of Emmit Stone's boat. Then Leeland climbed aboard and carelessly heaved the sheriff's body over the other side as if it were nothing more than useless flotsam.

"You!" he barked at Madison. "Get in here. Get on top of him. We need to keep him warm or he'll die from the shock."

Madison looked at her husband, whose face was set in a grim mask of anger. His hair was now plastered to the sides of his head. She was afraid he might do something crazy.

"Cody, it's all right," she said, calming him. "Maybe we can save Luther."

"If he dies," Leeland said to them in a pitched voice, "I'll kill you both. I'll find you, and I'll kill you."

Madison climbed in and lowered herself to the floor of the boat beside Luther. A bolt of lightning electrified the gloom and exploded with a deafening crack. Leeland found a tarp underneath one of the seats and threw it over them.

"Get him to a hospital," Leeland ordered as he climbed out of the boat and steadied it for Cody to get in.

"Go!"

Cody didn't have to be told again.

Leeland lifted the bow from the sand with Herculean strength. As Cody fired up the engine, Leeland pushed the boat out into the rolling water, wading past the floating body of the sheriff. Then he ran back to the beach yelling gibberish loudly to himself.

It took Cody a moment to get the pitching boat turned around. Then he surveyed the dark sky, trying to orient himself east toward Canal Point. Just as he began to push the throttle open, there was another horrible shriek from the shore. Cody looked back through the rain and lightning to see the half-naked Leeland Zorn, standing on the beach holding Kratch's decapitated head like an offering to whatever storm gods swirled within his tortured brain.

"What was that?" Madison said from her place on the floor of the boat. Only her head protruded from the tarp.

"It's him. He's completely insane," Cody told her, turning his attention back to the boat. "Are you all right?"

Madison nodded her head yes.

"You're all right," Cody said, reassuring himself that it was true. He sat down in the driver's seat of the boat and put his free hand gently against his wife's upturned face. Beside her in the pouring rain was a man he had thought was a killer, a man he was certain would now die in their care if he wasn't dead already. Cody wondered what would happen. He wondered if there could ever be a place that could keep them safe from a man like Leeland Zorn. At this moment, it didn't matter though. They were safe for now.

Cody opened the throttle full. Madison closed her eyes against the pelting rain and the storm that had yet to play itself to an end.

Epilogue

The jury filed into the courtroom and took their seats. Their foreman stood with a single sheet of paper in his hands.

"The defendant will . . . the defendant will sit up straight and face the jury," the judge ordered from his bench above them all.

Luther Zorn closed his eyes briefly and did as he was told, straightening himself as best he could for a man who had been partially paralyzed by a gunshot wound. His eyes then bore into the foreman's with regal defiance. Only Madison knew he was scared. She reached over and clasped his hand. It was cold and damp where it rested on the arm of his padded electric wheelchair, but he squeezed back and held her fingers.

With her other hand, Madison grasped the forearm of Mel Rosen. Since she had been an actual witness, she had only been able to serve as Mel Rosen's second counsel during the trial. It had been her strategy and even her words, however, behind the entire defense. Luther had insisted on that.

"On the first count of attempted murder . . ." the foreman read from his paper and then paused.

Madison couldn't help herself from looking down at Luther's face. He closed his eyes tightly and winced, as if he was about to be struck.

". . . we, the jury, find the defendant not guilty."

Luther's face showed momentary relief, and a murmur ran through the spectators and the press. It was good news, but it did nothing to relieve the tension Madison felt. The first charge was for the shooting of Detective Lawrence. Since Lawrence had fired several shots at Luther first, without provocation, the jury's acceptance of self-defense was not extraordinary. His shooting of Gill, however, was much more of a stretch. To shoot a policeman who hadn't fired a shot was tough to defend, even though Madison had been able to portray Gill as a crooked cop.

In fact, Madison had suggested conspiracy among Wilburn, Pallidan, Leeland, and Kratch and his men to the jury. She had hoped that the jury's knowledge of the entire story would help exonerate Luther. Madison had been around long enough to know that the whole story could sometimes do that.

"On the second count of attempted murder," the foreman continued, "we, the jury, find the defendant . . . not guilty."

There were several other counts as well, all of them less serious than the first two. But certainly they were significant for a man in Luther's condition. Even the smallest amount of time in jail would be incredibly painful. The jury, however, found Luther Zorn innocent on every count.

As the judge pronounced the defendant a free man, Luther put his head back, smiled at Madison, and closed his eyes like a tired soldier giving thanks at the end of a battle. Mark

Berryhill pursed his lips in a frown, but came over to shake the hands of both Madison and Mel Rosen.

A bailiff ushered Chris Pelo and Jamal out of the crowd and through the narrow gate that separated the players in the drama from the audience. The scrawny black child was an incongruity in the adult white world of crime and punishment. But Luther was now his legal father, and that certainly transcended any notion of decorum. Jamal grabbed hold of Luther and hugged him tightly. Chris put his arms around Madison and did the same.

"Congratulations, counselor," Chris said to her, clearing his throat to hide the embarrassment at his own show of emotion.

"Not bad for a sports agent, huh?" Madison replied with a warm smile.

"No, not bad at all."

Before the summer sun went down that day, Madison was out on her back deck beside the pool.

"Watch this, Mom!" Jo-Jo hollered before doing an awkward back flip off the board.

"I wish he wouldn't," Madison murmured to Cody.

"He's ten," Cody reminded her.

"I know," she acknowledged.

"Good one, Jo-Jo!" she cheered when her son came up for air. "Now listen, sweetheart, I want you to go in and get some clothes on. We'll be eating in about fifteen minutes."

"Okay, Mom," he said.

They watched Jo-Jo towel himself dry and then trot off to change. Cody got up and turned the hot dogs that had begun to sputter on the grill behind them. He sat back down in his lounge chair beside Madison, took a long drink from his sweaty beer bottle, and looked out over the golf course at the setting sun.

"Do you think they'll ever find him?" he asked abruptly.

"Leeland, you mean?" Madison said, also looking off into the same distance from behind her sunglasses.

"Yeah."

Madison shook her head sadly and took a sip from her drink. "I don't know, probably not," she said. "He seems to have the capacity to appear and disappear at will. They probably won't get him . . ."

"So Wilburn and Pallidan and Vivian Chase go free then, don't they?" Cody said.

Madison nodded her head. "I don't think Vivian actually had her husband killed. I don't think she was sad to see him dead, but I don't think she had a hand in it either.

"As far as Wilburn and Pallidan and Rivet himself," she continued, "the police and the FBI haven't been able to build a strong enough case against them to do anything."

Cody shook his head. "It's unbelievable . . . to get away with all that."

"The guy who really made out is Aaron Crawford," Madison reminded him. "He's made a fortune on the team's move, from what I hear. I guess he owns pretty much everything for about three miles around the stadium site. People are saying that his development plan is going to be a model for the interaction between sports and commerce for the next century."

"It's amazing," Cody pondered. "As scandalous as the whole thing was, Crawford still got exactly what he wanted."

"I think people these days care a lot more about what you do than how you do it," Madison said. "Memphis has its team. Crawford has his billions."

"That's America," Cody pronounced, finishing off his beer.

"Still," she said, "I like to think that sooner or later, every-one gets what they deserve."

"Maybe they do, Madison," Cody said. "Maybe they do."

It was well into the Caribbean night, and the three men who were enjoying the fruits of their labor were gathered around a table playing cards. The air was thick with the smoke of hand-rolled Cuban cigars. A steward appeared periodically with fresh ashtrays and to pour an unblended M. Ragnaud Le Paradis Cognac. The one-hundred-sixty-foot yacht owned by Aaron Crawford was anchored off the coast of To-bago. The three men were taking a holiday.

No one was particularly disappointed at the news of Luther Zorn's acquittal earlier that day. Luther had simply played his part in their drama. And now, no one, not even Wilburn, begrudged Luther his freedom. He had paid a dear price already for his intrusion into their plans. He would never again play the game that made him who he was. He would never even walk.

These men were celebrating because their patron, the great Aaron Crawford himself, had graced their presence for the past three days and had unfolded yet another plan. He had rewarded them liberally for their handling of the Ma-rauders, and they were now rich men. A helicopter had lifted their leader from the deck of the ship that very afternoon. Crawford had left them to enjoy his hospitality and their tremendous success with a smile and a congenial wave.

The negative publicity and the wild speculation of racke-teering and murder meant nothing to Crawford. Only results mattered, and they spoke for themselves. The team had been moved. No concrete connection had been made between Leeland Zorn and the Crawford empire, let alone any of the three men personally. That would happen only if Leeland were ever to turn up in the hands of the law, something they all felt confident wasn't going to happen. Leeland Zorn, they knew, was a man who had the capacity to live undetected somewhere for the rest of his life.

At that moment Leeland was, indeed, undetected. He was fastening a brick of C-4 to the hull of the yacht, which was anchored in seventy feet of water about two miles from shore.

Leeland set the timer and gave himself enough time to swim the quarter mile back to his skiff. He removed his air tank and lifted it into the boat. Then he slid over the side and sat back to wait. Overhead, the black sky was aflame with stars. A soft breeze dried Leeland's face, and he actually felt a moment of peace. He regretted the fact that Aaron Crawford had flown off that afternoon. It would have been nice to be able to include him in the grand finale of the night's festivities.

Suddenly an orange ball of flame lit the water's surface. An instant later the boom of the explosion crashed around Leeland's ears. He smiled to himself and started the little outboard motor. The ship went down faster than he thought it would, and soon the flames that leapt from the burning hull were extinguished. Leeland wondered if they had had time to get off. He hoped so. He would hate to have it end for them so quickly.

Of the three, only Rivet seemed to have gone down with the ship. Leeland puttered about in the wreckage, mercifully putting bullets into the heads of four crew members, who although burned to a man, had survived by clinging to the flotsam. With Wilburn and Pallidan, Leeland used his knife and took his time, bathing in the red-hued violence of the act. He wanted them to know exactly who was killing them and why.

By the time Leeland finished, the wind had picked up. As the little skiff mounted wave after wave on the way back to shore, two heads bumped ghoulishly about on the floor like forgotten coconuts. They would be the last. It would end now. Everything wasn't exactly right, but things were as good as he could make them. Leeland steered his boat around to the far side of the island and disappeared into the darkness.

More
Tim Green!

Please turn this page
for three
bonus excerpts,
one from each of his previous novels!

OUTLAWS

TITANS

RUFFIANS

Outlaws

1

THE OFFICES OF GEM STAR TECHNOLOGY were on the third floor of a mid-sized office building just off Congress Avenue on Eighth Street in downtown Austin. The rest of the floor served as the library of the Ridley & Shaw office and was accessible only from the firm's office on the fourth floor. It was rare for anyone other than William Moss or Clara Jones to get off the elevator on the third floor. In fact, very few people knew there even was an office on that floor. That was the way Bill Moss liked it. He didn't want people around, didn't want them to see him come or see him go. Clara knew that went for her as well.

Clara had been working at Gem Star Technology for seven years. She worked regular hours, was paid and treated well by her boss, and really didn't have very much to do. In fact, she often wondered how the firm stayed open at all. Bill Moss seemed to do very little business. He rarely had her type a letter, and he received very few calls. Mr. Moss, when he was in at all, would most often sit in his high-backed leather chair behind an ornate mahogany desk, listening to classical music and staring off into space. What she did know of his business seemed to explain his strange comings and goings, and how one man could maintain such nice offices and her salary on so few transactions.

Clara knew that Bill Moss sold weapons. There were many manufacturing plants in Texas that produced weapons. She had a cousin who worked at the American Arms Company just north of Austin, and she knew there were lots of others like it. Texans, she knew, liked their weapons. Clara herself wasn't against weapons, only handguns on the streets. What Mr. Moss did was different. Clara had typed letters to people in strange places, arranging for shipments of things like automatic rifles, grenade launchers, camouflage clothing, even tanks, armored personnel carriers, and missiles. These letters were copied to officials in Washington, D.C., who held positions in places like the Treasury Department, the Pentagon, and the FBI, so she knew that what was happening was legitimate. She wouldn't have said anything if it wasn't. She was the kind of person who just lived her life and hoped no one bothered her. But things were not going so well at the present time.

Clara chewed her lower lip and wondered if her boss would ever arrive. He had been out of the country for two weeks. She knew he was due back this morning, and usually after a long trip he would appear like the ghost he was, silently entering his office. Occasionally though, even after she knew he was due back, he wouldn't appear in the office for weeks.

Part of her wished that would be the case now. She dreaded asking her boss for anything, but this was an occasion where she felt she had no other choice. Mr. Moss was quiet and strong, and that made her nervous. Although she had worked for him for seven years, she could count all the conversations they'd had on one hand. The most talking he had ever done was during her interview for the job. He had given her the idea that he would be an amiable and pleasant person to work with. He wasn't unpleasant, but certainly no one would describe Bill Moss as amiable either.

She hated to ask him for anything, especially a favor, but this was certainly one time she could make an exception. The constant terror in which she and her son were living was making life unbearable. Something had to change, or else she would have to leave Austin. The only place she could really go would be to her sister's in Chicago. Clara's home, small and simple as it was, was not even close to being worth what she had paid for it. She'd have to walk away on the bank to get out of her neighborhood, and if she did that, she'd ruin her credit. She'd do it, though, and move, if something didn't change soon.

She knew, though, if there was one thing Mr. Moss didn't want, it was to be involved in her private life. She knew that from the beginning. He had told her so, and it had never bothered her. But now she had no one to turn to. She needed help. The police refused to take action; the school said there was little they could do. All she had lived and worked for over the last sixteen years and the health of her son were in danger. He'd never been entirely well, and the pressure he was under was becoming too much for him.

At first it was simply name-calling. She had expected that. Reggie had a clubfoot, and he stuttered. When he was very young, Reggie didn't go to a normal school. That was fine with her. She loved him. She wanted to take care of him. Then someone who didn't know any better decided that kids like Reggie should be in the regular schools. Things got bad.

When the boys in the neighborhood became teenagers, things got worse. Reggie began returning home from school with feces and urine smeared into his clothes and hair. Clara kept him inside after school, but they still got him between the bus stop and the front door. They were a sick bunch of kids. She knew that. They were part of a gang—a bad one. There were three of them, and they had taken it upon themselves to torment and terrorize Reggie as part of their daily routine.

Next came the beatings. She called the school. None of the abuse took place on school grounds, so school officials told her to call the police. Reggie was hysterically afraid of the police. He screamed uncontrollably if she mentioned calling them. She knew his tormentors had told him the police would take him away forever because he was a retard and a loony. He believed them. When she came home from work one day to find him under her bed with cigarette burns on the back of his hands, it was too much. She called the police. Reggie wouldn't tell them anything. The police were sorry. There was nothing they could do. They had people being killed every day. A few burns on the hands of a frightened teenager did not rank high on their list of things to fix.

Clara had no one. She needed help. The only person she could consider turning to for help was Mr. Moss. It was almost unthinkable, but she had to do something or face throwing herself at her sister's feet and living on charity until she got herself back together. She looked up at the clock. It was after noon. She pulled a brown bag from her bottom drawer and had begun to unfold her lunch when her boss walked in through the heavy wood door. Clara uttered a quiet greeting and stood up. Mr. Moss was in his office and already shutting the door before she could even get his attention.

Finally she blurted out, "Mr. Moss."

Striker looked at his secretary as if seeing her for the first time. It was unusual for her to speak to him. She knew he didn't like to speak. And he knew that didn't bother her, which was one of the reasons he'd hired her and paid her good money to do relatively little work. He knew everything about Clara Jones before he hired her. She was a large, homely woman who'd moved to Austin from Chicago when she learned she was pregnant. She had never been married, and he guessed she never would be.

Striker knew she was ashamed, and that was just as well. She had no friends or family close by, and she didn't want any; she had her son. He was fine, too. Striker even knew the son was not retarded. His IQ was slightly below normal, but his stutter and his physical deformity had tracked him in special education classes at an early age. He was a good drain on Clara's time. Striker didn't want Clara to have time for friends or family. He kept her on for as long as he did because she kept to herself, almost completely.

"Can I speak with you about something, please, Mr. Moss?" she said.

"Come in, Clara," he said in a way that was not unfriendly.

Clara nearly tripped over the chair trying to get her bulky figure out from behind her desk. By the time she got into Striker's office, he was already seated in his chair, his feet propped casually up on his desk.

"Sit down, Clara," Striker said.

"No, that's all right, Mr. Moss," she said, keeping her eyes trained on the floor in front of her.

"So, what is it?"

"I—I—I don't know how to start," Clara said, wringing her chubby hands as she looked up meekly. Striker could see that she had tears in her eyes.

"Clara," he said in a gentle voice she had never heard before, "take your time. Tell me what's wrong."

Clara took a deep breath and began. "It's my son, Mr. Moss. Me and my son. I have a problem. I don't have anyone, I'm sorry. I have to ask you for help. I know if you were to call, then the police might help. They won't listen to me—"

"Wait a minute, Clara," Striker said, holding up his hand abruptly. She thought he was going to rebuff her.

"Tell me what you're talking about," he said.

Standing there, wringing her hands as if she could wash the whole thing away, Clara breathed a sigh of relief and told her boss the entire story of the boys who were tormenting her son.

"If something doesn't change, Mr. Moss," she finally said, "I'm gonna have to leave."

"What do you mean, 'leave'?" Striker said. The last thing he wanted right now was to lose her. He didn't have the time it would take to hire someone else. He needed a secretary now that he could trust and rely on. The timing was horrible.

"I mean," she said hesitantly, staring at her shifting feet, "that I would have to go north, Mr. Moss. I'd have to leave here and go live with my sister."

Striker didn't have to ask why. He knew her financial situation. It was the way he wanted it, to keep her on a tether, not paying her too much, not paying her too little. Simply buying out her mortgage to the bank wouldn't do either. That would draw attention.

Striker sat pensively for a few moments with his chin resting on his steepled fingertips. He then asked her a few questions about the thugs. Clara couldn't help becoming excited. This was what she had hoped for.

"Well, Clara," Striker said finally, "I think the best thing is for you to call the police again. This is something that they should take care of for you. Maybe things will work out."

Striker took his feet off the desk and began going through some papers that were on the desk. Clara stood for a few embarrassed minutes before she realized that he was through with her. She said nothing. Her fingers trembled as she reached for the door handle and pulled it closed behind her. The phone on her desk rang mercifully. She pulled it from the receiver and answered it as she plopped down into her seat.

"Gem Star Technology," she said in the same flat voice she had used to answer the phone for the past seven years. She was too numbed with disappointment to feel anything. But later she would feel the full weight of his crushing rejection, and the hopelessness of her situation would tear her insides apart.

They came again that same night. The gang tormented her and her son, banging on the windows and doors, laughing and mimicking the terrified screams they heard from within. Finally, she pulled Reggie into a closet and held him close, humming to him in an attempt to drown out the noise. After a while the boys grew tired and left. Clara wondered how long it would be before the gang wanted more, before they broke into the house and . . .

Striker watched them as they left. It wasn't hard to follow the three hoods. They left a trail of broken bottles and headlights, and made plenty of noise. There was one among them who was the obvious leader. He walked slightly behind the others, who pranced around him like circus dogs, checking to see that everything they did or said met with his approval. He was the skinniest of the three and not the tallest, but Striker knew he was not only the leader but the most dangerous. He kept his hands in the big front pocket of his large, hooded sweatshirt, where Striker suspected he carried a gun. That was smart, keeping his hands on his weapon, but Striker knew the punk wasn't too smart or he wouldn't be wasting time terrorizing a disabled teenager and his mother.

Striker kept back and walked down the sidewalk on the opposite side of the street. He was dressed in dark jeans, a black T-shirt, and a black jacket. Those who saw him suspected he was crazy. Any white man dressed the way he was and walking in that neighborhood after dark was just asking to get killed.

Occasionally a chrome-lit foreign car would creep down the street, sending a heavy bass sound pounding through the windows of the tiny row houses that lined the block. The three punks darted into the shadows when one of those cars passed, like minnows scattering from the big game fish that had wandered into the shallows. Striker faded, too, when such cars approached. They would be trouble, and he was not there to clean up the streets. He was focused on a single purpose.

Striker watched patiently as his quarry openly sold drugs to other teens at street corners and in garbage-strewn driveways between gutted buildings. Finally one of them cajoled a bum into buying a case of Colt 45 Malt Liquor from a run-down corner store, and the three made off toward an empty garage in an abandoned lot. The garage was the only thing standing in the empty lot, which was surrounded by what Striker knew must have been a picket fence. Nothing was left of the old house that had once been there except some scattered pieces of brick and charred lumber covered with twisted rusty nails. Tall weeds poked through the uneven, garbage-covered ground and dotted the lot with menacing silhouettes.

After a few minutes, a glowing orange light shone through the broken windows of the garage. Striker saw smoke billow up through breaks in the roof before it disappeared into the clear night, and he let them get settled inside for a while. The night turned chilly, and he zipped his jacket up to his chin and pulled it up over his mouth to stay warm. Occasionally gunfire would split the night. Striker thought about going in. He could do what he had to with the three of them stone sober and armed to the teeth. But out of habit Striker would give himself the absolute best possible advantage. He would wait until they were intoxicated.

At twelve-thirty Striker limbered up, rotating his arms and legs. He removed his gun from inside his jacket as he crossed the lot and slipped into the abandoned garage through the side door. Two of them were sitting in old beat-up armchairs while the third, the fat one, stood by the fire gesticulating wildly as he told some story. Striker instantly zeroed in on the skinny one, the leader, and leveled his long sleek .22 at the youth's head. The end of the barrel was fitted with a silencer. For everyday use Striker carried a Beretta 9mm, but when he had a special job, he brought Lucy, his .22.

"Stand up," Striker ordered in a calm voice. The skinny kid gave him a smart-ass grin, and Striker put a bullet through his ear just to let him know that he wasn't a cop, and that they didn't have any rights. The blood drained from the kid's face. He grabbed at his torn ear. Blood seeped between his fingers, and he grimaced in pain. The other two remained frozen in disbelief. The quiet spitting of the gun almost made the whole thing seem like some kind of gag.

"Now stand up," Striker said in the same tone. Before he could blink they were all standing, facing him with their hands in the air.

"What the fuck?" the fat one whined.

Striker stepped in and whipped a front kick into the punk's groin. The kid collapsed in a heap, gasping for breath. Striker never let the gun waver from the skinny one. He knew better. There was no fear in the skinny one's eyes, and Striker knew that he was dangerous. The realization gave Striker a rush. He would have to change his plans. He knew better than to let an animal like this kid see another day. This kid would get him if he didn't get the kid first. It was too late to go back.

Striker stepped forward, but the skinny kid was expecting it, and he ducked under Striker's kick and went for the gun in his sweatshirt pocket. Instead of backing away, Striker shifted his weight while his kicking leg was still in the air and landed solidly right beside the kid. At the same moment that his foot hit the ground, his elbow smashed into the side of the kid's head and knocked him unconscious just as he pulled a Glock from his pocket. The gun clattered on the concrete floor. The other kid, whose face was riddled with acne, froze in his spot.

Striker aimed his gun at the boy's face and slowly advanced the muzzle toward him until it tickled his nose.

"Pick up the gun," Striker said in that same voice.

The kid bent down and picked up the Glock.

"Now, take the money out of your buddy's pockets," Striker said. This kid had seen enough to know that anything but obedience would be trouble. He pulled wads of money from the skinny kid's pants pockets.

"Now," Striker said, "put the gun up to his head, right to his ear. Right there!"

"Oh, man," the kid whined, "oh, man. Oh, no, no man, no . . ."

"Shut the fuck up," Striker snapped. "Now, pull the trigger . . . I said *pull* the trigger, you piece of shit, or I'll blow your fucking brains out!"

The kid began to cry, and Striker put the barrel of his gun to the kid's ear. He pulled back the hammer. The kid was hysterical.

"Do it!" Striker screamed in a rage. The tiny garage exploded with the sound of the big-caliber gun. The kid dropped the gun and collapsed to the ground, sobbing. Brains and blood were all over the place. Striker got a charge out of the mess, the hysterics, and the hot, pungent smell of the gunpowder. The fat one started to squeal on the floor in terror, and Striker kicked him hard in the side of the head to shut him up.

"Now pick up the fucking gun again, you piece of shit!" Striker had a crazed look in his eyes. He was riding a crest now, and he let it carry him. This pimple-faced kid would take the rap, no fuss, no muss.

"Pick it up!"

The kid did it.

"Shoot that fat fuck in the head."

"Oh, fucking man, oh, motherfucking man!" cried the kid, pulling the gun behind him as if he could hide it. "Why? Oh man, fucking please, no man . . ."

"Go ahead," Striker growled. "You want to be a big fucking bad guy. You want to scare people! Do it, bad guy!"

Striker grabbed a handful of the kid's nappy hair and twisted it hard, forcing him over toward the fat one. Then he put a vise grip on the boy's wrist and forced the gun up to the fat one's ear.

Striker punched his thumb into the pressure point between the kid's thumb and his wrist and screamed right into his ear, "DO IT, YOU MOTHER-FUCKING BAD GUY! DO IT! DO IT!"

The Glock exploded, and before the terrified kid knew what had happened, Striker was gone.

Titans

1

TONY RIZZO PULLED BACK THE HEAVY crimson drapes and looked out at the gloomy Manhattan day. Central Park was covered with a blanket of snow, and a gray mist hung in the air. He couldn't even see the Dakota. The barren trees were a dark, inky web against the pale sky. Rizzo smiled and stretched; he had just gotten out of bed and it was already two in the afternoon. It was Sunday, a day to build a fire, sit on the couch in a big soft robe, and watch the game. Then he remembered that he had to work, and he frowned.

But business was business. Rizzo went to his closet, grabbed a T-shirt, and strapped a 9mm Beretta semiautomatic under his arm. He stepped into some ratty jeans and pulled a heavy cardigan sweater on over the T-shirt and the gun. He grabbed a faded army coat from the back of the closet and checked the pockets. In the right was a snub-nose .38. In the left was a silencer—both came from New Orleans and could never be traced. He slipped on a pair of black Reeboks and headed for the door.

"Tony?" called a sleepy voice from the bed.

Rizzo stepped back into the bedroom and gazed appreciatively at the long blond hair and shapely figure beneath the satin sheets. He loved models. They were like toys, playthings he picked up at the Manhattan clubs that he visited nightly.

"I'll be out for a while," he said. "Stay if you want to. If you leave, just lock the door on your way out."

Rizzo turned his back and let himself out. He knew she'd still be there when he got back. If there was one thing a girl like that couldn't stand, it was indifference.

He walked down the hall. Expensive white paper embossed with thin gold columns hung on the walls. Plush red carpet covered the floor. Tony walked past the elevators and headed for the stairs. It was a long haul to the basement, but the old clothes he had picked for today would raise more than a few eyebrows in a building like his, and he wanted to slip out quietly. Only the garage attendant would see him this morning, and Willie was used to his unorthodox comings and goings. Having to sneak about stairwells was enough to make him think seriously about his uncle's repeated requests that he move back to Brooklyn, where the rest of the family lived and where he could come and go as he pleased without having to worry about his privacy.

Mike Cometti and Tommy Keel were parked right next to Willie's booth in an old beat-up maroon Fleetwood. Rizzo gave Willie a wink and climbed into the backseat.

"You wanna coffee, Tony?" Cometti asked as he pulled the steaming cover off a white Styrofoam cup and handed it back.

"Thanks, Mikey. Where's Angelo?" Rizzo asked in a displeased voice while absently considering the back of Tommy Keel's head.

"Your Uncle Vinny called him this morning and said he needed him. Ang couldn't think of a reason for saying no to your uncle, since you don't want anybody wise to this . . ."

"Tommy's gotta get his feet wet," Cometti added.

"You up for this, Tommy?" Rizzo said in a harsh tone, looking at Mikey all the while. Mikey shrugged and nodded apologetically.

"Yeah, I'm OK, Tony," Tommy said looking over his shoulder. "Like Mikey said, I gotta get my feet wet sometime."

"OK," Rizzo said flatly. "Let's go."

Tommy Keel put the car in gear and lurched out of the garage into the gloom. He took them straight down Fifth Avenue to Washington Square Park, then wove his way through the narrow streets of Greenwich Village until they found themselves parked in a dirty alley behind a row of buildings just off Bleecker Street. Steam billowed from a grate, and the stench of garbage caught in their throats.

The three men got out and walked around the block to a bar called Ironside's. The place was only half-full, and they were able to find a booth in a dark corner near the back. From there they could observe the other patrons in the bar without really being seen themselves. They ordered three beers from the waitress and settled down to watch the pregame hype on the big-screen TV.

Before too long the bar was full, but not crowded. Ironside's was not a popular place, but you could always count on the regulars to show up for an event as big as the Super Bowl, this year between the Titans and the 49ers. Mike Cometti spotted an enormous fat man squeezing through the door and taking off his coat. He nudged Rizzo. The Fat Man was wearing a black T-shirt and baggy dark green pants. He was breathing heavily as he

made his way to the bar. Two grimy-looking characters
vacated their seats to make room. The Fat Man was obviously an important figure at Ironside's.

"There he is," Mikey murmured, his brow darkening.

Rizzo only nodded and took a gulp of his beer. His face
turned to stone. The bar got noisier as game time approached.

At the kickoff, everyone except the three in the corner
cheered. Tommy glanced nervously at Rizzo, Mikey, and
the Fat Man. The longer the game went on, the more
Tommy's knee shook under the table. Rizzo counted the
empty draft pitchers as they were periodically removed
from in front of the Fat Man, who had begun sweating
profusely. Both Mikey and Tommy ordered another
round whenever the waitress happened by. Rizzo nursed
his first beer and ordered a second one only two minutes
before the end of the half.

When the half ended, the Titans were trailing the 49ers
17–3. Mikey stood up and turned to Tony, "I gotta piss
like a racehorse," he said apologetically.

Tommy slid out of the booth at the same time, and
mumbled, "Me too."

Rizzo continued to watch and wait. When his two
companions returned, they seemed less uptight. It was
well into the third quarter when the Fat Man sent away
his fourth empty pitcher.

"OK, Tommy," said Rizzo.

Tommy looked frightened, and Rizzo grabbed Tommy
tightly by the arm and shook him a little.

"Go," he said between clenched teeth.

When Tommy had disappeared out the back toward the
bathrooms, Rizzo turned his eyes on Mikey.

"You sure about this five-pitcher shit?" he said.

Mikey nodded. "Tony, I told you a thousand times. Every time the Fat Man finishes his fifth pitcher he makes his move on the john. Zeke says he's like clockwork, says the slob would piss his pants if he drank any more without pissing. He says he can't figure how the guy can go that—"

"OK, OK," said Rizzo. "Gimme some snort."

Mikey looked around cautiously, out of habit. Everyone's eyes were on the game. He took a little silver box from his inside pocket and handed it over. Rizzo fished beneath his T-shirt for a tiny gold spoon that hung on a chain around his neck. He took two big snorts, closed up the box, and returned it to Mikey. It was six minutes into the fourth quarter and the Titans were down 20–9 when the Fat Man finished his fifth pitcher.

The Titans were driving and their quarterback, Hunter Logan, ran a bootleg across the fifty yard line. A cheer went up in the bar. All eyes were fixed on the game. For a moment Mikey was afraid the Fat Man wouldn't leave his seat in the middle of such a crucial drive. Tony would not be happy if he was wrong. Then the Fat Man lurched from the bar and swung his bulk toward the bathrooms.

Logan faded back to pass. All the Fat Man could do was give a fleeting glance before he disappeared into the back. Rizzo and Mikey eased themselves out of the booth and followed the Fat Man as nonchalantly as they could. No one noticed. Tommy Keel was in the back of the hallway. He had checked both bathrooms to see that they were empty, then kept a watch to make sure no one came in from the kitchen. He gave Rizzo a thumbs-up. Rizzo looked back to see that Mikey was standing at the other end of the hallway with his back to the bathrooms. He stuck his hands in his coat pockets and went in.

The Fat Man had somehow wedged himself into the

stall. His pants were down to his knees, and his head was bent over in an attempt to see. He relieved himself with an audible sigh. From his pockets Rizzo removed the pistol and silencer. He moved quickly, but appeared to be in no great hurry as he screwed the two pieces together. Finished, he stepped forward, put the barrel of the gun to the back of the Fat Man's skull, and pulled the trigger.

The Fat Man jerked forward but remained nearly upright, wedged in the stall. His feet were crooked, and they twitched slightly. His bladder continued to empty into the bowl even after he was dead. Rizzo leaned into the stall and stretched his arm over the Fat Man's enormous back. Carefully he put two more slugs into the Fat Man's brain. He then broke down his weapon and jammed the pieces into his pockets. They would be at the bottom of the East River before the end of the game. Rizzo flipped off the light switch and quickly left the bathroom. He glanced left and gave Mikey a low whistle. Mikey gave a quick final glance around the bar. The crowd erupted in a cheer as Logan connected on a touchdown pass. Everyone's eyes were glued to the TV to catch the instant replay. Mikey turned and followed Rizzo and Tommy out the back door.

With their previous drive, the Titans had narrowed the gap, leaving the score 20–16. A touchdown was all that stood between them and the championship. Hunter Logan faded back to pass. He'd missed the blitz and knew none of his receivers were hot. He tucked the ball in tight and prepared for impact. The strong safety hit him at a full sprint. The instant Hunter felt the blow, he spun his body and ducked at the same time. The safety fell uselessly to the ground. Hunter's spin put him outside the pocket, where the rest of the 49ers defense was pouring through. His ducking caused the defensive end who had contain to miss him as well.

Now Hunter rolled out to his right, running for his life. Just before he reached the sideline, Hunter leaped in the air, twisted, and launched the ball twenty yards downfield. The tight end, who had seen the predicament, had broken his route to provide him with a safety valve. The tight end caught the ball at the same instant three pursuing 49ers crashed into Hunter, driving him four yards outside the boundary. Yellow flags flew from every direction.

Hunter lay dazed under the pile. He heard cursing and flailing. Above him, his own teammates were violently removing the defenders who lay on top of him. Leading the ruckus was Hunter's best friend, the Titans noseguard, Bert Meyer. Bert yanked the biggest 49er, Olson Fain, by the face mask and savagely twisted him back to the ground.

"That's our quarterback, you piece of shit!" roared Meyer as he delivered an open-handed whack to the head of the six-foot-six, three-hundred-pound Fain. Another yellow flag was tossed into the melee. Fain would have retaliated with more than a stream of obscenities if he had not been on the Titans' sideline surrounded by the entire team, all of whom were pushing and shoving him. The referees quickly interceded.

"You son of a bitch!" screamed a purple-faced official who had seen Bert's blow to Fain. "That's dirty play, you bastard! Another stunt like that and you're gone!"

Bert paid him no mind. He was too busy helping a disoriented Hunter Logan to his feet.

The trainers and team doctors quickly surrounded

Hunter, who was trying to push his way back into the game.

"Hunter!" barked the team physician. "Are you all right?"

"Yeah, I'm OK."

"Hunter," the doctor continued, "what's the score?"

"I don't know. I'm OK."

"Do you know where you are?" the doctor asked.

"I'm OK," replied Hunter as he tried to break free from Bert and the trainers.

"OK, OK," the doctor said, "just tell me how many fingers you see and we'll send you right back in the game."

"Three," Hunter said.

"OK, you guys, get him to the bench," said the doctor as he held up a single finger for them all to see.

Hunter struggled. "Let me go, you assholes! I've got to get in there! I'm gonna win this son of a bitch!"

"Hunter, come on," Bert coaxed, "you'll get back in there. Just get yourself together first."

Time was running out. The Titans sent second-string quarterback Bob Dunham in to replace Hunter. The penalties offset each other, but the Titans still had the ball on the 49ers twenty-one yard line. The Titans ran a sweep that went for twelve yards. The crowd roared. It was first and goal from the nine. With Dunham cold off the bench, the Titans would attempt to run the ball into the end zone.

Dunham fumbled the snap on first down. The Titans recovered, but they were now second and goal from the fourteen. They tried a draw that got them only three yards. It was third down and everyone in the world knew they would have to go to the air.

"What the hell's going on?" Hunter demanded as he tried to peek through the medical staff.

Dunham dropped back and threw a quick and wild ball out of bounds to avoid the blitz. It was now fourth and goal from the fourteen. There were only thirty-seven seconds left in the year's most important football game. A field goal was useless.

Pop Peters, the Titans head coach, called a time-out and came over to the bench. "Doc!" Pop bellowed. "What's the fucking status? I need Hunter in there, damn it!"

Hunter jumped from the bench. "I'm there, Coach!" he announced.

The trainers and doctors grabbed him by the arms.

"What the hell, Doc?" said Pop.

"I can't let him in there, Pop," the doctor replied. "I don't give a good goddamn if it's the Super Bowl or not. This guy isn't right. He can't even see straight. I won't take that risk. He won't do you any good as he is anyway!"

"Check me, Doc!" Hunter implored. "Check me again!"

Behind them all, Hunter grabbed his friend by the arm. He shot him a quick pleading look. Bert nodded.

"OK," the doctor said, holding up three fingers, "how many?"

Bert gave Hunter three quick pinches on the ass. "Three," Hunter said.

"Wait," the doctor said. "You said that last time. How many now?"

Bert gave Hunter two quick pinches.

"Two."

Everyone looked at the doctor.

"Jesus!" said the doctor. "His pupils are still dilated as hell . . ."

"Time, Coach!" the side judge bellowed at Pop.

" . . . OK, go!" said the doctor.

"Roll right ninety-two fade!" screamed Pop, as Hunter dashed out onto the field.

When he reached the huddle, Hunter bumped into his center, stumbled, and almost fell.

"Hunter, you OK?" asked Murphy, the center, as Hunter knelt in the middle of the huddle.

"I can throw this bitch in my sleep," Hunter said.

"Get it to me, Hunt," said Matt Brown, Hunter's best wideout. "I'll make the play."

"No," Hunter said firmly. There was no time to argue. "They're gonna have two men all over you, Matt. I gotta go to Weaver. Weaver, you know what to do. Roll right, ninety-two, fade, on one . . . ready . . ."

"Break!"

The Titans lined up on the ball. Hunter got up to his center. He couldn't really tell what defense the 49ers were in, but he knew they'd send every man on a blitz and go man-to-man coverage on his three receivers. Hunter steadied himself on the center and barked out the cadence.

"Down . . . set . . . hut!"

Hunter dropped four quick steps and rolled three more to his right before he lofted the ball. He was immediately engulfed by defenders. Weaver ran straight to the goal line, then broke for the corner of the end zone. Only when he was two yards from the corner did he look up. The ball was there, and Weaver pulled it in, dragging both feet in bounds before he collapsed outside the end zone with the defender on top of him. Touchdown! Weaver jumped up and held the ball overhead for the whole world to see, as the crowd roared its approval.

Ruffians

1

THE CONCRETE WAS COLD and made Clay's bare feet clammy. Stripped to his underwear, he stood in a line of about thirty other half-naked young men that extended around the room and out the door. The vaultlike room was cramped. Its high ceiling was a maze of corroding pipe and mold-stained ductwork. One of the players behind Clay laughed abruptly in a nervous and muffled way. Everyone turned. A fidgety silence settled among them once more. They were the rookie class of the National Football League. Every year, like cattle to the auction, the league harvested the finest football players from universities across the nation. Before the merchandise was bought and paid for, the buyers were given generous opportunity to inspect the meat.

Over three hundred college players had been flown into New Orleans from universities as far away as Hawaii and Boston College and as close as LSU and Auburn. Many, like Clay, were subdued even before they got inside. The big, dirty city offered little in the way of a warm welcome. Damp, fetid air from the distant Gulf of Mexico was tainted with smoke belched from factories and power plants. The New Orleans Superdome stood out like an enormous white spaceship, an anomaly in a town whose main attraction was the old French Quarter.

"DL7," called out the pale, spectacled man in a white lab coat.

It was Clay's turn to step onto the scales. The number had been given to him when he arrived at the NFL combines. It was printed in large letters on his T-shirt, and had been printed on the back of his hand in indelible ink as well. For as long as he was at the combines, he was DL7 and not Clay Blackwell.

"Two hundred seventy-three pounds . . ."

The lab technician paused as he jammed the metal arm hard down on the top of Clay's head.

Large and mostly overweight middle-aged men in ill-fitting clothes sat crammed into desk chairs that filled the center of the room. There were five or six rows of about ten chairs. The men were NFL scouts, and they wrote everything the lab man said like enthusiastic schoolboys, looking up only to eyeball the next slab of human flesh on the block.

The lab man said, ". . . six feet, four point one inches. Next."

Clay stepped off the scale and was pointed in the direction of a steel door at the back of the room. Not knowing what was scheduled next, he wordlessly followed a red-headed guy ahead of him who had DL6 printed on the back of his T-shirt, and stepped through the steel door into another cold concrete room.

"Walk to the yellow X and then back again," shouted a shape from behind a set of bright lights.

Clay did as he was told.

He had to squint to see that there were several lab men in this room and only a few scouts. Two cameras filmed Clay as he headed to the yellow marker on the opposite side of the room. Many coaches and scouts around the league believed a lot could be learned about an athlete's balance and speed just by the way he walked across the room.

Clay was dismissed and told to go dress himself, then report to Room C.

Strength testing was conducted in Room C. This room, too, was crowded with NFL scouts and coaches. They were packed in a circle around a single bench press like men in a barn about to watch a cockfight. The weight bar held 225 pounds, and the object was to press the bar as many times as possible. The last of the offensive line group, OL43, had set the standard at forty-four repetitions. As Clay's turn approached, his armpits dampened with nervous energy. He wanted to be the best at everything he did, but he knew he couldn't match forty-four. Still, the six DLs that preceded him had all got somewhere in the teens, so Clay adjusted his goal to be the best of the defensive linemen and not worry about the entire group.

The call came, "DL7."

Clay got down on the bench, and with a slight tremor in his hands he lifted the bar off the rack and began to press. With the first few reps his arms felt weak, not as strong as they should have been. But he figured nervous energy was sapping his mind, not his body, and he finally established a comfortable rhythm. Nineteen . . . twenty . . . twenty-one . . . twenty . . . two—his arms shook with real fatigue—twentyyy . . . three . . . twentyyyy . . .

"Aghhh!" Clay grunted as his arms gave out and the heavy bar sped toward his chest.

Two lab coats, one on either side, mechanically caught the bar and returned it to its rack.

"DL7, twenty-three reps," said one of the lab coats blandly.

Clay looked around for a sign of approval, but the only ones who weren't scribbling were other players who were not especially interested in seeing him succeed.

Clay left Room C following large arrow-shaped cardboard signs marked THIS WAY, and found himself walking through a maze of damp locker rooms in the bowels of the Superdome. Turning a corner, he was abruptly confronted with the huge expanse of the unnaturally green turf field. Artificial lights buzzed from above like monster insects, and the shouts of players, striving to run faster agility drills, echoed off the distant stands and roof.

While Clay waited for the rest of the DLs to arrive, he watched the last remnants of the OL group run through a series of drills and sprints. Clay's muscles began to twitch as he watched. He grinned to himself. This field was where he would set himself apart. For a man who was six-foot-four and weighed 273 pounds, Clay's agility and speed were remarkable. He knew that, and he knew that after he finished these drills, everyone else in the place would know it, too.

When the group of DLs was finally complete, Clay was assigned to a subgroup that consisted of DL1 through DL8. A lab technician led them to the vertical jump area. Clay watched his competition. His turn came. A lab coat marked his fingertips with chalk. Clay crouched beside the wall where he was to jump. He bounced several times, as if he was going to jump, but returned to his crouch. He got himself into a rhythm. Muscles in his legs and shoulders rippled with tension. Then, when his weight felt right, he sprang. The red marks he left on the wall were a good six inches beyond anyone else's.

"Thirty-seven and a half," said the lab coat who stood above them all on some scaffolding.

Clay couldn't help noticing the incredulous looks he was drawing from the other DLs.

"Hell of a jump," DL8 said, shaking his head as he passed Clay to take his place against the wall.

The jump was only the beginning. With each passing test, more and more scouts and coaches gathered around Clay's group to watch him perform. By the time Clay got to his last test, the forty-yard dash, almost half of the people in the Dome were clustered around him to see how well he would run. This was the benchmark for football players. From the time they are ten years old, football players talk about their speed in terms of the forty. Clay had worked for weeks on improving his start, and he now carefully placed his hands and feet in their proper places. He lifted his hindquarters, began breathing deeply, then exploded off the line. Once up, his motions were smooth and fast, almost liquid, but violent, like a tethered stallion cut free. His strides took up enormous sections of the turf. If it had been colder, steam would have burst from his nostrils as he churned across the finish line. The time: 4:63, the best any DL would run.

A coach who wore a Dallas Cowboys sweat top leaned over to the scout standing next to him, and whispered, "That's a Thoroughbred."

Clay had to wait until all the DLs were done in the Dome before the group would be taken by bus to the hospital for physicals. A lab coat announced there would be no lunch and that the bus would not be leaving for at least another hour. Clay shrugged, pulled on his Northern sweat suit, and sat patiently in a remote corner of the Dome reading a ragged paperback copy of Hemingway's *For Whom the Bell Tolls* that he had kept hidden in his bag.

At the hospital, the DLs were seated in chairs that lined

both sides of a long corridor. At the end of the hall was a door that every three or four minutes would expel one player while the one seated closest would get up and enter. Each time this happened, the entire forty-odd remaining players would get up and advance one seat closer to the door. For fifteen minutes Clay silently refused to participate. But after five empty chairs separated him from DL20, the glares from his frustrated counterparts became so malicious that he found himself distracted and unable to concentrate, rereading the same sentence in his book several times. To restore order, and his own peace of mind, Clay decided to play by the unwritten rules of the game and moved closer to the door.

As he sat, a man made his way down the hall. He wasn't a lab coat, but he carried a clipboard, a caliper, and a tape measure. He bent and fiddled briefly over each player before scribbling on his board. It wasn't until he was three seats away that Clay was able to figure out what he was doing.

"Fist," said the man when he reached Clay.

Having watched DL20, who in turn had watched DL3, Clay knew to hold out his fist at arm's length while the man measured the circumference of Clay's fist and the distance from his big knuckle to his elbow. The man then said, "Head," and fixed the caliper to his skull, measuring its diameter from front to back and side to side.

When the man had moved on, DL20 leaned over and murmured quietly, "That's the Seattle guy. I heard the Seahawks have some chart that tells how good you'll be in the league just by those measurements."

Clay gave him a knowing look.

"I'm Donny Drew," DL20 said. "You're Clay Blackwell, huh?"

It was the first time that day Clay had heard mention of his name. He nodded his head to the oversize Nebraska farm boy.

"Yeah," he said. "I don't remember when we met . . ."

"Oh, I never met you," Donny said, "but shit, everyone knows you. Northern U. superstar. Grew up somewhere around there in New York, didn't you?"

"Yeah," Clay said, "kind of born and raised, I guess you'd say."

"You're one of the top guys in the draft this year."

"Well, you never know . . ."

"Oh, my agent knows. You're a first-round pick, a one for sure. I know about all the DLs, you know, D-linemen coming out in the draft.

"I'm a three to five," Donny added rather proudly.

Finally inside the door, Clay was given a folder with eleven empty boxes on its cover.

"DL7 . . . Clay Blackwell?" asked a woman looking up at him from the desk.

Clay nodded.

"Fill each box with a circle. There are eleven stations in this room. You get one circle at each station. Don't come back until every box is filled."

Seeing that no further explanation was forthcoming, Clay turned to assess his situation. The room was cavernous, and seemed to be a cafeteria whose tables and chairs had been cleared away. There were large booths separated by heavy blue curtains. Each booth had a number over its entrance. Players milled about between booths and queued outside others. Clay headed for Booth 11, which had no line.

He entered this "station" to find two lab coats and a dentist. Clay sat on a stool while the dentist pulled back his lips.

One of the lab coats took a picture of Clay's teeth. The dentist fished around Clay's mouth with a mirror, making comments into a Dictaphone. When he was finished, the dentist turned his back abruptly on Clay, and the second lab coat stepped forward to give him a round blue sticker with the number 11 on it, which he stuck on the appropriate box of his folder.

This is a cinch, he thought.

Clay entered Booth 4 after waiting in a short line. Along with a booth for teeth and eyes and knee ligaments and body symmetry, there were seven additional booths. These housed a few lab coats and four or five physicians, one from every team represented and a corresponding trainer. Booth 4 was one of these. Someone grabbed his folder from his hand.

"DL7," that someone called out.

One of the physicians checked his hand to see that indeed he was DL7.

"Take off your shirt," someone said.

Clay did it.

"Bend down and touch your toes."

Clay saw by the stethoscope that it was one of the physicians who was speaking. The same one ran two fingers down the length of Clay's spine. Clay jumped.

"That hurt?" asked the doctor gruffly.

"Tickled," Clay said with a sheepish smile that was not returned.

"Any injuries?" asked another doctor.

Clay didn't quite know how to answer. He had no current injuries, but over his lifetime he had had his share. He couldn't think of anything worth mentioning though. He had never missed a college game because of an injury. If it wasn't serious enough to miss a game, then it certainly wasn't worth mentioning to this group.

"No," Clay said.

"No injuries, none?"

"I never missed a game," Clay answered.

It was quiet in the booth except for a lab coat who pounded furiously on the keyboard of a computer. Suddenly he looked up from the screen menacingly. "What about your elbow, fall of 1989?"

Clay thought. "Yes," he said, "I ruptured a bursar sack in my elbow, but I didn't even miss a practice."

"On the table, please," said a doctor who stepped up and grabbed Clay's arm at the forearm and the biceps. The doctor bent and twisted Clay's elbow in such a way that would have hurt any healthy elbow.

"That hurt?"

"No," Clay said.

Another doctor stepped up to the table to do more of the same. As he held Clay's arm, he noticed a scar on his knuckle. He held Clay's hand up to the light.

"What's this?" he asked.

"Oh, that was from a fight when I was in high school," Clay said.

The doctor looked up and said to no one in particular, "Make a note of that."

"What about your left knee?" said the lab coat at the computer. "Didn't you sprain your left medial collateral in spring of 1990?"

"Yeah, well, it was spring ball. I only missed a couple of days of practice, and I played in the spring game."

Every doctor was interested in this, and now each one, as well as each trainer, had a shot at not only his left knee but his right. That done, there was more general poking and prodding which had no apparent pattern. It was the guy at the computer who finally gave Clay back his folder with a green 4 fixed in its box, but not before he flashed one final look of hostility.

By the time Clay had all his boxes filled, his joints ached from twisting and turning and poking and prodding. He gave his folder to the woman at the desk. Without looking up, she told him to report to the fourth floor, Room 459 for EKG, X-rays, blood and urine, and his internal. Clay's eyes narrowed at the word *internal*.

"After you've completed that," she said, "you can wait for your group in the main lobby. Someone will take you back to the hotel."

On the fourth floor, a doctor whom Clay had never seen before ushered him into a small examination room and asked him to drop his shorts and hop onto the table in the middle of the room. The doctor began talking about the lobster bisque at a French Quarter restaurant called Arnaud's. Clay would have been somewhat interested had he not been on all fours atop the examination table with the doctor's latex-covered finger shoved up his ass. Clay's Adam's apple bobbed as he gulped the bile that filled his throat. The doctor handed him a box of tissues and left the room. Clay got down from the table and wiped the lubricant from between his cheeks with handfuls of Kleenex.

He was just pulling up his shorts when the doctor returned. He held out his hand for Clay to shake, and said, "Well, that does it for you. It was nice having met you."

Clay excused himself with a nod and a wave. "See you," he said as he shut the door. Clay could only frown and shake his head when the three other DLs outside the door looked up at his face for a clue.